Nichole Severn writes expl[osive romantic suspense featuring] strong heroines, heroes who [dare challenge them and a] hell of a lot of guns. She resides with her very supportive and patient husband, as well as her demon spawn, in Utah. When she's not writing, she's constantly injuring herself running, rock climbing, practising yoga and snowboarding. She loves hearing from readers through her website, nicholesevern.com, and on Facebook at nicholesevern

By day, **Maggie Wells** is buried in spreadsheets. At night, she pens tales of intrigue and people tangling up the sheets. She has a weakness for hot heroes and happy endings. She is the product of a charming rogue and a shameless flirt, and you only have to scratch the surface of this mild-mannered married lady to find a naughty streak a mile wide.

Also by Nichole Severn

New Mexico Guard Dogs
K-9 Detection
K-9 Shield
K-9 Guardians
K-9 Confidential

Defenders of Battle Mountain
Dead on Arrival
Presumed Dead
Over Her Dead Body
Dead Again

Also by Maggie Wells

Arkansas Special Agents: Cyber Crime Division
Shadowing Her Stalker
Catching a Hacker

Arkansas Special Agents
Ozarks Missing Person
Ozarks Double Homicide
Ozarks Witness Protection

A Raising the Bar Brief
For the Defense
Trial in the Backwoods

Discover more at millsandboon.co.uk

K-9 JUSTICE

NICHOLE SEVERN

OZARKS CONSPIRACY

MAGGIE WELLS

MILLS & BOON

All rights reserved including the right of reproduction in whole or in part in any form. This edition is published by arrangement with Harlequin Enterprises ULC.

This is a work of fiction. Names, characters, places, locations and incidents are purely fictional and bear no relationship to any real life individuals, living or dead, or to any actual places, business establishments, locations, events or incidents. Any resemblance is entirely coincidental.

This book is sold subject to the condition that it shall not, by way of trade or otherwise, be lent, resold, hired out or otherwise circulated without the prior consent of the publisher in any form of binding or cover other than that in which it is published and without a similar condition including this condition being imposed on the subsequent purchaser.

® and ™ are trademarks owned and used by the trademark owner and/or its licensee. Trademarks marked with ® are registered with the United Kingdom Patent Office and/or the Office for Harmonisation in the Internal Market and in other countries.

First Published in Great Britain 2025
by Mills & Boon, an imprint of HarperCollins*Publishers* Ltd
1 London Bridge Street, London, SE1 9GF

www.harpercollins.co.uk

HarperCollins*Publishers*
Macken House, 39/40 Mayor Street Upper,
Dublin 1, D01 C9W8, Ireland

K-9 Justice © 2025 Natascha Jaffa
Ozarks Conspiracy © 2025 Margaret Ethridge

ISBN: 978-0-263-39711-6

0525

MIX
Paper | Supporting responsible forestry
FSC
www.fsc.org
FSC™ C007454

This book contains FSC™ certified paper and other controlled sources to ensure responsible forest management.

For more information visit: www.harpercollins.co.uk/green

Printed and Bound in the UK using 100% Renewable Electricity at CPI Group (UK) Ltd, Croydon, CR0 4YY

K-9 JUSTICE

NICHOLE SEVERN

To all the readers who believe love can't conquer injuries.
You're going to hate this book.

Chapter One

The cartel had come for one of their own.

Ivy Bardot tried not to let the heat get to her, but there was no fighting it. The body had been left in the middle of the desert. Just like the others. A message. For her.

Dark hair splayed out from around a thin face. Wide eyes that had seen so much within the walls of Socorro Security stared into the sky without any life behind them.

The elements had done their job, stripping moisture from the victim's ocher skin and leaving nothing but a thick rawhide behind. *Victim.* That word wasn't supposed to fit. It wasn't supposed to touch anyone on her team. She'd tried to make sure of that since founding Socorro. Every operative was trained to take care of themselves. No matter the circumstance. Search and rescue, emergency protocols, food and supplies in every vehicle, combat training. It didn't matter the face staring back at her had seen more violence and blood out of the field rather than in. Ivy was responsible for all of them.

What had Dr. Piel done wrong?

"That her?" Chief of police Baker Halsey let his shadow cast across the cracked desert floor. Alpine Valley's protector had done his job. He'd taken Ivy's suspicion and run with it. Right out here into the middle of nowhere.

Only problem was, this wasn't the first time she'd been here.

In this exact spot. Staring at another victim who'd been stripped bare and left to rot. Not just one. Three before now. Déjà vu grabbed hold and refused to let up, dragging her back three years, when she'd still been working for the FBI.

"Yeah. That's her." Ivy tried to swallow around the mass in her throat, but there wasn't going to be any relief here. Sweat gathered beneath her blazer, and her mouth dried. "Do we know anything about where she's been the past three days?"

Right on time. The killer she'd known had taken and held his hostages for three days before dumping them in strategic locations in the middle of the New Mexican desert. She and her partner had never been able to narrow down the location of their final moments. Though, looking back, she'd known this day was coming. That she would pay for letting a killer get away.

She just hadn't expected it to happen so soon. Or to one of her own.

"Nothing yet. The medical examiner is stuck in Albuquerque. Won't be able to retrieve the body for a couple more hours," Halsey said.

"She deserved better." A pressure she'd become familiar with over the course of the past two years bubbled behind her sternum. Purpose replaced the cold leaking of grief in her gut, and the distractions bled to the back of her mind. Ivy cataloged everything she could about the scene. No tire tracks. At least, none that they would be able to match to a specific make and model. The man who'd done this was careful, calculating. He'd gotten the best of her once upon a time, but she'd changed. She could be just as calculating when she had to be. "Grab some gloves. We need to turn her over."

Halsey seemed uneasy at the idea. There were rules in a crime scene. No one touched the body until the coroner or the medical examiner had a chance to do an external exam and document and photograph the victim, but they didn't have two hours to wait for the right authorities to get here. The relentless heat could be destroying evidence as they spoke. "Like I said, the ME won't be here for a couple hours."

"I know that. I'm asking you to break protocol." Ivy hated the manipulation lacing her voice, but there were times when it was all she could do to keep the bad guys from winning. "I need to see her back."

Halsey considered her a moment. He'd been involved with one of Ivy's operatives enough to get a read on her himself. That was one of the things she liked about the chief of police. Always asking questions, never satisfied with the answers. Eager to dig beneath the surface and find the truth. Whatever Halsey saw in her expression then had him convinced what she was asking was worth the risk of contaminating a crime scene. He pulled a set of latex gloves from his back pocket and shoved both hands inside before crouching beside the victim. "Looking for something particular?"

"I'll know it when I see it." Her breath seemed to double inside her chest, taking up too much space for her lungs to function properly. Nervous energy skittered up her spine as the chief gently rolled Dr. Piel onto her front.

And there it was.

The markings she'd decoded—too late—carved into the woman's back. Fresh. Jagged. Unrepentant.

"What the hell is that?" Halsey asked.

A bead of sweat escaped her hairline, dissolving her controlled appearance in an instant as the secure world she'd built around herself cracked wide open. "A message."

A shift rippled through the chief as the implications of her answer settled in. "A message. For who?"

She didn't have all the information yet. She could be getting ahead of herself, but instinct said this was the same man. The same killer. The one she'd fought to what she'd believed to be his death two years ago at the hand of her trusted pocketknife. Only to learn he'd escaped that dark basement when she'd recovered. There was something she had to do. "Take care of her, Halsey. I'll be in touch."

The chief repositioned the body as though they hadn't just broken the entire rule book of their investigative training manuals. "Where are you going? We need to coordinate so we can figure out where she's been the past few days."

"I need to make a call." Ivy forced herself to take even steps in the direction of her SUV. To prove she could. That another body—a colleague—killed in the same manner as the victims from her last investigation for the FBI couldn't get to her. That she was as untouchable as she'd convinced herself she was when she'd built the most resourced security company in the world. But she was quickly learning that no amount of training or weapons, no amount of operatives and their K-9 units, could protect her from the failure clawing up her throat.

She locked herself inside her SUV, not even giving herself the chance to find relief from the heat. Halsey blocked most of her view of Dr. Piel through the windshield as he draped a tarp over the body. They couldn't risk the sun speeding up decomposition if they wanted an accurate assessment of time of death, but the woman's feet were still visible. This wasn't supposed to happen. She'd worked too hard and too long for the past to be able to reach her now. Ivy punched the vehicle's start button with her thumb, and the engine came alive.

This wasn't a onetime incident.

Her stomach rolled at the idea of another one of her operatives turning up dead. Jocelyn, Scarlett. But that wasn't the only way to hurt her either. While the killer preferred female victims over male, every one of her operatives had bound themselves to their significant others and partners in the past two years. They'd built their own families, one even welcoming their first child. If anything happened to any one of them…

Nausea churned hot and acidic as she pulled away from the scene. She'd built Socorro Security out of a need to protect those who couldn't protect themselves. Those like the three women abandoned and killed for no other purpose than to draw Ivy and her partner in. Cartels like *Sangre por Sangre* fed off innocent lives, poisoned the very people they went out of their way to use, abducted children into their ranks and killed anyone in their way. But Socorro had put a stop to that. Ivy and her operatives had sacrificed and risked their lives for this. They'd made a difference. According to their inside source, upper management within the cartel had gone into hiding. The few remaining lieutenants were on the run. She'd done that. She'd saved lives.

And yet she hadn't been able to save one of her own.

Tears blurred her vision as she checked the rearview mirror. The crime scene was long behind her, but the weight of loss clung tight.

Dr. Nafessa Piel had been one of the first contractors Ivy had taken on. The work she and her operatives had engaged in came with casualties, mostly in the form of physical injury in the field. Bullet wounds, concussions, stab wounds. The cartels didn't fight fair, and they certainly didn't have any remorse for doing whatever it took to achieve their mission. Dr. Piel had been there right from the beginning. Ready to send contractors back into battle, a little more worn, but stronger.

Socorro Security was supposed to save the world.

Who was going to save its operatives now?

Ivy accelerated toward Albuquerque, letting the hour tick by without much thought. There was no point in heading back to headquarters now. She didn't have answers for the team, but from the soft ping of her cell phone every few minutes, that didn't stop them from trying to get them. She turned her entire focus on the mental map directing her to Fairview Memorial Park just as the air conditioner was beginning to penetrate through her slacks and blazer.

The cemetery wasn't large in any sense of the word, but it had been constructed in that unique Mexican-inspired architecture of sandstone monuments, bare patches of dirt and white grave markers. Light stuccos and black metal rods made up the columns standing guard over the souls forever resting inside. Ivy parked along the side of the road, gazing through the gate. She'd never come here before.

There hadn't been a need until now.

Ivy shut off her phone, disabling any kind of GPS. Though it wouldn't be hard for her security consultant to track her down if Scarlett put her mind to it. That was what Ivy paid her for. Only it hadn't saved Dr. Piel when they'd needed that skill the most, had it? Whoever'd killed their physician had known Socorro would find her. That had been his plan all along.

She shouldered out of the vehicle and rounded the hood. Slipping her hand into her blazer pocket, Ivy felt for the pocketknife she'd carried since leaving home at seventeen. The one that had saved her life when it mattered. She navigated through the gate and around the first few headstones. Once-pristine landscaping—dying grass, interestingly enough—spread out in front of her and made her search easier. A slope arched from her left, creating a slight hill with hundreds of markers, some a century old, staring back at her.

Seven from the right. Two back.

Ivy pulled the pocketknife and set it on top of the headstone of a name she'd never been able to forget. The third victim of her last investigation. The one that had led them straight to her killer. "It's time for us to finish this."

CARSON LANG WAS waiting for her.

Tucked into the corner of the apartment in one of the well-loved chairs. Out of sight. Clear line to the front door. Just in case he had to make a quick escape.

He hadn't bothered with the lights. Too exposed. Shadows hid the minute details of a woman who escaped here more than she wanted others to know. A knitting project—half-finished—splayed across the side table, her most recent read beneath it. This one a psychological thriller. Seemed she didn't get enough real-life mind games and danger in her work. She had to seek them out in fiction. It all added up to a woman who took charge of her circumstances. Who didn't wait for permission to take action or walk a straight line to get what she wanted, but there were softer sides to her, too. Ones she'd tried to hide her whole life. To prove she was worthy. That she wouldn't fail. That she'd climbed free of her past.

The scar directly over his right kidney testified to her softer side.

He didn't have to learn what kind of woman Ivy Bardot was by being in her personal space. He'd been watching her for a long time.

The front-door dead bolt flipped. The door cracked. Slower than he expected. Her outline maneuvered inside and closed the door behind her. Blocking his exit. A strong inhalation crossed the space between them. A distraction for him to focus on as she unholstered her sidearm.

She was good.

"Don't bother with the lights." He could practically feel the battle-ready tension ripple down her frame from here.

"It will look more suspicious if I keep them off." Her voice erased years of doubt, secrets and violence in a single sentence. Hell, he'd missed it. That connection to the outside world. A place where he'd once thrived with her at his side. "Not to mention it'll be harder to shoot you for breaking into one of my safe houses."

"You're the one who called me, remember?" He held up the pocketknife in front of the window to his right. Just enough light for her to register it. A piece of her he'd known had taken everything for her to leave on top of that gravestone and walk away.

Ivy set her bag on the entryway table beside the door, moving slower than he knew she wanted to go into the living room. Gun still in hand, she reached beneath the lampshade on the opposite end table. The entire space burst with brightness, and it took too long for his vision to adjust.

Except he couldn't take his eyes off her. Under the wrong circumstances the perps they'd apprehended had made that very same mistake, only for an entirely different reason. Her guard was up, based on the way she was scanning the rest of the apartment with those intense eyes that seemed to know far more than she let on at any given moment.

Something had changed.

Something had gone wrong.

She crossed the room and retrieved the pocketknife. As though she physically needed it in her possession. "I had no other choice. Where's my dog?"

Of course, that would be her most pressing question in this little exchange. It always was when they managed to debrief every few months.

"Max is downstairs in the SUV." The German shepherd had been a parting gift before he'd gone undercover. One that had ended up saving his life a couple of times. "Couldn't risk her drawing attention."

"Right." Ivy hadn't moved.

"What do you mean you had no other choice?" A heavy weight pinned him into his seat. Carson sat forward. This wasn't like her. Not the real her. Sure, she had to keep that legendary emotional armor in place when in the field and directing her team and Congress, but she didn't need to do that with him. They were partners. Didn't matter they were on two opposite ends of the spectrum at the moment. They would always be partners. "What happened?"

"One of my operatives is dead. Our physician." Ivy disappeared behind the wall separating the living room from the kitchen, her heels echoing through the safe house. Her direction changed, farther down the hall as she swept the rest of the place for threats.

He wouldn't take it personally. The things they'd seen as partners had nearly destroyed them. Any slipup, any mistake on their part, meant risking the very lives they were working to save.

"I'm sorry." Carson shoved to stand with every intention of pulling Ivy into his arms, but she wouldn't let herself slow down long enough for that to happen. Not now. "How?"

She slid back into his vision, holstering her weapon beneath the navy blue blazer that brought out the depth of emerald in her eyes. Ivy leaned into the wall, crossing her arms across her frame, and exhaustion caught up in her expression. "Did you know?"

"Know what?" he asked.

"That he was coming for me." There was a bite in her voice. Accusation. "Our last case together. When three women were found dead in the middle of the desert with symbols carved into their backs. We caught up with the killer. We barely made it out of that house alive. He got away through an escape hatch that led beneath the house and emptied out onto the back of the property."

"I remember the case, Ivy. The son of a bitch nearly killed you." Where was she going with this? Why had she pulled him out of the field? Why had she risked blowing his cover? To rehash an old investigation? "If it weren't for that case, we wouldn't have known about *Sangre por Sangre* until it was too late."

Sangre por Sangre. Blood for Blood. The cartel had clawed its way to the top of the food chain through brutality, abductions, underage recruitment, drugs and women. The organization demolished competitors and left nothing for police and the DEA to tie back to them. Socorro Security and Ivy's team of private military contractors had been the only ones to ever get close enough to bringing the cartel to its knees. With him feeding her the information she needed to do it. Now *Sangre por Sangre* was on the run. Desperate to keep itself alive. Carson was close to identifying the head of the cartel.

"He's been out there all this time, but no matter where I look, he's a ghost. We agreed you would go undercover in the cartel to find him. I quit the FBI because I didn't think the federal government could protect you as well as a private organization could, and I've kept my end of the deal. I built Socorro Security for you. You said you would find him, and we would end this. It's been two years, Carson, and we're as clueless as when we started." She slid away from the brace of the wall, standing on her own two feet when it looked as though she wanted nothing more than to collapse right here in the middle of the floor. "Who is he?"

"What is this?" She was so close, it wouldn't take much for him to reach out for her. But the distance she was purposefully putting between them set his nerves on edge. This wasn't the Ivy he'd gone undercover for. This was his former FBI partner, before they'd risked their lives for one another. Before he'd been injured in the field. Before she'd donated a piece of herself to save his life. And, damn it, he hadn't missed this version of her. He wanted more. He'd always wanted more for them. "Why the sudden interest in our last case? What is it you're not telling me?"

Ivy turned on her heel, heading for the bag she'd left at the front door. In seconds, she'd pulled something from inside and thrust it against his chest, every ounce the woman with the capability to bring the world to a stop with a snap of her fingers.

He grabbed for the paper crumpled under her grip. Not a piece of paper. A photo. Carson slipped it from her hand, instantly victim to the softness of her skin against his. The past two years had put him in a position of power, of respect, of camaraderie within the cartel. He was trusted by upper management. Though he'd never met the leader of *Sangre por Sangre*, Carson had proved himself time and again as a valuable asset. He'd made friends. Some of whom he'd fought beside as they'd taken their last breath in the field. Some who'd sat beside him in cuffs when an assignment went south. His fellow soldiers had been there for him. And, yeah, there'd been women. Cartel bunnies who were always more interested in what his position could give them rather than what he craved. But this... He'd missed this connection. The feel of Ivy. Her warmth. Her compassion. His heart rate ticked up at her mere touch.

Until his brain cleared enough to process the subject in the photo.

Dr. Nafessa Piel. Dead. Exposed. Left to decompose alone. Complete with added wounds carved into her back. Carson had seen this before. He'd lived it. Only it had been a different woman then. The symbols were different this time, too. This wasn't the same message the killer had left him and Ivy two years ago announcing *Sangre por Sangre*'s rise. "When did this happen?"

"The medical examiner hasn't been able to determine time of death yet," Ivy said. "But she'd been missing for three days."

"Same as the others. Let me guess—nothing but mucus in her stomach? Dehydrated, starved and tortured." The details would line up. She didn't have to respond. The answer was written all over her face. Carson forced himself to study every detail of the photo in an attempt to pick up on something they'd missed before. "And the message?"

"I pulled the old case file and compared these symbols to the ones left on the other three victims. He's evolving. Using a variation of the original, from what I can tell." The fight seemed to drain right out of her then. "I have a member on my team who may be able to speed up the decryption, but it's still going to take some time."

"Why now?" Carson offered the photo. "Why her?"

"Socorro has practically driven *Sangre por Sangre* underground, thanks to your intel and our manpower. This could be a final attempt to survive." Ivy stared down at the photo of her colleague, and a sadness Carson couldn't stand etched deep into her features. She would blame herself for this. And without hesitation she would take on the entire cartel to make it right. It was one of the things he admired most about her. It was why they'd gotten this far. She swiped her hand under her nose and grabbed for the photo. "As for why he targeted Dr. Piel, I was hoping you might have some insight."

He wanted to give it to her, but despite his years undercover, she knew everything he did about the cartel. "The last three victims betrayed the cartel. They were used as a warning to those who stepped out of—"

A red laser cut through the room between them.

"Get down!" Ivy lunged for him.

Just as a swarm of bullets exploded through the window.

Chapter Two

She was already reaching for her go bag.

Debris and glass rained down from above as the safe house's living room wall disintegrated under fire. Picture frames seemed to explode above her. Photos of happier times, of family she'd lost touch with years ago, of commendations from her career in the FBI. It was all being ripped to pieces by hot lead.

Ivy fisted the backpack she'd stashed beneath a section of the couch and kicked off her heels. Rolling off Carson, she dragged the go bag into her chest. The safe house she'd built to escape the day-to-day violence was falling apart around her, but she couldn't think about that right now. They had to get out of here. "Get to the bedroom!"

Whoever was on the other side of that gun would expect them to go for the door. But Ivy didn't like to follow expectations. Not even when it had come to taking the beatings her stepfather doled out on a regular basis when she'd been a child. Who would have thought a ten-year-old could shoot a man who was supposed to protect her? Based on his final expression, certainly not him.

Her partner was already moving. Carson shoved to his feet, fingers encircling her arm. They moved as one, as though a single day and an entire war hadn't kept them apart for two years. He took the lead, surely already having mapped out this apartment. Leaving no chance for surprise.

Bullets punctured through the wall to their left. Every single one of them seemed to hike her nerves higher. Moonlight pierced through the holes left behind.

Ivy crawled on hands and knees down the hall right behind Carson. The bedroom was positioned at the end. Drywall and dust worked into her lungs, but she couldn't pay attention to the tightness in her chest right now. Sooner or later the gunfire would stop. The shooter on the other end would breach the apartment. They'd want to make sure they had hit their target. But she and Carson wouldn't be here. She had to make sure of that.

"Go, go, go!" The orders were unnecessary. What was he going to do? Stop in the middle of the hallway to have a chat? But the need to be in control, to feel as though she was doing something to get them out of here, had taken hold.

A single round ruptured through the wall in front of her face.

Ivy pulled up short as Carson turned back and locked his gaze on her, facing the reality the bullet could've dropped her right here and now. Too close. She forced herself to shake it off. They were going to die if they didn't pick up the pace.

Except the gunfire had stopped.

One second. Two. Longer.

No more shattering glass. No more close calls. No more attack.

They were out of time. "They're coming."

Carson lunged for the bedroom and somehow managed to land straight on her king-size bed.

She was right behind him, kicking the door shut. She

threaded both arms through the backpack straps and secured it in place. Ivy unholstered her weapon and hit the release for the magazine. Fifteen rounds. Plus more in the go bag. They had a fighting chance.

"This is nice." Carson slid his hands over the comforter sprawled across the bed. "Much softer than that crappy mattress you had in your last place."

"It's one of those mail-order mattresses." She crossed to the corner window facing the next building over. It was one of the features she'd specifically required when she'd found this place. Corner apartment. Alley escape. Higher chances of getting out alive in case of an ambush. Most people didn't live that way. But she did. She had to. Unlocking the window, she pried the pane up and pushed the screen free. "No squeaky mattress springs. Memory foam. I sleep like the dead."

"Maybe one of these days I'll get to try it for myself." Carson was already on her heels as she maneuvered one leg through the window opening.

"Watch your step." She latched on to the overhead stucco ledge framing the window and tucked her toes into an identical one under her feet. The framing only extended the length of the window. They were going to have to make it to the railing on the floor directly beneath her. She'd practiced a handful of times, once scaring the crap out of Mrs. Orson, who'd taken to doing yoga outside, but Ivy wouldn't regret it now. "It's a long way down if you're not paying attention."

A hard thud registered from inside. Then another. The shooter was trying to breach the front door. It would take a while since she'd replaced the short screws holding the hinges in place with much heavier-duty ones. That, and she'd added a couple of dead bolts. It would take him at least—

The heavy door slammed into the wall behind it.

Not as long as she'd hoped. "Come on."

Stucco bit into her fingertips as she shuffled off to one side, out of line of the window, to make room for Carson on the ledge. He didn't waste time in joining her outside. These frames weren't meant to hold weight. They were purely decorative, and the longer they held on, the higher chance the construction would fail and they'd both die sooner than they'd planned.

Movement echoed through the apartment. Crunching glass. The shooter was on the hunt. For them.

Ivy steadied her breathing and turned her attention to the railing below. Ten feet down, five feet to the left. She hadn't jumped with the added weight of her go bag yet. She'd been building up to it in preparation for this exact scenario, but now she didn't have any other choice. They were going to have to risk it. She whistled low to catch Carson's attention, then nodded downward.

Disbelief and something along the lines of defiance spread across what little she could see of his expression. He shook his head.

All she could do was nod in response. A single word could give away their position. She'd already lost Carson to the cartel once, and it had changed the entire course of her career and her life. She couldn't do it again. Ivy spread her weight evenly between both feet.

The movement inside the apartment was getting louder. Closer. They had a minute—maybe less. They had to do this now.

The weight of her backpack was beginning to wear on her. There was no encouraging Carson through facial expressions alone. She forced her attention to the target. Mrs. Orson's second-floor railing. Ivy redirected everything she had into her toes to give her the distance she needed. Her stomach vaulted into her chest as gravity took hold. The metal railing rushed up to meet her. Faster than she expected. Her fingers grazed the metal.

Then slipped.

She was free-falling. Every cell in her body screamed in warning.

Just as she clutched on to the bottom rail.

Her head hit the section of stucco holding up the second story. Her concentration frayed, and her hand lost some of its strength. Her legs swung out of control and twisted her body to one side. The ground seemed to move beneath her, threatening to swallow her up.

Metal reverberated through her a split second before a strong hand wrapped around her wrist and drew her gaze upward. Carson. He'd taken the leap. He was the only one keeping her from falling. His strength gave her enough direction to swing her legs back around. They still had another floor to go before they landed on solid ground, but right then it felt a little more possible with him watching her back.

Movement registered from her bedroom window.

"Watch out!" She pulled Carson over the railing as the gunman took aim. His weight intensified the pain in her shoulder and nearly dislodged her hold altogether. They had nowhere else to go. The first spray of bullets missed by a hair. The gun jammed, the click of an empty magazine echoing through the alleyway. Ivy had the feeling they wouldn't be so lucky the second time. The small muscles in her arm stretched longer than they were meant to. Any second now she'd drop him. "I can't hold on."

"Ivy, you have to let me go, or we're both going to die."

Her partner seemed to gauge the distance between them and the ground.

Let him go? Had he lost his mind? No. She wasn't letting him go. She needed him alive. There was no way she could find Dr. Piel's killer without his insight into the cartel and the man she believed responsible for the murder.

The shooter slammed a new magazine into place and lowered the barrel of his assault rifle. At her. And yet Ivy couldn't seem to let her hand relax. Carson's weight was tearing her apart from the inside. She couldn't let him go. Not again. Not after everything they'd already survived together.

"You can do this. You have to do this, Ivy." Carson stared up at her, those dark eyes as familiar and foreign as she remembered. "I'll be fine."

She released his hand.

Carson hit the ground. At least twelve feet below. He landed hard enough for his legs to buckle, but then he was rolling out of the shooter's range. Ivy didn't hesitate. She released her own hold on the railing. The ground rushed up to meet her harder and faster than she expected. Her knees launched into her chest, but her backpack forced her to roll and redistribute the weight to save her from breaking her legs.

Asphalt exploded around her, and she forced herself to her feet. "Run!"

Only Carson wasn't there. He wasn't anywhere.

A high-pitched whistle from the end of the alley pierced her attention. Ivy pushed everything she had into pumping her legs. The gunman was three floors up. He would have a hell of a time intercepting them.

Unless he had a partner.

Drawing her weapon into her hand, she registered a cascade of police sirens in the distance as she rounded toward the front of the building. Mrs. Orson probably wasn't the only resident to call 911 at the sound of gunfire. Ivy just hoped no one had been hurt in the ambush. As much as she could leave the apartment and anything else connecting her to this life at the drop of a hat, the people in this building didn't have that luxury.

She caught up with Carson at the corner and followed him down the street to a black SUV stashed in one of the parallel alleys. Her vehicle wasn't an option. Whoever had targeted the safe house would already have her registration details, and if this was some kind of coordinated effort to hunt down and ambush Socorro operatives, none of them were safe.

"Get in." Carson climbed behind the wheel, with Ivy collapsing into the front passenger seat. Max made her presence known with a series of too-loud barks that could summon demons under the right circumstances, but apparently, Carson didn't have the heart to quiet her excitement for seeing Ivy. The engine growled to life at the touch of a button, and they sped onto the street. Keeping an eye on the rearview mirror, her partner relaxed over a series of seconds. "The life you built is over, Ivy. From here on out, we can only trust each other."

HIS HEART RATE hadn't come down yet.

Seemed no matter how many miles Carson put between them and Ivy's safe house, having his former partner here kept his entire nervous system on edge. Adrenaline had started to drain and left him feeling keyed up and exhausted at the same time. A dangerous combination when facing the possibility his cover had been blown. That he'd been followed. Or that someone had come for Ivy.

"Where are we going?" She stroked Max's fur with a soothing calmness that, at that moment, Carson wished she'd paid toward him, but two years was a long time. They'd kept in touch. Him slipping her cartel intel, her providing him the plan to dismantle *Sangre por Sangre* and the warning to steer clear of Socorro's next move. They worked well together in that respect, but in this case, time had made their wounds deeper. Not given them a chance to heal.

She didn't like not knowing every detail ahead of time, and she sure as hell didn't like not being in charge, but there were certain things he couldn't tell her just yet either. At least, not without him logically defending his use of cartel resources available to him, and he wasn't running on logic right now. "We'll be there soon enough."

"You're very good about avoiding having to answer questions," she said.

"How do you think I've been able to survive this long undercover?" He'd meant to lighten the mood. Because they both knew, out of the two of them, the FBI had chosen the wrong agent to send undercover within *Sangre por Sangre*. The only reason it hadn't been her was because of his skin color. His mother's Asian roots had made their mark around his eyes, but it was his father's Mexican heritage that defined him on the outside. That heritage had given him an entry point inside the cartel, but to survive its ranks, he'd learned the rest violently and strategically.

Ivy directed her attention out the passenger-side window but stayed physically connected to the dog they'd once shared as a couple. "Good point."

They'd gotten out of the city without incident, heading north, but it was only a matter of time before whoever'd come for Ivy scorched through the rest of her life as they had her safe house. Which meant her team could be at risk, too. And not just them. Anyone connected to Ivy. Operatives' families. Clients. Any family she might have left.

"The shooter was sporting an M4 assault rifle. Exclusively a military model with a high-capacity magazine. Not something you would normally find on the streets." Ivy's voice had taken on that tone she used for interviewing witnesses and suspects. Strangers. "Which makes me think Dr. Piel's murder and this ambush are tied back to the cartel. The timing would be a hell of a coincidence if they weren't."

He'd made the same connection. "She was your friend. The way you talk about her. It's not the same as when you've talked about your other operatives."

Ivy rolled her head back toward the center console. "It didn't start out that way. I hired Dr. Piel because she was the most qualified for the job. She was a general surgeon at Columbia University. The only female in the entire emergency department. I saw how hard she had to work just to prove she was meant to be there, while getting a fraction of the salary as others less qualified. Not just as a woman, but as a Black woman." There was that sadness again. A mere hint of the grief Ivy was most likely hiding from him. "She reminded me of…me. Of my time in the FBI. So I made her an offer on the spot. I convinced her to uproot her entire life to come to New Mexico. I provided her a surgical suite and clinic, paid her three times what she was worth and watched her do what she did best. Saving the lives of my operatives. Without her, Socorro wouldn't have been possible. I owe her a lot. Only I'm just now realizing I never took the chance to tell her that."

The SUV's headlights bounced as he turned onto an unpaved road cutting off the I-25. It wasn't well-worn like most others. Practically hidden in the expanse of the desert. Purposefully out of reach of wandering hitchhikers and curious civilians. Carson carved up the single-lane dirt path partially overgrown from lack of use. He couldn't remember the last time he'd been out here. Didn't know what was waiting for them at the other end either. "Did Dr. Piel talk about her personal life? Maybe a falling-out with friends, family, a neighbor?"

"No. Not that she mentioned." Ivy stared out the windshield, the lights from the console glimmering off the line of unshed tears in her eyes. His partner never cried. Not even when she'd believed she was about to die. Then again, a lot could change in two years. "And before you ask, I've already looked into her finances and phone records. She didn't have any money problems, and there wasn't any suspicious activity in her messages or calls. We drug test regularly due to the nature of our work and the missions we take on. Her results have never given me reason to believe she's anything more than the woman I believed her to be."

"Then we need to assume she was killed because of you. Because of your connection to her." Carson pulled the SUV in front of the safe house. Well, *safe house* was a bit modest of a description. This place was more like a compound. A base *Sangre por Sangre* upper management utilized in case of emergency. Only it hadn't been used much in the past six months for the simple fact there wasn't much management left, thanks to Ivy and her team. He switched off the engine but didn't move to get out. Not yet. "Ivy, we knew this would be a possibility going in. You've spearheaded Socorro's creation and this war against the cartel. You've rallied the entire United States government to back you without hesitation and put *Sangre por Sangre* in a position of battling for survival.

Dr. Piel's death, the attack at the apartment... This is just the beginning. They will not stop until they've destroyed everything and everyone you love."

"What is this place?" Ivy leaned forward in her seat, taking in the expansive landscaping, architecture and driveway leading to a three-car garage off to the left. She didn't wait for an answer and shouldered out of the vehicle. Rounding to the front of the SUV, she turned on him as he climbed out of the driver's side with Max following suit. "Did you bring me to a cartel safe house?"

"It's the last place they'll look for you." He didn't know how else to explain his decision. In his head, bringing her here made sense. Whoever had come for her at the apartment was well resourced, had access to military hardware and was not afraid to hurt bystanders. This was the best option to keep her safe. Right under the cartel's nose.

"Or I'm walking right into their hands." Her concern was valid. For as long as he'd been embedded within *Sangre por Sangre*, there were still some things he'd been kept separate from. The head of the cartel's identity, for example.

"I would never knowingly put you in danger." Carson couldn't take this distance between them anymore. Not just physically, but emotionally. He might've been on assignment for two years, but he was still the same man she'd fallen in love with during their last assignment. They were supposed to be a team. Not...whatever this was. "You know that."

"Do I?" Her jaw set hard enough to cut glass, but there was still an edge of nervousness. As though she expected to have to make a run for it at any second. "Because it was easy to contact you those first few months, Carson, but you stopped contacting me altogether. After a while, I was the one arranging our meetings. I was the one having to pull intel out of you instead of you offering it. That wasn't how this was supposed to work, or did you forget that while killing anyone the cartel pointed you at?"

Tension bled into every muscle along his spine. Every shot, every kill, had been ingrained into his head. There was no way he'd ever be able to forget the voices that had begged for their lives. No way he could ever forgive himself for the futures he'd stolen in the name of *Sangre por Sangre*. No matter their level of evil. But her accusation that he'd forgotten his purpose in all of this—that he'd defected into the enemy's ranks—gutted him. "I couldn't blow my cover. Every time I reached out increased the chances of exposing our operation and putting your life in danger. We knew what we were getting into when the special agent in charge approached us with this assignment, Ivy. You're the one who stepped away from the FBI's support and took it upon yourself to compartmentalize who was involved. You agreed to all of this."

"I thought you were dead. Do you know what that feels like? To believe that your partner can't get word to you that he's in danger? That you're helpless to do anything about it?" Ivy swiped at her face. She lost the battle of facing off with him, escaping back to the SUV. Except she didn't stop at the SUV. She kept walking. Heading toward the main road.

Carson didn't have an answer for her. Not the kind that would make her feel any better when exhaustion, adrenaline and anger were working to undermine her executive function. He trailed after her, keeping his distance. For now. "Where are you going?"

"I'm not just going to hide out in some cartel safe house and wait for the son of a bitch who killed my operative and came after me to make his next move. I need to know if the rest of my team is in danger." She pulled a phone from her blazer pocket. The screen lit up around her as she pressed her phone to her ear. "I can have an extraction here in twenty minutes."

Carson grabbed the phone from her hand. He tossed it on the ground and stomped it into the dirt with the heel of his boot. The metal and glass protested, but he couldn't risk broadcasting their position. "Whoever killed Dr. Piel wasn't responsible for what went down at the safe house tonight."

"You needed to destroy my burner to tell me that?" She seemed to come back into herself, the anger bleeding from her expression. "How can you be sure they're two separate incidents?"

Max whined between them as the tension thickened.

"Because the killer we're looking for prefers a blade. He likes to get close to his victims and make examples out of them. A gun is too messy. Traceable through ballistics." Any second now, he'd lose what little trust was left between him and Ivy. He couldn't let that happen. He couldn't lose her, too. "My guess? The ambush was a distraction. Something shiny for us to chase. And if I'm right, that means whoever killed Dr. Piel is already using it to his advantage."

Chapter Three

She felt as though she needed to wash off the evil.

It seemed to seep in from the walls, the floors, the top-of-the-line appliances and pretty tile. The bedding calling to her very sleep-neglected brain. She wouldn't touch any of it. This entire compound had been bought with the blood of thousands of innocent lives. Lives she'd sworn to keep safe from the cartel. Most she'd been too late to save.

Carson must've come here before. During his assignment.

Their conversation wouldn't stop replaying in her head. She'd accused him of losing perspective over the course of this assignment. She'd practically called him out as a cartel soldier who mindlessly followed his next order, and she hated herself for it. But worse, she hated her admission of how much she'd worried about him while he'd been undercover. Feelings weren't her strong suit. They'd done nothing but betray her and had been used against her in the past. And some habits died hard.

"Hungry?" He was the only one who could breach her personal space without triggering her defenses. Carson offered her a bowl-like plate of something orange and creamy with beans. "Cannellini beans with garlic, cherry tomatoes and onions."

"You just happen to have all the ingredients for my favorite comfort meal on hand?" She couldn't resist the promise of food or the fact that he'd taken the time and consideration to cook for her after what they'd been through tonight. Was it tonight? She wasn't sure how long ago a gunman had ripped apart the life she'd built separate of her crusade.

He withdrew the plate a couple of inches. "Is this your way of saying thank-you?"

A tendril of shame heated in her cheeks, and she took the plate. She was boxing him in as a potential threat when Carson had done nothing but fight beside her in the limited time they'd been thrust together. "Thank you."

The heat felt good in her hand. Grounding and strong. Or maybe it had nothing to do with the plate and everything to do with the partner handing it to her. A partner she'd missed more than anything. Ivy took her time with the first bite, letting the combination of garlic and onion soothe her down to her very bones.

Carson backed off, giving her space in a seemingly endless expanse of emptiness surrounding them. "Better?"

"Much." Calories had a way of making everything better, but she'd never gotten over his cooking. No matter how many times she'd tried re-creating the recipes in the old recipe book his mother had put together for him when he'd gone off to college, it wasn't the same.

"Still think I've been brainwashed by the cartel?" he asked.

The soup lost its taste, and suddenly she wasn't as hungry as she'd thought. "You've been invested in learning everything you can about *Sangre por Sangre* for the past two years. You've done things for them. Gotten to know the men and women that make up their ranks. Is it so hard to believe you may have started coming around to their way of thinking?"

"Going so far as to serve you up on a silver platter?" He was right there. No longer concerned with her need for personal space. The heat of his body drove through her T-shirt and soothed the aches of hitting the railing.

Ivy directed her gaze to the plate of food in her hand. He knew her better than anyone else in the world—inside and out—and there was a part of her that wanted to convince herself he would use that information against her. Only that part was lying to her. "We've been fighting this virus for so long, sometimes I start seeing threats where they don't exist."

Carson slipped his index finger under her chin and notched her gaze higher to meet his. "I'm not the threat, Ivy. Not for you. Ever."

Her nerves frayed under his touch, and she was instantly lost in the feel of him. Of having him this close. How long had they starved themselves of moments like this? How long had they let the job rule how they interacted with one another? Pretended their mission was more important than their feelings for one another?

Too long.

She was the one to maneuver the food he'd made from between them. The plate missed the edge of the kitchen island and fell. Glass exploded from the impact, spreading far and wide with the soup across the tile. She didn't care. Neither of them cared as she rose onto her toes and crushed her mouth to his. Ivy arched into him, pressing against him in an attempt to make them one, and the hollowness she'd suffered without him these past two years waned. In seconds, she was breathless. He did that to her. Had from the beginning.

It didn't matter that they'd been partners, that the FBI had put rules in place to keep agents from getting romantically involved. There'd always been a loyalty from Carson she couldn't ignore. Not just to the job. To her. In a lifetime of always looking for the best way to survive, for once, she'd felt as though she had someone at her back. And, damn it, he felt so good.

"I've missed you." Her words vanished into his mouth. In his arms, she wasn't the head of the Pentagon's only weapon against *Sangre por Sangre*. She wasn't calling the shots or grieving the loss of one of her best operatives, and with that came a sense of freedom. Of unburdening. It had been so long since she'd given herself permission to drop the weight of responsibility at her feet. But Carson made it easy to be herself. Safe.

"I missed you, too." He moved his hand over her rib cage—right where she needed him—but pain spiked into her chest and down her hip.

She sucked in a hiss of air, pulling back, as she grabbed her side. Lightning streaked across her vision. Ivy tried to swallow the nausea climbing up her throat, but there was no stopping it as long as her ribs were screaming for relief.

"You're hurt." Carson didn't waste time waiting for her to deny it. Dropping behind the island, he pulled a first aid kit from underneath one of the cabinets.

"It's nothing. Just a bruise." Reality was rushing back. Too fast. She wasn't ready to let go of the past few minutes. Because she wasn't sure how much longer it would be until they allowed themselves to drop the roles they'd taken on again. "Is there a bathroom in this place?"

He stood there. Waiting. Waiting for her to let him help her. To be the one who burst into the room and fixed everything, as he had during their last case together. But the truth was, they weren't those people anymore. Time and violence and death had contorted them into something hard and unrecognizable. "Yeah. Down the hall. Second door on the right."

"Excuse me." Ivy wouldn't question his confidence. He'd been here before. In this place. In what capacity, she didn't know, but he was obviously more familiar with the cartel's setup than he'd reported.

She memorized the layout as she moved into the hallway, catching an office first. Cleaned out. What were the chances *Sangre por Sangre* had left something behind for her to use against them? What resources had they been forced to give up when the last few remaining lieutenants had gone underground? Her fingers itched to find out, but the pain in her side hadn't subsided.

She bypassed the bathroom as her legs threatened to collapse right out from under her. Adrenaline had run out within minutes of the ambush. She hadn't eaten anything other than that single bite of dinner in close to twenty-four hours as she'd tried to piece Dr. Piel's movements together from the past few days. Her go bag was stocked with food and water, but she'd left it back in the living room. As much as she hated to admit it, a piece of her needed the distance from Carson. To work this out. To put things back in perspective.

Ivy leveraged her hand against the wall as she moved down the too-long corridor. Room after room, stripped, abandoned. Papers discarded, shredders overflowing. Until she found one room furnished with an actual bed. The pressure of keeping it together popped before she managed to close the door behind her. Big breaths did nothing to counter the hurt pressing into her from all sides. Her nervous system was processing Dr. Piel's murder, the ambush at the apartment, the reunion with the man who'd promised her forever, the kiss they'd shared. The reminder a killer had slipped out of her reach. It was trying to bring her back to neutral, but there was just so much stuff in the way. She barely had time to take in the setup of the rest of the room before hiding away under the covers.

Cutting off her senses was the only proven method of bringing her out of a tailspin. It had been a long time since she'd felt this...powerless. But the past few days had compounded until she wasn't sure she was strong enough to take her next breath. At least, not anytime soon.

A low moan registered through the heavy comforter a split second before the mattress bounced with additional weight. A wet nose prodded underneath the seam of the blanket until Max had fully made her way inside the barrier between Ivy and the rest of the world.

"You always seem to know when you're needed." She wrapped one arm around the German shepherd, giving in to the warmth and the weight of the symbol of the relationship she and Carson had once created together. It all seemed so broken now. Foreign and strange. The longer Ivy stroked Max's fur, the sooner the pressure subsided, until she almost felt like herself. Almost. There were still a few pieces missing and unsure, but Max made the edges less sharp.

If she was being honest with herself, Carson had, too. He'd helped get her out of the apartment. Protected her when the gunman had taken aim. He'd risked his life to ensure she kept hers. That hadn't changed in the years they'd been apart.

But as sleep dragged her into unconsciousness, a single thought followed her under. One Ivy hated to consider at all but would be reckless to ignore.

That despite the attack on the safe house tonight, Carson was still utilizing cartel resources. And she wasn't sure she could trust him anymore.

SHE AND MAX had fallen asleep together.

Carson couldn't tear himself away from the sight as the past superimposed over the present. Of Ivy surprising him with the pup once he'd been released from the hospital at the end of their last case. Of the sheer look of joy on her face, so different from the woman he'd come to know as a partner. No longer burdened. But free. They'd been through hell together. Nearly died for one another. He'd lost one of his kidneys in the process. The kidney his mother had donated to keep him alive when he'd gotten sick a few years ago, but Ivy had done something unthinkable at the time.

His partner had given him one of her own.

She'd saved his life in more ways than one.

It was a miracle their blood types had matched. Her work with the FBI and her crippling terror of becoming victim to any kind of vulnerability had kept her healthy and strong, and when the time had come, she'd been there for him when it'd mattered most. Had brought them closer together than ever. But something had changed.

Ever since he'd accepted this assignment.

These past two years had separated them physically—he couldn't deny the shift—but what he hadn't expected was the emotional fallout keeping them apart now. The fallout that made him feel like he'd made up everything between them up to this point.

This job, the one he'd taken to find the killer they'd let slip away, had been their only chance to cut *Sangre por Sangre* off at the knees, and they'd done a hell of a job together. The cartel was dying off. What else could he do but finish what they'd started together as a thank-you for everything Ivy had sacrificed for this cause?

The transplant scar—doubled in thickness now—prickled with awareness as Carson watched the slow rise and fall of Ivy's shoulders. Secret exchanges of information, coded messages, slipped documents—they were nothing compared to being with Ivy in person. Feeling her pressed against him, hearing her breathing change as he got close. He'd taken a risk going to that apartment last night. Now, faced with the possibility his cover within *Sangre por Sangre* had been blown, Ivy was all he had left.

A stab of regret cut through him. Rising through the cartel's ranks hadn't been a singular event or a solitary one. The men and women—the soldiers—he'd fought beside had become friends in a sense. People who considered him one of their own. He'd laughed with them, mourned with them, fought with them. Most of them were dead now, but there were a few who'd gone to ground. If he wanted to find the bastard who'd killed Dr. Piel and the three women before her, he'd need their help.

"It's rude to stare." Ivy shifted on the bed, careful not to wake Max. They'd both learned early on how illogical a German shepherd could be when ripped out of her beauty sleep, and they'd paid for it several times in the way of torn clothing and chewed shoes. Neither of them could risk it at this point. The clothes they were wearing were all they had for now. But all Carson could do right then was admire the sunrise coming through the window framing Ivy's face. "How long were you going to let me sleep?"

"As long as you needed," he said. "Figured you could use the rest before we decide where to go from here."

"And by here, you mean using a cartel property as a safe

house." The severity in her expression had drained in sleep, leaving a hint of the woman he remembered before they'd gotten themselves in this mess.

Coming here might not have been the best choice, but they'd made it through the night. He probably wouldn't have been able to say the same for a Socorro property. *Sangre por Sangre* had learned the locations of each and every hideout Ivy's operatives utilized. Carson didn't know where upper management had gotten the intel, but he hadn't been willing to risk putting her in more danger. Not when he'd just gotten her back. Keeping her here—close—was his only option. "Not going to let me live that one down anytime soon, are you?"

"No." She maneuvered out of bed with nothing short of grace despite her constrictive clothing and the sidearm holstered beneath her blazer. Her blouse had earned a few more wrinkles, almost making her human. She let her hand sweep down Max's back. "I can't believe how big she's gotten. I remember bringing her home the night you came home from the hospital. Neither of us could even get off the couch after the surgeries, but she didn't seem to mind. She just wanted to be held, and we all ended up asleep in the living room of your tiny apartment."

A warmth he'd convinced himself he'd been cut off from a long time ago prodded at his chest. That night had changed everything. Given him a small glimpse of the future he'd do anything to have. With Ivy. Little did either of them know it would be one of their last together. "A lot can change in two years."

"Yeah." She seemed to come back to the moment right then. Stiffening. Treating him as though he were a stranger despite her very blood coursing through his veins. "Does this place have coffee?"

"Already brewing." Carson dipped for the duffel bag at his feet. He tossed it Ivy's way. She caught it, but he hadn't expected anything less.

"I'm going to get cleaned up. I think there's still glass in my bra." His former partner disappeared into the attached bathroom. Within seconds, the sound of water hitting tile emerged underneath the door, with a thin veil of steam escaping with it.

It would be easy to cross this room, to open that door and reclaim what they had. He'd strip her free of that makeshift armor she presented to the world and join Ivy underneath the water. He'd memorize her body—her taste—all over again and remind himself what he'd been fighting for all this time.

But he wouldn't.

Max stretched across the bed, rolling to her back. The German shepherd was still half-asleep. As though these four walls could protect them from what was coming. Carson knew better. There was no escaping the cartel. Least of all for him. And he wasn't going to take Ivy down with him.

He peeled himself away from the bedroom door and forced himself down the hall. Mere weeks had passed since the last time he'd holed up in this compound. Upper management had given him the responsibility of recovering a large fentanyl shipment moved from one of their distribution warehouses during a Socorro raid. Scarlett Beam and her DEA partner had torn the place apart in an attempt to recover the boy *Sangre por Sangre* had abducted to force the DEA agent's compliance. Billions of dollars in fentanyl had simply disappeared into thin air. No trace. No witnesses. No profit for the cartel.

Carson had made sure of it.

Though a handful of soldiers had paid the price. People he'd gotten to know in this very compound. Through late nights. Rounds of beers. War stories. Family regrets. A hook had caught in him. One that refused to let go. No one else could see it. No one else understood. He'd been tasked to walk a line between two competing worlds, and his loyalties had split over the course of this assignment. His heart and soul had been committed to ending the cartel's evil influence on innocents, to stopping the destruction they'd caused from the very beginning. But living among *Sangre por Sangre* had shown him there were innocents caught on both sides. Family members of soldiers, even some soldiers themselves whose loyalty had been based on fear more than respect. He couldn't abandon them. Now one of those worlds was on the brink of destruction. What was he supposed to do then?

Carson shoved the memories to the back of his mind as far as they would go at the sound of movement from the hallway. Max's nails ticked off the tile as she searched for breakfast. "What'll it be today?"

She gazed up at him with those big black eyes that had seen too much in their short amount of time together. More than a companion should see.

"All right. Pancakes it is." They were Ivy's favorite, and since he'd taken the liberty of stocking this place back when he'd been working for the cartel, he was sure they had the ingredients to do it. Carson went through the pantry cupboards surrounding the refrigerator. "Any opinions on toppings?"

"I'm partial to raspberries." Her voice struck him harder than he expected. As though his entire nervous system had been waiting for a hit of her. Stepping into his peripheral vision, Ivy scrunched a towel into her hair, the ends of which contrasted with her light skin tone across her shoulders and collarbone. She took a seat on the other side of the island. "But I'll take anything other than a granola bar at this point."

His breath seemed to catch in his throat. The black tank top and cargo pants weren't anything special, but they weren't Ivy. Not the FBI agent and security CEO he'd come to know. The woman across the kitchen from him was the one he'd gotten to know behind closed doors. In the privacy of their homes as they'd figured out how to become more than professionals. More than partners. And he couldn't help but stare. "You clean up nice."

"It's amazing what a toothbrush and a shower can do, isn't it?" She tossed the towel onto the back of the other bar stool. "There was talk of coffee."

"Help yourself." He motioned to the mugs and pot on the counter to his right as he grabbed for the base pancake ingredients. "Sorry to disappoint, but there aren't any raspberries."

"I'm not hard to please when it comes to food." Ivy maneuvered into the kitchen—close enough for him to feel the leftover heat of her shower—and filled two mugs with straight black coffee. The way he'd come to like it given the cartel didn't spring for sugar and creamer on most jobs. Handing one of the mugs off to him, she seemed to melt at her first sip. "Hunger is the worst feeling in the world. I'll do whatever it takes to avoid it most days."

He couldn't help but laugh at the memories of the few times they'd been caught in the middle of a stakeout without something to eat. He'd never seen a more perfect example of Dr. Jekyll and Mr. Hyde in those moments. To the point he'd started packing snacks in his vehicle. For her. "I remember."

A softness filtered across her expression then. "Everything seemed so much easier back then. We took orders, we did our jobs and we went home at night. There wasn't this... nervousness that followed us around."

"What do you have to be nervous about?" Making pancakes slipped off his priority list, much to Max's annoyance as she poked her nose into the side of his leg. But all Carson had attention for was Ivy. For this sudden introspection she seemed to fall into. "You and I are more than equipped to handle anything that comes our way. We've proved that a dozen times during our time with the FBI alone."

"You mean apart from the possibility the cartel could come through those doors at any second and kill us both?" Ivy wrapped both hands around her mug as though it were some kind of life vest. "This feels different."

"Because we don't have the resources of the FBI behind us?" he asked. "Or because you think Dr. Piel might've been involved with *Sangre por Sangre*?"

Chapter Four

"That's not possible." She hadn't wanted to say the words out loud, but the dark temptation was there. It came from her investigative training, the same training that had helped her connect the dots between three dead women in the desert and their killer.

The idea one of her operatives could be involved with the very cartel responsible for most of the holes Dr. Piel treated made her sick to her stomach. But there was a pattern. The man who'd strangled and murdered those women and then left their bodies in the desert for her to find two years ago had done so as a warning. To encourage those who attempted to leave *Sangre por Sangre* to reconsider.

There's no escaping Sangre por Sangre.

The message carved into those women's backs hadn't been clear from the beginning. Their killer had used an encryption that had taken too long for Ivy to solve. Not to mention decomposition, swelling and the heat had warped the carvings in their skin. That case had nearly cost Ivy her life in the process. Had Dr. Piel gotten caught in the cartel's web? Two years was a long time. The son of a bitch responsible could've come at Ivy at any point during that time. Had good reason to as she and her operatives had chipped away at the killer's layer of protection. *Sangre por Sangre* didn't extend their protection services for nothing. The killer would have to have already been a member. Or given the cartel something they'd wanted.

In the end, it didn't matter. She'd made a promise to those women. She was going to finish this. And she wasn't going to let a drug cartel get in the way.

"As much as I hate to think someone in the cartel got that close to you, you and I both know it's a possibility, Ivy. But something must've changed. Dr. Piel must've tried to get out. This could be the killer's way of punishing her like he did with those other women." Carson always seemed to be able to read her. Better than anyone else. It was the small considerations that showed how fiercely he committed to others. How intensely he loved the people in his life. His mother before she'd died, Max, her. Equally, that intensity could turn him into the worst enemy if given enough heat. "Do you have any reason to believe Dr. Piel might've needed the cartel for something? Does she have a relative in their ranks?"

Acid surged into her throat, and Ivy suddenly didn't have a taste for coffee anymore. She set the mug on the counter, nerves raw. "No. Like I said, her financials and phone records don't indicate any contact with anyone on the cartel's roster. But we both know once you ask the cartel for help, you're theirs forever."

Goose bumps prickled down her arms, and in that moment, she'd never felt more naked despite her clothing. A tank top and jeans were logical in case they needed to make a quick escape, but her blazer and slacks had served her well in the past. With her uniform—brought into her security life from her time in the FBI—nothing was impossible. She could command armies, raise funding for missions, train

K-9s and protect her team. But now…there was no clear path here. No agenda she could pinpoint, and that left her exposed in a way she'd avoided since she was ten years old. "In truth, I think I'd rather this be about me. At least I would have something to aim at."

"It's still a possibility, especially considering the attack at the apartment, but as long as we're working blind, you're going to have to avoid everything and everyone you know." Carson got to work mixing whatever ingredients he'd pulled from the pantry in a metal bowl. He knew exactly where everything was in this kitchen, and the realization hurt more than she expected. He was comfortable here. In a compound owned and operated by the very people tearing their cities apart, people they'd vowed to bring to justice. Just how deep had he committed himself to their cause during his assignment? "That means Socorro hideouts and resources."

Her gut hollowed. The comparison wasn't lost on her right then either. How the killer they were hunting had hidden behind an impenetrable wall of cartel protection while she'd built her own layer of armor with Socorro. Without her team and resources, they wouldn't survive. The cartel would find them here. Maybe not tonight. Maybe not tomorrow. But soon. Every single cartel safe house she and her team had raided came with security measures patched into a mainframe that fed back to an undisclosed location. There might not be many members of *Sangre por Sangre* left, but security would be a priority. Someone would figure out this compound wasn't empty. "You're asking me to trust you with my life."

Carson's grip on the whisk tightened, but his rhythmic mixing didn't even falter. "You've done it before. Is it so hard to believe you can trust me now?"

She didn't know how to answer that. What he wanted from her. At the start of this, she wouldn't have hesitated, but now? Her partner was right. A lot changed in two years. "You've been chasing this killer since you've gone undercover, Carson. All that time, you've supplied me and the Pentagon with information on cartel shipments, safe houses, lieutenants, soldiers and plans. Complete with names and photos of every soldier. Invaluable information that has brought the cartel to its knees." She regretted putting her mug down so quickly, leaving her empty-handed and cold. "But every time I asked for intel on the man who killed those women, you haven't been able to supply anything useful. No photos. No names. No ranking. According to your reports, he's a ghost. At first, we thought he might be a lieutenant, but they're all dead now. There's the possibility he's one of their contracted killers, but his MO hasn't turned up anywhere else in the country, according to Alpine Valley PD."

A knot of tension built between her shoulder blades. She watched him. For a change in his expression. For something to tell her she was wrong. "I was willing to believe your theory he's a lowly soldier for a while, but what are the chances you wouldn't have come into contact with him all this time? Which makes me think maybe you did find him. And there's some reason you're not telling me. So, yes, Carson, it's hard for me to trust you with my life right now. Because I'm not sure I know who you are anymore."

"And bringing you here?" Carson ceased his mixing then, turning to face her. "Risking my cover to help you escape your apartment last night? You think I would do that just to hand Socorro's founder over to upper management on a silver platter?"

"I don't know why you brought me here. Other than you've

obviously been here before. You know where everything is. You knew what was stocked in the pantry, that this place would be empty." Her lips dried the longer she scrambled to put the pieces of the past twelve hours together. "Or maybe that was all part of the plan to gain my trust. So you could feed me whatever reason you have for lying to me all this time."

He backed out of the kitchen as though she'd physically assaulted him. His voice lost the confidence she'd always felt from him. "You saved my life, Ivy. I have one of your organs keeping me alive. You've known me for years. We were partners. We had each other's backs. Do you really think I could just hand you over to the people who want you dead like that?"

"Then tell me who he is." She couldn't help but counter his retreat, closing the distance between them. "Give me something to go off of, something I can use to make him pay for what he's done."

"I don't have what you want, Ivy. I've handed over every piece of intel I've uncovered while on assignment within *Sangre por Sangre*." He wasn't trying to escape anymore. He'd taken a stand. "What I can tell you is that there hasn't been a single day I haven't regretted going undercover within the cartel or leaving you to fight this battle on the outside alone. I knew what I was getting into, but I sure as hell never expected my own partner to question my loyalties."

She didn't know what to say to that, what to think. He was right. She'd been the one attacking *Sangre por Sangre* from the outside, taking the credit, making the big moves to dismantle the cartel while he'd been forced to keep to the shadows, to give up everything he'd known and cared about. Carson had never been one for glory. It wasn't in his nature, even as a rookie agent closing his first case. And he deserved a hell of a lot better from her. "I'm sorry. I think I've been at this for so long now, I'm constantly on the lookout for the next threat, and without one staring me in the face, I maybe started creating one where there wasn't any danger."

"I know exactly what you mean." He reached for her then—as though she hadn't just accused him of betraying her, their cause and their country—and pulled her against his chest.

Right where she needed to be. She didn't like being caged, but in his arms, the thud of his heart took off the edge. It was a rare occurrence for her to relax with anyone else around, a gift from the chaotic and abusive childhood she'd endured for so long. But Carson had been the first person she'd given herself permission to trust. Because he'd earned it. "I just want this to end. I want everything to go back to the way it was."

"There's no going back, though, is there? Not for us," he said.

"No. I suppose you're right." They'd left everything they'd known as a couple behind when he'd gone undercover. Left the FBI, left their homes, left their partnership. They'd set out to create something new—to do something good in the world. And this...this was new territory for them both, a crash of two worlds that didn't quite fit together. Ivy deadened the anxiety of not knowing what came next with a deep inhalation, pulling away. Pulling herself together. "Which means the only way out of this is *through*."

"Where do you suggest we start?" he asked. "The killer we're looking for is really good at staying under the radar."

"Then we work backward," she said. "We start with figuring out if Dr. Piel was involved with *Sangre por Sangre*."

Alpine Valley PD had cordoned off the property, but from the look of the seal on the front door, the official search hadn't been conducted yet.

Dr. Nafessa Piel's single-level home sat back away from the road with a dozen other cookie-cutter houses lining both sides of the street. Hardscaping had been maintained—no stone outliers on the driveway or pavers waiting to trip some kid on the sidewalk—in a simple design with sections of different rock to create movement across the flat stretch of land. From what Carson understood of the victim, extravagance had never been one of Dr. Piel's values, mostly noted in the lack of polish on the woman's nails and a single item of simple gold jewelry in the crime scene photos Ivy had shown him. He expected nothing but that same conviction inside.

Ivy pulled her pocketknife from her jeans and slid the blade along the sticker sealing off the home from nosy neighbors and murder groupies. She hesitated just before pushing inside, glancing back at him. In that moment he was thrust back into the partnership they'd each given up for this cause. One where she took the lead and he could do nothing but follow. Only that couldn't be the case anymore. They had to do this together. "All of our operatives are supplied with a security system when they sign on with Socorro. The alarm will trigger the second we open the door if Alpine PD hasn't already disabled the system. I could put a call in to my security expert, but if you insist on not using Socorro resources, I'll have to enter the override code manually."

The alarm could alert the neighborhood and the police to them breaking a threshold they had no business crossing during an active homicide investigation. But the punishment for giving *Sangre por Sangre* any kind of lead on Ivy's location was far worse. "Then we make this quick."

"All right. I've been here a few times since the installation. The panel is in the entryway, on the right wall." Ivy tested the doorknob, and it turned easily in her hand. She pushed inside.

But there was no sound of the alarm.

Shadow stretched out in front of them, and Carson's nerves rocketed into overdrive. Every cell in his body wanted to maneuver Ivy behind him, to protect her from any threat that came their way, but doing so would deepen the cracks in their partnership. She'd trained with the best, employed the best and worked tirelessly to become the best. That hadn't changed.

"The police department must've already disabled the alarm." She unholstered her sidearm. FBI agents and officers alike knew without a doubt house calls were the most dangerous part of the job. No telling what waited for them on the inside of a home. Or if a homeowner had set a trap to avoid containment. Her boots echoed off ugly tan tile lining a vaulted entryway, common in New Mexico houses.

Carson closed the door behind them.

The entryway dumped them into a front room furnished with leather couches, a mounted TV, a coffee table and an expansive rug to absorb the cold chill shooting down Carson's spine. Light filtered in through the back of the house from the kitchen, currently out of sight. "You said you've been here before. Anything different from your last visit?"

The admission hadn't meant much to him on the other side of the door, but he saw the relevance now. Ivy had been here several times, enough to know where the security panel was located and the basic layout of the home, past the fact her company had installed it. Which meant she and the latest victim had more than a professional relationship. They'd been friends. And not in the way a boss protected and interacted with her employees. There was a heaviness in the way she moved. As though expecting Dr. Piel to greet her with a smile and announce this had all been a misunderstanding. Why wouldn't Ivy have told him of their personal connection from the beginning?

"No. Everything looks the same, as far as I can tell." Ivy motioned to her right, down a length of hallway that angled into a different section of the house, as she took the left.

The place was much larger than he'd originally estimated, with multiple bedrooms and bathrooms. It was a lot for an unmarried woman who lived alone and spent most of her days patching up a team of private military contractors. He kicked at the base of the first door branching off the hallway and took aim inside. Empty. Gray carpet—new, from what he could tell—stretched out beneath a queen-size bed made up for guests. Another TV had been mounted on the wall. Nothing in the closet. No attached bathroom or signs of recent use.

Carson forced himself to move on. There was something off about this place. Why the hell had their victim bought such a large property? He searched the next bedroom, then an office and the primary bedroom. Everything in order. Everything in its place. No backups of lotion or conditioner or cleaning products. Personal photos and memorabilia were sparse and primarily in the largest bedroom. It was as though this place didn't really serve as a home.

More like a safe house.

Tension ratcheted into Carson's shoulders with every second he was separated from Ivy. Holstering his weapon, he retraced his steps until he located her going through drawers in the kitchen. "This place has four bedrooms."

"I know. No bugs or surveillance, from what I can tell, though." Ivy closed one of the drawers and moved on to another. "I would tell you this place was for friends and family that stayed frequently, but from what Nafessa has told me about her past, she didn't have anyone close, and she didn't like to host. She mostly kept to herself. Talked very little of her life outside of Socorro. It took months working with her before she let the smallest detail slide."

There were pieces of this puzzle that were starting to line up, but Carson didn't want to bring those into her awareness. Pieces he couldn't prove. Yet. "That's the first time you called Dr. Piel by her first name. Why didn't you tell me you two were closer than her as a contracted employee with Socorro?"

"Because there's honestly not that much to tell. She lived alone. Kept to herself. Whatever was between us was…new, in a way. Just within the past few months." Ivy abandoned her search of the kitchen. "It started as greeting each other in the halls, to sitting at the dining table during lunch."

"Who instigated conversation?" he asked.

"I don't remember." A healthy dose of suspicion tainted her voice, and right then, it felt as though the years hadn't torn them apart.

This was what they were good at. This was what they did best. Working off each other, testing theories, testing statements. He'd missed that. More than he thought he had.

Carson memorized the decor and personal touches, which didn't take long. Everything seemed to have a sense of order. Everything in its place. Or at least that was what the victim had wanted them to believe. That someone lived here. That this place was nothing more than a cookie-cutter home that served as a refuge to a private security physician. He moved into the living room, picking out more details. The lack of wear or imprints on the couch. The dust settling over the bookshelves. Adults played victim to their habits. A favorite spot on the couch while watching TV, a stack of books on an end table, even a preferred burner on the stove. But from what he could tell from this place, Dr. Piel didn't have any. "Did she ever ask about you personally?"

"Of course. That's what people do when they're becoming friends." Confusion deepened the lines etched between Ivy's eyebrows, but it didn't last long. She was never one to let an emotion—any kind of emotion—linger longer than necessary. She'd never seen a reason to. "If you're worried I gave away your undercover identity, you can relax. Nobody in my office but my counterterrorism agent Granger Morais knows that information. He figured it out a few weeks ago, and he isn't the type to spread the news."

"And what did Dr. Piel tell you about herself in return?" Every relationship in existence—biological, romantic, created—was transactional. Give and take. There were rules to follow and expectations to meet.

"She came to New Mexico from Columbia University when I offered her the contract. General surgery. Before that, her background was in emergency medicine at an array of different hospitals." Ivy folded her arms over her chest as she settled back against the kitchen counter. "She was an only child to a single mom. Her mom passed away when she was a teenager. Drug overdose. She put herself through school and went to medical school on scholarships."

"Did you speak with her references before you offered her the contract with Socorro?" He pulled the couch cushions up, one by one. No crumbs. No loose change. Nothing to suggest this couch had been here more than a few days.

Hell, he could still smell the plastic covering it had most likely been delivered in.

"Of course I did. She came highly recommended from each of her supervisors, especially at Columbia." The defensiveness he'd come to expect played around her eyes and straightened her shoulders.

"Who reached out first?" he asked. "When you were looking for a physician, was she the one to make the initial contact?"

"Yes. I put the word out I was looking for a physician through my contacts in the Pentagon. She was one of the first who submitted her CV, and I made an on-site visit to Columbia." Ivy rounded into the dining room, just within his peripheral vision. "What are you doing?"

"Has this couch always been here?" There was a fire burning beneath his skin now, feeding into a theory he couldn't ignore anymore. "The times you visited, was this the same couch that was here?"

"What?" A realization seemed to spark in her eyes. "No. I… I spilled wine on the cushion last time I was here. She must've replaced the couch."

"Why not just have the cushion cleaned or replace that single piece?" Instinct drove him to throw each cushion out of the way. "Why replace the whole couch?"

"What the hell does a couch have to do with anything?" There was a bite in her words that hadn't been there before. A raw nerve he'd touched. "The woman's body is decomposing in the refrigerator of Alpine Valley's only emergency clinic with strangulation marks around her neck and knife wounds in her back, and you want to focus on the fact she bought a new couch?"

"Yes, because I don't think Dr. Piel bought it. It smells

too new." He shoved the couch free from its position in the living room. And found exactly what he was looking for. "And I don't think she pays the mortgage on this place or actually lives here."

"What are you saying?" She couldn't seem to keep herself away, coming closer. "Is that…?"

"Blood." Carson fought to keep his breathing steady as he studied the brownish-red spread that hadn't come clean from the tile's grout. He couldn't help but lock his gaze on hers. "It's likely Dr. Piel was killed right here."

Chapter Five

Alpine Valley PD had taken control of the scene. She hadn't had any other choice but to notify them since this had likely been the location of Dr. Piel's death.

The other women they'd recovered in the desert, the three who'd lost their lives on her last case for the FBI, had been killed in and around their homes. This case seemed to be hitting the same markers.

"What were you and Mr. . . . ?" Chief Halsey left the question open, a pen raised over the notebook in his hand, but she wouldn't finish that sentence for him. Carson Lang no longer existed. Her partner had become Dominic Rojas, a *Sangre por Sangre* cartel soldier with a rap sheet longer than the US Constitution, and there was no way in hell she'd take the chance of compromising his cover by putting his name on paper. If she hadn't compromised it already.

"What do you think we were doing, Baker?" She hadn't meant the words to sound so harsh. Baker Halsey had gone above and beyond to overcome his resistance to accept and collaborate, but it had taken falling for one of Ivy's operatives to bring him around. "Nafessa Piel was one of my employees, and now she's dead. Did you really think I was going to sit back while your department investigated her murder?"

"I was hoping you would pay me the same respect to do my damn job as I give you and your team, and I seem to remember sealing this door so as not to disturb a potential crime scene. From the look of it, the seal was cut through. Most likely with a blade." Intense blue eyes the shade of a clear sky centered on her, but Ivy wasn't the type to fall for a pretty face or drawn-out silences. She'd faced down senators and military officers. She'd built a security company from the ground up when it became clear the federal government couldn't protect Carson on the inside of a cartel. Chief Halsey had a job to do, but she'd learned police tactics a long time ago. They wouldn't work now. The notebook disappeared into his uniform jacket pocket. "Any idea how that happened?"

Red and blue patrol lights swept across her face from the chief's vehicle parked in the driveway, almost hypnotizing. The events of the past hour raced through her head. Cutting through the seal, searching the house. Finding evidence of blood beneath the couch. Carson's accusations replayed on repeat, no matter how many times she tried to override them.

That Nafessa Piel had targeted Ivy and Socorro. That the physician had worked her way into Ivy's confidence with patience, probing questions and expertise. That the house they were standing in right now hadn't been a home, but a safe house.

No. She wasn't entertaining this idea. It was crazy.

Okay. Yes, Dr. Piel had been the one to reach out to apply for the position. Yes, she'd been the one who'd initiated her and Ivy's friendship. She'd been the one to take that first step and invite Ivy over for drinks, and Ivy had said yes. Because the thought of going another two years without direct contact from her partner had made the black hole in her chest so much worse, and having a friend—someone she could connect with—had felt important.

Ivy's mouth dried as she was forced back into the moment. "No. I don't know how the seal on the door was broken."

"I see. And what about him?" Alpine Valley's finest was smarter than that. Chief Halsey nodded toward Carson, standing with a deputy she didn't know on the other side of the room, but there was something along the lines of humor playing in the corners of Halsey's mouth. "There a good reason the founder of Socorro Security has partnered with a cartel soldier on your little rogue expedition?"

Panic infused the muscles down her spine. Ivy breathed through her initial response to deny the truth. "I don't know what you're talking—"

"That man saved my and Jocelyn's lives," he said.

The intensity she'd noted a few minutes ago drained from around the chief's eyes.

"To be honest, I still don't know why," Halsey said. "We were in their territory, fair and square. I was ready to tear their entire building down to get Jocelyn out alive when he walked in with six armed cartel soldiers. He took one look at Jocelyn, and it was like he knew her. Like they'd been friends for years."

She let his assumptions hang between them.

"He's one of yours, isn't he? Planted in *Sangre por Sangre*'s ranks." She hadn't given Chief Halsey nearly enough credit in their short time working together. The man had definitely earned that badge and the title of Alpine Valley's hero. He directed his attention to the living room. "Too bad I got here after the people who'd broken into this property had already gone. Didn't get a chance to get their statements. Sure was lucky I discovered the bloodstain beneath the couch, though."

His meaning took a moment to sink in.

"Yeah. Lucky." She detached herself from the gravitational pull the chief seemed to exude by taking a single step back.

"One more thing, Ms. Bardot." The chief pointed the end of his pen at her. "Heard about what went down at your apartment. Jocelyn has been calling me nonstop since the news broke. I'm guessing there's a reason you're not in touch. All this have something to do with keeping them in the dark?"

"I'm not sure yet, but I have a feeling it won't be long before I find out." Nervous energy played at the tips of her fingers. The longer she and Carson stayed in one place, the more attention they were bound to garner from the wrong people. But she couldn't leave until she got what she came here for. "Has the ME finished the autopsy on Nafessa Piel's body?"

Halsey lowered his voice, coming in a few inches closer. "I took your advice and reached out to your old special agent in charge for the file on your last case. The FBI isn't usually so agreeable, but once I mentioned your name, he was all too willing to cooperate. I read through your notes and passed them on to the medical examiner. Three women left in the desert, strangled, with messages carved into their backs. Despite the variation in the characters recovered on Nafessa Piel's back, the ME has ample reason to conclude this latest murder fits the MO of the killer you were chasing back then. He's willing to state there's a connection between both cases."

Confirmation. Her stomach knotted tighter. She'd been willing to make the leap based off unproven facts, but there was no denying the truth now. The man they'd let escape two years ago was killing again.

"Watch yourself, Ivy. I've seen firsthand the lengths the cartel will go to to get what they want, and I know you have, too." A sadness she couldn't begin to understand creased in his jaw. "I've got this covered. Whatever it is you're after, I trust you know when to bring me in."

"There is something I need you to check for me." Dread pooled at the base of her spine, but she hadn't built her career without considering all the options. No matter how hard it was to swallow. "I need to know if Nafessa Piel has an off-the-books connection to *Sangre por Sangre*. No matter how small. Anything they could've used to manipulate her. Quietly, please."

"Those other women's deaths you investigated, you theorized they were all trying to get out of the cartel's grip, and that's why they were targeted. To send a message to deserters." The chief's gaze bounced around the house, as though the walls were listening. "You think that's the case here?"

"I'll be in touch." She nodded thanks. Carson followed her out of the house. It wasn't until they'd pulled away from Dr. Piel's home that she had the guts to break the silence between them. "It's him, Carson. The medical examiner confirmed a connection between Dr. Piel's murder and the case we worked back then."

"We're going to find him." Confidence resonated in every word. He reached across the center console and took her hand in his. Warmth spread up her arm from the contact and chased back the chill that had taken hold from searching that cold, empty house. "He's going to pay for what he's done, and we're going to finish this. Together. I give you my word."

His reassurance was enough to ease her denial of Dr. Piel's

involvement in her own demise. For now. They'd potentially uncovered the scene where Socorro's physician had been killed, but there were still so many questions they didn't have answers to. And Ivy wasn't sure she wanted those answers. She stared out the passenger-side window as the houses in the neighborhood ticked by, begging her mind to switch off. To forget the outline of a pool of blood stained into the tile of her friend's home. Her only point of grounding contact was the hand still in hers. "Is it hard for you to be undercover?"

He didn't answer for a few breaths. "In some aspects. Not so much in others." She'd resigned to not getting more than that from him, but Carson went on. "There were things I missed at first. My own bed being one of them. I was never alone. The lieutenants exerted power any chance they got with orders and privileges. Metias Leyva—the lieutenant your forward observer went up against to protect Leyva's ex-wife—was probably the worst. Our meals were cold and few and far between. We mostly slept on cots or the ground or in the back seat of our vehicles. We're tools to be used. Nothing more."

Everything he'd described stabbed deeper than she expected. The conditions he'd suffered would've broken any man, but Carson had held on. For this assignment, for their agreement to not let the *Sangre por Sangre* virus spread. She studied their interconnected hands resting on the center console. That was one of the things she'd loved about him. His loyalty. His commitment. No matter how much risk came with his decision, he'd always been one to stick through it. "What aspects weren't so hard?"

"There were things that made taking orders easier. Knowing why I was there, knowing our end goal, helped. After a while, I started to get to know some of the other recruits.

Some of us got…close." He brought the back of her hand to his mouth, planting a kiss there. "Most of all, I guess the thing that made everything not so bad was knowing, sooner or later, I was coming home to you."

A battle ensued within. Warning spiked in her gut at his mention of the other cartel recruits with such…fondness, countered with the warmth of his simple assurance. But Ivy couldn't trust her instincts right now. Carson's theory concerning Dr. Piel—that one of her own people might've been involved with the cartel she'd taken an oath to dismantle—was starting to make sense.

Ivy directed her attention out the window. And started planning her next move.

CARSON HAD GONE through the crime scene photos a dozen times.

Nothing had changed.

The FBI had done nothing more to find the man responsible for three women's deaths once Carson had agreed to go undercover within *Sangre por Sangre*. The case had been abandoned on their end. No new evidence. No witnesses coming forward. It was as though the federal government had simply given up. The victims' bodies had been released to their families, the evidence cataloged and filed away in some storage locker that would take an act of the director himself to release.

Exhaustion blurred the reports in front of him. They'd come back to the cartel safe house to regroup, but they were getting nowhere. No matter which way they looked at it, they were right back at square one. Just as they had been before he'd gone undercover. The medical examiner was in possession of the most recent body. There was little chance he and

Ivy would be allowed anywhere near it, and he couldn't risk taking the chance the cartel already had eyes on Dr. Piel's remains. All he and his partner knew was there was a solid connection. The man who'd killed those victims two years ago had come after a Socorro physician. But why now? After all this time, the son of a bitch Carson had been hunting had lain low in the cartel's ranks. Was this about Dr. Piel? Or was this about Ivy?

"Anything new?" Her voice had lost its assertiveness in the past couple of hours. Draining with every dead end they came across.

He pushed back away from the kitchen island. Crime scene photos, initial reports, his own handwritten notes from another lifetime ago covered every inch of the quartz surface. None of it had done him a damn bit of good. "I've been through everything. Twice. The house we cornered the killer in two years ago has since been sold and bought by an elderly couple with clean background checks, and the two soldiers I fought that night trying to get to you in time are still serving time in prison."

He scrubbed at his face. How long had it been since he'd slept? Twenty-four hours? More? He couldn't tell anymore. Adrenaline reserves had run out a long time ago, and the pancakes they'd had this morning had already been spent. This was the part of the assignment he hated the most. The dead end. Serving the drug cartel had been simpler, in a way. He'd taken orders and carried them out. There'd been bullets occasionally, but for the most part, he'd been secure in knowing he wasn't the one responsible for any kind of loss of life. Not like he had been with the FBI.

"I've been through every piece of paper the cartel left behind in this safe house. There's nothing here." Ivy moved in close, directly over his shoulder, and invigorated his senses with a hint of vanilla and soap. It was enough to keep him from spiraling in the moment, but the effect would wear off the more he starved himself of sleep and calories. "What about the intel you gathered within the cartel? Anything that might give us a lead? You said you got close to some of the other recruits. Maybe one of them mentioned someone within the organization that liked to strangle his victims before carving messages into their backs?"

She was fishing for information, and hell, Carson didn't blame her. It was in Ivy's nature to have a plan worked out in her head before she took the next step, but a defensiveness that had no business coming between them surged. The people he'd gotten to know within the cartel's ranks had been sources. Nothing more. And yet there was a part of him that needed to protect them as much as they'd protected him since he'd joined their ranks. "I've kept records of everyone I came into contact with since the moment I joined *Sangre por Sangre*, but the people I worked with were foot soldiers. Grunts who didn't know anything. It was the lieutenants that issued the orders. The founder of the cartel kept his identity in the dark by making us go through them."

His mind went straight to the one man who'd gotten him through most of the assignments that'd left his hands covered in too much blood. Sebastian Aguado had been with the cartel nearly his entire life. Saved Carson's life on more than one occasion. And was rewarded for that loyalty with the loss of his wife and children—violently—after a rival cartel had abducted and killed them in retaliation. *Sangre por Sangre* hadn't done anything to stop the slaughter. Leaving Sebastian with nothing. There was a chance his old friend might want to even the playing field by helping him and Ivy root out the head of the cartel. Hell, he might be the only resource they could rely on.

Ivy's exhalation brushed the back of his neck. Too close. Too familiar. Too dangerous at a time like this. Because the moment he took his eyes off the end goal, the cartel would strike. He couldn't risk making any mistakes. Not when it came to Ivy.

She shifted her weight away from him, as though sensing his need for space. "And from what you've reported..."

"They're all dead. Socorro made sure of that." He hadn't meant the statement to take the shape of an accusation, but there it was. They were in an impossible situation. One he didn't know how to fix.

Other memories, of Carson having to step up and be the man of the house when his father had left him and his mother high and dry, surged forward. He hadn't been able to fix anything for his mother either. It didn't matter how good the grades he earned were or how much money he contributed to their expenses when he was old enough to get a job—he couldn't fix other people's mistakes. And now the one person he had left in this world—the one person he trusted—was caught in the result of his own failure. There'd been a time when all Carson wanted was to do something good with the second chance he'd been given after his mother had donated a kidney to save his life. Then again when he'd lost that kidney in a fight for Ivy's life and taken on one of hers. But this... Nothing concerning this case gave him hope this could end in anything but misery. "I'm going to get some fresh air."

Ivy didn't respond as he shoved away from the kitchen island and headed for the back door. He clocked the cameras positioned at the exit, but he'd ensured the cameras installed around the perimeter of the property had been taken off-line weeks ago.

Carson wrenched the sliding back door open with a bit too much force, earning himself a bark from Max. She followed him out the door beneath the covered porch. New Mexico had a peculiar habit of being too hot and too cold at the same time. Or maybe it was just his brain playing tricks on him as he stared into nothing but a fenced yard of dirt and weeds in the middle of January. Every piece of evidence, every witness statement, every lead jumbled through his mind. Out of order, upside down.

Despite years of undercover work—of following orders, of taking out every target required, of watching his fellow soldiers bleed out beside him and giving up everything he'd known in the process—he was nowhere near closing in on the killer who'd nearly taken Ivy from him. Who'd killed those women.

His phone weighed heavy in his pants pocket. There was still one option left. Sebastian had been able to avoid being buried six feet under with the rest of the cartel. Within the past month, whatever remained of *Sangre por Sangre* had scattered, "every man for himself" style, and his mentor had been no exception. Carson had heard whisperings the lifelong soldier in his fifties had fled back to his hometown of Aztec, but they'd just been rumors.

Carson forced himself to take his next breath slower than he wanted. Reaching out to anyone in the cartel directly—even with his cover intact—could unleash a hell neither he nor Ivy was prepared to deal with. Not to mention it could give Ivy reason to distance herself from him even further.

But what other choice did they have at this point?

Ivy had been targeted. Not just at her apartment, but possibly by a sociopath sending her a direct message by taking out one of her employees, and there was no way he would sit back and lose her. Not again. They'd fought too hard and for too long to let someone else have a say in their future. Least of all a killer. His fingers tingled with the need to send that message. He checked over his shoulder. For Ivy. But she must've remained in the kitchen. Most likely to go through the files they'd built over the past two hours. Carson unpocketed his phone.

Max locked her gaze on him, cocking her head to one side. In judgment.

"You want to go home, don't you? You want to go back to sleeping in a bed with your mom instead of on the ground with me?" He was more than aware of the ridiculousness of expecting his K-9 to answer back. He was also cognizant of how he was projecting onto his partner his own internal motivations for even considering contacting a man who'd dedicated his entire life to *Sangre por Sangre*. But Sebastian had roots deep into the organization. Twenty years' worth of experience, loyalty and know-how pertaining to all cartel business. Carson had heard the stories—the legend—of the soldier who had single-handedly undermined the DEA investigators over the years. Didn't hurt that Sebastian owed him a favor.

The German shepherd licked one side of her mouth.

"That's what I thought." He tapped out the message one-handed and hit Send. "Time to pay up, old man."

The back door protested on dirty tracks, centering Ivy over the threshold. "Thought I might join you for that fresh air."

Carson slipped his phone back into his pocket, just out of her line of sight. "I've had worse company."

"You're talking about Max, right?" A smile cracked at the corner of her mouth. Something private and meant only for him. It was her tendency to only reveal bits and pieces of herself to people she trusted that had first gotten his attention in the FBI. Why he'd requested to become her partner despite his lack of experience and the fact she'd driven most of her previous partners into early retirement. He'd wanted to be one of the few she trusted. Considering their partnership had dipped into a personal relationship, Carson would say he'd succeeded. Until she determined otherwise. Ivy crossed the porch to the railing at the edge of the cement, fingers interlaced as she searched the backyard. He'd never seen anything more beautiful in his life, never seen something more worth fighting for than her. "It's peaceful out here. I can see why you like it."

He joined her at the railing. "First time I came here, I was part of a security detail for a lieutenant named Tolenado. Turned out I had the most experience of anyone else on the team. Tolenado noticed. Decided to bring me on as one of his enforcers."

His pocket vibrated with an incoming message. Sebastian's response.

"I remember Tolenado. He abducted and tortured a war correspondent for three days. Intended to kill her, too. Right up until my operative Jones Driscoll pulled her out." She seemed to memorize the layout of the land spanning behind the house. "That correspondent was the one who broke the news a state senator had allowed *Sangre por Sangre* to kill ten US military soldiers to undermine Socorro. He failed, though."

"That's because you believe in what you're doing out there," Carson said. "From the very beginning, you were willing to do whatever it took to protect the people who couldn't protect themselves. Including me. I like to think that conviction has rubbed off on me."

"Except I couldn't help Nafessa or those other women from getting killed." Her voice hooked into him. "I went back through the intel you've gathered over the past two years along with the locations of the cartel's safe houses and the names of every *Sangre por Sangre* operative you encountered. At this point, we're treading water with no land in sight."

Carson pulled his phone to his side and read Sebastian's message. The old man had come through. "Then we start swimming. Right into the belly of the beast."

Chapter Six

Turned out the belly of the beast Carson had mentioned took the form of a small town she'd never heard of. Aztec, New Mexico, stood as home to an array of natural arches, forgotten ruins and six thousand people at the very top of the state. The town itself sat so close to the border between New Mexico and Colorado, they could practically cross state lines within minutes. Was that why *Sangre por Sangre* had chosen this location? Or was there anything here at all?

She studied the grid-like design of every street, the homes surrounded by dead lawns and bare earth. Cement driveways had cracked over time, giving up the ghost to overgrown scrub brush and cacti. There was an expansive difference between Albuquerque and towns such as Aztec. While big-box stores and skyscrapers moved in to mask cultural origins and wipe slates clean, places like this went out of their way to protect tradition and the history of their people. She could see it in the architecture. Not forced or inauthentic but preserved. "What makes you think the cartel has any resources here?"

"Rumor has it one of the cartel's top soldiers survived Socorro's purge. From what I've learned about him in the past, he considers Aztec a safe haven. Someplace no one will come looking for him." Carson kept his gaze on the road ahead. "I haven't been able to verify the intel. Honestly, I'm not sure there's anything for us here, but I figured if we were going to get any information on Dr. Piel's killer, this could be our best shot."

A lead. Her stomach fluttered, and for a reason unknown to Ivy, she wanted nothing more in that moment than to unholster her sidearm. "And if this cartel soldier doesn't want to share what he knows?"

"That's why we brought Max. She has a way of making people talk." He flashed her a smile meant to extinguish the nerves funneling through her chest, but Ivy felt nothing but apprehension at the idea they were walking into a *Sangre por Sangre* trap. "There's an entire arsenal in the cargo area, too."

"Who is this guy? And why hasn't he come up before?" The more information she had, the better decision she could make. That was the way this worked. Learning about this lead two days into their investigation didn't sit right. Though there wasn't a single bone in her body that believed Carson would put her in the cartel's crosshairs on purpose. Up to this point, he'd gone out of his way to ensure her safety. Hadn't he?

"Sebastian was my recruiter when I first joined the cartel. He watched over me, brought me into his circle. Trained me." There were emotions in those few statements Carson tried to bury, but she'd become an expert at reading him in their partnership. Something wasn't right here. There was something he wasn't telling her. "I saved his ass during one of Socorro's last raids on *Sangre por Sangre*'s headquarters a few weeks ago. Your counterterrorism agent Granger and his partner brought the entire place down on itself by taking out the underground tunnels the cartel was using to continue operations. I kept Sebastian from becoming one of the casualties."

"So he owes you his life." Why didn't that fact make her feel any better? "And you think an active member of *Sangre por Sangre* would be willing to turn on the cartel?"

"Sebastian has only one priority—survival. Whoever provides him the ability to do that the best is his friend. And at this point, Ivy, he's our only chance. No one but the lieutenants and the founder themselves have been with the cartel as long as this guy," he said. "If the killer we're looking for is active again, Sebastian can tell us who he is. For a price."

She wedged her boots into the floor as Carson maneuvered the SUV onto a barren street along the north edge of town. A beaten sign that was too difficult to read this time of night swung from rusted-out chains with a short burst of wind ahead. "I'll have to trust you on that."

He slowed his approach as oversize metal gates materialized through the darkness. A motion sensor–activated spotlight beamed to life, shining directly through the windshield.

Ivy brought her hand up to block the assault. Blind to any threat that might be waiting for them in the darkness.

"We're here." Carson shoved the SUV into Park and switched off the ignition. Max maneuvered her head between the front seats as though in an attempt to get the lay of the land before having to exit the safety of the vehicle.

Ivy felt the need to do the same, but the spotlight had yet to relent. She shouldered free of the SUV, her boots sinking into softened dirt. The gates stood as sentinels keeping unwanted visitors out, but the open structure and years of wear allowed her to see past the form-fitted plastic blocking most of her view inside. "Sebastian No-Last-Name lives in a junkyard?"

"A place like this comes with a lot of benefits. It's off the grid, you have to deal with very few visitors and there's access to a variety of vehicles in case of emergency." Carson rounded the head of the vehicle, the SUV's headlights exposing every strained vein in his forearms. No matter how much he trusted his own intel, there was obviously still a good amount of unknown he hadn't accepted.

Ivy joined him in front of the gate, responding in a singsong rhythm. "And there's plenty of places to hide a body or two."

Max huffed between them. Almost desperate to get this over with. The pressure growing heavier in Ivy's chest agreed. The sooner they could get out of this dark, rotting hellhole, the better. Preferably alive. The main building spread out to her left. She clocked two single roll-up doors and an expansive warehouse built from white metal sheeting. No vehicles parked in front. Aboveground power lines cut across the single-lane road they'd taken to get here and disappeared into the dark. This place was isolated. Far from prying eyes. And much larger than any auto recycling operation she'd come across before. "I hope this isn't a mistake."

He raised his gaze to the corner of the gate. "Smile for the camera, Ms. Dixon."

Dixon. She hadn't used that alias in years. Which meant Carson didn't trust Sebastian with her real identity. Why?

Her curiosity got the best of her, and Ivy directed her attention to the surveillance camera mounted overhead. The gate snapped open without being touched, and Carson pushed inside. Remote locks. The spotlight died out the moment she followed after, leaving white spots across her vision. Disorientation acted as an operative's best friend, and whoever the hell was inside knew it.

Ivy itched to unholster her weapon, but a move like that would put both her and Carson in danger before they'd gotten the information they needed. She followed her partner's lead, Max trailing a few steps behind. Only a few dimmed lights punctured into the overhang of the main building lit their way. Multiple rows of cars—every make and model—had been arranged in rows as far as the eye could see, and she couldn't help but wonder if *Sangre por Sangre* had utilized their pick of illegal VINs over the years. Perhaps switched out a few license plates. "I hope you know what you're doing, Rojas."

The back of the property rose into somewhat of a hill and showcased additional vehicles parked facing toward them, adding strain to her already-tight muscles.

"That's far enough, Rojas," a voice said from the shadows clinging to the warehouse. "You know the drill. Weapons, please."

Carson slowed, then pulled to a stop at a side door to the building. Unholstering his sidearm, he spread his arms wide before tossing the weapon a few feet ahead of them. "I come in peace."

"Does she?" a voice asked from the dark.

An invisible pool of dread leaked into her gut. There was no way in hell she was giving up her weapon. Not to a man tied to the very organization who'd killed innocent people for profit and domination.

Putting her in his sights, Carson nodded at her sidearm. "He won't talk to us unless we're unarmed."

"Then I guess this was all a waste of time." Ivy searched the darkness for a shape, an outline, for any evidence they weren't walking straight into a cartel ambush. One hand on the butt of her weapon. The weight of Carson's gaze remained on her in expectation, but she wouldn't budge. Not for the slim chance of getting what they came for. There had to be another way.

Carson lowered his arms, turning to face her. In an instant, he'd closed the distance between them, each footstep punctuated with the groan of wet gravel and dirt. He slipped his palm over the back of her hand set against her sidearm. "For Dr. Piel."

Three words. That was all it took for her to release her hold. To give up her only protection. Because the truth was Ivy owed Nafessa Piel whatever it took to bring her killer to justice. Months of conversations, of shared meals, of invites into personal spaces. Thousands of texts and emails. For the first time—possibly since she'd been ten years old—she'd had a friend. Someone who wasn't scared of her murderous past or holding a personal agenda. It didn't matter Socorro's physician might have had a connection to the cartel. Ivy didn't care. This killer—the man who'd targeted four women—used those victims as a warning to those wanting to leave the cartel behind. Which meant it was possible Nafessa wanted to leave the cartel behind. She'd wanted out.

Ivy's hands shook as Carson drew her weapon from her shoulder holster, tossing it beside his before turning back to the owner of that mysterious voice. Disorientation. Vulnerability. These were the attributes of someone who liked to be in power. In control. But Ivy wouldn't give in.

"That's better." Movement registered near the building, but the moon's light wasn't strong enough to reach into those dark places, leaving Ivy blind. "Now, to what do I owe this visit from my old friend?"

As though Carson Lang had never existed, Dominic Rojas took shape in her partner's features. Harder, more intimidating, stronger. The kind of man who used that strength to overpower others. It was an impossible—almost supernatural—shift that left her cold. "I'm calling in my debt, Sebastian."

"I see." Gravel crunched beneath heavy footsteps as Sebastian moved to the edge between light and dark. Though Ivy still couldn't see his face, the gun aimed at her and Carson was perfectly clear. "In that case, come on in."

"TE VOY A MATAR." I'll kill you for this. His Spanish had gone rusty in the years he'd chosen to speak his mother's language of origin, but the message was perfectly clear. Sebastian would pay for this. Every defense Carson owned shot into the forefront of his mind as he raised his hands, palms forward. He maneuvered in front of Ivy. "We had a deal."

Max growled low in her throat, ready for the command to strike, and Carson was almost ready to give it.

"And yet you brought Socorro's CEO straight to my door, *mi amigo*. Did you honestly believe I wouldn't recognize the woman responsible for *Sangre por Sangre*'s destruction?" Sebastian kept his face in shadow, using the warehouse behind him as an added layer of protection. "Because of her, our brothers and sisters are six feet underground."

He had a decision to make, a split-second reaction that would either get him and Ivy killed or give her a chance to walk away. Carson turned on Ivy, advancing with every pound he had on her. "Is that so? You told me your name was Christine Dixon, and you sure as hell didn't say anything about being involved with Socorro Security."

Ivy notched her chin higher, but there wasn't an ounce

of confusion in her expression. She was good at this. Had trained him well in their too-short time together as partners. "Would you have brought me here if I had?"

He reached for her. Secured a hand around her neck and pulled her into his chest. Not in the least bit hurting her. It was all for show. A way for them to get out of this alive together. Her hands latched around his wrists, her thumb directly over the thinnest section of skin. His pulse skyrocketed as he tried to find a way to get her out of here. "I don't like being lied to."

Carson cut his gaze toward the back of the property, where the lights from the warehouse didn't reach so easily. She was going to have to run.

"I'll send you an apology card." Her shoulders tensed. A split second before she rammed her knee into the top of his thigh.

Pain lightninged down his leg, but it was nothing compared to the real thing of taking a strike to the groin. He released his hold on her neck and hit the ground. Ivy took off, kicking up gravel and wet dirt behind her.

A gunshot exploded from behind as Sebastian attempted to stop her from escaping. The bullet ricocheted off the nearest vehicle with a spark. Missing his partner.

Max shifted on all four legs. Her bark echoed off the cars surrounding them as Carson got his bearings. The junkyard stretched several acres in each direction. With any number of hiding places. She just had to disappear until he could neutralize the threat himself. *"Pass auf!"* Sebastian didn't speak German. There was no way he'd be able to understand the command for Max to protect Ivy.

The K-9 bolted straight ahead and into the dark. She would

do whatever it took to keep Ivy safe. "Split up. She can't get far without a weapon," he said to Sebastian.

In reality, Ivy's survival training had readied her to thrive in the worst circumstances. It was her way of protecting herself, of being prepared for any situation and coming out on top, and she'd ensured each and every single one of her operatives could do the same. Including Dr. Piel.

"You find her, bring her to me. She's mine. Understand? Those Socorro sons of bitches are going to pay for what they've done." Sebastian split off to the left as Carson followed after Max.

"We'll see about that." His boots suctioned into soggy dirt as the land failed to soak up the last of the winter rainstorms. The ground had acclimated to extreme dryness over the decades. A single storm could wash out roads, flood towns and trigger mudslides without warning.

He shouldn't have brought her here. Ivy was out here, forced into a position of self-defense because of him, but there was no point in shaming himself now. There was no way in hell Sebastian would give him the intel they needed now. Not unless Ivy was dead at his feet.

Carson maneuvered through the maze of vehicles, keeping low and moving fast. He searched each one, but Ivy had taken this game of hide-and-seek seriously. A low whine called to him from the right, four rows from the warehouse, and he picked up the pace.

Max's tail set a new speed record as he approached. She danced in excitement of seeing him and to show off her expert skills of protecting the woman at her back.

"How's the leg?" Ivy pressed one side of her body into the rusted-out sedan she'd taken cover behind. Mud caked up her shins and covered her boots, most likely leaving a trail straight to her. It was going to take them working together to get out of this mess.

"I'll live. Thanks for not going for the full monty." Carson struggled to catch his breath as he surveyed the junkyard. Cars stood as silent soldiers all in line, ready to serve. No movement between them, but the moon had disappeared behind a cloud overhead, and his vision had yet to adjust.

"Can't have you slowing me down, can I?" She leaned back to get a view over the rear end of the vehicle. "Where's your friend?"

"South side of the lot. I can give you a head start, but I'm going to have to sell my part." Carson turned on his heels, staying low enough to avoid drawing attention. "I'm sorry about this, Ivy. I failed to account for the cartel recognizing your face."

"It's not your fault I've got such a pretty face. This is God-given." Her attempt to lighten the tension closing in worked, but it didn't last long. The cars in this lot weren't stacked on top of each other. Any move on their part would give away their location. "Still think Sebastian will give us the information we came for?"

"As long as we put you in the position of power." He scratched at Max's head to get her to settle down. "Until we have every last soldier and contact in *Sangre por Sangre* in custody or buried, I'm not sure it's smart to risk my cover. Including Dr. Piel's killer."

"What if we just ask for his identity nicely?" she asked.

"Sure. Let me know how that goes." He caught movement out of the corner of his eye. A mere two rows to their left. Damn it. Carson reached for his weapon, but he'd left their sidearms where he'd tossed them. "Think you can get to your gun if I distract him?"

"This mud isn't very forgiving." She hiked onto her heels, bracing both hands against the sedan. The car wobbled and groaned under the leverage, and he realized all four wheels had been scavenged. The metal body had been suspended by blocks. "But I can make it."

They had to try. Carson wrapped one hand around her arm and pulled her in. Not unlike when he'd crushed her against his chest a few minutes ago. Only this time, his mouth came down on hers. This kiss was quick and desperate, but it was enough to reenergize his nervous system and keep his head in the game. "Take Max. I'll draw him away. Be careful."

Ivy rolled her lips between her teeth in the dim light given off by the moon above. "You, too."

He crouched low and headed farther back in the lot, the opposite direction of Ivy and Max. This would work. It had to work. Because losing her once had nearly killed him and had taken one of his kidneys. He wouldn't recover if something happened to her again. His breathing shallowed as he tried to listen for squelching footsteps, but there was nothing. No sign of Sebastian. No gunshots. No insect noises coming from the desert spanning out on every side of the junkyard.

Everything had gone dead silent.

A barrel of a gun pressed into the back of his head.

Carson froze.

"I knew there had to be someone on the inside. It was the only explanation for how Socorro and the feds managed to find us time and time again." Sebastian's voice no longer held that mentor quality Carson had associated with him. Instead, this was the cartel soldier who would do whatever it took to survive. "On your feet, Rojas."

Without a weapon of his own, Carson didn't have a choice. He failed to catch sight of Ivy or Max as he shoved upward.

There was a part of him he'd had to hide from her these past two days. A monster he'd fed with every innocent life taken and order fulfilled within the cartel. It clawed to the surface now, changing him, pushing out all emotion and feeling. "Call me dirty one more time, and I'll feed you that gun, *amigo*."

He didn't give Sebastian a chance to counter. Dodging to one side, Carson grabbed for the gun, ripped it from the man's hand and took aim. All in the span of a blink of an eye. "This right here? This is what those Socorro dogs want. For us to turn on each other, but we're smarter than that."

He relaxed both hands around the weapon.

"These people have driven us out of our homes and into the ground. They've destroyed our futures, our *familia* and murdered our friends." Carson offered the weapon back. "Don't play into their mind games. Don't give them what they want."

A smile creased Sebastian's mouth, one of pride, as he accepted his weapon. "You always were my favorite, Dominic. Out of all my soldiers, I knew you had a bright future in *Sangre por Sangre*. Come." His mentor navigated down the row of cars, toward the gate blocking Carson's SUV. "The *gringa* isn't going anywhere."

He scoured the visible layout of the junkyard for any sign of Ivy, but all had gone still. A sick knot twisted in his gut. "What do you mean she isn't going anywhere?"

Sebastian waved the gun over his shoulder. "You think this is how I wanted to spend my retirement? In a junkyard? No, no, no. This place isn't one of the fancy safe houses the lieutenants run to." The cartel soldier lowered his voice, slowed his pace. As though they were approaching a cornered animal. "These cars are part of a maze. They funnel trespassers right where I want them. Like a spider catching a fly in her web."

A bark echoed through the property. Then another. Though Carson didn't have eyes on Max's location or Ivy, he forced himself to remain.

Sebastian brought him to the edge of a dark expanse of dirt tucked between two rows of vehicles. No. Not dirt. A massive hole nearly invisible at this time of night.

And there at the bottom lay his partner. Unconscious. Unmoving. Max circled around Ivy's body, staring up at him for help.

"This is where *el jefe* sent his enemies to be questioned and die." Sebastian smiled, proud of his accomplishment, before turning back to Ivy at the bottom of the hole. "He sent them to me."

Carson didn't have a chance to process what Sebastian meant as his recruiter shoved him forward. The ground rushed to meet him. Too fast. And the world went black.

Chapter Seven

Something grimy coated the inside of her mouth.

Her pulse pounded at the back of her head as she tried to bring herself back into consciousness, but the delirium of sleep worked to drag her back down. There was no pain there. No pounding in her ankle. No headache.

Warmth framed her jaw, turning her face this way and that. Too easily. As though she were nothing but a rag doll. "Come now, *senorita*. It's no fun if you're not awake for this next part."

Next part? What was the next part?

Ivy put everything she had into forcing her eyes open. But the world seemed to have turned upside down while she'd been asleep. Not asleep. Knocked out. The outline of a man shifted in front of her, letting her brain first take in the position of her body. Gravity pulled on her every muscle, pain igniting in her feet. Like they'd fallen asleep. No. Like the blood supply had been cut off.

She dragged her chin to her chest, a feat in and of itself. Upside down. A prickling took hold in her fingers. Her hands had been tied behind her back. With a zip tie, from what she could feel.

"Ah, there we are." The man in front of her took his seat.

Though she couldn't pick out any distinguishing features with the lighting so low. Little of her surroundings were distinguishable, but he seemed to be avoiding showing his face altogether. "That's better, don't you think?"

His voice grated against her nerves. The kind of voice that visited in nightmares. Gravelly but calm at the same time. Low and threatening.

Ivy pulled at the zip ties binding her wrists at her lower back. She'd trained her operatives to beat such flimsy safeguards. It wouldn't take much to break through the thin plastic, but the angle had to be right. Upside down was not a good angle. "Where…?"

Snippets of memory—of running for the gate of the junkyard—pieced together as slowly as the puzzle she'd been working on since Christmas. She and Max had gotten sights on the gate. They'd run while Carson intercepted Sebastian. Then…inky blackness.

A hole. Her stomach lurched as she recalled the sensation of falling. She'd landed feetfirst, but her right foot had made contact with a rock protruding from the basin. Her ankle had shot one way while her foot had gone the other before her head had collided with another rock jutting out from the side of the dirt wall. And Max… Where was Max? Where was Carson? "Where am I?"

"Does it matter?" Her captor shifted in his chair, but there was a hint of resistance in the movement. As though his body were fighting against him. She hadn't been able to estimate his age without looking at his face directly, but the thin, papery skin along the backs of his hands said older rather than younger. Crusted jeans were stained with what looked like oil and grease, but from what little light illuminated the room, she noted perfectly clean, trimmed nails.

Not the mechanic he wanted her to believe he was.

Interlacing his hands against his low belly, Sebastian waited. It was an interrogation technique. Silence created pressure to fill the void. Lawyers, law enforcement and her own operatives used it as a weapon, but Ivy was conscious enough to recognize it for what it was: establishing power. He wanted her to believe he was in control. That the only way out of this was to comply, but she'd been through worse. Had survived worse. And he sure as hell would have to try a lot harder to get anything out of her.

Sebastian reached for something off to one side, pulling a sidearm into view. Her sidearm. "No wallet or keys in your possession. Just a gun, a little pocketknife and a lie about who you are. You failed to realize I knew exactly who you were before you showed up at my gate."

"Then why let me in? Why go through this whole charade?" Ivy tried to take in the rest of the room. Find any potential objects that could be used as a weapon. But despite what her brain wanted this place to be, she couldn't pick out equipment, tools or machinery relating to a junkyard warehouse. No. This place, this room, was something far more dangerous. Unique.

"To cut the head off the snake." Sebastian detached the gun's magazine from the main frame, seemingly counting the bullets lined up like little soldiers inside. "You and your private military contractors have torn *Sangre por Sangre* limb from limb. You've hunted us, stolen from us, murdered us."

"Yes. Well, I'm so sorry about stopping your lieutenants from slaughtering thousands of innocent lives so you can push your drugs, steal their women and children and make a profit off other people's misery." Pure vitriol spread through her at the thought of all the damage the cartel had inflicted. All the hatred they'd created. The families they'd torn apart and the homes they'd destroyed. Raids, explosions, underage recruitment. Socorro had saved lives, and now he was going to try to convince her she was the bad guy? "I won't do it again. Promise."

Sebastian's low laugh brushed against a buried part of her memory. As though she'd heard it before. Except that was impossible. Running Socorro kept her out of the field, and there hadn't been a single instance in which *Sangre por Sangre* had succeeded in getting past her security measures. "I can see why Dominic likes you so much. Why he couldn't kill you himself."

Carson. Her heart jumped into her throat. Nothing in her peripheral vision suggested Carson or Max had been invited to this little party. The lack of windows in this place kept her from deducing how long she'd been unconscious, but her internal hunger cues gave a few clues. Not enough time for her insides to start eating themselves. Couple of hours. Maybe less. Which meant they had to be somewhere else. Somewhere within the warehouse or on the property. Sebastian wouldn't have had time to dispose of their bodies and conduct this worthless interview.

The cartel soldier shifted forward, dark hair coming into view as he stood. Heavy footfalls seemed to echo through her with each connection to the cement floor. Sebastian circled to one side, just out of reach. "I imagine you're the reason for my protégé's recent lack of commitment to the operation. Why he's been so…distracted."

"What can I say? I'm in very high demand." Ivy took the opportunity of being out of his direct sight to study the apparatus keeping her hoisted above the floor. While Sebastian had secured her hands with zip ties, he'd doubled up on chains around her ankles, hanging her from an oversize metal hook used to tow vehicles. And considering Carson most likely hadn't helped secure her for the impending torture coming her way, Sebastian would have needed to lift her in place himself. Meaning he wasn't as invalid as he wanted her to believe.

A fist rocketed into the side of her face.

Lightning exploded behind her eyes. Her teeth cut into the soft tissues of her mouth and forced blood to the surface. Momentum swung her body away from her attacker. Sebastian caught her before the pendulum could be completed, and a visceral stain of evil leached through her clothing and deep into bone from his touch alone. "Why don't you tell me what you managed to get out of Dominic, eh? What was your end goal?"

"If I told you that, I'd have to cut this conversation short." Ivy struggled to breathe through the blood clogging her airway. "And we just started to get to know each other."

Another strike spun her a full one hundred and eighty degrees. Only this time, one of her back teeth dislodged. Her face pulsed in anger. The adrenaline that had numbed the area was already dissipating, and pain moved in to replace it. Her vision wavered. She fisted her hands in an attempt to stay conscious, but there were no guarantees.

Searing pain spread across her scalp as Sebastian pulled her head back by her hair. Exposing her throat. A small blade pricked at the thin skin there as he got close enough to whisper in her ear. "You know, I've seen a pocketknife like this before. A few years ago now. You don't realize how very sharp they are until someone stabs you with it."

Warning pooled in her gut.

"I know why you came here, Agent Bardot." Puffs of air tickled her ear and triggered a shiver, but she wouldn't let him see the effect he had on her. That his proximity had on her. "I know you've been searching for me all this time. That I'm the one who haunts your dreams and influenced every decision you've ever made in the past two years. You built Socorro to protect yourself from me, but where is your team now? Hmm?"

Agent Bardot. Not *Ms*.

Ice coursed through her veins as that voice took its rightful place in her memory. There was a reason it had felt so familiar, why he'd tried to hide his identity.

Sebastian moved into her line of view, fully exposing his face in the light, and her insides knotted tight.

"You." All this time, Carson had been tasked to uncover the identity of the man who'd killed three women from within *Sangre por Sangre*. And the son of a bitch had been in front of him the entire time. Though it wasn't clear until this moment—hanging upside down from her ankles with blood trailing into her hairline—that Carson hadn't set eyes on the man who'd nearly killed her.

That night, those memories she'd tried to bury, flooded through her mind in a rush that stole her breath. Of waking in a basement not unlike this room, of feeling the killer's hands on her. Of knowing there was a possibility she would die, that she'd never see her partner again. In an instant, Ivy was right back in that position. Vulnerable, helpless. It was all too much of a reminder of those nights her stepfather had drunk too much and exerted his power over her mother with flying fists, hard shoves and broken bones.

Until she hadn't been able to take it anymore.

Ivy saw herself in her mind's eye pulling her stepdad's

gun from his nightstand as a ten-year-old. She saw herself fisting her pocketknife in that basement two years ago.

And in this moment, she saw herself snapping through the zip tie binding her wrists and ending this for good.

"That's right, *senorita*. Me." Sebastian released his hold on her hair, letting the blade of her own pocketknife cut through the first layer of skin at her neck. "You and I have some unfinished business to attend to."

ALL HE COULD hear was barking.

Incessant and sharp and panicked.

Carson felt as though an elephant was sitting on his chest, ready to crush him to death. He tried to reorient himself, but he couldn't seem to get his body to obey. The last memory—of falling, of being shoved, of trying to avoid landing on Ivy—took center stage.

Sebastian. That son of a bitch had captured Ivy and Max. And now… Now Carson didn't know what had happened to his partner. Though from the sound of it, Max wasn't too far away. Her barks cleared the haze from his head second by second.

He tried to bring his head up. Too fast. His forehead collided with something metal and large. Lightning exploded behind his eyes, and he fell back. Cement smacked against the back of his skull. If he hadn't sustained a concussion from the fall into a dark hole in the middle of a salvage yard, he sure as hell had now.

His next inhalation caught hints of motor oil, gasoline and rust. His chest seemed to fill any available space, but it was too dark to get a sense of his situation. It was like he'd been sandwiched between two oversize forces. Carson maneuvered his hands at his sides. His weapon had been taken from him. Sebastian hadn't wanted to take any chances of him shooting his way out of...whatever this place was. Not a surprise but still a disappointment. He'd been positioned on his back. Cement beneath him had been sealed. Most likely a floor. Inside the warehouse? He couldn't be sure yet.

Another round of barking pierced into awareness.

"Max?" Carson's vision adjusted the longer he focused, but there was still too much unknown for him to create a strategy to get out. Her responding whine confirmed what he needed to know. She was alive. She was okay. "Good girl."

He managed to get his elbows into his rib cage and feel the wall hoisted above him. He followed the curves of what felt like car parts. Only there was something distorted about their shape. As though they'd been crushed. Burned crust flaked off and fell into his eyes, nose and mouth. He spit at the chemical bite, but there was nothing that could get rid of the taste of asphalt and heat. "Damn it."

Sebastian had pinned him beneath a crushed car somehow.

The narrow cavity giving him enough space to keep breathing must've been maintained by one of the hoists. Though the son of a bitch had set it on the lowest level. Without the vehicle's tires, there was no room to navigate an escape.

He was trapped.

An animal-like scream escaped his chest as Carson shoved against the vehicle balanced above him with everything he had. It echoed off the warehouse walls but failed to change anything. He needed to get out of here. He needed to locate Ivy.

He'd brought her here to ease the pressure of this investigation, to give her hope the past two years hadn't been for nothing. But all he'd managed to do was make things worse.

He'd trusted the wrong person, and now she would be the one to pay for his mistake.

Carson braced both palms against the underside of the car. The muscles in his neck and shoulders strained against the weight of the vehicle. There was no moving it. Not on his own. "Come on!"

There was no telling what Sebastian would do to Ivy. How much pain he would inflict. Or if the bastard would just kill her for her connection to Socorro.

Max's barking seared his nerves with every protest. Until it was all he could focus on. His heart rate ratcheted into his throat as he released his hold on the vehicle above. He couldn't lose Ivy. Not after everything they'd fought for. Not after what they'd survived. They'd sacrificed too much to only come this far and get nothing in reward. He didn't want to imagine all the ways Sebastian was punishing her for her crimes against the cartel, but he couldn't stop the thoughts either.

He'd taken this assignment to do something good with his life. To earn the kidneys both his mother and Ivy had donated to save his life. But what had he really accomplished? What did he have to show for it? There was no end to the amount of evil and violence he and Ivy took on every day, and no matter how hard he fought, it felt as though every step forward was ripped out from underneath him. He'd given up his friends, what little remained of his family, his life. All he had left was Ivy.

"And Max." Carson shifted his body weight to one side of the cavity stabilizing the hoist. There wasn't enough room for him to roll. He had to leverage his heels and palms into the floor and slide. Dim light bled through the gaps between the crushed vehicle and the platform meant to support the tires. He could make out movement through the holes. "Max."

Stillness followed her gruff response.

More details came into focus the longer he forced his brain to account for the obstacles in his vision. He could just make out the K-9's paws if he concentrated hard enough. "Come here."

Max took a few steps forward but was prevented from making it to his position. Which meant Sebastian had most likely tied her to something in the shop. Only Carson couldn't tell with what. There was a difference between a chain and a section of rope. She whined about not being able to fulfill her orders. "It's okay. We're going to get out of here. We're going to find your mom. I promise."

Though how he was going to do any of that still hadn't made itself clear. Either way, he wouldn't give up. Not on them. Not on their future. One they'd earned through the countless hours of blood, sweat and tears. Of losses on both sides and the hurt they'd inflicted. On victims who hadn't been given the justice they deserved. Because he believed in them. Him and Ivy. These past two years had been about doing what they each thought was best to protect those who couldn't protect themselves, but no future was worth not having her in it.

Carson angled his head in a way to give him a better view of whatever had been tied around Max's collar. An earthquake-sized relief rocked through him. Rope. He and Max had trained for this in the times they weren't assigned perimeter security or guard duty. It had taken up silent hours waiting until the next Socorro raid, and he'd never been more grateful for those hours now. "Max, *packen*." Bite.

The German shepherd stared at him as though trying to

decipher if a crushed car was the one giving her the order. Carson fit his finger through one of the gaps in the metal. *"Packen."*

His K-9 partner took the command to heart, turning on the section of rope securing her to something out of sight. She clamped down on the twine and got to work. Within minutes, Max had chewed through the rope and gained her freedom. A few feet of rope still remained tied to her collar, but she didn't seem to mind. Charging for his position, she put some bounce in her step. Showing off. She pressed her nose against his exposed finger.

"Good girl. Good girl. I'm getting you the largest steak I can find as soon as we get out of this place." Carson rubbed at her nose, but the affection fell short. "Okay. We need to find the controls to get this thing off of me."

How the hell he was going to manage that in his current position, he didn't know, but Max was smart, and he'd prepared her for anything. He didn't have a whole lot of knowledge when it came to mechanic shops and salvage yards, but there had to be a button or lever that would lift the vehicle. *"Knopf."* Button.

Max sniffed at his finger for a few more seconds, then pulled back. Out of sight. Her nails clicked against the cracking cement. Strong at first, then less so. A rise of panic coated Carson's throat, but as long as he was trapped here, Max wouldn't leave. It wasn't in her nature to abandon the people she loved.

"What do you see, Max?" He tried to maneuver farther down the cavity, but the angle of the tire platform dropped off toward his feet, and his toes hit the underside of the vehicle. *"Knopf?"*

No answer. No sound of her nails on the floor.

"Max?" he asked.

The car jolted above him.

His nerves spiked into dangerous territory. Carson braced for the potential of the two-ton vehicle to drop directly on him, but nothing happened for a series of seconds.

The car shifted again. This time increasing the light coming in through the gaps between the hunk of metal and the hoist. It was moving upward. A laugh clawed through Carson's chest. "Max, *knopf*!"

A mechanical groan filled his ears, and the car lifted higher. It cleared the platform, but there still wasn't enough room for him to squeeze through. Not yet. "Keep going, baby." Another round of moaning raised the oversize paperweight higher.

The hoist continued its upward ascent. Any mechanic would've spotted the signs the weight had been unevenly distributed and stopped, but he couldn't expect that from a German shepherd.

The vehicle had started tipping toward him. Off-balance.

But there still wasn't enough space between the bottom of the car and the tire platform for him to escape. Carson didn't have a choice. He had to move. Now.

He kept his attention locked on the unbalanced vehicle as he hauled himself over the brim of the cavity holding him hostage.

Carson hit the cement floor, free of his makeshift prison.

Just as the vehicle dropped.

Two thousand–plus pounds of metal screeched from the impact. In the exact same location as he'd been held hostage. Shattered glass escaped the confines of the car's shell and skimmed across the floor to his position.

Max's bark called to him from the back of the hoist. He

scrambled to his feet, out of breath and in one piece. Because of his K-9 partner. Max nearly knocked him over as she stretched onto her hind legs to give her version of a hug. He buried his hands into her fur. "You're getting as many steaks as you want tonight."

She licked at his face, then sneezed from the amount of crust that covered his skin, before dropping onto all fours.

"Had I known you were going to kiss me, I would've showered first." He caught sight of a toolbox splayed open with an array of potential weapons. Sebastian might've taken his gun, but the son of a bitch wasn't going to take anything else from him. Carson collected a heavy wrench capable of a lot of damage if swung hard enough. "Now, what do you say we go get your mom?"

Chapter Eight

The crash jolted her awake.

Though she wasn't entirely sure she'd fallen asleep as Sebastian—if that was his real name—fed into his own desperation for answers. Where was her team? Where would they strike next? Had they learned about this location? Her body hurt. Every inch. Blood dripped from her hair onto the floor below, staining the cement.

A bark reached through the haze closing in around Ivy's awareness. Through the seal her brain had created to protect itself. She knew that bark.

"I never liked that dog." Sebastian stepped into view, her pocketknife in hand. Coated with her blood.

"She's a…good judge of character." She'd lost count of how many lacerations he'd cut into her arms, legs and stomach. Nothing vital. He knew what he was doing, how to bleed her to death without so much as raising her body's alarm systems until it was too late. Her mouth felt full. As though she'd attempted to swallow a handful of bees. Adrenaline had left the party a while ago. She couldn't count on it to get her out of this as she had so many times before. Adrenaline didn't consider logic or others. It was pure survival. Her arms ached as she attempted to break through the zip ties one more time. In vain. The angle was wrong. Not enough force.

"Don't go anywhere. We're not finished." He flipped the pocketknife to face down in his palm and stabbed it into the drywall near a door she hadn't noticed until then. In a single breath, her abductor—her torturer—was gone.

A sliver of hope that had no business sparking lit up inside of her. The crash. She wasn't sure of the source, but given Max was alive, Ivy was willing to bet Carson was, too. That he'd been the one to cause the disruption of Sebastian's latest masterpiece. Ivy struggled against gravity and exhaustion to duck her chin into her chest. There wasn't much she could do in the way of getting her hands around her feet for better access.

But there was another way.

She forced air into her lungs, then breathed out harder than necessary. It had been years since she'd dislocated her shoulder, courtesy of her stepfather, but old wounds never really healed right. There was a chance this could work. If she was willing to endure just a little longer. For Carson. For Max. For the family she'd created in a world full of nothing but brutality and betrayal. Ivy clamped her back teeth together, stretching her bound wrists toward the floor.

The idea of inflicting pain on herself when she'd intentionally built Socorro to protect her and others from going through what she had as a child gripped her hard. But the possibility of losing everything—her partner, her team, her dog—hurt so much more.

"One." Her stomach protested the pain coming. "Two." She bounced her straightened arms to get a feel for the momentum needed. "Three."

She put everything she had into disconnecting her right

shoulder. The muscles screamed as they twisted in the entirely wrong direction. Inky blackness encroached into the edges of her vision, but she had to hang on. She had to keep going. Her wrists followed the path of the zip tie as she brought them forward. Every breath helped ease the pain, but her body had hit a wall. It couldn't take much more.

Ivy fought through the drowning sensation pulling her into unconsciousness. If she blacked out now, Sebastian would have free rein to kill her and everyone she loved. There would be no one to stop him. No. She couldn't give in. No matter how much she wanted to. She'd survived before. She could—she would—do it again.

Reaching for her feet, she attempted to curl her upper body forward. But the lacerations across her midsection only slowed her down. She fell back and let the relief take hold. Just for a moment. There was a chance she'd never be able to lift a weapon with her damaged arm, but for now, all she needed it to do was get her closer to the tow hook holding her hostage. Ivy tried again. A groan backed up in her throat as her fingertips brushed the end of the hook.

"Closer." She collapsed again. The room swirled in her vision as she released the air she hadn't realized she'd been holding on to. Time seemed to slip through her fingers without any effort. Seconds, minutes, an hour. She wasn't sure how long she hung there. The rhythmic patter of blood dripping onto the floor kept in time with the pulse thudding in her throat. This wasn't how it was supposed to end.

She pried her eyes open.

And stared straight into the face of a dead man. As real as Sebastian, as Carson, as the operatives on her team. He hadn't aged a day despite twenty-seven years since she'd seen him.

"What did I always tell you, Ives?" her stepfather said. "You're not strong enough to beat me."

"You're not real." The words slurred due to the swelling in her face and lips. "You're not here."

His sneer pooled dread at the base of her spine. It was that same sneer he'd given her when he'd dared her to pull the trigger that night. Right before he'd lunged at her to take the gun. She'd shot him at just ten years old, scared, desperate to help her mother, to keep him from killing them both. Then she'd shot him again. He'd dropped to the floor right there in the entryway of their small Jacksonville house, hand to his chest. And she'd stood over him, watching. Waiting for him to take his last breath. Her mother had called the paramedics with a broken arm and two missing teeth, and the EMTs had somehow kept him alive. Only he'd never come home after leaving the hospital. He was still out there. Still haunting her memories, her nightmares.

"You're a coward, Ives. Same as you've always been." Her stepfather moved in closer. So close, she could almost smell that sickening scent of his aftershave. "You think you're protecting people, but the truth is, you're just protecting yourself. Like a child. All you ever cared about was yourself, what you wanted. That's why you shot me. It wasn't to protect your mama. Look what happened to her after that night."

"No." Tears burned in her eyes, giving away the echoing feelings of helplessness when faced with this particular threat. She didn't want to think about that. About how after the incident her mother hadn't been able to find a job, how she hadn't been able to put food on the table and then just gave up trying. Life had beaten her mother down long after her stepfather had gone, had stolen any glimpse of hope.

Until there was nothing left but drugs, a revolving door of men and a final overdose.

"She died because of you. You know that, right?" His words surfaced and took shape from within; they'd followed her through high school, college, into the FBI, and were controlling her now. "If you hadn't shot me, she'd still be here. You're pathetic, Ivy Bardot. You're nothing. You can't save anyone. You can't even save yourself."

"Stop." Tears mixed with blood across her face. The image—the hallucination—of her stepfather waned. Years of building her personal armor, of becoming the woman she was, seemed to disintegrate at the accusations living in her head. Ivy shook her head as though it would make him go away. "It's not true."

The thing that made everything not so bad was knowing, sooner or later, I was coming home to you. Carson's words cut through the self-hatred and worked to repair the damage done to her heart. They burned through her, cleansing and clarifying. Ivy set her attention on the figment of her imagination. Carson was out there right now. Fighting to survive. Fighting for her. Just as he'd done during their last case together. They were still here because they'd refused to give up on one another. And she wasn't going to let the past stand in the way now.

"You're wrong." Confidence replenished some of the strength she'd lost since coming to this hellhole. "I was a child, asshole. Everything that happened in our family was the responsibility of two adults who should've made better choices."

Anger creased her stepfather's expression. He reached for her, but Ivy thrust herself upward with everything she had left. Her fingers latched on to the tow hook. She gripped the cold steel with force enough to crush a diamond, hauling her bound ankles over the lip of the hook. Just as quickly, her strength gave out. She hit the floor, her legs collapsing out from under her. It was enough. She was free.

Her stepfather had returned to the small space in her head where she'd buried the memories of him. At least he'd been good for something after all this time. She managed to untangle her ankles from the rope, but the filaments of torn muscle in her shoulder wouldn't like what came next. Hiking her hands above her head, she slammed them down against her thighs with as much force as she could muster. The zip tie broke. Setting sights on the door, she fought through the dizziness closing in and locked on her pocketknife stabbed into the drywall there. "That's mine."

Crusted blood stained the handle and blade, but it would be enough in the coming fight. Because this wasn't over. Throwing open the door, Ivy stepped out into a black expanse of warehouse. Her ankle ached under her full weight, but she couldn't stop now. She had a family to protect. Every cell in her body homed in on picking up the threat before it slapped her in the face. A single fluorescent light flickered at her left, and she scanned for movement.

"You were right, Sebastian." Her words bounced off the sheet-metal walls, and the confidence in her voice invigorated her to keep moving. "You and I have unfinished business."

No answer. No sign of Max or Carson. It would be easy to panic if she let herself, but she'd just conquered one of the demons that kept her up at night. Now it was time to face the second. Gripping her pocketknife in her nondominant hand, she pressed her back into the walls of whatever room Sebastian had held her in. "Come out, come out, wherever you are."

"Are you sure you want to play this game, little girl?" Sebastian's answer felt far away and yet too close at the same time. "The last time I checked, you weren't cut out to face me."

She'd sustained a good amount of injury hung upside down as his personal punching bag. Her brain could be messing with her, but Ivy got the feeling her perception hadn't changed. Sebastian knew this warehouse better than she or Carson. There were spaces he'd most likely created to track his enemies, watch them, ambush them. He wouldn't be so lucky today. Memories of that voice threatened to slow her down, but she'd already made up her mind. There was no turning back.

A shadow shifted in her peripheral vision.

She didn't hesitate. She arced the blade of her undersized weapon.

And hit something soft.

"My pocketknife says otherwise." Ivy fisted Sebastian's collar and dragged him into the light. Victory charged through her as pain creased into his face. "This is for Nafessa Piel."

Agony seared through her side. Exposing a thin saw blade where her right kidney used to be.

"And this is for stabbing me two years ago," he said.

She stumbled back, forced to leave her pocketknife in his shoulder.

And dropped to her knees.

"No!" Carson watched on as though things unraveled in slow motion.

Ivy pressed a hand to her side. Then turned her gaze to him down the length of the maze of in-progress automobiles before going limp. She hit the floor with nothing more than the sound of a feather landing lightly.

Everything in him froze. His worst nightmare had come to fruition. He'd lost her. Carson's bellow filled the entire warehouse.

Sebastian wasn't ready for the rage boiling over inside of him.

Carson raced to close the distance between them. He swung the heavy-duty wrench with every ounce of control he had left. Sebastian dodged the first attempt but couldn't avoid the second. Metal connected with bone in a sickening crunch that would haunt Carson for the rest of his life. The man he'd once considered a mentor within the cartel—a friend, even—had taken away the only person he had left. There was no one left to ground him to this life. His father had left when he'd been a kid; his mother had died after an infection started eating her from the inside. The FBI wanted nothing to do with him, and the men and women he'd fought beside on the battlefield were six feet underground. And now Ivy. Taken by the very person he'd saved from being buried under megatons of rock, cement and steel.

He swung the wrench back for another blow. To end it.

Only Sebastian wasn't ready to accept his fate. The cartel soldier caught Carson's wrist, but the wrench's momentum ripped the tool out of Carson's hand. It skidded across the cement and was lost to shadow in an instant.

A fist rocketed into Carson's face. Once. Twice. Lights exploded behind his eyes, but it wouldn't slow him down. Sebastian held on to his wrist. Except there was more than one way to win a fight. Carson thrust his forehead into the bastard's face. *Sangre por Sangre*'s most fearsome killer fell back, releasing his hold with a groan. Another fist came at him, and Carson raised both forearms to block it.

"Max, *bring*!" Retrieve. The K-9 leaped from her hiding place with a sharp protest, vaulting for Ivy. She'd never had to pull an entire person out of a hostile situation before, but Carson had his faith placed in her. It was the only way they were all going to get out of this alive. The German shepherd latched on to Ivy's boot and started jerking Ivy out of sight.

"I'm going to cut you and gut you for what you've done, Rojas. You should know better by now. No one escapes *Sangre por Sangre*." Sebastian added some distance between them, swiping the back of his hand beneath his shattered nose.

"What did you just say?" That phrasing. He'd heard it before. No. He'd read it before. Carved into the backs of four women, one of whom had been killed a mere two days ago. But…it wasn't possible. Was it? The man standing in front of him—who'd served as his recruiter and guided him through the ranks of the cartel—couldn't be the same one he'd been searching for all this time.

"There's no saving Agent Bardot. Even if you make it out of here alive, I will hunt you both for the rest of your lives." Sebastian's threats were more growl than words now. "You will never be safe. You will never have a future. I'll make sure of it."

Agent Bardot. Not Ivy Bardot of Socorro Security. Sebastian had known Ivy since before she'd founded her private military contractor operation. But it didn't matter what the son of a bitch called her. Every second Carson wasted here was another second Ivy didn't have. She'd been stabbed. He didn't know how badly, but he'd lived through the experience enough to tell him there was a chance she could bleed out if he didn't get to her.

"We've survived worse than you." Carson kicked out. His heel connected with Sebastian's midsection and sent the cartel soldier straight back into a tool bench.

"You have no idea who I am, do you, boy? What I can do to you and your partner?" Sebastian grabbed for a section of chain coiled on the surface and whipped the heavy metal. He was grabbing for anything and everything. Always putting his own survival first. It was a wonder Carson had gotten this far within *Sangre por Sangre* without seeing it until now. "You've never known the kind of pain I will bring down on you."

Sebastian lashed out with the chain.

The links snapped against Carson's raised wrist as he attempted to block the strike and coiled around as tight as a boa constrictor might. Muscles burned as he, in turn, pulled the chain tighter and brought Sebastian into his personal space.

A fist thrust into his kidney.

Carson arched backward as the pain lightninged across his back and down into his legs. Three surgeries—two transplants and a stab wound—should have prepared him for the pain, but the opposite seemed to be true. One knee bit into the ground. Sebastian released his hold on the chain. Only to secure it around Carson's neck in his next breath.

The metal dug into Carson's flesh. Pinched his skin between the links as his air supply lodged in his throat. He couldn't breathe. Couldn't think. Pressure built in his chest to the point he was convinced his lungs might pop. He tried to twist out of the man's grip, but Sebastian only held on tighter.

Black waves pierced into his vision. Trying to convince him to give up, to sink into the gravitational pull of unconsciousness. Carson threaded his fingers around the chain, but it was no use. Sebastian had the upper hand. He put everything he had into his heels, kicking back. But the leverage did nothing to relieve the weight of suffocation.

Sebastian's hands shook from the effort. The only reminder the cartel recruiter was human. That he could bleed just as well as Carson. As Ivy.

Max would get her out of the warehouse. She and Ivy were going to make it. His partner had out-strategized some of the top supervising agents back in the FBI. When she set the rules, failure wasn't an option. There was only winning in her book. And she wouldn't let something like a stab wound slow her down. Not when there were potential lives at risk. The partners who'd come before him had seen her as a narcissist, selfish, someone bent on having control and only concerned with her own survival. He'd been warned of her intensity, that she tended to mow people down—partners, witnesses, supervising agents—to get her way.

But that wasn't Ivy at all. Not the real her. Not the woman she'd allowed him to see underneath that battle armor. Though it had taken both of them nearly dying for Carson to see the truth. That intensity every one of her former partners had feared had been built on survival. They'd been right about that. But not hers. She fought for the victims. For the potential victims. For those who'd been taken advantage of and those too scared to stand up for themselves. She fought a war no one else could see to ensure the evil would never touch them. Hell, he admired her. Wanted to be half as strong as her.

And he would make sure she got out of this alive.

Because the cartel wouldn't stop, and the innocent lives in

their path deserved someone to protect them. They needed her to keep fighting for them. She was all that mattered.

Carson grabbed for the old man's forearms with both hands. Sebastian had the upper hand, the higher ground, but Carson had the strength. He put everything he had into shoving to his feet. Sebastian was forced to adjust his hold.

And Carson took advantage.

He hauled the cartel soldier over his back and slammed the bastard onto the cement in front of him. Air crushed from Sebastian's lungs as Carson unraveled the chain from around his neck. His cough filled the warehouse as his lungs tried to remember how to breathe. He tossed the length of chain. "You're not strong enough to take her on alone. No one is. So tell upper management if they want a war, they'll have it, and they will lose. Because you have no idea what you're up against."

The old man grabbed for his back, rolling onto one side. Giving up the fight.

Carson stepped over the son of a bitch, and exhaustion hit hard. He'd been running off fumes and adrenaline. A potent combination that only inflicted more damage the longer he pushed himself. He located the point where Ivy had collapsed, noting the trail of blood left behind as Max had dragged her out of the building. He had to go. He had to get her to the hospital. Now.

"You don't get to walk away from this. None of us do." Sebastian's voice was the only warning Carson received as a pipe came down on his shoulder.

The pain exploded through his neck and down his arm, but it wasn't enough to stop him from turning on his former mentor. He caught the pipe on Sebastian's second attempt and ripped the weapon from the man's hand. Immediately returning the attack. The end of the pipe connected with Sebastian's face, and the son of a bitch hit the floor. "Go back into hiding, Sebastian. That's the only way you're going to get out of this alive."

He tossed the pipe to one side, jogging for the exit. The trail of blood took a right turn. Headed straight for the nearest door. "Good girl, Max."

Carson shoved through the barrier and out in the New Mexico sunrise. Cold air burned down his throat as he sighted the German shepherd struggling to get her human across the salvage yard gravel. His heart double-timed as he picked up the pace. "Ivy."

Max released her hold on Ivy, pouncing on all four paws.

He skidded to a stop, kicking up gravel as he hauled Ivy's upper body away from the ground. Her head fell back. Swelling blocked out one of her eyes, bruises already starting across her jaw. But it was the blood that nearly stopped his heart.

Cuts covered her arms, legs and torso. Dozens of them. Something dangerous and more familiar than he wanted to admit clawed through him, and if Ivy weren't in a position of bleeding out in his arms, he would go back into that warehouse. He would make Sebastian pay for what he'd done.

But he didn't have time. Ivy didn't have time. Carson threaded his arms behind her shoulders and knees and shoved to stand. Max followed on his heels, her attention fixed on the woman in his grasp. "I've got you, partner. I've got you."

Chapter Nine

People were dying to get into their graves.

Ivy wasn't one of them.

Bright fluorescent lighting agitated the migraine somehow behind her eyes and every other inch of her brain. She wanted to go back to sleep, but the damn rhythmic pulse on the EKG machine wouldn't let her. The IV line in the back of her hand itched and hurt at the same time. And the bedsheets had obviously come straight from hell.

Ugh. She'd been admitted to a hospital.

"You're awake. That's a good sign." The voice she expected was not the one speaking to her now. Styled dark hair consumed her attention. Not a single hair out of place. White coat—physician.

"I don't know you." Her heart hurt at the reminder Dr. Piel wouldn't be the one to clear her for fieldwork or to go head-to-head with Congress again. Ivy scanned the room, but there was no sign of her team. No sign of Max. Or Carson.

She didn't know what to think of that right then. Didn't really want to think about it.

"No. I expect you wouldn't." Her doctor faced her, his clipboard leveraged against his lower abdomen. Sharp features built out a handsome face. A little too perfect for her taste. She'd always been attracted to men who had a little wear on them, a little life experience. This one was brand-new. "I'm Dr. Cavill. I'm your attending physician during your stay here."

"And where exactly is here?" Ivy tried to sit up, but her body seemed to have other plans. In the way it screamed at the slightest movement. How her right shoulder refused to take any weight. She could see out of both eyes. That was comforting. The swelling she'd sustained from Sebastian's fist colliding with her face multiple times had gone down. Which meant she hadn't just taken a nap in the time she'd passed out and woken here. It was now most likely days since she and Carson had stepped into a fight they hadn't been prepared to handle.

"Alpine Valley." Dr. Cavill made a note on the clipboard. Presumably in her chart.

"I'm in the clinic." That explained the sheets. Alpine Valley, while home to almost two thousand residents, kept a small-time feel with family-owned businesses and a medical clinic that mostly handled broken bones and people who knew each other's names. "Can I get an early checkout?"

"I'm afraid not." His laugh did nothing to ease her discomfort. "You're lucky to be alive, Ms. Bardot. You've suffered from multiple blows to the face, dislocated a shoulder, and we can't forget about that nasty stab wound in your side. If you still had a kidney, we probably wouldn't be having this conversation."

"Don't forget the sprained ankle." Her nerves were ticking higher with every pulse of that damn machine. She'd never liked being held against her will. Though she'd have to say this was far more preferable than being hung upside down from a tow hook and used as a piñata. "As for the kidney, someone else is borrowing it."

Dr. Cavill set the clipboard on the side table and unwound the stethoscope from around his neck. Practiced movements. As though done thousands of times. Maybe he wasn't so brand-new after all. "Yes, I've read your medical history."

Goose pimples spread over her skin as he slipped the cold metal between her shoulder blades. She tried to keep her breathing steady, but the more she tried to force herself to relax, the farther away she seemed to get from her goal. "Not sure how you would, seeing as how that is confidential information."

"I contacted your employer when we couldn't find any next of kin to ask permission for your history. One of your employees—Cash, I think his name was—was kind enough to send it over while you were recovering. He's in the lobby with a couple police officers waiting to take your statement about how you ended up in my clinic. Along with what I believe is everyone else who works for Socorro." Dr. Cavill withdrew his probing and recentered the stethoscope around his neck.

Her team was here?

"I have to say it's a miracle the damage you sustained wasn't any worse. The dozen or so lacerations over your body were all relatively surface cuts. We've cleaned and bandaged each one." The physician picked up his clipboard once again, making another note. "As for the stab wound, we sewed you up with two levels of stitches. We found some rust flakes in the wound, so we made sure you were up-to-date on your tetanus shot. You should make a full recovery with no ongoing issues as long as you take it easy for the next few weeks, but based off your past X-rays, I'm willing to bet this isn't the first time you've dislocated that shoulder."

Her past X-rays. Dr. Piel had insisted on collecting as much past medical history and films as possible for each Socorro operative. Ivy couldn't even remember the number of broken bones she'd sustained the first ten years of her life. Each had healed, in their own way. None perfectly. "No. Not the first time."

A deep ache that had nothing to do with her injuries took hold. "What happened to the man who was with me? Carson—" She had to stop herself. Because Carson Lang didn't exist anymore. That part of his life had ended a long time ago, and there was no getting it back. Not as long as *Sangre por Sangre* still had power. "Dominic Rojas. He would've had a German shepherd with him. Is he here?"

"He was." Dr. Cavill finally looked up from that damn clipboard. He pointed to the door with the end of his pen. "I think one of the nurses finally convinced him you would be okay if he got a few hours of sleep. I'll see if my staff can locate him."

Something released inside of her. He was alive. They both were, and it didn't escape Ivy that they'd been in this situation before. Not that long ago they'd faced a killer in a cartel hideout. The same killer. A sinking sensation interrupted the steady rhythm of her heart rate on the EKG, but Dr. Cavill didn't seem to notice.

"Try to get some rest. You've been through a lot." The physician headed for the door. "I'll be back to check on you in a couple hours. Until then, try not to make matters worse by thinking you can check yourself out, Ms. Bardot."

Before he could exit, Dr. Cavill stepped back as the heavy

metal door opened from the other side. Carson. "Well, that saves me having to track anyone down."

The doctor closed the door behind him, sealing her and Carson in the same room.

"Hi." As a professional, she ran a multibillion-dollar security firm. She lobbied for additional resources from the Pentagon. She shot down congressmen and made public statements. And the only thing she could think to say when seeing her partner was *hi*.

"You're awake." Carson moved deeper into the room, heading straight for the side of her bed.

"That's what they tell me." She grabbed on to her injured shoulder wrapped securely against her chest. "Can't say it's been a great experience thus far, but it's better than being used as a punching bag for a cartel soldier."

He settled on the edge of the bed, the mattress dipping under his weight, but there was a distance between them. Something thick and unspoken she didn't want to deal with right now. "Ivy, I'm sorry. I made a mistake—"

"Stop. It's…" Well, it wasn't fine. It wasn't close to fine, but blaming him for what had happened wouldn't get them closer to bringing Dr. Piel's killer to justice. "It's him, Carson. Sebastian. He killed those women."

Understanding slid into his expression. "All this time I've been looking for the man who abducted you—almost killed you—and he was standing right in front of me."

"What better way to hide than in plain sight?" Images kept coming back to her. Of the warehouse. Of seeing Carson before she collapsed. There were sensations and memories and confusion. And it had all led to this. To them. Ivy shut down a shiver prickling along her spine. "Did you…? Is he dead?"

"No." Regret laced that single word. "I sent him back to

upper management with a message. They want to come for you, they'll lose. I'll make sure of it."

The wrongness of that statement collided with her need to know she wasn't alone in this and pressed the oxygen from her lungs. A warning that had been there since the moment she'd found him in her apartment slithered into awareness. It had taken a back seat in her subconscious over the course of two days, but it was growing now. "You had the chance to put an end to this, and you let the killer off with a warning?"

"You'd been stabbed, Ivy. You were bleeding everywhere. I wasn't sure how long you had until…" Color drained from his face. "I didn't want to lose you again. I did what I thought was right."

Right. Of course he had. Because that was what partners were supposed to do. Ivy chastised herself for seeing a potential threat where there was none. She didn't know whether it was from the painkillers or the trauma she'd sustained that raised her defenses, but there had to be a point where she let herself take something at face value. There wasn't always a hidden agenda. She reached for his hand, pressing her thumb between his first two knuckles. "Thank you. For getting me out of there."

"Actually, that was Max," he said. "Turns out she's a lot better at retrieval than I gave her credit for."

"I'll be sure to thank her, too." Ivy pulled on his hand until Carson's upper body had to come with him.

"You're going to have a hard time getting her attention with all your operatives keeping her busy out in the parking lot." A smile pulled at one corner of his mouth, instantly erasing the memory of Dominic Rojas. The partner she'd fallen for locked his gaze on hers as he leaned into her.

"In that case, I think we should enjoy this time we have alone together," she said.

"Believe me, Agent Bardot." Carson pressed his mouth against hers, and the pain, reality and a whole lot of bad disappeared at the contact. "I intend to."

They couldn't go back to the cartel safe house.

Not as long as Sebastian—or whoever the hell the killer was—was alive. Whatever remained of *Sangre por Sangre* had been called to a final fight, with Sebastian at the forefront. There was no going back. There was no more Dominic Rojas or the connection he'd built over the past two years. No resources. No team he could rely on. And Carson couldn't help but feel a hole beginning to develop at an entire two years of his life gone just like that.

Once they'd given their statements to Alpine PD, they'd been permitted to leave the clinic. As long as Ivy promised to rest. An impossible task for a woman determined to take on the weight of every suffering human and find a dozen solutions in the process. He pulled the SUV off to the side of the road of a little neighborhood he hadn't stepped foot in since he'd gone undercover. Max's tail hit him in the face as she climbed over the center console and across Ivy's lap to look out the window. "Get out of here, you giant fur ball." He tried to maneuver her into the back seat, but there was no derailing the German shepherd.

She was home.

"What are we doing here?" Ivy studied the small house with its pristine stucco, traditional-style roof and maintained front lawn. The tree out front looked much bigger than he remembered the last time he'd been here, and the garage had been painted black instead of its original white, but everything else pulled memories from a happier time.

A time when he knew who the hell he was. Where he belonged.

The bruising along one side of Ivy's face had darkened to a sickening purple and blue but told him Sebastian favored his right hook. Something to keep in mind the next time they met. "You realize I don't live here anymore, right? I live part-time in that place full of bullet holes we escaped four nights ago and the other part in a stronghold with a team of mercenaries."

Carson shouldered out of the vehicle. His forearms ached with the use of the small muscles extending from his wrists to his elbows. Protecting his head from being bashed in with a pipe had left its stain beneath his skin, but it was nothing compared to the pain Ivy had to deal with. They needed somewhere she would be safe, that gave her the time she needed to recover. Where nobody could find her. Rounding in front of the SUV, he felt Ivy's eyes follow him as he approached her door. He opened the passenger-side door and offered his hand. "Trust me."

Max took the opportunity to spring out of the vehicle. She bounded up the driveway and pranced around the front yard as if she owned the place.

Ivy stared at his hand, then cut her gaze to the house behind him. He could practically see the wheels turning in her head, considering all her options. Trust him or die at the hands of a killer who'd been playing mind games with them all this time? The choice should've been easy, right? Slipping her uninjured hand into his, she let him pull her and her go bag from the vehicle. "What did you do?"

"Nothing big. Just convinced the people who bought the

place from you to sell it to me." Carson led her up the driveway, slower than he wanted to go but fully aware of her limitations after surviving what she had.

Disbelief and something along the lines of joy etched into her features. Ivy couldn't seem to take her eyes off of the house. "When did you do this?"

"While you were recovering in the hospital. Not sure you know this, but you were asleep for a long time." A move of this magnitude had taken precision planning and people skills. But, in the end, he knew it was worth the effort. Just for the look on her face. "I know you had to give this house up when I went undercover. We couldn't hold on to our old lives when we started this war, but considering our options are limited to using *Sangre por Sangre* resources or putting you in the crosshairs with a Socorro safe house, I figured this would be the best place to lie low for a couple days."

"How…? How is this possible?" she asked.

Carson offered her the key. "Want to go inside?"

She nodded, seemingly incapable of responding. They moved as one up the rest of the driveway and past the black iron gate protecting the front door from solicitors and anyone else looking for their pound of flesh. Ivy slid the key into the dead bolt and turned.

Max pushed past both of them, nearly knocking Carson off-balance. Her nails clicked against the simple, oversize tile installed throughout the entryway as she raced through the maze of rooms. The rug positioned to greet visitors crumpled behind her.

"Knock it off! You're going to break something." Carson guided his partner over the threshold, and for a moment, he couldn't help but think of the night Ivy had invited him inside this place for the first time. How she'd kissed him right here at the front door. It had been a simpler time then. All they'd had to contend with was the FBI's rules on office romances. Everything had gotten so…out of order since then.

"It all still looks the same." Ivy unwound her hand from his and limped down the narrow hall leading to the rest of the house. "What did you do, ask the previous owners to leave their furniture and belongings and get out?"

"Something like that." A lot like that actually. Though he'd certainly made it worth their while. Hundreds of thousands of dollars over value. The thing about working for criminals for so long was he'd learned to become one. He'd known his days as Dominic Rojas would have to come to an end eventually. He hadn't known the exact moment when, but Ivy's influence had trained him to prepare for every threat. Every possibility. The cartel wouldn't get the drop on him. No matter the circumstance, and so Carson had ensured his own future. With the help of *Sangre por Sangre*. He set Ivy's belongings by the door and followed after her into the kitchen. "It's purchased under another alias for obvious reasons. Your operative who works your team's security—Scarlett—helped with the details."

Ivy ran her uninjured hand the length of the expansive kitchen island. Large enough to seat four people, though Carson had never known his partner to invite anyone into the space but him. The tension drained from her shoulders minute by minute. "I didn't think I would ever get to be inside this place again. I drive by it sometimes. Wasn't too happy with them painting the garage a different color, but they took good care of it, from what I can see." She surveyed the kitchen and the attached living room. "Do you think there's a chance they left anything to eat?"

"Already on it." Carson dodged Max's beeline for the living room couch. "If you don't calm down, I'm going to put you outside."

Ivy's laugh followed her into the living room, where she sat down on the sofa beside the German shepherd, and in that moment, it was easy to imagine they were on the other side of this investigation. That they'd survived *Sangre por Sangre* and Sebastian and everything else the world threw at them, and all that was left was...this. This peace.

It had been so long since he'd allowed himself to relax, he wasn't sure he knew how to anymore, but right now, here with Ivy, he saw their future. A future he'd killed for, had nearly died for and sacrificed for.

In an instant, guilt—thick and hot and acidic—burned in his gut, eating away at his stomach lining. He'd built a life within the cartel. Dedicated himself to protecting the people he served with. They'd become his team at a time when he'd needed them the most.

But choosing Ivy meant abandoning them. Delivering them up to the slaughter when Socorro brought down the final judgment.

His fellow soldiers. The people he'd laughed with around bonfires in the middle of the desert while they waited for their next orders. Who'd pressed their backs against his in the middle of a firefight with the DEA. Who'd stood watch over him so he could grab a couple of hours of sleep out in the open. For the first time since he'd lost his mother he'd had a family of his very own.

Sebastian had been included in that group. Now there wasn't anything Carson wouldn't do to keep him from putting his hands on Ivy again, but his insides still raged as the two lives he'd created battled for dominance. "I'll see what I can scrounge up for food."

He set to work on inventorying the cabinets. Lucky for him, the previous owners had left a good amount behind. While he'd never been anything but a ramen chef as an FBI agent, there were some skills he'd been forced to rely on within the cartel. Being able to create a densely nutritional meal out of few ingredients, for one. Within minutes, Carson plated a sizable helping of homemade macaroni and cheese complete with hot dogs and brought two plates to the couch.

Max eyed him scornfully as he handed off Ivy's plate.

"Yours is in the kitchen. Try not to make a mess," he said.

The K-9 took that as permission to fly off the couch and skid across the tile floor. Only she failed to stop in time, crashing into the lower cabinets.

Ivy's laugh interrupted her initial bite, and she had to cover her mouth to keep the macaroni from falling back onto the plate. "Happy to see she's held on to some of that puppy excitement. It's nice, knowing she's still the same troublemaker I brought home so long ago. I missed that."

He had to remember that. That as much as Carson had missed of the real world over the past two years surviving and thriving within a drug cartel, Ivy had missed a lot, too.

"You should see her when I manage to get my hands on those special chips you used to eat." He took his first bite, and his entire body clung on to that single influx of calories as though he'd gone weeks without food rather than twelve hours. "You think she's hyper now. She practically flies on that stuff."

"Salt-and-vinegar chips aren't special." Ivy took another bite and seemingly melted as quickly as the cheese. "Kind of a delicacy for a cartel soldier. Apart from the fact the one time I offered you one, you threw it into the neighbor's backyard. I think you said something like vinegar isn't meant to be consumed."

"Yeah, well." He couldn't help but smile at the memory. A sliver of time when they'd been allowed to be nothing but themselves. "I might have changed my mind a little."

"Good to know." She speared her next bite of macaroni onto her fork, only didn't bring it to her mouth. In fact, Ivy let the fork skid along the outside of the plate. "Is there anything else you might've changed your mind on I should know about?"

"Yeah. There is." Carson set his unfinished plate on the coffee table. He'd been putting this off long enough. Unwilling to let go. But there was no future for him in the cartel. Not anymore. "I'm ready to come home."

Chapter Ten

Carson rolled into her from the other side of the bed, jarring her back into the present.

She'd been awake for hours. Replaying Sebastian's claims. That he'd killed Dr. Piel and those other women, that he'd been biding his time, proud of himself for taking up so much of her life. Every cell in her body wanted to live in denial, but none of it did his victims a bit of good. And that was all that mattered. The victims.

Ivy turned her attention to Carson. It hadn't mattered before, but she needed to know. Had Dr. Piel been involved with *Sangre por Sangre*, or had Sebastian used Socorro's physician as bait? To lure Ivy out into the open. To take someone she cared about away. To hurt her. The last few seconds before she'd collapsed into unconsciousness played at the edges of her mind. Of seeing Carson in the middle of the warehouse. Of not knowing which side he would choose in the face of her death. Would he have gone back to the cartel given the chance? Or had he meant what he'd said earlier about coming home?

Her mind was playing tricks on her again. Trying to create a threat when she was positive one wasn't there. It did the same thing every night, keeping her awake for hours. Imagining scenarios in which everything she loved was taken from her. Where the Pentagon refused to re-up Socorro's contract, leaving her team ungrounded and scattered. And where she learned of Carson's death. Two years was a long time to give her anxiety the playground it needed to thrive. But, at the same time, had prepared her for the worst.

There was no way she was going to be able to sleep tonight. Dr. Cavill's orders to get as much rest as possible could go to hell. Ivy slipped from the bed she and Carson shared, careful not to wake the mound of fur at the end. Her go bag had supplied everything she'd needed to survive for up to two weeks, but somehow she'd forgotten to pack something to sleep in. As though she'd tried to convince herself that survival didn't require sleep. Instead, she'd taken one of Carson's extra T-shirts. It was too big and drapey and exactly what she'd needed. Something comfortable that didn't scratch at the dozens of bandages keeping her from falling to pieces.

She tiptoed to the bedroom door, looking back to ensure she hadn't woken either Carson or Max. And froze. She'd come close to losing them back in that warehouse. She never wanted to feel that way again.

Ivy navigated through her old house as easily as she had done years ago. Muscle memory. This place... It had been her safe haven. Not just a house. She'd come to think of it as home. The first place she felt comfortable enough to be herself, to let go of the hurt and the pain and the defenses she'd weaponized on the job. Something entirely hers. Not connected to her past or her origin. Though there were times when those memories penetrated these walls, they didn't have as much hold on her as they had back then. This was where she'd become her own person. Separate from the trauma and abuse and sexism.

It hadn't been until Carson signed on as her partner that she'd imagined this home as anything more than her own personal barricade against the world. It had become something more. He'd somehow maneuvered his way into her life and made himself at home. As though he'd always belonged here, and, in a way, he had. He'd even made it easy. And when she'd brought Max home to meet him, it had felt like they'd become a family of her own creation. A team.

But when he'd accepted the assignment to go undercover within *Sangre por Sangre*, everything had changed. She'd no longer had the option to fantasize about the future. She had to give all that up in an attempt to keep him alive.

Ivy couldn't help but run her fingers the length of the hallway as she headed toward the kitchen. This home was supposed to be theirs when the time was right, but that didn't feel possible anymore. She spotted her go bag by the door where Carson had left it and dragged it to the kitchen counter. He'd made it clear she couldn't contact her team or use any of the devices registered in her name, but she wasn't going to sever herself from the intel she needed either. "Thank goodness for VPNs."

Her operatives were equipped to handle any situation, including disappearing off the grid. While she preferred to use the resources available, she couldn't risk bringing the cartel down on Carson and Max. Ivy unpacked a clean laptop, formatted and wiped thanks to her security operative for situations just like this. The subscription and credit card she'd registered the VPN under was set to an alias she'd used while in the FBI. Still active the last time she'd checked. The payments were made through an endless loop of shell corporations set up to keep anyone trying to track her going in circles. To give her the time she needed to drop off the radar. Just in case.

"Show me what you've got." Ivy took a seat at the kitchen counter and logged in to her Socorro email. Hundreds of unread messages filled the queue. But she was only looking for one. "Bingo."

She tapped the bolded message from Chief Halsey. Incident report: 914 NM-516, Aztec, New Mexico.

Followed up on your statement. Partnered with Aztec PD to raid the salvage yard. Suspect has not been located. See report attached.

Halsey had always been a man of few words. Maybe that was why she'd always liked him. His significant other, Jocelyn, was the complete opposite. Always offering a baked good in hopes of getting people to open up. They were perfect for each other.

The Alpine Valley chief of police would've had to pull a good amount of strings to get his hands on the incident report from another jurisdiction, but she couldn't think about how she'd repay him right now. Opening the email, she scanned the first page of the file before moving on to the crime scene photos.

Yellow tents punctured through the whitewash of spotlights directing investigators to evidence. A saw blade tipped in blood, a stain directly below a hook mounted to the ceiling in the back office. A wrench angled diagonally across the floor twisted with dark hair.

Every image resurrected the pain in her side, but she moved on, forcing herself to take it all in. To relive the hours that would haunt her nightmares for years. There had to be something. Something to tell her who Sebastian really was. Blood, sweat, hair, fingerprints, cell phone GPS. It was impossible to interact with an environment and leave nothing behind. Especially given the advancements in forensics and technology.

She made a mental note to have Alpine Valley PD look into the Sensorvault data during the duration of her and Carson's stay inside the warehouse. If Sebastian had a cell phone on him, the largest collection of phone GPS in the world would register the number. Possibly even locate it. "Come on. Give me something I don't know."

"Still talking to yourself?" Carson's voice hitched her heart rate higher. He turned on the lights, coming into the kitchen. "You know that's considered a red flag, right? I bet your Socorro psychologist would be very interested to hear about it."

The onslaught to her vision receded after a few moments but broke her concentration. "The FBI didn't seem to think it was a problem, and my current boss doesn't give a crap. She just wants results. And Socorro doesn't employ a psychologist."

Which felt like an oversight on her part right then. Her operatives had come close to death, each and every single one of them, and while she believed in the power of love and finding their significant others to share that burden, love wasn't always a solution.

"The FBI didn't know about it. And your current boss is you." He moved into the kitchen, opening the first cabinet. Only he didn't seem to find what he was looking for. He continued on to the next and grabbed a glass from the shelf. "Still not sure how you were able to pass the psych eval after everything you've experienced."

"Compartmentalization is a superpower." She was only half invested in this back-and-forth they'd always had together. It had become something of a habit in the course of their partnership, but her attention was almost entirely focused on getting through Aztec PD's crime scene photos.

"And is running off no sleep a superpower?" He filled his glass with water from the fridge and took a drink. "You were stabbed less than forty-eight hours ago, Ivy. You lost a lot of blood. When are you going to give your body a chance to slow down and heal?"

"As much as I appreciate your concern, it's actually none of your concern." Her own words pulled her out of the flow state she'd sunk into while studying the photos, and Ivy regretted them instantly.

Carson stepped back as though he'd been sucker punched. He stared down into his glass, and she couldn't help but wonder if he was wishing he hadn't come out here at all. "And here I thought we were still partners who gave a crap about each other. Has that changed?"

"We are. I do. I'm sorry. I just…" Ivy tore her attention from the computer. Because this…they were important. "I didn't mean that the way that sounded. Of course I give a crap about you."

"And yet you're not convinced you're worth giving a crap about." The accusation hit harder than it should. "Do you know why I asked to be your partner all those years ago?"

That information caught her by surprise. "I wasn't aware you had a choice."

"I did. Your former partners, none of them wanted to work with you anymore. They saw you as a wild card who would do anything to close a case. No matter who you had to bulldoze in the process. You were difficult to work with, too blunt, too brash, too intense. Yeah, you closed more cases than anyone in our office, but it was at the expense of being one of the team." Carson set his water glass on the counter. "I saw an agent who needed to know she wasn't alone. That she had someone she could rely on, someone she could trust. I've tried to be that person for you, Ivy, but you're still operating as though you're the only one who can finish this mission."

She didn't know what to say to that, what to think. Except the truth. "I've always felt better alone. Because then no one could hurt me."

"Do you really think, after everything we've been through, that I would hurt you?" he asked.

"Everyone is capable of hurting the people they care about." Ivy let her gaze drift back to the computer. And she froze. Her brain latched on to the photo within a photo on the screen. "What the hell?"

Carson penetrated into her peripheral vision, coming around to get a better look. "What is this?"

"Crime scene photos. Of the salvage yard. It's a long story." She pointed to the burned remnants of paperwork and photos captured by Aztec PD. "Look at this. Where is this?"

"I don't know. I didn't come across a room like that," he said. "It looks like an office."

"It's not the room I was hung upside down in. This is someplace new." She tried to enlarge the photo, but there was only so much her laptop could process.

"So?" Carson didn't see what she saw. Not yet.

"So, look at this partially burned photograph. Sebastian didn't burn the entire thing before leaving it behind." Dread spilled into her gut. Ivy shoved away from the counter and tipped her go bag upside down. She grabbed for the burner cell stuffed deep inside and punched in one of the numbers she'd memorized in case of emergency. Like now. "I've seen it before."

"What am I missing?" Agitation tensed his shoulders.

"Dr. Piel wasn't involved with *Sangre por Sangre* like we originally believed." The phone rang. Once. Twice. Three times. Voicemail kicked in. *Hey, it's Jocelyn. Leave your—* Ivy hung up and dialed again. No answer. "I think she was just the first target."

"Can you make this thing go any faster?" Ivy held on to the handle above the passenger-side door as they raced into Alpine Valley. She'd tried calling her logistics coordinator, Jocelyn Carville, a dozen times without any answer.

Alpine Valley's chief of police wasn't answering either.

Carson floored the accelerator. Dirt gusted across the unpaved road in front of them, blocking out his view of the lights up ahead. Months ago an entire cliffside had buried Alpine Valley after a bitter chief of police attempted to bring down *Sangre por Sangre* himself. Even before that, the cartel had raided secluded towns like this, burning everything in its path.

Now a killer could be loose in Alpine Valley's streets.

The engine revved higher at his touch, and the SUV bolted forward. "Try the police chief again."

Ivy allowed herself a moment of unbalance and grabbed for her phone with her uninjured hand. She wasn't supposed to be here. Her physician had specifically instructed her to rest, but trying to talk her out of helping one of her fellow operatives had been out of the question. She raised the phone to her ear. And waited. "No voicemail. It just keeps ringing. It's like his phone is turned off. That's not like Baker. He's never been out of reach."

Carson didn't want to offer theories as to why Alpine Valley's chief of police suddenly wasn't available. No good came of catastrophizing. But there was a chance Sebastian or someone within the cartel had gotten to the chief and his Socorro partner first. There was no other reason why a photo of Jocelyn should've been in that warehouse office. "This isn't your fault, Ivy. You didn't bring this down on them."

"That's easy to say when you aren't the one who is supposed to protect them." She inhaled audibly. "My operatives—my team—have been there from day one. They believe in the cause just the same as I do, if not more. They're the ones who are in the field. They're the ones getting shot and stabbed and abducted. Because I pay them to. They risk their lives and the lives of the people they love because of me, and it's up to me to make sure they make it out of this alive."

Carson checked the rearview mirror, targeting Max lying across the back seat. The K-9 locked her gaze on him. "Max has been undercover with me since the day I was recruited by Sebastian. It was a risk bringing her with me, especially as young as she was, but I knew I needed the extra protection. I didn't have anyone else as long as I was part of the cartel. She's risked her life for me more times than I can count. Not because I asked her to. But because she loves me. Those operatives you have working for you, Ivy, they're not just doing a job because you give them a paycheck in return. They believe in you. They trust you. They would've found a job that doesn't get them shot and stabbed otherwise."

She was quiet for a moment. "Should you get the chance to meet my team, I don't recommend you tell them you just compared them to a German shepherd. It might not go over well."

He couldn't help but smile at that, at her willingness to add a bit of humor to a terrifying situation. Carson set his hand on her knee and squeezed. "It's going to be okay. I promise."

"I'm not sure that's something you can promise, Carson." Ivy faced him, the dim glow of the SUV's control panel washing her in a blue tint. "We don't even know what we're walking into."

"It doesn't matter." He didn't know how to explain his own brand of confidence right there in that moment. "Because we're walking in there together."

Carson followed the navigation mounted between them, taking a hard right onto Alpine Valley's Main Street. Evidence that the cartel had left its mark was everywhere, in half-burned buildings, new construction, and shaded windows this late at night.

"Up on the left." Ivy was already peeling herself out of her seat by the time he came to a full stop in front of the modest rambler coated in a dark stucco. The house itself stuck out among the ones on either side of it with their traditional Mexican style and coloring, making it an easy target. She unholstered her weapon with her nondominant hand, but not as awkwardly as he'd assumed she would. Which meant she'd practiced shooting with both hands. Always ready for the next threat. "No lights on inside or vehicles on the streets. Do you see any movement around the perimeter?"

Carson shoved the SUV into Park, getting Max's attention. She perked up in the back seat, then scanned her surroundings out the window. Ready. "No. Nothing."

Still, something didn't feel right. It was the same sensation of dread he'd experienced inside the salvage yard. He pulled his backup sidearm and checked the rounds left in the magazine. "We go in together. You go where I go. Understand?"

The last time they'd entered into a house with cartel inside,

Ivy had ended up under the killer's control, and it had taken Carson losing another kidney to get her back. He couldn't go through that again.

"I understand." No argument this time. No trying to take control of the situation. She was trusting him to put her operative and the chief of police at the top of his priority list. "They have a German shepherd. Maverick. He's a bomb detection K-9 and fiercely protective of Jocelyn."

"In that case, we'll let Max go first." Except Carson didn't want to leave the safety of the vehicle. No. It wasn't that. He'd gone headfirst into any number of situations with higher stakes. He didn't want Ivy to leave the safety of the vehicle. But asking her to stay behind would betray their partnership, and he couldn't turn back on his decision to come home now. Not when he was so close to getting the future he'd always wanted. "On three."

"Three." Ivy didn't wait for the countdown. Every second they hesitated could cost her teammate, and she was the kind of person to take mistakes personally.

So Carson followed. He let Max out of the back seat, approaching the front door low and fast. Ivy moved in time with him despite her injuries. Whether by force or by habit, he wasn't sure. They reached the front door, but Carson was the one to pull back the heavy metal screen protecting the aged wood. It was a recent installation. Considering the nature of the couple's work, he was willing to bet the Socorro operative had added the extra measure of security. "Does your logistics coordinator have a Socorro security system, too?"

"No. Baker wouldn't allow it. He doesn't particularly agree with our values, but I imagine he's got his own security system in place." Ivy stood back enough to give him room to swing the screen door wide and test the doorknob.

The dead bolt hadn't been engaged.

"Is he the kind that dares criminals to break into his home, or was this supposed to be locked?" Carson tried to make out a layout of the home with his limited vision, but the only way to get a read on the place was to step inside.

Ivy raised her weapon, taking the first step over the threshold. She led him straight into the living room with a hallway branching directly to the back of the house and what he assumed was the kitchen. Another branch went right. Most likely to the bedrooms. She scanned the living room gun first and allowed his nerves to take a step down. "Clear."

He moved in behind her, then pushed ahead down the hallway. Max beat him to it, her tags tinkling together as she advanced. The kitchen was small and looked to be original, from what little he could see of the streetlights coming through the windows. No movement. No one waiting to ambush them. "Clear."

They turned their attention to the hallway. "I'm thinking nobody is here, or Maverick isn't a very good guard dog."

Ivy didn't answer, seemingly bracing herself as she moved into the hallway. The first bedroom housed an office. It belonged to the chief, from the disarray of paperwork on the surface of the desk. No logistics coordinator would be so careless. The room straight across from it looked to be a guest bedroom. Made up nice and tidy. Small bathroom with no windows midway through. A heavy metal garage door on the other side. Locked.

Two bedrooms sat at the end of the hall, almost making a T formation. Ivy took the one on the right. Carson the one on the left. He kicked the door inward. But the door stopped short of hitting the wall behind it. He hit the light switch near the door.

And found a body.

"Son of a bitch." Holstering his weapon, Carson dropped to both knees and flipped the uniformed officer onto his back. Blood leaked from a head wound most likely caused by someone bashing his head in from behind. The man's phone lay in pieces beside him. Would explain why Ivy's calls never made it through. "I'm guessing this is the chief you're looking for?"

Ivy abandoned her search. "Baker. Damn it."

"He's alive." Carson almost lost himself in the relief at the feel of the chief's pulse against his first two fingers. Broken skin and blood across the officer's knuckles told a good story. "Busted up, from what I can see. Man put up a fight. Whoever was on the other end isn't going to get far."

More details came into view as Max bounded for another body across the room. Only this one wasn't human. She sniffed at the unconscious German shepherd in concern.

The chief's groan filled the room. Baker Halsey blinked at Carson a few times before some deep-rooted pain no one could see set in. Alpine Valley's elected hero pushed his upper body off the floor. "Please tell me you're here to get the recipe of Jocelyn's famous chocolate chip cookies."

"Chief, you were attacked," Ivy said. "Did you see by who?"

"No. Sons of bitches caught me from behind. Must've been waiting behind the front door when I got home." He set sights on the K-9 still unmoving a few feet away. Chief Halsey practically crawled to the dog and brought the German shepherd into his lap. "I got you, bud. Hell, Jocelyn's going to murder me for letting them touch Maverick. Where is she?"

"She wasn't with you?" Carson asked.

"What? No. I just got off shift. I came home. The house was dark, but I saw Maverick..." Fear contorted the chief's face, and he maneuvered Maverick off his lap. Baker shoved to stand—unbalanced and grabbing for the nearest wall. Carson moved to assist but was rejected. "Jocelyn never goes anywhere without Maverick. They're a team. Ivy, where the hell is my partner?"

Chief Halsey didn't wait for an answer. He shoved into the hallway. "Jocelyn!"

"We've already searched the house. She isn't here." Ivy tried to keep up with the chief of police. In vain. The man was on a mission, the same kind of mission that had held Carson in its grip in that damn warehouse: getting to the woman he loved. "Baker, think. What can you remember up until you blacked out?"

"Jocelyn!" Baker flipped on every light in the place. The chief was reaching for his weapon, but the holster on his hip was empty. Whoever had attacked him had stripped him of his weapons. The man was close to losing it. He threaded both hands into his hair. "All right. Give me a minute. The sliding glass door. It was open when I came home. I thought something was off. We never go out there."

Ivy bolted for the kitchen and out the back door.

"Stay here, Chief." There was no telling what they would find. Carson followed Ivy into the backyard.

"Go to hell," Baker said. "That's my partner."

The motion-sensor spotlights lit up.

Exposing the woman left for dead in the middle of the yard.

Chapter Eleven

"He's targeting us one by one." Ivy couldn't forget the images of Jocelyn as she'd lain there. Left in the middle of her own yard. The message gouged into her back was the same as the one found on Dr. Piel.

There's no escaping Sangre por Sangre.

Except Jocelyn had somehow survived. EMTs had managed to get a breathing tube down the logistics coordinator's throat in time. Ivy's operative was recovering in the hospital with Chief Halsey and Maverick refusing to leave her side. The dog had been taken down with a sedative but would make a full recovery.

It had been too close.

Too personal.

Ivy stared out the wall of windows in her office. The weight of her team's attention pressed between her shoulder blades. She was supposed to keep things like this from happening. She'd been responsible for training them, for getting them through the hard assignments and out onto the other side. Now two of her operatives had been attacked, with one of them dead.

"I've sent Elena and the baby to her parents' house." Cash Meyers, Socorro's forward scout, prided himself on seeing the threat from a distance, on knowing when an attack was coming. But there was no way for him to see this. His new family had been put at risk. Because of her.

This threat had come directly from Ivy's past. Something she'd never shared with any of them. She'd never seen any value in being anything more than their fearless leader. Who would follow her if they knew she couldn't face the nightmares she'd created, let alone send them out into the field to confront new ones? She faced what was left of her team and, in that moment, felt considerably under-experienced in finishing what she'd started two years ago.

Carson stood in the corner of her office, so out of place, and yet necessary. To this mission. To Socorro. To her. He hadn't contributed to the discussion, and the truth was, she hadn't expected him to. It was easy to imagine him shouldering the responsibility of what had happened, just as she had. Being crushed underneath it. The only way they'd get through this was together. He'd said that. "What about Maggie, Jones? Have you been able to get any information?"

Jones Driscoll—Socorro's combat coordinator—wouldn't take an attack on this team lying down. He'd risked his life to pull a war correspondent out from the cartel's grip without hesitation and brought down a corrupt senator in the process. Of every operative she employed, he would be the one to burn everything to the ground. And maybe that was exactly what she needed now. "We thought *Sangre por Sangre* had gone to ground before—the entire organization is a ghost now. No chatter. No corner deals on the streets. I've been monitoring the smuggling routes, but all I found was a bunch of abandoned trucks with product still inside. The cartel's been forced to cut back on operations over the past few months. Now it's like they've given up entirely. Maggie reached out to a couple of her contacts, but all she's managed to uncover is a couple of low-level soldiers who don't know what the hell is going on. We've got them in one of the holding cells downstairs, but they're not talking. Whoever killed those women and attacked Jocelyn is staying to the shadows. Feels like he's waiting for something."

"Not waiting. He's compartmentalizing." Carson unfolded his arms and raised his chin. Confident and ready to take charge. Ivy needed a bit of that right now. "There are protocols the cartel follows when it's in danger. First, consolidate information. The fewer people who know of his plan, the less chances there are of a betrayal. Sebastian will only trust the people he's known since he joined the cartel twenty years ago. Next, he'll take an account of *Sangre por Sangre*'s assets. Safe houses, cash, product and alliances. The cartel hasn't had any luck attacking Socorro directly. Picking us off one by one is his only option, but he won't do it slowly."

"And you know all of this how? Who are you?" Granger Morais's graveled advice had been Ivy's voice of reason from the beginning. The former Department of Defense counterterrorism agent was the first operative she'd recruited, and he in turn had brought Socorro's security consultant on board. He pushed for the logical decision in every scenario, questioning every turn and vetting every fact. Without him, Ivy wouldn't have come this far.

"You don't recognize him?" Scarlett Beam—Socorro's security expert—studied Carson from head to toe. Her fiery red hair only gave a glimpse of the wild card underneath. Scarlett was the type of operative to make her own rules while still getting the job done and protecting the people she cared about. Her DEA partner and his son could attest to that after Scarlett had managed to uncover a massive shipment of cartel fentanyl and somehow managed to bring the boy home alive. She genuinely worked to protect and defend, and she took the safety of this team personally. "You're in the presence of our very own undercover source within the cartel. The guy who's been giving us all the good info on *Sangre por Sangre*'s lieutenants, shipments, targets and assets to hit."

"This is Carson Lang, though some of you may know him as Dominic Rojas. He's been vital to neutralizing the *Sangre por Sangre* threat for the past two years," Ivy said.

Except Carson was more than a tool Socorro had used to its advantage. He was Ivy's partner. The man who'd saved her life. Twice. Who'd sacrificed everything he'd known and loved, to protect her and bring a killer to justice. He was passionate for their cause, carrying around a heavy heart that had lost too much over the years. A misfit who'd never really adapted to anyone except the chosen few he allowed into his life. He was creative and isolating and seemingly stuck in a never-ending cycle of loss.

And she loved every facet of him. Would give up this entire company if asked to keep him in her life. Because they belonged together. They were partners.

Granger seemed to grow in size as he crossed Ivy's office and closed the distance between him and Carson. Max shook herself out of a deep sleep and got to her feet in response. At the ready for a confrontation. "You're the one who told us the cartel was targeting Charlie Acker and using her extremist family to strike the state capitol building last month."

"Yes," Carson said.

The counterterrorism agent extended his hand. "Thank you. For saving her life. If it weren't for you, I wouldn't have made it to Charlie in time."

The men shook, and an air of agreement wove through the office.

"Aah, I can feel the love." Scarlett leaned back in her chair, smile wide. Pulling her phone, she skimmed her finger across the screen and raised the device. "Now hug. I want it for the company newsletter."

"I will kill you and your little dogs, too." Granger shot her a look that would send any cartel soldier running for cover, but it had no effect on this team. They were all well aware of when an empty threat wasn't so empty.

"Good luck." Scarlett snapped a photo and sat back in her chair. "I'm teaching the twins some new commands. Primarily how to break into locked rooms. You'll never hear them coming, Granger."

"As much as I hate to break up…whatever is happening here, we need a plan," Jones said. "I don't know about any of you, but I'm not willing to sit back and let these sons of bitches pick us off. What's the move, boss?"

The team looked to Ivy.

And she…looked to Carson. For a little bit of that confidence and maybe some assurance. She'd built this company from the ground up. She'd battled against corrupt congressmen and Pentagon officials. She'd coordinated with local law enforcement, her old FBI office and the DEA on assignments. There wasn't a single battle she wasn't willing to take on alone. And yet, right then, she felt the need to rely on him.

The shift rocked through her. Because he'd been right: she didn't have to do this alone. Not anymore. Maybe she never had. She had an entire team willing and waiting to fight this war alongside her. But constantly living on the edge of survival had left her feeling isolated. Convinced her threats were everywhere even when there weren't any, lied to her about who she could trust. Carson had seen through all of it. He always had.

"The man we know as Sebastian seems to hold a good amount of power within *Sangre por Sangre*." Ivy filled her lungs to the point of stretching the stitches in her side. "He's made connections and most likely built a few of his own he'll be calling on to come after us individually. We're not going to let that happen."

She steepled her fingers on the surface of her desk, looking at each one of her operatives in turn. "We've been fighting this war through small assignments and conflicts up to this point. We've been shot and stabbed and tortured for information. There have been broken bones and explosions and entire buildings coming down on top of us. Our loved ones have suffered. We've lost team members and people close to us. We've watched entire lives be destroyed by the cartel. Homes gone, towns buried underneath mudslides, families ripped apart. Our K-9s have stood by our sides, risking their lives to please us. All of that has led us here. To the end of the line."

She set her sights on Carson. "I'm not going to pretend I'm not responsible for what's happening now. This killer is targeting each and every one of you to hurt me. To force me to watch as I lose everyone and everything I care about because I have declared war on the cartel. He won't stop until he's put every one of us in the ground and burned this building to the ground. So I'll give you a choice."

Ivy held herself a little taller. "You can walk away. All of you. You can go home, be with your families. I will write you references for your next job, and I'll pay your severance for your service to this company and to me. I'll provide new identities, if that's what you require, and there will be no hard feelings. But I'm realizing now I can't do this alone. I need you at my side. All of you. I need my team. Will you help me?"

Silence ate into her nerves as she dared study her operatives for a reaction. Seconds ticked off, excruciating and hard to swallow.

Until Scarlett shoved to her feet. "Looks like Hans and Gruber will get to test out those new commands we've been working on after all."

Jones stood. "It's about time we finish this."

Granger nodded, sharp and curt. He was in.

Cash folded his arms across his chest. "I love seeing Bear take bites out of cartel soldiers. I'm in, whatever you need, boss."

Ivy turned to Carson. The same speech applied to him. He could walk away from this. From her. No hard feelings. She would acquire a new identity from her contacts at the Pentagon and pay him the severance he'd risked his life for. But a large part of her needed him more than anyone else on this team.

Carson pulled his phone from his pocket and headed for her office door. "I've got to make a call."

CARSON PICKED UP his pace toward the elevators.

The call was a ploy. To get out of that room. Away from Ivy's team. Honestly, he had no idea where the hell he was going, but one of the operatives had said the cartel soldiers they'd brought into custody were being held downstairs. He'd find them sooner or later.

He hit the elevator's down button with a little too much force and stepped back. Max caught up without so much as a huff. As though she was as disappointed in him as much as he was with himself.

Movement registered in the reflective stainless steel, and he turned to find Ivy standing there. She'd changed back into her slacks and blazer, washed her hair, scrubbed the dirt and blood from her skin. The woman he'd pulled out of that warehouse was buried beneath the armor she'd built for herself over the past two years. Never to surface again as long as she could help it. "Tell me what's going through your head."

He didn't want to have this conversation. Not yet. Not here. Carson hit the elevator call button a second time, but the damn thing wouldn't speed the hell up. "You did a good job rallying the troops in there. I can see why they've stayed on with Socorro as long as they have. You should start working on your strategy to track down Sebastian. Every second counts."

"And what will you be doing?" The fabric of her slacks rustled as she moved in close, and a flare of heat shot up his neck.

It spread down his spine and wrapped around his rib cage, squeezing him in some invisible vise. "There's something I need to take care of."

"Would it have anything to do with the two cartel soldiers Jones brought in?" she asked.

He didn't want to lie to her. She deserved better than that. The elevator arrived, doors parting, and Carson took a step into the car. Max followed, planting her butt at his feet.

Except Ivy was right behind him. She threaded her arm between the doors and prevented them from closing. "Just tell me what's going on, Carson. After everything we've been through the past few days, everything we've promised one another, you at least owe me that."

She was right. Of course she was right. That same sinking feeling he'd experienced before Sebastian had betrayed him at the salvage yard took hold. He was standing on the edge of a blade. Tip too far in one direction, make one choice, and he lost the family he'd found within the cartel. Tip too far in the other, and he lost Ivy. His cartel world and his personal world were mutually exclusive. He couldn't have one without losing the other. The idea of helping Socorro slaughter and arrest the soldiers—the people—he'd come to know and rely on surged acid into his throat. There were good people in those ranks. Not just killers. People who'd had no other choice than to join the cartel to save their families, their friends, their way of life. At the same time, these were men and women he'd only known through becoming someone he wasn't, and choosing them over Ivy threatened to tear his heart in half. "I think you already know the answer you're looking for."

Color seemed to drain from her already-pale skin. Her mouth parted on a strong exhalation, but it was the only sign she'd filled in the blanks. Like always, she was trying to hold herself together, to keep anyone from seeing her vulnerabilities. "You're going back. To the cartel."

"I don't have a choice," he said. "There are people there who were just following orders, Ivy. They don't have anything to do with calling the shots. They weren't the ones who targeted Alpine Valley or retaliated for a missing fentanyl shipment. They were just trying to survive. Like me. They deserve a chance to get out while they still can."

"If by survive you mean kidnap an eight-year-old boy to force his sister to turn herself over to their lieutenant." Ivy's voice lost the confused quality it had taken a minute ago, growing stronger. Puncturing him like a thousand needles. "Or when they abducted and tortured a war correspondent because she witnessed the cartel slaughter ten American soldiers in the desert. How about when they put a bounty on an innocent woman's head because she refused to be connected to her extremist family of preppers? Was that your friends' way of surviving? Was it yours?"

She could list a dozen more incidents. With good reason. A chill spread along his back as he realized the position he'd put himself in. If he wasn't choosing Socorro—if he wasn't choosing Ivy—he was choosing to become her enemy. Black and white. No going back. "That's not the least bit fair, and you know it. I agreed to go undercover. We both knew what that would entail, what I would have to do to work my way up the ladder and gain the cartel's trust, but I don't expect you to understand what it means to be part of a team. All your former partners were right. You bulldoze anyone and everyone to get your way and solve a case, and I was fine with that for a long time. Because you provided justice to those who deserved it. You kept more people from getting hurt and you saved lives. But you're so blinded by one man's atrocities that you're not willing to see there might be more innocent lives involved in this investigation than the ones you found in the desert."

Silence built between them. Heavy and thick and unrelenting.

Ivy stepped over the threshold into the elevator, her heels on the verge of getting caught in the tracks.

"I have watched the cartel tear apart people's lives. They've sold girls and women for profit. They've spread their drugs and killed children. They punished Dr. Piel and Jocelyn for simply having a connection to this company, and they'll continue killing my team unless I put a stop to it. Do you know what that tells me?" Ivy didn't let him answer. "That tells me that every single soldier, contracted killer, lieutenant and supplier is complicit in the cartel's actions. You talk about the low-level soldiers, these friends you made while undercover, as innocent? There are no innocents inside the *Sangre por Sangre* cartel, Carson, and I will not let any of them walk away without answering for their crimes."

"And that's why I have to leave," he said. "I have to give them a chance. Just one of them. Please."

She smoothed her expression, as though he were a stranger. "From the moment I found you in my safe house four nights ago, there was a part of me that wondered where your loyalties really fell. Your insistence on hiding out in a cartel safe house was just the start, but I think it was your connection to Sebastian and your willingness to consult with a cartel soldier on this investigation that gave you away. I convinced myself I was being paranoid, that there was no way my partner could've been turned, but all of that paranoia was with good reason. Because you're not my partner anymore."

His heart shot into his throat with denial. But Carson only let her words hang between them.

She dropped her hand away from the elevator door sensors and allowed the elevator to start closing. "You have two hours before Socorro comes for your organization, Dominic Rojas. I suggest you get the people you're trying to save as far from here as possible. Before you're caught in the fight."

The doors sealed between them.

Carson stared into his reflection as gravity shoved his stomach higher in his torso. An emptiness he'd managed to keep a rein on grew bigger, as he added more distance between himself and Ivy.

Max moaned at his feet, echoing the hurt and the pain doubling inside his chest, but there was no going back for them. He'd made his choice, and Ivy had made hers. Neither of them was willing to consider the other's position, and everything he'd hoped for the future—for them—stayed behind in Ivy's office.

Second by second, the Carson Lang he'd been over these past few days slipped to the back of his mind. The elevator doors parted on the level below, and he stepped into a black-on-black corridor. Every inch the cartel soldier he'd trained himself to become. Within minutes, this building would become enemy territory. A maze meant to confuse and trap him and keep him from getting what he wanted. He had minutes to locate the two soldiers taken into custody and get out.

Carson's fingers tingled to unholster his weapon, but any threat inside the building was sure to alert the security system and the woman behind it. He and Max moved along the corridor with an abstract idea of how the building had been laid out, according to Ivy's and the other operatives' descriptions.

It was enough.

They made a right at the end of the main hallway, coming face-to-face with a wall of glass. Not so much a window. One-way glass that looked into a single interrogation room. Carson recognized the woman inside. Her dark hair had been braided back tight enough to pull at the frame of her face. She paced back and forth, stripped of her weapons. She'd never liked being put in a closed-off space with no exit. Always had a knack for finding the best way out of any given situation. It was one of the reasons he'd been able to get himself and Sebastian out of the cartel headquarters when the entire building had started coming down on them. She'd been the one to lead them out.

He went for the door and threw it open.

She turned on him. Every inch of her lean frame ready for a fight. Confusion creased her wide, heart-shaped face, and she backed off, lunging for the door. "Dominic? What the hell are you doing here?"

"Getting you out of here." He didn't wait for her response, moving on to the room next door. Carson threw the second door open, confronted with one of the younger recruits brought into the cartel within the past couple of months. The rookie didn't have a lot of know-how about how things worked yet, but he'd been willing to learn from the beginning. "Come on. We don't have a lot of time."

"How did you find us?" the first soldier asked. "How did you know we were here?"

"I've got my ways." They didn't have time for twenty questions. There was no telling if Ivy's two-hour head start would hold with the other operatives. They had to move. Right the hell now. "Do you want to get out of here, or do you want to wait to see what Socorro is going to do to you to get you to talk?"

"Right behind you." The second soldier added a hitch to his step, and the three of them and Max retraced Carson's steps. He hit the elevator call button, every cell in his body on fire considering the possibilities waiting for them downstairs.

But Ivy had kept her word.

Carson, Max and both cartel soldiers hit the parking garage, located an SUV with keys sitting in the front seat and sped out of the garage. Leaving Socorro—and Ivy—behind.

Chapter Twelve

"You're just going to let them leave?" Granger's logic wasn't going to help her right now.

"Carson made his choice." Ivy watched plumes of dirt kick up behind the SUV racing across the New Mexico desert. Her heart twisted hard every second it kept driving away. "Give them thirty minutes, then activate the GPS."

Though she already had an idea of where Carson and his fellow soldiers were headed. This final war between *Sangre por Sangre* and Socorro had practically been fated. She'd only let him leave because they could track him.

"Do you know what it took to capture those two?" Jones extended one hand toward the massive wall of windows, motioning to the retreating vehicle. "The woman nearly gutted me like a fish. I'm lucky to be alive, and you're just letting them leave?"

"Easy, tiger. The boss knows what she's doing." Scarlett's insistence on being the voice of reason didn't sit well. Socorro's security operative didn't usually agree with Ivy's strategy, which had led to the installation of a hundred pounds of C-4 lining every hallway in the building in the past in an effort to protect the team. It had worked. And also destroyed the garage during a cartel ambush a few months ago. Scarlett's calm demeanor made Ivy wonder what the woman had up her sleeve. "You gotta make them feel safe, give them a reason to let their guard down. Then when they least expect it, you trigger the explosive."

"Come again?" Granger asked. "Are you telling me you've wired our SUVs to explode? How far is the frequency?"

"Anywhere in the world. That's the beauty of satellites," Scarlett said. "Don't give me that look. The next time you or Charlie or any one of us is abducted, you'll be begging me for a kill switch. This way, we're prepared."

"Wait. Does King know about this?" Jones asked. "Does he let you drive his son around in an SUV wired with explosives?"

"I'm not allowed to drive Julien," the security consultant said. "But that's not connected to the C-4. No."

"Enough." Ivy couldn't deal with this right now. She swallowed to counteract the emotion clogging her throat since her final conversation with Carson. But, worse, the idea of coming face-to-face with him on opposite sides of the divide triggered a grief so intense she couldn't breathe. She'd trusted him. Counted on him. She'd…loved him, damn it.

They'd agreed how far they would go to see this through, and now… Now he was choosing the wrong side. He was choosing the enemy over her. Over their partnership. To make matters worse, he'd taken her dog in the process. Part of her was still in denial. She'd wanted him to turn back, to choose her over the mission. Wondered if she'd been right in letting him go, but if he was hell-bent on saving a few cartel soldiers, she'd at least use his exit to her advantage. "Jones, check in with the hospital. I want an update on Jocelyn's recovery. Get ahold of Chief Halsey if you have to, and let him know of our plans to initiate contact with *San-*

gre por Sangre. Granger, contact the medical examiner and see if he has any more to add from Dr. Piel's autopsy. And, Scarlett, get those explosives off my SUVs before someone ends up hurting themselves."

"Yes, ma'am," Scarlett said. "But to be clear, it's not easy to trigger the explosives. There's a whole security code you have to put into the system to connect to the devices, and—"

"Thank you, Scarlett. That will be all." She just needed to be alone. To figure out what to do next. She'd given Carson a two-hour head start with the intention of providing him the opportunity to change his mind, but he'd called her bluff.

Movement registered behind her as the team headed for her office door. And her heart hurt, damn it. As though Carson had taken it between both hands and squeezed as hard as he could just to see what would happen. Air rushed from her lungs as the betrayal hooked into her. She was about to fall into a thousand shards of glass from the invisible pain.

"Boss." Granger's reflection took position behind her injured shoulder. Then Jones and Scarlett and Cash. "We're your team. Every single one of us has experienced loss and betrayal. Sometimes from the people we love the most. You don't have to hide from us. We've got your back. Whatever you need."

"I need..." She didn't know what she needed. A single tear escaped her control, and a rush of embarrassment flooded through her. Ivy immediately swiped it away as she turned to face them. The men and women who'd devoted themselves to carrying out her own personal crusade. Except two had been taken from their ranks. Jocelyn was recovering, but Dr. Piel would never step foot in this building again. "I need this to make sense, but no matter how I reframe it or pull it apart, it just doesn't."

"Which part of this war has made sense in the past two years, Ivy?" Cash asked. "*Sangre por Sangre* doesn't follow the rules. Because no cartel has gained this much power in the entire history of the drug epidemic. This is all new territory, for all of us. But we knew one day they would come for us. They've tried en masse in the past. Now it seems this Sebastian guy has figured out how to slide the blade in without us even noticing."

"Doesn't mean he gets to walk away in one piece," Jones said.

That hadn't been at all what she'd meant, but exposing her lack of judgment—her grief—wasn't in her DNA. Maybe that was the problem. She and Carson were supposed to be partners. Had made a commitment to one another. They'd started this war against the cartel together. Only now… He was gone. He'd been there when she'd needed him the most, but had she returned the investment? Had she been as committed to him as Carson had been to her, or had she let her past dictate their relationship? Was her stepfather still finding ways to show her she wasn't strong enough—for this job, to finish what she started, to keep a partner—from beyond the grave?

Ivy wanted to deny that man had anything to do with the life she'd built for herself, that he'd encouraged her to rise above her trauma and finally take control. Except she couldn't. Every experience, every conversation, every fantasy and hope she'd had since the age of ten had made her into the woman standing in this office. Including the abuse she'd suffered at the hands of a parent who was supposed to protect her. She couldn't forget any of it, and that failure to disassociate from that part of her life had followed her into the most important relationship she'd ever had.

And cost her everything.

What that meant for the future, she didn't know. All she could do was focus on the next step. "Every battle between this team and the cartel has ended in one place."

"*Sangre por Sangre*'s headquarters." Granger folded his arms across his broad chest. "Hell, is there even anything left of that place? Charlie and I were nearly crushed to death when all of the new underground tunnels collapsed last month."

She remembered. Having been the one to pull him out of the collapse. "Check out the latest satellite images before disabling the explosives you installed on the fleet, Scarlett. If there's movement, we'll have a better idea of what we're up against."

"I can bring it up now." Scarlett took her phone out from her back pocket and tapped both thumbs against the screen in a nonsensical order to anyone but her. "I'm repositioning the Pentagon's satellite over the headquarter coordinates. Should take just a couple minutes."

Scarlett's phone chimed. "That's not good."

"That might be the worst response you could possibly come up with." Jones had never been one to hide his criticism of others, but there'd been less of it since he and Maggie had gotten involved in the past year.

"Is there a problem with the satellites?" Ivy asked.

"No. I was able to reposition them without any problems." Scarlett turned the phone to face Ivy. "This is the problem."

Ivy lost control of her exhalation and took the phone from the security operative. "When were these images taken?"

"Less than an hour ago." Scarlett looked to the men at her side. "Seems *Sangre por Sangre* isn't on its last legs as our intel suggested. There has to be at least a couple hundred vehicles parked around that building."

"It's Sebastian." Ivy didn't know where the theory had come from. She felt it as nothing more than an instinct that had been trying to warn her over the past four days. But now, staring at the screen, she'd never been more sure of anything in her life. She handed Scarlett's phone to Granger, who in turn tensed as though he'd watched someone kick his K-9.

"What do you mean, boss?" Cash took the phone next, refusing to allow his expression to give away the dread they were all feeling.

"There's no way a low-level cartel soldier would have been able to round up this many recruits in a matter of two days. Not as long as upper management was still in control and as sure as hell not just because of me or Carson." Energy she had no idea what to do with skittered through her as the pieces started falling into place. "This kind of power only comes from years of earning your subordinates' respect, of sending warnings and exacting punishment when orders aren't followed, and people try to get out."

Granger seemed to grow another two inches. "You're not saying—"

"We've been looking for the identity of *Sangre por Sangre*'s founder since we got into this mess. Carson was never able to get a face-to-face. Didn't even have a clue as to his whereabouts or his name. Lieutenants were handed orders through coded messages and delivery services. Everything was hands-off. Every soldier we've gotten to talk has only called him *el jefe*, and I think now we know why." She slapped her hand against the nearest window. The entire pane shook under the force, but it was nothing compared to the frustration burning through her now. "He was right there in front of his own soldiers the whole time. Pretending to be one of them, keeping an eye on them, making sure they did what they were told."

"You mean this Sebastian, the guy who attacked you at the salvage yard, is actually the leader of the cartel?" Scarlett asked.

"It's the only way this makes sense." Ivy was still trying to process this new possibility. Her mind was working faster than her mouth. "He killed those women to send a message. *No one escapes* Sangre por Sangre. But in the two years Carson has been undercover, no one was willing to offer information on a killer in the network who carved symbols into his victims' backs. Because they knew who was responsible and what would happen if they identified their leader."

"Wait." Cash stepped forward. "Then doesn't that mean this Sebastian would've had to have known that Carson was part of an undercover operation from the beginning? I mean, he couldn't identify the top brass for two years."

Acid pushed into her throat. Ivy raced for her cell phone and pressed the autodial to call Carson. Despite the lingering effects of their last conversation, she couldn't let him go through with this. "He's walking straight into a trap."

This place was on the verge of total collapse.

Carson wasn't sure the structure could take much more.

The multistory building had been designed to hide in plain sight. Meant to bring the cartel together, to pool resources and serve as a headquarters as efficient and deadly as the very people trying to destroy *Sangre por Sangre*. But a handful of explosives had broken it down, eroded its foundation and turned it into something worthless.

Not entirely unlike the emptiness coiling through him.

"Get rid of the vehicle." He tossed the keys into the back seat to the youngest of the soldiers and shoved free of the SUV. Knowing Ivy, he was sure she'd have equipped her fleet with GPS and possibly even better countermeasures. But she had promised him a two-hour head start. He trusted her to keep her word—for now—but her patience would run out sooner or later.

There was a small chance Sebastian had managed to contact upper management since their showdown in the salvage yard, but the way Carson had left him unconscious and bleeding would buy him the time he needed to defend his case. At least, that was the hope.

The soldier positioned behind him had caught the keys and gotten out, letting Max hop down from the back driver's-side door. In less than a minute, dirt kicked up behind the stolen vehicle but disappeared over the ridge of the man-made bowl acting as a defense system around the building. If anyone came close to this place, the cartel saw them coming. Especially now that upper management seemed to have called in every asset, soldier and resource on and off the books. "There a party I don't know about?"

His female companion didn't answer, taking the lead into the partially collapsed garage. In truth, she probably didn't know what the hell was going on either. Both she and her younger associate had been apprehended downtown for a number of hours.

Though Ivy's operative hadn't said where. If the street dealers had been pulled off their corners, why had two soldiers been left behind? Carson's curiosity had always gotten the better of him. He'd never been able to look an answer straight in the face without questioning the premise. It was one of the reasons the FBI had brought him on board. Why they'd trusted him to go into this assignment.

He followed in his companion's tracks through debris, pools of water and what looked like pulverized cement toward the entrance into the building. One point of entry. One point of exit. He gauged the chances of being able to turn back now and scanned the property over one shoulder. They weren't looking good. "So how did Socorro get the drop on you two?"

"It was stupid, really." She led him into the building, and a sensation of being crushed took hold, with a healthy hint of resistance. Though his companion kept moving as though they couldn't possibly die within these walls. "We were on a stakeout, and my phone died. We didn't get the word about pulling back until it was too late."

"A stakeout?" Carson hadn't received a single order the past month, but apparently, that wasn't the case for the rest of the soldiers he'd served beside. It didn't make sense. Someone was still operating the cartel despite the limited resources and manpower, and yet they'd managed to pull this many soldiers out of thin air. His gut clenched tighter with each step he took deeper into the belly of the building. He took the time to memorize the route they were taking through the maze of corridors. Or maybe *Sangre por Sangre* wasn't as injured as upper management wanted everyone to believe. "Whereabouts?"

"Across the street from that Socorro bitch's apartment. The one who runs the place." She slowed her pace. Just enough to maneuver behind him in the narrow corridor. "We were told there was a potential rat in our ranks, and that he would be there. Our orders were to drag him back to face his punishment."

Carson scanned the hallway up ahead. They hadn't come in contact with anyone else from the cartel, but his instincts said the moment they did, he was out of options. He slipped his hand into his opposite pocket, out of his companion's sight, and secured Ivy's pocketknife in his palm. He hadn't meant to hold on to it, but the chaos of the two days since the battle in the salvage yard had prioritized more important things. "You got a name of this rat?"

"Funny you should mention it," she said. "Because I was told it was you."

She didn't hesitate to make the first strike. His companion latched on to his shoulder and dug her fingernails into his skin. He arced the pocketknife toward her temple, but there was a reason she'd been recruited into *Sangre por Sangre*. Her background in street fighting had only served her when cornered. She blocked his attack. Carson took the opportunity to go for the other side of her head.

Max's barks filled the hallway and threatened to trigger a ringing in his ears from her proximity. She waited for her turn to attack, but he wouldn't give the order. Not yet.

His fist connected with the soft tissue of his companion's cheekbone. He brought his heel up and kicked straight into her chest.

She fell back into the corridor wall, sliding down until she hit the ground. Out of breath.

"Come on, Max. We gotta get the hell out of here." Carson didn't wait for his companion to get back up. He bolted back the way they'd come, playing through each turn they'd taken in his head. Except there seemed to be no end to this place. He picked up the pace. The cartel's top brass knew he'd handed intel from within the organization to Socorro. They knew about his relationship with Ivy. And if they were waiting for him at her apartment, they'd most likely intended to use her to punish him. "Where the hell is the exit?"

This was the way they'd come. He was sure of it. Only now…

A barrage of flashlights assaulted his vision as he took the next turn.

Carson pulled up short, though every cell in his body screamed for him to turn around. He brought one hand up to block the brightness of the flashlights, but his vision refused to adjust. It was no use. They had him pinned. Going back would only extend the inevitable.

Max made her discontent known almost instantly, her low growl threatening anyone who dared touch her handler.

"Dominic, you made it." An outline shifted forward through the wall of individual lights. And presumably the weapons trained on him. Sebastian had somehow remained in one piece. Considering the beating Carson had given him, his quick recovery only credited the complicated design to the mask the cartel soldier seemed to wear. This was no ordinary recruiter for a drug cartel. Carson didn't know what the hell he was. "We were getting worried."

This was it. The moment he'd dreaded for two years. His cover had been blown, and there was no going back. Not to Socorro. Not to the cartel. Not even to the FBI.

They'd all abandoned him. But, worse, he'd abandoned them. The power of knowing an entire organization—that a partner—had his back in case the cartel had learned of his true identity wasn't there anymore. He was on his own.

"Sorry I'm late." He tried to count the soldiers at Sebastian's back through the shadows. Too many for him to number. Too many for him to fight alone. His blood ran hot at the idea of dying right here in this place. With nothing but his weapon and Ivy's pocketknife on him. And Max. She'd be forced to watch before Sebastian had her put down and buried somewhere nobody would find her remains. Hell, she deserved better than this. "Hell of a party you're throwing."

"All in your honor, my friend. Please." Sebastian angled one side of his body, completely at ease with the potential of an attack. In fact, Carson had the feeling the son of a bitch was betting on it. "Join us, won't you? This moment has been coming for a long time."

Carson didn't have a choice. He scanned the walls, clutching on to Ivy's pocketknife—just to have something to keep him in the moment—and took a single step forward.

Pain splintered across the back of his skull.

He fell forward, losing his grip on the pocketknife, and hit the floor on all fours. Lightning didn't come close to describing the patterns exploding behind his eyes. Max's revolt went into overdrive as she lunged at his attacker. Loud screams pierced through the haze closing in around Carson's mind. He couldn't think, couldn't force his limbs to obey his commands.

"Enough," Sebastian said.

A single shot sucked the life out of Carson.

The K-9's whimper etched into his brain and refused to let up. Then silence. It bounced off the cinder-block walls and dug deeper holes into his heart. His pulse rocketed higher as rage spread hot and thick through his veins. Carson shot to his feet, turning on his heel. His fist connected with the soldier who'd clocked him. The man dropped hard beside Max's still frame. "No!"

His knees couldn't hold his weight anymore as grief overwhelmed any thought of his own survival. Carson pressed his face into Max's, and she licked at the tears. She was alive.

For now. He skimmed his hand down the length of her body, coming away with blood. He'd done this to her. He'd trained her to protect him, and now... Now he was going to lose her.

Fingers fisted into his hair and pulled him away from his partner.

"I'm sorry to say dogs are not invited to this fiesta." Sebastian dragged him across the dirt and tossed him back onto the front lines of infantry ready to fire.

Flashlights danced around Carson as he looked up at the man who'd brought him into the cartel. A man whose life he'd saved. "I'm going to kill you for that. Every single one of you."

Sebastian's knees popped as he crouched beside him. Fisting another handful of hair, the cartel leader forced Carson's head back. The physical damage from their brawl had darkened, sharpening some features and downplaying others on the older man's face. "You asked me to give my bosses a message the last time I saw you. Consider your message delivered, Agent Lang."

Chapter Thirteen

She'd already lost one of her operatives.

She couldn't lose another.

Ivy massaged her uninjured palm into the steering wheel, but no amount of distraction could take away from the desperation clawing through her chest. Carson had made his choice to go back to the cartel in an effort to warn the friends he'd made of the danger headed their way. She should let him deal with the consequences of that choice. But she couldn't. She couldn't leave him to Sebastian's sadism. She couldn't let him suffer as she had in that small room at the salvage yard.

She was angry with him—more than she'd been when he'd taken this assignment—but that didn't mean she'd stopped caring about him. Loving him. Nobody, not even her worst enemy, deserved that kind of pain. She'd watched her mother endure it for years and had finally gotten the strength to put it to a stop. It had taken everything she had, and she wouldn't give anything less now.

Because she loved him.

Because the best thing she could do with this life was to protect someone else. But Carson hadn't seen her devotion to stop the pain of this world from touching those she cared about as selfless. His accusation, that she bulldozed everyone and everything in her path to get what she wanted, had left her feeling carved out and empty. She'd known what her former partners had thought of her. She'd heard their whispers and knew about their transfer requests. With Carson... she'd been different. She'd let him through her guard. She'd smiled more. She'd laughed. Their banter had kept her from spiraling into the nightmares of the past, and his touch had kept her warm.

But old habits died hard.

She could see where she'd messed up, like a long line of dominoes. Tip the first one and the others were bound to feed into the final outcome. The end of their partnership had been coming for a long time. The wrong turns she'd taken were clear as day as she looked back. By not fighting his acceptance of the undercover assignment. By keeping her distance when he'd brought back intel to Socorro. By telling him her safety and health weren't his concern. It was all there, staring back at her in a mirror of failure. She'd just been too late to put a stop to the final domino from falling.

"You're going to tear that steering wheel in half if you keep it up." Granger Morais kept his attention straight forward, his laptop open as he provided the GPS info on their stolen SUV. But she already knew where they were headed. No matter what the tracking said. "We're about a mile out."

"We're not going for the SUV. Send the coordinates for *Sangre por Sangre*'s headquarters to the rest of the team." She targeted each of the SUVs in her rearview mirror. Four vehicles in total with two police cruisers in the rear. She'd tried to convince Chief Halsey to stay with Jocelyn, but there'd been no persuading the man from getting his pound of flesh. Sebastian would regret the day he'd put his hands on one of her operatives.

The cartel would see them coming from a mile away. That was the point. To take a stand. To make a point. That nobody messed with Socorro Security.

"You're sure that's where this ends?" Granger was looking at every angle, every possibility. The idea of them showing up to an empty building was probably the worst that could happen in his eyes.

She directed her attention to the SUV up ahead. Angled off the side of the road. Abandoned. Except somewhere in the back of her mind she realized someone would've had to have driven it out into the middle of the desert. Someone most likely waiting to ambush them. "More sure than I've been about anything else in my life."

Ivy grabbed for the radio velcroed to the dashboard and hit the talk button. She'd had Alpine Valley PD tuned in to their private channel in case they got separated. "We're coming up on our stolen SUV. Be prepared to take on fire."

Granger reached into the back seat and pulled his Kevlar from beside his bull terrier, Zeus. The dog was more fat than muscle, but when it came to protecting his handler, the K-9 never failed. Mostly by sitting on anyone who dared get close enough. The counterterrorism agent threaded himself into his gear. He leaned forward in his seat, studying their SUV through the windshield, then took the radio and opened the line. "Movement. Passenger side, back wheel well. Scarlett, that's all you."

"Understood." The security consultant's voice crackled through the line.

Ivy sped past the sitting SUV, then watched as Scarlett hung back and let Alpine PD, Jones and Cash pass. The SUV at the rear of the pack moved out of line.

Then the shooting started. The cartel soldier presumably

responsible for ditching the SUV opened fire on the caravan. Bullets thudded against Ivy's back window but didn't penetrate, thanks to bulletproof glass and armored panels.

Scarlett's vehicle suddenly sped up.

And targeted the back quarter panel of the abandoned SUV. The security consultant rammed her vehicle straight into the other. The cartel soldier was caught by the collision and thrown clear.

"What the hell is she doing? I wanted her to trigger the explosive. Not ram the other vehicle." Slowing, Ivy brought the rest of the vehicles to a halt to assess the situation. She forced her upper body to turn in her seat. Waiting. The driver's-side airbag had deployed in the rear vehicle.

"Guess Scarlett has her own ideas of what qualifies as 'that's all you.'" Granger didn't seem surprised. Or worried. It was his calm nature that would get her through what was to come. "See? She's fine."

Ivy caught sight of her operator punching down the airbag. Scarlett shouldered out of the vehicle, not an inch worse for wear. In fact, a wide smile had taken over the security consultant's expression as she hitched a ride in one of the other vehicles. Ivy turned back to the road. "I need to up her liability insurance."

The radio staticked. "Am I supposed to ignore the fact Scarlett intentionally rammed another vehicle and most likely killed everyone inside?" Chief Halsey asked.

Ivy nodded to the radio. "That's all you, Morais."

Her counterterrorism operative fisted the radio. "Yes." One word. End of conversation.

The hum of tires on dirt worked to settle her nerves as they approached *Sangre por Sangre*'s headquarters, but she couldn't trust that feeling. Not yet. Not until they had a clear read on the situation and Carson's location. "Remember the priority."

"I got it." Granger thumbed bullets into the magazine of his pistol, laptop now angled sideways at his feet. "Get Lang out. Make sure Sebastian doesn't leave. Easy as... Jocelyn's homemade chocolate chip cookies."

"Have you seen the amount of ingredients that goes into those?" she asked. "They are not easy. But, damn, are they worth the wait."

He didn't respond right away, the pressure of his attention boring into her as strong and slow as an oil drill.

"She's going to be okay, Ivy. Jocelyn is strong," he said. "She'll be back in the field in no time."

Ivy's grip tightened all over again. "But will she forgive me for putting her in the crosshairs in the first place?"

Granger didn't seem to have an answer to that.

A chain-link fence materialized as they drew closer to the massive man-made crater protecting the cartel's hideout. It was a forty-five-degree angle down, but Ivy had prepared for this. "Hold on to something."

She pressed the accelerator as Granger grabbed for the dash. They closed the distance between them and the flimsy barrier and blew straight through it. Sparks lit up as metal met metal, but the fence had never stood a chance against her vehicle.

The SUV instantly dipped over the edge and down into the bowl. Gravity lost its hold on Ivy's stomach as they plummeted toward the basin. Four vehicles followed behind, all catching air as they launched over the rim and down. Her team had chosen to follow her into the depths of hell, and she would never forget it.

Ivy twisted the wheel as the SUV hit flat earth and got

out of the way of the convoy behind. Within seconds of touchdown, bodies started appearing through the wide field of cars preventing them from driving straight to the front door.

Another round of bullets bounced off the vehicle.

Granger shoved the magazine into his weapon as he fought to stay upright from the wicked turns she was forced to make. "Head for the garage. It's the easiest way in."

She forced the SUV into a skid in order to get as close as possible to the entry point. All four vehicles behind her did the same, setting up a semicircle of protection.

The radio lit up. "Get inside. Alpine Valley PD will cover you. We got this." Chief Halsey's insistence told her he was all too happy to pick off as many cartel soldiers as he could.

Ivy responded. "Copy that. Try not to get shot."

"Can't promise anything, but I'll keep it in mind." Halsey's patrol cruiser lit up, his voice registering over the PA. "This is Alpine Valley police. Put your weapons down and your hands on your heads. No? Okay, then."

Return fire thumped through the windows.

Ivy and Granger took advantage. She unholstered her weapon, using only her free index finger to go for the latch, and kicked the door open. The driver's-side door protected her from the spray of gunfire. She couldn't advance until the bullets stopped. She couldn't get to Carson and Max.

A length of silence punctured through her raised senses. She nodded at Granger over the hood of the SUV. "Go."

Ivy pumped her legs as fast as they would go. The stitches in her side screamed and stretched, threatening to tear from the effort, but she wouldn't stop. Not until she found her partner. They made it to the overhang of the garage and ran straight into shadow. It took a few seconds for her vision to adjust, but she refused to slow down.

"This way." Granger took the lead as Jones, Scarlett and Cash brought up the rear with their K-9s in tow. All free of bullet holes.

"I was really hoping I would never have to come back here," Jones said.

Cash moved to Ivy's left side. As though they'd each taken position as her personal bodyguard. "Imagine how I feel. I blew this place to hell and back with C-4, and it's somehow still standing."

"Did you use the right amount? You've got to get the measurements right or it does no good at all. I've told you that a dozen times." Scarlett was a little too buoyant for someone who'd just sent a cartel soldier flying through the air.

"Quiet." Granger pulled up short at the single entry into the building. He raised a hand, beckoning them forward.

Scarlett's twin Dobermans rushed through the door, and the other K-9s fought to catch up.

The team moved as one into the darkened corridor, and a dampness she didn't want to think about slipped beneath her blazer. "This place is worse than you guys wrote in your reports."

"You have no idea." Jones switched the flashlight mounted to his pistol on. "I got something over here. Oh, hell."

"What is it?" It took Ivy a second to get a visual as all four of her operatives crowded around some kind of mass in the middle of the floor. The K-9s were whining, shifting on their feet and circling. She saw the fur first. Then the watery black eyes staring up at her. Unblinking. Her stomach flipped as she lunged to put pressure on the German shepherd's blood-matted fur. "Get Chief Halsey in here! Now!"

So this was what dying felt like.

Carson's head skimmed the cement underneath him. Above him? He couldn't think straight. Whatever direction, there was no getting out of the mess he'd put himself in. Strung up by his ankles. Surrounded by armed gunmen willing to pull the trigger with a single word. Nope. He wasn't going anywhere. Not without a miracle, and he didn't see Ivy and her team showing him any kind of grace when they burned this place to the ground.

Blood coated the inside of his mouth. He'd lost one of his back molars during the many fists to his face. Turned out Sebastian had been hiding more than his true identity all this time. An aging old man, he was not. No. There was a contained strength hidden within the cartel recruiter's bones. Something Carson had never imagined.

And, damn it, he hurt. Everywhere. He spit the next rush of blood to clear his mouth. "Bet it feels good to finally be yourself, Sebastian. Hunting and killing those women must've been too easy."

Except the son of a bitch hadn't gone easy on Ivy. He'd done this to her. Tortured her, humiliated her, nearly killed her. Would have if she hadn't bested Sebastian with her training and will to live.

"Easy?" Sebastian wiped his bloodied hands on the shirt of another soldier on the periphery. His voice almost echoed off the open two-story cinder block that had taken too much damage over the years. "No. Those women, they fought. They begged. They made it fun. You? I just want to kill you."

It was the same room the war correspondent had been brought into and tormented for information concerning photos she'd taken over a period of three days—evidence of the cartel working in cahoots with a state senator. Carson had been powerless to stop it, and so he'd volunteered to take the place of her abusers. Holding back his strikes without giving away his intentions. He'd at least given her the chance to regain some of her strength, to escape. Thankfully, one of Socorro's operatives had helped her survive. "Then what's the holdup? You know who I am. You know what I've been doing inside *Sangre por Sangre* all these years. Why wait?"

Blood rushed to his head, darkening his vision. Lack of sleep. Lack of nutrients. Heartbreak. Possibly a concussion. They would all play a vital role in the next hours.

Sebastian finished cleaning his busted knuckles and turned his attention back to Carson with nothing but death in his eyes. "You know, I never married. Never had children. Building this organization took everything I had. The lieutenants I recruited became family. My soldiers, my children. We worked together to bring about change. To finally take what was stolen from us so long ago."

Sangre por Sangre's founder—Carson still couldn't wrap his head around that—withdrew a blade from one of the soldiers looking on. He moved faster than Carson expected. The blade stabbed through Carson's upper arm. His scream failed to drown out Sebastian's words. "Every single soldier I've lost in the past two years was because of you. Men and women who devoted their lives to my cause, who fought for me, bled for me and died for me. You're going to pay for their lives. Slowly. Painfully. Then I'm going to leave your body in the desert for Agent Bardot to find. Then I'm going to kill another of her operatives. Then another. Until she has nobody left, and she'll know the pain that you two have caused me."

Excruciating pain burned until it overrode every sense Carson owned. He lost his control to the point a laugh escaped his chest. It rolled through him, gaining strength, blocking out the pain. Blood dripped beneath his shirtsleeve and tendriled over his collarbone.

"This is funny to you?" Sebastian asked.

"This? No." Carson tried to shake his head. "I'm just imagining what Ivy's going to do to you. Especially if she finds out you shot her dog. You have no idea the kind of hell you've brought down on yourself. On the soldiers you claim to care about. You think you're some kind of protector. You have no idea what that word means compared to her. And I can't wait to see you fall."

A fist rocketed into his face. Carson's body swung away from his attacker, then back for another strike. His head snapped back. Pain unlike anything he'd experienced before kept him conscious and urged his body to shut down at the same time.

He wouldn't be able to take much more.

But of all the ways to go, he'd choose this a thousand times more. Because he knew the end result in his bones. He knew that Ivy would finish the assignment they'd started while they'd still been partners in the FBI. Despite his betrayal, she would remain the same woman she'd always been.

Valiant. Committed. Courageous.

He'd never been any of those things. Not like her. Carson had taken the easy way out. He saw that now. How going undercover within the cartel gave him the mask of hero, but Ivy had been on the outside. Fighting. Risking her team and her reputation and her own life. She'd earned a target on her back to protect him. How hadn't he seen it before?

Their last conversation played on repeat at the back of his mind. He'd accused her of doing it all for herself. For the glory, to keep building a wall between her and the rest of the world, but that couldn't have been farther from the truth. She was brave. Braver than Carson. He'd believed her inability to separate herself from their investigations over the years had built her into an unyielding, closed-off partner, but that wasn't the case at all. The hell she'd suffered as a kid had led her to use her work to distract herself from dealing with the trauma. The grief. At ten years old, she'd had to shoot a man who beat her and her mother. How could he have seen her intensity as anything more than a way to ensure she never had to suffer like that again? That all she needed was for someone to choose her? Ivy Bardot loved fiercely. The proof was right there in the two bullets still cataloged in evidence in her stepfather's investigation box. She risked everything in pursuit of holding on to the people who meant the most to her.

And he'd done the stupid thing and turned his back on her. He'd become a coward, so different from the times he'd come home with a black eye or a bloody lip because he'd refused to back down from the bullies who made fun of his mixed race.

Because he'd just wanted Ivy to choose him, too. To love him as much as he loved her. Losing his mother had taken everything from him, but Ivy had been there to step into that role of companion. And when he'd gone undercover and lost his constant connection to her, he'd tried to replace it with the very men and women who would kill him with a single order now. To live up to her expectations.

He'd relied on other people to love and support him without ever considering he could do it himself. That he was the one responsible for his own happiness. Not his mother. Not Ivy. Not the people he'd convinced himself could give him what he needed from within the cartel. Him. The realization hit him harder than Sebastian's next fist. And he wanted to figure out how to fix it. To move forward without that external validation. For once, he wanted to find out what made him happy. Other people's interests be damned.

Only that seemed impossible now. Hanging upside down in the middle of a drug cartel headquarters surrounded by soldiers ready to kill him.

"Unfortunately, I'm not the one who will be falling today, Agent Lang." Sebastian nodded to one of the soldiers off to one side. His female companion stepped forward. "Get him ready. I expect Socorro is already on its way, and we don't want to keep them waiting."

Socorro. Ivy. Carson pulled at the rope binding his hands behind his back with everything he had left. Which wasn't much. The threads didn't even stretch as the cartel soldier waved two more companions closer to assist. "You knew who I was. All this time. You knew what I was doing."

"Of course I knew," Sebastian said. "How else was I supposed to keep an eye on my old friend Agent Bardot?"

Son of a bitch. Carson had served within the cartel to provide Ivy and her team a leg up in this war, but he'd only been Sebastian's puppet. Putting Ivy and Socorro in danger. Drawing them into a trap. "You can't win this, Sebastian. It doesn't matter how many soldiers you throw at them or how many guns you buy. She won't stop until you're behind bars or six feet under."

Sebastian wiped blood from the blade used to stab Carson's arm on the same rag he'd used to clean his hands. "Don't worry about me, my friend. There's a reason I lured those Socorro dogs here."

"What are you talking about?" Carson struggled as three soldiers braced his shoulders and started hauling him down.

The world righted itself as they held him upright. They maneuvered him toward the corridor. Three to one wasn't good odds.

"Let's just say my focus is no longer on keeping operations moving or making more money. I've moved beyond mere survival." The cartel founder smiled, easy and relaxed, despite the monster hidden within. "It's all about the future now. I must thank you, Agent Lang. Without you, I never would've learned the identities of Socorro's operatives, their protocols, their weapons preferences. You will be the reason *Sangre por Sangre* lives on to fight another day. Thank you."

Carson hadn't provided any of that.

"You son of a bitch." He fought the strength of three soldiers as they dragged him toward the door. He didn't know where they were taking him. It didn't matter. What mattered was warning Ivy.

"Get him out of here, please." Sebastian rounded a table Carson hadn't noticed until then, turning a laptop toward him. Surveillance footage. Of the complex. And there, on the screen, a line of operatives making their way through the building. Ivy in the lead. "It seems our guests have arrived early. Let's give them a proper greeting, shall we?"

Gunfire punctured through Carson's shallow breathing a split second before Socorro's private military contractors breached the room.

Ivy took aim at the man of the hour as her team and their K-9s filed in behind her. "Who shot my dog!"

Chapter Fourteen

No one raised their hand.

That was okay. She would find the person who shot Max. She would tear this whole building down to do it, too. Until then, Chief Halsey was taking care of the German shepherd the best way he could. She lost count of the number of soldiers taking aim at her and her team. One wrong move. That was all it would take to tear apart both of their organizations. Ivy raised her weapon, at Sebastian. "I'm going to give you one chance to put your weapons down and surrender."

"You must be confused, Agent Bardot." Sebastian's laugh inspired the rest of his soldiers to participate. He spread his arms wide, motioning to the men and women prepared to shoot on his order. "You see, I have far more manpower. You, you have four operatives and some dogs."

"You're right. Doesn't feel like a fair fight, does it?" Ivy scanned the room. Instantly landing on Carson. He'd been bound, beaten. Blood dripped down his arm and slid between his fingers. "Would you like to invite more soldiers to come help you? We'll wait."

Sebastian's smile slipped off his face. He stepped away from the desk he'd put between him and her team. "You've been hunting me for two years. Sent your lapdog to identify me, to undermine my operation. You send your operatives to take out my lieutenants. All while you hide in your black tower. You are not ready for what's coming, little girl. You are not strong enough to fight me."

Strong enough. When the hell had she let other people determine what she was capable of? When had she let it haunt her to the point of paralysis? Ivy lowered her weapon. "Shall we finish what we started in that basement, Sebastian? You, me. No federal agents. No cartel soldiers to interfere. That's what you want, right? To prove *Sangre por Sangre* deserves to sit on the throne. That all of this leads to one outcome— you standing over the bodies of your enemies. I'll give you that chance."

"Ivy, what the hell are you doing?" Carson struggled to be free of his captives. In vain.

"I would love nothing more." A wide smile transformed the cartel founder's expression. "One weapon. No guns. To the death. I win, I will kill your entire team and your undercover operative. Socorro will be no more."

"And if I win, *Sangre por Sangre* surrenders to the Alpine Valley Police Department and Socorro. Never to operate again." Ivy passed her weapon to Granger, positioned behind her.

"Boss, you sure about this?" Scarlett kept her voice low, but the concern was louder than anything else in the room. "You're still injured from the last time you two were in a room together."

"I'll be fine. I have something he doesn't." Her gaze cut to Carson as she stripped out of the sling meant to help her dislocated shoulder heal.

"What's that?" Jones seemed to take inventory of the soldiers he would like to take out, that battle-ready energy coming off him in waves.

She handed off the sling to Granger and rolled her shoulder out. "A team who has my back, no matter what. As long as I have you guys, I can never lose. But for him? Every single one of these soldiers will put their own survival first if pushed." Ivy turned to face Sebastian as his soldiers cleared away the desks and debris from the middle of the room. "See the C-4 strapped to the major structural beams overhead? He's not confident in his plan to get to the rest of you. He plans on bringing down the building on top of us if this doesn't go his way. Make sure he fails. Understand?"

"I have some experience with that," Scarlett said. "I'll take care of it."

"Granger, Jones, Cash." She didn't want to say goodbye. She didn't want to admit that this was a bad idea and that she had no way of knowing if her reason would hold up against a man who'd already killed four women and put another in the hospital. Not to mention the thousands of lives his organization had taken over the years when Socorro had failed to protect the people they swore to protect. "The moment he attacks, he's going to let his soldiers have a field day. Don't let your guards down. And feel free to take as many of them out as you can. Just make sure Carson isn't one of them."

"Wait. Are we friends with this guy again?" Cash said.

"Enough waiting." Sebastian kicked a rock from in front of his foot. She'd misjudged him in the dark of a salvage yard before, then again when her eye had swollen to the point she hadn't been able to see. The man had claimed to spend twenty years building his empire, but there was still a youthfulness to him. A strength she hadn't considered before.

This was going to hurt. But the past no longer had a hold

on her. All that mattered was the future. Hers. Her team's. And Carson's. Ivy shrugged out of her blazer and handed it off to Granger. The muscles in her shoulder still ached. The stitches in her side warned her not to take another step, but she wasn't doing this to feed some ego-driven show of dominance. This was how she protected her family. Just as she'd done all those years ago.

Ivy took a literal and metaphorical step into the ring. "Sure you want to go through with this, Sebastian? That shoulder of yours isn't looking too good."

His laugh slid beneath her confidence and started to break it up into pieces. "How's the side, Agent Bardot?"

She didn't want to give away the pain she was already in. Not to him. Filling her lungs with as much oxygen as they could hold, she steadied her pulse with Carson in her peripheral vision.

"Ivy, you don't have to do this. You don't have to—" Her partner's words were cut short from the sucker punch to his gut. He doubled over within his captor's grasp.

Sebastian was the first to strike. He took advantage of her distraction and launched at her. She saw him coming. Ivy fisted his collar and rammed her forehead straight into his nose. The son of a bitch fell backward and hit the floor.

All hell broke loose.

Bullets sprayed across the room. Her team broke apart, each operative hunting for cover. Cash returned fire as his rottweiler, Bear, ran straight for the nearest soldier.

Ivy threw herself behind Sebastian's desk. A soldier reached over the edge. He grabbed on to her tank top and pulled her across the surface. A knife arced down toward her face. She managed to lean out of the way, letting it embed in the wood. Gripping the handle, she pulled it free and returned it to its owner. Straight into his chest. The soldier fell back, and she got to her feet.

Two more came for her. Both tried to cage her between them, but she was faster. Ivy ducked out from the reach of one and kicked his knee out from under him. The soldier slammed into the floor face-first. The other got a good hold on her from behind. Locking her arms behind her. Her shoulder threatened to dislocate all over again.

"None of you are getting out of here alive." Sebastian stumbled to his feet. Blood coursed from his nose and framed his mouth. Stained his graying beard. He withdrew a blade from a sheath on his belt.

"And here I thought we were going to play by the rules." Ivy rammed her heel into the soldier's foot at her back. He released his hold and tipped off-balance. He fell at her feet, and she made sure he would never get up again. Kicking her toes into his groin as hard as she could.

Just as Sebastian closed the distance between them.

He slammed into her. The knife grazed the outside of her arm as the cartel founder pinned her against the desk. She latched on to his wrist to gain control, but he was a hell of a lot stronger than he let on. Her shoulder screamed for her to let go. But she couldn't. Not yet.

Time seemed to slow.

Seconds distorted and stretched into minutes. Scarlett took a fist to the face as she tried to reach the laptop dislodged in the chaos. Cash blocked one attack while attempting to dodge a blade to the gut from the opposite direction. Granger had been pinned against the wall by no less than three soldiers. Granger's bellow filled the entire room as Jones used one of the cartel soldiers as a shield to avoid getting shot.

And Carson. He'd shoved one of his captors off but failed

to account for the soldier at his back. The butt of a weapon slammed down onto his skull. His legs collapsed out from underneath him.

They were losing. They were going to fail. Because of her. Because maybe her stepfather—maybe Sebastian—had been right. Maybe she wasn't strong enough to win this war. But she wouldn't stop trying.

"Look at them, Agent Bardot. See them suffer." Sebastian struggled to bring the knife down into her heart. Sweat dripped from his forehead and splashed onto her face. "I can make it all go away. All you have to do is give in."

The tip of the blade penetrated through her tank top. She couldn't hold him off much longer. A pinprick of pain registered just below her collarbone. "I gave my word to those women."

Ivy arched her hips off the desk and threw his weight to one side. Sebastian had no choice but to follow. She hiked his wrist upward, then straight down onto the edge of the desk. The crunch of bone pierced through the sound of gunfire and screams. Along with his scream. He stared up at her with nothing but violence and death.

"I was going to make you pay for what you did to them." Ivy kicked Sebastian's legs out from under him. Fisting his collar while he was down, she ignored the pain in her shoulder. And launched her fist into his face. Once. Twice. His head snapped back. Years of being told she wasn't strong enough to fight created a new energy that sizzled through her. "I keep my promises."

Sebastian's body went limp in her grasp. His eyes rolled back in his head. Unconscious. Ivy let him sink to the floor. It was over. The loss. The pain. The fear. Straightening, she left the cartel's founder there to suffer the consequences that had led them to this room.

The gunfire seemed to cease all at once as *Sangre por Sangre* came to terms with the end result. Jones ripped out of a soldier's hold, then pinned his attacker against the wall. Granger shirked off the three men trying to bring him down. Scarlett didn't seem to notice any change in her surroundings, her focus on the C-4 ready to explode at the touch of a button. Cash shoved one of the soldiers forward.

And Carson raised his gaze to hers through the blood seeping into his eyes. They'd done it. Together. As a team. It had taken so much longer than she'd planned, but they'd—

A gunshot exploded from behind.

Then came the pain. Ivy lowered her attention to the stain spreading across her tank top, then back to her team.

Right before the world went dark.

SOCORRO'S OPERATIVES FELL into action.

Each running to catch their boss before she met the ground.

Carson could only watch Ivy as she fell. The past superimposed the present as he simultaneously saw her collapse in the salvage yard warehouse and hit the floor now. Sebastian lowered his gun hand. A smile creased the outer edges of his face.

Carson's head pounded in rhythm with his increasing heart rate. He could barely see through the blood dripping into his eyes, but struggled to his feet. The soldiers on either side of him fought to keep him down. Under control. It wouldn't work. A fire had started burning in him, and there was nothing anybody could do to put it out. No one but Ivy.

Carson rammed his shoulder into the nearest captor,

throwing the son of a bitch off-balance. His female companion he'd gotten out of Socorro holding rushed at him. She didn't make it. He buried his heel in her stomach and took the air right out of her. Her knees dropped as she gasped for breath. Movement registered in his peripheral vision. Carson ducked to avoid the butt of the weapon coming at his face and swung around in time to let the soldier's momentum carry him into another moving in to subdue him.

A third attacker came straight at him. The bastard hiked his foot up as though to land a solid kick. Only Carson managed to capture the soldier's boot between his bound arm and rib cage. One tight jerk and the soldier's ankle practically broke off in Carson's grip. He forced the attacker to hop on one foot, angling the gunman right into another threat.

Pain spidered down Carson's back as a fourth soldier swung his weapon down. It gave *Sangre por Sangre* a chance to gang up on him. Two more attackers grabbed for his shoulders and arms. He took down another coming from the front and took out the soldier's knee. Carson ducked out from the son of a bitch on the left and crushed his head into the soldier's temple. Then had to quickly dodge a knife aimed straight for his spine. The bladesman overcorrected his momentum. But not in time to avoid Carson's knee to his face.

Men and women groaned at his feet. But the fight wasn't over.

Ivy's operatives were dragging her off the battlefield, toward the exit. She hadn't moved, hadn't opened her eyes. Even if she managed to survive, there was no telling when Sebastian would come for her again. Come for her team.

Carson had to end this now.

He caught sight of the cartel's fearless leader making a break for a door he'd once mapped as a secret escape from the building. Low-level soldiers had been kept in the dark. It was just like upper management to sacrifice the men and women they'd used to do their dirty work while keeping their own hands clean. "Sebastian!"

Carson crouched to pick up a fallen knife and sliced through the rope at his wrists. Blood rushed back into his fingertips as he followed after the man responsible for so much death. He'd been an idiot to believe there was an ounce of good within the cartel, that the people at the bottom were simply following orders. He'd been manipulated, used.

And now he was going to make sure it never happened to anyone else.

He dodged another attempt to slow him down. A second soldier pointed a gun at him, but one of Socorro's K-9s—a husky—intercepted and took the gunman down. Fierce growls let him know these dogs weren't in the mood for playing. They were here to protect their handlers. Well, except maybe for the one sitting on top of a cartel soldier off to his right. The bull terrier simply grinned at him as Carson cut across the body-strewn space. And, hell, he couldn't blame the K-9 for adding a bit of fun to this mess. Sometimes that was the only way to make it through the hard stuff.

Ten feet. Five.

Sebastian ducked through the door and secured it behind him.

Just as Carson lunged. His shoulder made contact, but the door had locked from the inside. He slammed both palms against what was meant to look like cinder block, but the exit wouldn't budge. "Sebastian! You coward! You can't run forever! I will find you!"

This was no time for caution. He had to get in there.

"We can help you with that, Lang," a voice said from behind.

Carson turned to find two Socorro operatives, armed to the teeth and not an ounce of exhaustion etched into their faces. To be fair, they hadn't been tortured for a couple of hours. He motioned them forward. Though he wasn't sure of their names, they each had the look of determination of seeing this through to the end. The same determination that had possessed him since coming back to the cartel. "By all means, be my guests."

The one he was fairly certain was called Cash—Socorro's forward scout—raised his weapon and took aim. Then fired. Once. Twice. The second operative—Jones, maybe—rammed the heel of his boot and forced the exit open. "You come for one of us, you come for all of us. Ivy says you're one of us. So go get that son of a bitch. We've got everything covered here."

One of them. Three words shouldn't have held so much weight, but Carson felt the beginnings of the support he'd been searching for all this time. First, with his mother, then through Ivy, and when he'd been required to distance himself from her, from the cartel. Only the people he'd fought beside in the field hadn't ever really felt the same for him as he had for them. It had all been a manipulation. An order. He saw the truth now. He knew what the future held and whom he wanted in his life, and it sure as hell wasn't *Sangre por Sangre*. The haze of revenge and rage lowered to a simmer as he processed the body count. Every Socorro operative was still standing. Apart from Ivy. "Thank you."

"Hey, Lang, hold up," Jones said. "There's something you should know about Socorro. We never go anywhere without our partners."

Both men parted, letting a stubborn, bleeding, protective

Ivy through. She held on to her side. Blood seeped between her fingers.

"What the hell are you doing? You were shot." He reached for her, unsure if she would appreciate the contact. "You need medical attention."

Somehow she'd lost even more color since she'd confronted him in Socorro's headquarters. "When have I ever let a wound slow me down? Besides, I may have played up the seriousness of the shot." She pulled her hand away, revealing a stained tank top. "There was no way I was going to be able to fight Sebastian on my own with a dislocated shoulder and a stab wound. So I let him take me out of the equation."

Disbelief stole the air from his lungs. "But the bullet—"

"Was very real." Her laugh took the tension out of his shoulders. She was alive. She was okay. Ivy lifted the edge of her shirt, showing off a line of blood and burned skin. "But it was just a graze."

"You guys know the longer you stand here, the farther our suspect gets, right?" Cash pointed toward the door.

Ivy set clear green eyes on Carson, and the entire world seemed to make sense again. As though for the first time in two years, he'd given himself permission to make his desires known instead of bowing out to everyone else's. "Are you ready to end this?"

"Let's do this." Carson shoved through the door. His heart rocketed into his throat every step he stumbled in the darkness. Grief charged through him at the realization he didn't have Max to help guide him with her higher senses. Except he wasn't entirely on his own.

He had his partner.

"I've never been through this corridor before." Carson

felt his way along the wall, following the sharp turns that seemed to never end. "This must've been how the cartel was still able to operate over the past few months."

"Where does it go?" she asked.

He didn't have a chance to answer as sunlight pierced into the darkened space up ahead. "I'm guessing outside." Carson offered her his hand. Which she took. "Come on."

Ivy unholstered her weapon—the same one she'd handed off to one of her operatives earlier—as they ran. They left the protection of the building and scanned the open desert. "Where did he—"

An engine revved from their left.

And shot directly at them.

Carson pulled Ivy with him, just as she'd done that night in her apartment when they'd been under attack. Saving his life. They hit the ground as one, and he tucked her into his body. Dirt worked into his mouth and nose with each roll, but they'd avoided dying. For now.

The vehicle crashed into the exit, sealing it off. Sebastian shoved free of the driver's seat, armed with what looked like a long piece of rebar.

Ivy was the first to get to her feet. And took aim. "Drop it, Sebastian. Or I will shoot."

"You took everything from me!" The cartel founder brought the metal weapon down on her forearm. The gun went off. A bullet shot into the wall of the building and spit dirt.

Ivy fell forward. The gun fell from her hand, out of reach, as she cradled her arm against her chest. Sebastian raised the elongated metal for another strike, and Ivy rolled. The rebar thudded into the cracked earth. "Now I'm going to take everything you love from you."

Carson dragged Ivy to stand, maneuvering her behind him. "It's over, Sebastian. There's nothing left of your cartel. Give yourself up, and you might live another twenty years."

Sebastian unpocketed some kind of device. A small black box with an antenna. A detonator? "Say goodbye to your team, Agent Bardot."

He hit the button.

Except nothing happened.

Carson waited. One second. Two. Sebastian pressed the button again, then once more. And the tension eased out of Carson's shoulders.

"Looking for this?" Scarlett Beam rounded the corner and into view. Tossing a brick of white... C-4? Jones, Cash, Granger and their K-9s followed. Each taking aim with guns in hand. "You can thank Ivy for that. She noted the C-4 wired into the structural beams of the building. I took the opportunity to reprogram your detonator. To mine."

The security consultant showed off her phone. Then tapped the screen with a smile not meant for life-and-death situations.

The explosion started within, bringing the building in on itself in a series of blasts but containing it at the same time. It was the perfect system.

"You're finished, *el jefe*." Ivy rounded into Sebastian's vision, seemingly memorizing his realization that he'd lost. He'd outmanned and outgunned Socorro, but he couldn't beat them. Because they were a team. "*Sangre por Sangre* is dead."

Sebastian sank to his knees as he watched his headquarters collapse in on itself.

Sirens echoed off the sides of the man-made bowl. A patrol cruiser skidded to a stop behind Carson, and Chief Halsey pulled a set of handcuffs from his pocket.

"Sebastian Aguado, you are under arrest for a whole lot of shit." Halsey pinned Sebastian's arms behind his back and hauled the cartel founder to his feet to install the cuffs. "Namely, coming after my partner, but that one will be the least of your worries. Because you get to ride in the back seat with her German shepherd. We've got two years of charges you've earned. And I'm going to make sure every single one of them sticks."

Carson couldn't help but etch this scene into his brain. To convince him it was real.

Alpine Valley PD shoved Sebastian headfirst into the back seat of the patrol car. Chief Halsey secured the cartel founder inside with a nod in Ivy's direction.

"It's finished." Ivy stared after the cruiser, the sun highlighting the bruises and scrapes along one side of her face. "After two years, we finally took down *Sangre por Sangre*."

Chapter Fifteen

Three days later

She was supposed to feel some kind of relief, wasn't she?

Ivy moved the paperwork that had stacked up over the past week to the other side of her desk. This office had been her command center. She'd stood at this company's helm, given orders and developed strategy to keep her operatives safe and a drug cartel from spreading across the state.

And now? Now she didn't really know what she was supposed to do. A nervous energy urged her to review the dozens of threats that had crossed her desk and pick one to focus on. The Pentagon, of course, was appreciative of her and her team's effort in neutralizing *Sangre por Sangre*, but the cartel had merely been a drop in the bucket. There were a handful of other cartels the DEA, the FBI and the ATF were trying to get a handle on, and not just in the drug arena.

At the same time, the muscles in her shoulder were protesting, and the stitches in her side had torn during the fight three days ago. She hadn't been sleeping since walking away from the cartel's headquarters after Scarlett had finally brought the whole structure down on itself, and her team… Well, they all had families to go home to. Lives to maintain.

She had a bullet-ridden safe house or the couch in her office. She'd gone for the couch the past few nights. The regret had started instantly. Ivy stretched the muscles in her neck on either side. She should replace it with a pullout until the building owner could patch up the holes in her walls. Which, according to him, wouldn't be for another two weeks.

The state prosecutor had made the argument to try Sebastian—actually identified as Silvio Juarez, according to his fingerprints taken in early arrest reports from two decades ago—on a federal level. The US Attorney General was inclined to cut out as many obstacles in the case as possible. Though Ivy was sure Sebastian's lawyers would do their best to slow everything down.

The low-level cartel soldiers who'd managed to survive the final minutes of *Sangre por Sangre*'s demise had been offered deals. Testify against Silvio Juarez or face a life in prison. Most of them had taken the deal. They'd given their statements and signed affidavits negotiating their sentences down to two to three years. It was the best they were going to get. The shooter who'd ambushed her and Carson that first night had admitted to being ordered to shoot Carson if he came into contact with any operatives from Socorro. And considering her partner had waited inside her apartment, the shooter had taken it upon himself to follow through.

Two *Sangre por Sangre* soldiers had admitted to replacing the couch in Dr. Piel's home after Sebastian had killed her. A deep dive into the physician's background, another pass at her references and interviews with others within Socorro had convinced Ivy of what she'd known from the beginning: Nafessa Piel had not been involved with the cartel. She'd just been the target of a man devoted to making his enemies suffer.

As for the gunman who'd shot Max, his or her identity had yet to come up in Alpine Valley PD's interviews. Whether out of fear or because the cartel soldier hadn't survived, she didn't know. Either way, they would get what they deserved. Max herself was recovering nicely in Socorro's vet clinic. She'd been pampered with top-of-the-line meals, round-the-clock care and all the attention she could possibly want or need.

And Jocelyn was recovering just as well. Though slower than Max. Chief Baker had sent regular updates, but if Ivy knew her logistics coordinator at all, Jocelyn was most assuredly enjoying the time off.

Three knocks pulled her out of convincing herself she should take a look at the case files the Pentagon had sent her way. They wanted her and her team on the next assignment. But something inside of her needed the breather. Two years without a vacation or so much as a night off of being on call had compounded into this…exhaustion. It was something she'd never allowed herself to feel before. But her body wouldn't heal unless she gave it the chance.

Ivy brushed the imaginary wrinkles off her blouse and raised her gaze. And locked on Carson. "Oh. Hi. I wasn't…" A rush of heat stole her train of thought. "I didn't know you'd been released from the hospital."

The bruises he'd sustained from Sebastian's assault had gone from swollen and dark to a little lighter. The shape of his face had changed slightly, mostly in his nose. Possibly broken. Though she hadn't followed up with him since he'd been taken in one ambulance at the site and she in another. With his wounds fresh, the EMTs had determined the clinic wouldn't be enough. He'd been brought to one of the hospitals in Albuquerque to recover. Fortunately, no one else on the team had been injured. They'd somehow gone up against an entire army and come out the other side unscathed. Apart from the bullet graze along her ribs.

"I checked myself out." Carson stopped at the door. As though he was on his way out. "I couldn't sit there anymore."

"I know how that feels." She traced her fingers over the stack of proposals. Stories of *Sangre por Sangre*'s defeat had hit the media within hours. Mostly thanks to Maggie Caldwell, Jones's partner. Per Ivy's past agreement on all things cartel, the war correspondent had written an exclusive and sold it off to the highest bidder. From there it was just a matter of time. Companies from all over the country, some international, wanted Socorro's expertise in their security needs. "I was going to come visit once I got through these proposals. Not sure if you've heard, but things have been a bit crazy around here."

"I've been watching the news." He took a couple of steps into the office. Studying it while trying not to look at her in the same way he did when faced with a stranger. Was that what they were now? Strangers? A lot had changed in the hours he'd chosen the cartel over siding with her and Socorro. But there had to still be some kind of feeling for her in there, something worth keeping. "Though I was surprised you weren't the one running the press conference."

"I would have been, but I'm still recovering from Sebastian's work. There isn't enough makeup in the world to cover this up." She was trying to make light of the events they'd suffered over the past week, but the humor failed to make her feel any better. Ivy tried to distract this…incompleteness from taking over by moving the files back to the center of her desk. "Granger did well. He's a natural. We've got more contract proposals than we know what to do with. Seems Socorro Security has made a name for itself this week."

Carson seemed to lose his will to keep his distance. In a matter of three steps, he'd rounded her desk. "I didn't come here to talk about Socorro, Ivy. I came here to talk about us."

"Us." The word thrilled her and yet felt so foreign at the same time. There had been a gaping hole in her heart since their conversation in the elevator. The edges were still raw and pulsing, preparing for the next injury. "I contacted the special agent in charge of your undercover assignment. The FBI has closed the investigation into the deaths of the three women we were looking into two years ago. Now that we know Sebastian—Silvio Juarez—killed them and Dr. Piel, your assignment is complete. You are officially released from federal duty, if that's what you want. You're free to go."

"Where am I supposed to go, Ivy?" The regret and heavy dose of sadness deepening his expression pulled at her insides. But this wasn't a decision she could make for him.

She tried to keep her voice light. Tougher than it should've been. Ivy sucked in a deep breath to steady herself and turned back to the files she didn't actually want to go through. To detach herself from the emotion working through her. To give herself a chance to keep the upper hand. "Anywhere you want."

"And what if the place I want to go is home with you?" he asked.

She jerked at the possibility, catching her knuckle on the edge of a piece of paper. The paper cut stung more than the freaking stab wound she'd sustained in the salvage yard. Not really. But close. "Damn it."

Carson was there. Folding her hand between both of his. He swiped the blood rushing to the surface with the pad of his thumb. "I was wrong to believe I could save anyone from the cartel alone, Ivy. I... I thought I'd had something with them that I'd lost with you, and before that with my mother, but it turns out I was being lied to the entire time. I've been seeking this sense of family since my father walked out on us when I was a kid. I wanted that connection with my Hispanic heritage, and I thought I found it with the people I was in the field with. I convinced myself they were just following orders like I was, that they didn't have a choice. I was trying to re-create that feeling of having a support system that I missed since going undercover, and I'm sorry."

Her heart sank at the thought of how lonely and isolated he must've felt during his time with the cartel. Just as she had been on the outside. "I'm sorry, too."

Confusion etched three distinct lines between his eyebrows. "You don't have anything to be sorry for."

"Yes, I do." The paper cut didn't hurt so much in his hands. "I chose to delegate intel exchanges between you and Socorro over the past two years. I was afraid if I saw you, I would ask you to give up your assignment and come home. And I knew you would do it because you were my partner, and then all of this would be for nothing, and people would keep dying. So I distanced myself from you. I fed into my isolation to complete this mission, putting everything I had into this company and my team, but all I ended up doing was hurting you. I kept you on the outside the same way I keep other people out, because that's what was easiest. But you deserved so much better. Because I love you."

"I love you, too." His smile broke through the hurt and started to piece her back together, one step at a time. "We're messed up, aren't we?"

"A little bit," she said. "But if I've learned anything over the past week it's been that I need a partner. I need a team. I can't do all of this on my own. I need you. Here, with me, and at home. Where you belong."

"Is that a job offer?" he asked. "Because, to be honest, I think I'm unemployed—"

She kissed him. Totally and deeply. With everything she had. A fury of relief coursed through her veins as Carson secured her in his arms. The graze on her side put up a little bit of a fight, but she didn't care. He couldn't hurt her. Not as long as they were on the same team. "Welcome back to the land of the living, Agent Lang. From here on out, Dominic Rojas is dead. Think you can handle that?"

"With you at my side, Agent Bardot?" He kissed her again. "I can handle anything."

* * * * *

OZARKS CONSPIRACY

MAGGIE WELLS

To everyone who was a little too quiet, or a little too different, or a little too much. Don't let the 'little' people convince you that you aren't living life large.

Chapter One

Hannah Miller tucked an annoying chunk of hair behind her ear and stepped back to survey the fronds of thick greenery she'd stabbed into the green floral foam to start a standing spray arrangement. Mrs. Grace Templeton had been one of Hannah's grandmother's closest friends. The two women had been tennis partners in their youth, then bunco buddies, and finally, founding members of the Eureka Springs Swingers—a club for senior citizens who loved swing dancing and double entendres.

When her grandmother had been diagnosed with cancer, Mrs. Templeton insisted on driving her to her treatments while Hannah finished up the coursework for her Master of Design Studies degree in Fayetteville. The two old friends sat holding hands and shedding tears as they watched Hannah cross the stage at the commencement ceremony. Then, she and Mrs. Templeton sat by the side of Gran's bed the night pneumonia set in, and the doctors did everything they could for her.

It wasn't enough.

And now, Mrs. Templeton—Grace, though Hannah was never comfortable with calling the older woman by her given name—was gone as well. Hannah was sitting in the shop her

Gran left her, designing the floral arrangements her grandmother would have wanted for her best friend.

She picked up one of the snowy white gladioli she'd trimmed to the exact length she needed and pushed it into the presoaked foam. Her movements were deft and sure. She'd been helping around the shop ever since she came to live with Gran, the day after her parents had been killed in a car accident the summer Hannah turned twelve.

Grace Templeton drove Gran up to the church camp outside the Mark Twain National Forest to help Gran bring her back to Eureka Springs with them. Now they were both gone, and here she was, using her master's degree in architecture and design to find the right balance between lavish and elegant, and wondering if the green-white hydrangeas she planned to use in the center of the spray would provide enough contrast—

An odd screeching sound from the back alley behind the shop made her freeze. The stem she'd been ready to insert dropped from fear-numbed fingers as she glanced at the steel door, wondering if she'd remembered to lock it when she opened the shop that morning.

Were the thugs who'd broken into Mrs. Templeton's antique store coming back? Would they dare to rob a place in broad daylight?

Whoever had broken into Antique Like Me had thought nothing about tying a woman in her late seventies to a chair and stuffing one of the dozens of delicately embroidered doilies she used throughout the shop into her mouth so she couldn't scream. They left her there, alone in the dark storage room. The coroner said Mrs. Templeton suffered a stroke at some point during the night. By the time her assistant found her the next morning, the bustling, vibrant woman Hannah considered a second grandmother was gone.

And she was alone. Again.

Hannah flexed her hand as she bent to retrieve the flower she dropped. "Someone throwing something in the trash," she murmured to herself. Still, she pulled the shears she used to trim stems from her apron pocket as she straightened.

With a swift, jabbing motion, she thrust the stem into the foam. Then she backed away to peer out into the storefront again. There was no one there. Not a surprise.

Flora's Florals didn't get much foot traffic. Located on a side street off Main, her grandmother catered more to the residents rather than the tourist crowd. Flora's was tied in with all the national florist networks, of course, so they did a steady business in baby bouquets, prom corsages and funeral arrangements, but her grandmother refused to stock the trendy souvenirs found in the town's multitude of gift shops and quirky artist galleries.

Returning to the work bench, she cocked her head as she surveyed the half-formed arrangement on its tripod stand. It didn't feel right to replicate the mix of greens, creams and whites she'd used for the casket spray. Mrs. Templeton had been bold and vibrant and unique. Would Gran have created something so neutral for her?

She was carrying the hydrangea stems back to the cooler case to swap them out for the gorgeous violet blue ones when she heard another *ka-thunk* from the alley. This time, whatever it was had landed against her back door.

Hannah dropped the flowers back into the bucket beside her. Shears in her right hand, she scrounged around in her apron with her left, wondering where she'd managed to leave her cell phone. Casting around, she spotted it on the workbench, half-hidden by leaves she'd stripped from stems and a tangle of florist wire and cream ribbon with gold edging.

She was about to lunge for it when something hit the metal door again, and this time it swung open.

Hannah's jaw dropped as several people wearing dark windbreakers tumbled into the workroom with weapons drawn. Instinctively, she moved toward the front of the shop. But the tinkle of the bell above the front door announced the arrival of more company.

A slender man, with close-cropped hair and a jacket with some sort of badge screen-printed on it, made a beeline through the shop displays to the back room, gripping a handgun with both hands and shouting orders. "Police! Drop your weapon."

She stared at him blankly. Could he not see he was in a flower shop?

One of the officers knocked a ceramic planter shaped like a bunny holding a basket from a shelf, and it shattered on the ancient tile floor near Hannah's feet. All the guns swung in her direction.

Afraid she was about to be caught in the crossfire of whatever this was, Hannah instantly dropped to her knees, her hands high in the air.

"Drop your weapon," the man shouted again.

Heart hammering, Hannah glanced over her shoulder where the others stood. They wore navy blue jackets, but the police officer wore black. Was this some kind of gang-related dispute? Why did they have to come through her store? And why wasn't anyone lowering their guns?

The man in the black jacket moved closer, and she shrank back. His eyes were hard. The deep, forbidding blue green of Beaver Lake on a stormy winter's day. But it wasn't winter, and the storm seemed to be blowing through her shop.

"What's happening?" she asked in a voice so shaky she barely recognized it as her own.

"Drop. Your. Weapon," he repeated, enunciating each word as he glared at her.

Only then did Hannah realize he wasn't talking to the windbreaker-clad militia assembled behind her. He was speaking to her.

"Weapon?" she repeated, trying to process the request.

"In your hand," he clarified, his stare unwavering.

Confused, Hannah looked up at her hands. A piece of damp leaf clung to her left palm. In her right she held a pair of pruning shears. Were they considered a weapon? Sure, she could cut someone with them, but the curved blades weren't more than two inches long. Bewildered, she lowered her arm and let them fall to the floor with a clatter.

"Hands up," he said, gesturing with the gun he kept trained on her.

She complied. "I don't under… What's going on here?" Hannah managed to ask as the team behind her spread through the workroom, stepping into the walk-in. She could hear them knocking buckets over and winced on behalf of her bruised and battered inventory.

"Are you Hannah Miller?" the man demanded.

"I am."

He jerked his chin up, then spoke to the clumsy agent beside him. "Cuff her."

Shards of ceramic bunny rabbit crunched beneath the officer's boots as he moved behind her. Before Hannah could wrap her head around what was happening, he clapped a cold metal bracelet around her right wrist and pulled her arm down.

"What's happening here?" she demanded, her voice rising with panic. "Why are you busting into my shop?" She jerked her left hand from the officer's grasp. "Why am I being handcuffed?"

"Hey, now, I don't wanna hurt you," the man behind her said in a tone so gentle, she couldn't help but relent. Surely this was nothing more than a big misunderstanding.

Tears gathered in her eyes as he tightened the cuff. She stared up at the man standing in front of her. He was holstering his weapon, thank goodness, but kept his feet braced wide. "I don't understand."

"Hannah Miller, are you the owner of Flora's Florals?" He addressed her with almost robotic stiffness.

"I, uh…" She glanced nervously around the shop she'd always considered her grandmother's, never hers. "Yes." She swallowed the hard lump of emotion knotting her throat. "I mean, it was my grandmother's, but, yeah, I, um, inherited it."

"When?" he demanded without missing a beat.

There was another crash, but this time whatever fell was made of glass.

"Be careful," the man barked. Then, he turned laser focus back on her. "When?"

"When what?"

"How long have you had the shop?"

Hannah shook her head, unable to piece her thoughts together while they continued to tear the place apart. "I, um, almost two years, I guess."

"You guess?"

"She was sick for a long time before she passed, so I've

been running it longer," she explained curtly, anger bubbling up through the morass of fear and confusion. "Why do you care? What's going on here? Why are you trashing my business?"

But rather than answering her questions, he came back with more of his own. "And your website? Do you run the website?"

"Website?" she asked blankly, confused by the sudden turn the conversation took. Flora's Florals was a small business serving the local community. They didn't ship arrangements or even deliver beyond a twenty-mile radius. Was this some kind of scam? "We don't have a website."

He pinned her with a hard look. When she didn't respond, he raised skeptical brows. "You don't have a website," he repeated, his voice flat.

She shook her head. "We don't do internet orders."

"You are not the owner of the florasflorals.com domain?" He pulled out a mobile phone and started scrolling.

"Can I…" She trailed off, wincing as she shifted her weight from knee to knee. "Would it be possible for me to get up? Or sit?" she offered, when he looked up, brow furrowed. "The tile is hard, and I'm sure I have bits of broken pottery poking through my jeans."

"Fine." He stepped back, his face going blank as he gestured to the guy who'd put the handcuffs on her. "Help her up." He turned in a tight circle, then craned his neck to look behind the cash wrap counter. "Do you have a chair?"

"There's a stool in the back."

He nodded, then gestured for them to proceed.

Hannah let out a soft gasp when they came around the corner and she saw the wreckage of what was once her orderly workroom.

"Oh no," she whispered, eyeing an overturned bucket of white roses, the water pooling beneath the delicate petals of the partially open blooms.

The tears her initial fears had held at bay broke loose on a huge gasping sob. With her hands cuffed behind her, Hannah had no way to stifle the flow. The officer holding her arm guided her to the stool she'd pushed away from the worktable, then quickly backed away. She couldn't blame him. The sight of Mrs. Templeton's funeral flowers bruised and scattered on the floor seemed to have uncorked her.

Behind her, the man who seemed to be in charge snapped, "Pick those up," and one of the men in a windbreaker announcing he was with the Bureau of Alcohol, Tobacco, Firearms and Explosives scrambled to do as he was instructed.

"Is this how you conduct a search?" the man in charge demanded of the others. "You realize that you may have contaminated any evidence we might have found," he continued, his tone hard and scolding. "Clean up the glass," he ordered, pointing to the remains of a shattered vase.

"Evidence of what?" Hannah cried, trying to lift her shoulder enough to wipe some of the moisture on her shirt. "Who are you, and what are you doing here?"

There was a beat of supercharged silence, then the man in the black windbreaker stepped in front of her. Still gripping his phone in one hand, he pulled a leather bifold wallet from his windbreaker pocket.

"I'm Special Agent Simon Taylor, of the Arkansas State Police Cyber Crimes Division," he informed her, holding his badge and identification up for her to inspect.

Hannah blinked rapidly as she rubbed her cheek on the opposite shoulder, trying to clear her vision enough to confirm the man's claims. On a shuddering breath, she leaned in and peered at the photo identification slotted opposite the state police shield.

"Why are you here? This is a flower shop," she added, though she knew the clarification was utterly unnecessary.

This man knew her name.

They hadn't burst through her door accidentally.

The bell above the door rang out again, and she heard her best friend, Mia, call out, "Han? Are you okay?"

"Mia?" she answered, feeling buoyed by the presence of her lifelong friend. "I'm not sure." Then, she decided it might be good to call in reinforcements of her own. She'd taken her grandmother's spot in the local chamber of commerce and was on friendly terms with the police chief. "Would you call Mitch Faulk for me?"

"Mitch? Sure, but what are all these…" She trailed off. Leaning forward on the stool, Hannah saw two of the officers attempt to turn Mia away. "What's happening?"

"I think it's all a misunderstand—" Hannah began but she was cut off.

"Ma'am, we're going to need you to step outside," one of the men in a state police jacket said firmly.

"Han?" Mia called as the bell rang again.

Before she could answer, Hannah heard the dead bolt being thrown and deflated on a long exhale.

The special agent guy snapped his bifold shut and shoved it back into his pocket. "Who is Mitch Faulk? Your attorney?"

She stared back at him, defiance warming her cheeks. "No. He's the chief of police," she shot back. Then she frowned. "Wait. If you're really the police, wouldn't you know?"

The agent who'd put the cuffs on her wrists leaned closer

to the other man. "He's the one I left the message for, telling him the operation was a go," he said in a low voice.

Annoyed at being left out of a conversation that so obviously concerned her, Hannah swiveled toward them on the stool, nearly losing her balance on the precarious perch, thanks to the fact her arms were trapped behind her back. "What operation? What are you doing here?"

The man with the cool lake water eyes turned back to her, his expression stoically blank. "I think you know what operation I'm referring to."

She stared at him, uncomprehending. "This is a flower shop," she repeated.

"Yes." He turned to a few of his compatriots, a brow raised in unspoken question. They each shook their heads. "And our search has confirmed you are not keeping your inventory on the premises, but—"

"My inventory of what?"

"Spirits," he answered as if she should have somehow intuited as much.

Maybe he had her mixed up with one of those bogus 1-800-PSYCHIC scams? Or one of those rip-off ghost tours? Eureka Springs attracted thousands of tourists interested in paranormal activity each year. Maybe he thought she was running some sort of scam out of the shop?

"Spirits?" She huffed a harsh laugh and shook her head. "I mean, if you're looking for a bogus ghost tour or something, you need to head up to the Crescent Hotel. They've been saying it's haunted for decades, but I've never seen anything out of the ordinary there."

"Ms. Miller, this investigation is not a joke," he informed her sternly.

"Obviously," she shot back. "These cuffs feel real, and

you've trashed hundreds of dollars in inventory, and I have no idea why," she said, practically shouting the last word at the man.

But rather than raising his voice, he lifted his phone and tapped on the screen until he found what he wanted. He thrust it at her, the screen coming so close to her nose, she reared back. There on the screen was an e-commerce site featuring some standard-looking bouquets and centerpiece arrangements.

"Okay," she said slowly. "What am I looking at?"

"Your website," he replied, impatience turning the three syllables into a growl.

"I don't have a—"

He pointed to the address bar on the screen. "You registered the domain florasflorals.com five years ago. This SiteStructure website was created the same day."

Hannah stared at the generic layout, shaking her head. "I bought the domain name for my grandmother and started creating the site, but we never published it. It was a shell. I never even uploaded a photo."

"I have data showing this site has been active for nearly three years," he refuted.

"No." She wagged her head so hard she almost toppled off the stool. "I tried to get my gran interested, but she wasn't. Then my classwork picked up, and a year or so later she was diagnosed…" She trailed off, unable to think too hard about all that came after. "I did not create that site."

"The metadata says you did," he countered.

"Hey, uh, Cap?" the officer beside her interrupted, his tone cautious, but firm.

"What?" the man in charge snapped.

The agent who'd spoken cast a wary eye at the other windbreaker-clad officers now milling and lounging around the shop. "Maybe we can turn the other guys loose and interrogate, uh, I mean talk, to Ms. Miller in priv—"

He was cut off by a hard banging on the glass door. Hannah swiveled with the rest of them, and there on the other side of the glass stood the police chief. Mitch was flanked by Mia, Mrs. Hopkins from the yarn shop, and... She frowned at the sight of the man who stood scowling beside the police chief. Was that Russ Whitman? Had all of Eureka Springs come out to witness her humiliation?

"Chief Faulk is here. Let him in. He knows me," Hannah said, her voice rising on a tide of panic-tinged relief. "I don't know what's happening here, but it's not whatever you think it is."

The taller agent glanced at his boss. "I think we should."

"Let him in," the man in charge said, never breaking Hannah's gaze. "But only the police chief." When the other man pivoted to head for the front door, he leaned in close. "We've been tracking your delivery van. We know what's happening here."

"My van?" Hannah stared back at him, stunned. "What do you mean?"

"I think you know," he returned, pulling away as the other agent escorted the police chief to his side. Thankfully, they'd left the other lookie-loos he'd gathered on the sidewalk locked out of the shop.

"Mitchell Faulk," the chief said, extending his hand.

"Simon Taylor," the other man replied, but offered nothing more.

"Mind if I ask what y'all are doin' with Miss Hannah here?"

Simon Taylor's jaw tensed, and for a moment she was

afraid the taciturn man would refuse. The silence stretched a beat too long before he pulled a piece of paper from an inside pocket and handed it to Mitchell. "We are investigating Ms. Miller's business practices as part of a joint task force investigation between the Arkansas State Police and the Bureau of Alcohol, Tobacco, Firearms and Explosives."

Mitch's bushy gray-brown brows rose as he took the paper and held it at arm's length to read it. "A joint task force? You afraid our sweet Hannah here is smuggling poppies into the county or somethin'?"

"Or something," Simon Taylor repeated, plucking the paper from the older man's hand, then holding it out for her to read.

She saw it was a warrant to search the premises of Flora's Florals, the delivery van and her home.

For the life of her, Hannah could not connect the dots. Flora's was an established business with a steady stream of income. She'd never get rich owning it, but she managed to keep up with the bills and fill the fridge every few weeks. The cottage Gran and Gramps bought after they married was clear of debt. And the ancient delivery van was more often used to help friends and neighbors move furniture than deliver bouquets. What possible interest could they have in any of it?

"We believe Ms. Miller's establishment has been serving as a front for the unsanctioned distillation and distribution of spirits," he said flatly.

"Distillation and distribution..." Mitch Faulk repeated, his voice rough with shock. He shook his head like a retriever shedding water, then let out a guffaw so loud it made her flinch. "Hang on a sec... Are you fellas tryin' to tell me you think sweet little Hannah Miller is a bootlegger?"

Chapter Two

Simon Taylor could not fathom why the man doubled over in front of him—a sworn officer of the law, no less—was so amused by the notion of a major crime ring operating right under his nose. To his way of thinking, Mitchell Faulk should be ashamed of himself. He was the chief of police. He ought to be outraged.

"I don't understand why you find this funny," Simon said, his posture stiffening as the man let loose another whoop of laughter.

"Hannah Miller," he hooted, "a bootlegger!"

The man was shaking his head and bucking around like a bull turned loose in a rodeo. When Simon glanced over at the woman in question, he found she was as annoyed by the police chief's mirth as he was.

"This isn't funny, Mitch," she said in a taut voice. "I don't know if you've bothered to look past your nose yet, but I'm sitting here in handcuffs and these bozos have ruined half the flowers I needed to get ready for Grace Templeton's visitation this evening."

The police chief sobered at the mention of the upcoming funeral service. "Aw, Hannah, I'm sorry." He wiped the corner of his eye with the back of his hand, "It's so..." Then he turned his attention to Simon. "It's ridiculous."

Simon's spine stiffened. "We've been monitoring the activity of Ms. Miller's website for months. As stated by the warrant," he continued, waving the folded piece of paper, "we have had a tracking device on the delivery van. We have mapped the movements of the van, and they extend far beyond the city limits. Well past the county line," he added for good measure.

Hannah Miller frowned. Her response to this news came in a soft, measured tone. "Sometimes we make deliveries to outlying communities."

"And don't you loan the van out to any deadbeat with a sob story?" Faulk prodded. "Heck, I even told you to have the logo repainted with Hannah's Hauling after you let the Jurgen boy use it to move half his frat house home from Fayetteville." He turned to Simon with a knowing smirk. "He covered at least five counties."

His second-in-command, Wyatt Dawson, cleared his throat, drawing the attention of both Hannah Miller and this Faulk fellow. "We have data matching the movement of the van with sales made through the website."

"I told you, we don't have a website for the store," Hannah said tightly.

Simon could hear the impatience bubbling inside her. Maybe if he stayed the course, she'd crack, and it would all come out.

"Excuse me, Captain Taylor?"

Simon turned to find one of the ATF agents assigned to the team approaching. "We searched the van in the alley. We didn't find anything. I think it's a dry well, sir."

Everything inside Simon clenched. He wanted to snap at

the young agent. To lord his years of experience over this green kid's head, but he didn't. Couldn't. Technically the Bureau had the lead on this case. Federal law was being violated in addition to state laws. He was nothing more than the guy tasked with finding the evidence. And so far, he was failing.

Turning to Special Agent Dawson, he spoke in a low voice. "Disband the team. We'll stay and talk with Ms. Miller. I'll call Agent Nelson later and fill her in on what went down."

When Wyatt turned away to gather the team in the storeroom, he turned back to Mitchell Faulk. "Why do you find it so hard to believe Ms. Miller is doing what we believe she is doing?"

Her tart reply came fast and furious. "Why don't you ask me?"

Simon inclined his head to acknowledge the validity of her question but stuck to his guns. He knew in his gut he was right about what was happening online. But this local law man found the notion of their suspicions… What did he say? Ridiculous? So, he tossed the question up like a jump ball.

"Why would it be ridiculous for Hannah Miller to be a bootlegger?"

The chief of police sobered instantly. "Because everyone knows Hannah doesn't hold with drinkin' liquor."

He must have looked as perplexed by the statement as he felt, because she jumped in to clarify. "I don't drink. Never have, never will."

Simon blinked. Her statement was so broad, so bald, he couldn't help but believe her. But not being one to partake didn't exonerate her from the crime. Not in this case.

"Ma'am, we're not accusing you of public intoxication or driving under the influence."

He spoke slowly, measuring each word as he checked

and double-checked his own line of reasoning. No. It was sound. Being a teetotaler didn't exclude a person from becoming a bootlegger.

"We have a record of sales made through a website operating on a domain name registered to you and a site created by you. These sales are for quantities of illegally distilled spirits. And we have GPS tracking reports correlating to the delivery of goods attributed to those sales. Some of them across state lines. All of them in violation of federal and state laws regarding said commerce."

"You don't understand, mister, uh, officer—"

"Special Agent," he provided.

"Special Agent Taylor," she enunciated carefully. "My parents were killed by a drunk driver when I was young. Not only do I refrain from imbibing, but I also actively encourage others to do the same."

"You're some kind of activist?" Simon heard the skepticism in his tone but was unable to modulate it.

She shot the police chief an exasperated look, but when she spoke her words were calm and measured. "I'm not an activist." She tipped her chin up. "But I did try to start a chapter of SADD at my high school."

"SADD?" The name rang a bell, but he couldn't quite put his finger on it. Thankfully, Wyatt had returned to his side.

"Students Against Driving Drunk," his right-hand man supplied.

She raised an eyebrow. "The name was changed to Students Against Destructive Decisions, but yes. But the chapter never took off."

"No?" Simon asked, unable to repress a scoff.

The police chief chuckled. "Agent Taylor, I know the rest

of the state skews toward the straight and narrow, but around Eureka Springs people tend to march to a different drum."

Simon knew he wasn't wrong. The area had long been known as "the place where misfits fit" and cultivated a reputation as a liberal oasis in the sometimes-rigid confines of the South.

The chief placed a hand on Hannah's shoulder and gave it a squeeze. "Our Hannah here earned a reputation as a Goody Two-shoes for her efforts when she was a kid, and it stuck."

"A reputation I didn't mind having," she shot back, acid in her tone. "Special Agent Taylor," she began hesitantly. "If I promise on my grandmother's grave not to run and Mitch here will vouch for me, do you think we can remove these handcuffs?"

Simon hesitated. Even if he was barking up the wrong tree, the evidence he had did not lie. Somehow this woman's establishment was involved in the case he'd been pursuing for months. He wasn't always the best at deciphering people's intentions, so he shot a glance at his second-in-command. Wyatt Dawson inclined his head a half inch, and he drew in a deep breath before granting permission.

"Take the cuffs off."

Hannah Miller let out a long, ragged sigh as she pulled her hands into her lap and rubbed at each wrist in turn. "Thank you."

"We're still going to search your residence," he said, feeling knocked off balance by her simple gratitude.

She met his gaze directly. "Fine. I have nothing to hide." She added a little extra emphasis to the words to let him know she was displeased, even if agreeable.

"I'll ask for both you and Chief Faulk to accompany us," he said, gesturing to the back door.

"I'd insist on it." She rose from the stool, but her steps faltered when she neared the partially constructed arrangement perched atop a spindly legged easel.

"Would you mind…" She turned a pleading gaze to the police chief, who responded with a sympathetic hum. "If I could finish this last arrangement." She pointed to the flowers in the buckets beneath her workbench and the rumpled blooms now scattered across the wooden surface. "The visitation begins in an hour."

She offered the last bit as if it should be some kind of free pass, and Simon bristled at the notion of this woman thinking she could go about business as usual during a federal investigation. "Ms. Miller, I'm not sure you grasp the severity of—"

"Grace Templeton was my grandmother's best friend, and a good friend to me," Hannah shot back. "She was a kind, good-hearted woman who was always there for her friends and neighbors. She didn't deserve to have her life cut short by some whacked-out jerk," she said vehemently.

Simon reared back. "Excuse me?"

"Mrs. Templeton was the victim of a robbery at her store two nights ago," the police chief explained. "She was bound, gagged and left in the storeroom. It's believed she suffered a stroke sometime during the night and passed away. Ms. Miller is preparing the arrangements for her services."

Simon glanced over at Wyatt and Agent Vance. For the first time since he took command of the Cyber Crimes Division he was completely at sea. Data he could handle. Hinky malware and sneaky culprits were no problem. But he wasn't used to dealing with the public in his investigations. Most of the time he hardly ever saw any of the people involved.

The chance to get into the investigation and truly mix it

up was one of the things that drew him to working on the joint task force. But now he was faced with, well, people problems, and he wasn't quite sure how to proceed.

Thankfully, Wyatt Dawson had been blessed with all the charm he lacked. "Why, of course you should finish," Wyatt said gruffly. He nodded to the police chief and then to Hannah in turn. "Our condolences. We can wait."

"Thank you," Ms. Miller said shortly. She swallowed hard and turned a cool gaze to him. "I'll get someone else to take them over to the funeral parlor."

"Don't you worry about a thing," Mitchell Faulk said, giving her arm a pat. "I'll have Deputy Mueller run them over. He's assisting with traffic and parking duties this evening anyway." The police chief started toward the front door. "I'll get rid of these nosy folks too."

"Thank you, Mitch," Hannah said, then she turned her back on them all.

Simon felt wrong-footed standing there letting a suspect dawdle. What if she had a partner or accomplice? What if they were cleaning out her house as they spoke? He watched as she planted her hands on the edge of the workbench and bowed her head, taking a shuddering breath. Afraid they were being fooled by delay tactics, he turned to his young agent, Tom Vance.

"Head over to the house. Don't go in, but make sure no one else goes in or out until we get there."

Her shoulders tensed, making it clear she'd heard the order. But Simon didn't care. If he was granting concessions, she had to allow him to preserve the integrity of his search. "Do you have an issue with my orders, Ms. Miller?" he prompted.

"No," she answered without hesitation. Her movements

jerky, she began to clear the ruined flowers from the work surface and gather her implements again. Once things were set to rights, she paused to take three deep breaths, inhaling through her nose and exhaling the last with a soft, but steely, "Okay."

Simon's gaze never left Hannah Miller as she moved from the cooler to the bench several times. She measured each stem with a precision he had to admire before snipping it to length with the shears she'd recovered from the floor of the storefront. Her hands moved as gracefully as hummingbird wings as she wrapped green wire around each stem for reinforcement. He was embarrassed to admit he jerked a little when she thrust the first stem deftly into the rectangle of green foam at the center of the arrangement. Thankfully, Wyatt and the police chief startled too.

With each flower she placed, a tiny trickle of liquid dripped to the floor. Simon found himself studying the process with a critical eye. He couldn't help but admire her economy of movement. She snipped, twisted and plunged each quivering flower into place with a surety he felt only when staring at rows of data.

Maybe he'd been foolish to think he could be as effective in the field as he was at a desk. But he'd been unable to pass on the opportunity to marry his unique skills with his training. Now he was paying the price for his own hubris. The raid he'd insisted was necessary had turned out to be a dry well, and now…

Now he was watching his primary suspect stab a block of foam with flowers.

If he couldn't find some connection between Hannah Miller and the transactions processing through the website using her domain, he'd be the laughingstock of State Police Headquarters. His phone vibrated. He pulled it from his pocket to find a text from Vance. The house was dark and quiet. No obvious signs of anyone having been there for hours.

"Damn," he muttered under his breath.

"Cap?" Wyatt asked, turning toward him.

"Nothing." He checked the time on his phone, then slipped it back into his pocket. He'd give her another ten minutes before they got this show on the road.

Hannah worked quickly and methodically, arranging the longer thinner stalks in an array around the outer perimeter, then filling in the center with big ball-like blooms. When it looked about as full as it could be he pushed away from the wall, ready to call an end to his indulgence, but she disappeared into the walk-in again. He started to follow, only to pull up short when she reappeared a moment later holding a handful of fern-like greenery.

Her sneakers squeaked on the tile floor as she drew up to keep from running into him. Dark eyes bright with unshed tears bore into him. But she shed no tears. Instead, a puzzled frown creased her brow. "Is there a problem?"

"Aren't you done?"

"No." She raised the hand with the green plumage. "I need to fill in the gaps, then we can go."

She stepped around him, and Simon whirled on his heel, annoyed at being put in his place and equally intrigued by the woman's ability to focus on the task at hand. The arrangement she'd created was lush and full. Creamy roses and white flowers climbing long stalks fanned out in every direction. The bluish-purple balls of flowers she'd used in the center looked like clusters of tiny butterflies. Vaguely familiar flowers of pale pink and white filled spaces between the roses. Tapping his fingertips against his thigh, he searched his memory.

Carnations. They were called carnations. He'd bought a wrist corsage made with carnations for Sally Baker when he escorted her to his senior prom.

Stepping up beside Hannah Miller, he surveyed the arrangement, tilting his head to the exact angle of hers, and wondered what he was missing. Without being asked, she pointed to two miniscule holes between the carnations and whatever the big blue flowers were.

"See the gap between the carnations and the hydrangeas?" she asked quietly.

He filed the name of the blue butterfly flowers away in his memory for future reference. "Not until you pointed it out," he admitted.

She snickered and poked a frond of greenery into one of the spaces. "Funeral flowers are about so much more than decoration, Special Agent Taylor." She continued stuffing the ferns into invisible holes as she spoke. "They're a reflection of everything the person stood for in life, and all the people left behind will miss now they're gone. Our community will feel the holes left behind by the passing of Grace Templeton for a long time," she murmured as she fussed with a few of the stems, adjusting their position. "But we'll find ways to fill those holes and hopefully, in doing so, make things a little nicer to honor her memory."

"I understand." Simon winced at his clipped tone. Sometimes he had difficulty modulating his patterns of speech to suit his sentiments. "I mean, it's pretty. Beautiful," he corrected.

The last bit may have taken it a step too far. Wyatt Dawson's eyebrows shot for his hairline. But it was the truth. And if he was known for nothing else it was for telling the truth.

"Ms. Miller, we wouldn't be intruding in your life if we didn't have solid evidence to back us up," he said in a reasonable tone.

"I would hope not," she said pressing the last stem into place. She took a single step back and surveyed the finished product. Then she turned to him and said, "Come on. Let's get this over with."

She turned and walked toward the door, leaving the men to scurry after her. Stepping into the back alley, she turned and faced the police chief. "Mitch, you'll see to the flowers?"

He nodded. "I'll make sure everything's taken care of. Lock up here, and I'll go with you to the house."

Hannah nodded and pulled a ring of keys from her pocket. She thrust one green-stained thumbnail into the ring and pried it apart. As she worked a single key free, she nodded to the van the team had already searched. "I don't suppose we can use the van to transport the flowers?" she asked, not looking in Simon's direction.

"We would prefer it if you didn't, ma'am."

She stopped struggling with the keychain and her shoulders dropped. "Mitch, I hate to…"

He held up a hand to stop her. "I told you I'd handle it. Now, let's get this nonsense taken care of so you can get changed and head over to Colson's. I know Miss Grace isn't going to rest easy until you say your goodbyes," he added, pinning Simon with a pointed glare.

"It isn't nonsense," Simon growled.

"We'll see," the police chief answered darkly. "Let's go."

Simon slid behind the wheel of his state-issued SUV

and let out an explosive breath. "Well, that couldn't have gone worse."

Beside him, Wyatt Dawson buckled his seat belt. "Now, come on. We both know things can always go worse," he chided.

But Simon was in no mood for cajoling. Starting the engine, he backed out of the parking space they'd claimed a block down from the flower shop.

"There's no shame in admitting you're disappointed in the way things panned out," Wyatt said quietly. "I am too. I thought we had them."

"We could still find something at the house," Simon said, making a too-sharp right turn onto the side street where Hannah Miller lived.

The house was only a few blocks from the business. It was a craftsman-style bungalow with a narrow driveway separating it from her neighbor. This close to downtown, parking was at a premium. Simon took his foot off the gas and slowed to a crawl, scanning for an open spot along the curb.

"I don't think we will find anything," Wyatt said softly. "And I believe what she says about the website. She didn't come across as a person with anything to hide."

The hell of it was, Simon agreed. And that left him with egg on his face when it came to reporting back to his counterparts at ATF—something he was already dreading.

He hit the brakes a tad too hard when they passed in front of her house. Tom Vance stood on the porch waiting for them. As he'd reported, the house appeared to be empty. A Eureka Springs Police Department squad car sat parked in the driveway. Chief Faulk and Hannah Miller climbed out of it.

Impatient, Simon hooked a left into the driveway across the street and shifted the car into Park.

"You're going to leave it here?" Wyatt asked.

"They can ask us to move it if they need us to," Simon said gruffly. "Come on. I don't want to waste any more time."

"Yes, sir," his second-in-command responded as they bailed from the vehicle.

Curtains twitched when they mounted the porch steps. A steady stream of deep, ominous barks echoed inside the house. As they assembled on the porch, she pulled the ring of keys from her pocket. "Let me go in and get my dog settled," she said, fitting the key into the front door lock.

All four law enforcement officers nodded and hung back. None of them were overanxious to enter a house guarded by such a ferocious-sounding creature.

Standing near the door, Simon could hear her crooning to the agitated animal. "Good boy," she sang to him. "Yes, you are a good boy, my sugar Beau baby. My best boy. You told them. Yes, you did. You told them to stay out of our house because it's your job, and you are such a good boy."

Beside him Wyatt chuckled. "If only someone would greet me like that at the end of a day."

"No kiddin'," Chief Faulk agreed genially.

"You mean Cara Beckett doesn't talk to you all sweet and soothing?" Vance asked, unable to resist ribbing his teammate.

"You wish you knew how Cara Beckett greets me," Wyatt shot back.

"I bet she doesn't call you a good boy," Simon muttered.

"Cara Beckett?" Chief Faulk asked. "Why does that name sound familiar?"

"Never mind," Wyatt said preemptively.

But Agent Vance spoke over him, all too happy to spill. "Special Agent Dawson has a fancy pants guru for a girlfriend. But apparently, she doesn't tell him he's a good boy when he comes home from work." He elbowed Wyatt. "I thought positive reinforcement was a part of all that touchy-feely stuff."

"It's obvious why nobody wants to get touchy-feely with you," Wyatt shot back, an eyebrow raised.

"Stop," Simon ordered, as if they were both misbehaving mutts.

The sound of the screen door opening captured their attention, and Simon noted the absence of canine disapproval. "Safe to come in?"

She smirked. "Safe as it will ever be. I put Beauregard in my bedroom. If y'all need to look in there, then you're going to have to give me a little time to get him resituated."

Wyatt smiled his easy charming grin. "I like dogs. And Beauregard is a great name. I had a black Lab growing up who was my best friend. Her name was Lucy."

"Best friend," Vance snickered.

Wyatt tipped his chin up. "I'm not ashamed to admit it. A man who can't say he loves his dog isn't much of a man at all."

"Agreed. But I'd prefer to keep Beau as calm as possible. He's a rescue and has a lot of anxiety issues."

"Don't we all?" Simon muttered under his breath.

Hannah Miller held the screen door open wide. "Go ahead and do what you need to do."

Chapter Three

While the three agents from the state police searched her home, Hannah went into her bedroom to soothe her overwrought dog.

"Shh," she whispered, though Beau stopped whining and barking the moment she sat on the edge of her bed. She could hear them moving around, occasionally calling out to one another as cabinets, drawers and doors were opened and closed. She didn't bother picking up the discarded clothing spilling from her messy closet or fret about the thin layer of dust coating the objects on her dresser. She hadn't invited them into her home. They were not guests, they were investigators.

And she was a suspect.

The notion should have made her laugh, but she was having a hard time finding even a kernel of humor in the situation. She'd spent her entire life trying to be as little trouble as possible.

"It's what you do when you don't belong somewhere, isn't it?" she asked, staring deep into her beloved companion's eyes. "But we belong to each other, don't we, boy?"

Beauregard, the last of a litter of puppies left in a cardboard box on the side of a country road, looked like a yellow

Labrador who'd been caught in some comic book villain's shrink ray. He was only knee-high, but barrel-bodied atop his spindly legs. His beige-gold fur was bristly along the ridge of his back, but his ears and cheeks were soft as silk. He stared back at her, dark eyes limpid with love.

"You and me," she whispered, leaning down to kiss the top of his head. "We're a pair."

Someone cleared their throat from the doorway. Her dog matched her beleaguered sigh when she looked up. "Yes?"

Simon Taylor waved a jerky hand. "May I?"

Her dog gave a low warning growl, but she stood, her fingertips trailing reassuringly along the top of Beau's head. "Of course."

She didn't leave the room. The bedroom she'd used since she came to live with her grandmother was a piece of ground she refused to cede. She could barely remember what the room she'd had at her parents' house looked like, but she knew every nook and cranny of this one.

She watched as he moved to her closet, stepping carefully around a pair of jeans left in a crumpled heap on the floor. "There's a chain for the light," she informed him, cringing internally at the eager note in her tone.

He tugged on the tasseled pull chain, and a small cut-glass enclosed bulb exposed the full extent of her domestic neglect. "I, uh, I haven't had time to clean—"

He cut her rambling off with a raised hand, then curled his fingers in until he was pointing to the closet ceiling. "Is there an attic?"

"Yes. More like a crawl space," she amended.

"Where's the access?"

She did her best not to bristle. If the man wanted to keep

things all business, that was more than fine with her. "In the hall."

"Attic access in the hall," he called over his shoulder.

"On it," one of the other men replied.

He pushed her clothes aside, then began thumping the back wall of the closet with the side of his fist. When the test failed, he bent and took a knee. Without waiting for permission, he started pulling shoes out of the closet, shoving them aside as he started testing the floor.

"There's no hidey-hole in the floorboards," she informed him haughtily.

"I'm afraid I can't take your word for it," he responded, continuing unperturbed.

Beau let out another low growl but leaned heavily into her leg. She couldn't help but smile. The phrase "all bark and no bite" suited Beauregard to a tee. He lacked the confidence to be a true guard dog, but he did a decent impression of one with his outsize bark.

Apparently satisfied he wasn't going to find what he was looking for in her closet, Simon Taylor sat back on his heels and turned to look at the dog. "I thought he'd be bigger."

"He's perfect," she retorted.

"I meant…his bark is big." He shrugged, then extended his knuckles in Beau's direction. "Good dog."

A part of Hannah wanted to melt at the sight of this strange man trying to make friends with her dog in the chaos of her room, but then she remembered how they got there. She was about to yank Beau out of reach, but then her bashful boy straightened up and leaned in to give the proffered hand a cautious sniff.

The thought of this invader winning her best boy over to his side was too much for Hannah. "Come, Beau," she said, mimicking the no-nonsense tone the dog trainer on the You-View video used.

Both man and beast looked up at her, confused by the abrupt change in tone. Hoping to appease the only one she cared about, she raised her eyebrows and used one of Beau's favorite words. "Outside?"

Without waiting for a response from either of them, she stalked from the room, certain her dog would follow.

The late afternoon sun slanted between the close-packed houses. She found Chief Faulk at the foot of the back porch steps, leaning against the house and smoking a cigarette. When she shot him a surprised glance, he dropped it to the cracked patio slab and ground it beneath the heel of his shoe. "Don't tell Betsy," he grumbled.

"I'm not the cop here," she retorted.

They lapsed into silence as Beau bounded around the small fenced yard, trying to decide which toy to play with first.

"I can't believe this is happening," she said at last.

"I can't believe anything that has happened this week," he said with a heavy sigh.

Hannah sobered, straightening her spine. She'd been so wrapped up in her indignation that she lost perspective. Turning to look at the chief, she asked, "Do you think there's some connection?" He slid her a sidelong glance, and she pushed harder. "Between Mrs. Templeton and whatever they're looking for?"

He only shrugged. "You know we get all sorts of shenanigans around here," he answered laconically.

"Shenanigans?" She pinned him with a penetrating glare. "An elderly woman was tied up and left to die in the stockroom of a store she owned for nearly forty years. Now I have some kind of task force busting into my grandmother's flower shop looking for illegal substances? My house is being searched, Mitch," she pointed out, her tone heavy with sarcasm.

"Ms. Miller?"

Hannah stiffened. There was something about the crisp edge in Simon Taylor's voice that drew her attention. It annoyed her to respond so easily to his natural air of command. Stubbornly, she drew in a deep breath and counted to three before sparing a glance in his direction. "Yes, Agent Taylor?"

"I believe we're done with the interior of the house," he informed her. She heard the groan of the old wooden porch steps and knew he was coming to join them in the yard. "One of my agents said you have a storm cellar back here?"

Hannah frowned, but she turned instinctively to the battered doors covering access to the subterranean cellar beneath the old stone cottage.

"A storm cellar? Yes." She nodded to the doors, with their peeling paint and weathered handles. "It hasn't been used in years. My grandmother kept some preserves down there," she told him.

"I'm afraid we're going to have to take a look in the cellar," he informed her stiffly.

She gestured to the wooden doors on their diagonal slab. "Be my guest, but I wouldn't go down there without a couple of brooms to beat a path and some industrial-strength pesticide if I were you."

The corner of his mouth twitched in what might have been the shadow of a smile, but she wasn't sure. "We'll take our chances."

She and Mitch stepped back as Special Agent Taylor and his two officers surveyed the gnarly old doors. The younger agent slid the block of wood used to batten down the doors free from the worn handles. Agent Dawson pulled on a pair of gloves before reaching down and tugging hard on one of the handles, stumbling back when it swung open smoothly.

She blinked, as shocked as the rest of them by the absence of squeaking hinges and the lack of protest from the aging wood. Agent Dawson glanced over at his boss, his brows raised. Simon nodded his head and Dawson shuffled to his left. He pulled the other door open wide and laid it to rest against the ground.

"Looks clean," he commented, peering into the depths. Glancing back over his shoulder he asked, "You say it hasn't been used in years?"

At a loss, Hannah shook her head. "I haven't been down there since I was a girl."

"Where do you go when a storm comes through?" Simon Taylor asked without glancing in her direction.

"I hunker down in the bath if there's anything severe." When all three men turned to glance over, she shrugged. "It's an interior room in a sturdy stone home. I'm as safe there as I am anywhere above ground."

"But you have an underground shelter available to you," Simon Taylor said, gesturing to the gaping dark hole.

Feeling defensive, she tipped her chin up. "And I choose not to use it," she said with a sniff. "The cellar isn't a place I would voluntarily spend time."

"You'd rather take your chances against Mother Nature?" he challenged.

"Any day," she responded without hesitation. "When's the last time you sat in an old storm shelter?" she prodded. "They're dirty and damp, and they're full of spiders." She shuddered involuntarily on the last word.

Simon Taylor's eyes widened for a second, as if he'd grasped some secret she'd given away. Perhaps she had, but a fear of spiders wasn't exactly unusual. Especially in Northwest Arkansas, where tarantulas, brown recluses and black widows were not uncommon.

"I see."

Wyatt Dawson stepped down into the space up to his knees, then paused to activate the flashlight function on his phone. He ducked his head and went down two more stairs, bending to peer into the gloom. A moment later, his head appeared. "Boss?" He ascended the stairs as quickly as he had gone down, handing his phone to Simon Taylor like a runner passing a baton. "You're gonna wanna take a look."

"Okay." Agent Taylor took the phone and made his way cautiously down the steps.

Hannah glanced over at Mitch. "What in the world?"

The police chief only shrugged. "There was a time people might have busted into the place to steal some of your grandma's peach preserves," he said with a wan smile, "but those days are long past."

Hannah nodded. Sadness twisted in her belly, and a wave of all-too-familiar grief washed over her. She wished now she'd taken the time to help her grandmother more in the kitchen, to learn the family recipes, to have a part of her heritage to hang on to. Now she was alone in the world, and no one other than a dwindling number of friends and neighbors would ever know the joy of Flora Fontaine's peach preserves.

Simon Taylor's neatly combed head appeared, but she couldn't take the time to wonder at how the man remained so preternaturally unsullied by a search of an old dirt-floored cellar. The expression on his face was too grim.

Shaking her head, she flashed a nervous smile. "Y'all are scaring me now." She darted a glance at Agent Dawson, then at Mitch. "Don't tell me there are bodies buried down there or something," she said, choking out a harsh laugh.

"Ms. Miller, you have not been in the cellar in how long?"

the special agent said as he signaled to his agents to close the doors and put the wooden slat back in place.

"Years," she said, her voice weak with disbelief. "What's the matter? What's down there?"

He came to a stop in front of her and Mitch, his expression somber. "It's not a matter of what's down there so much as what's not."

She raised an eyebrow. "Can you cut out the cryptic bit and give me a straight answer?" she snapped.

"No spiders," he said, looking her straight in the eye. "No spiderwebs, cobwebs, snakes, frogs or any sign of damp or scent of mildew. No dusty jars of preserves on the shelf," he informed her gravely. Then he shrugged. "No shelves."

"No shelves?" She shook her head, confused. "I don't understand. She always said my grandfather built those shelves for her..."

"Is it possible Miss Flora had somebody clean the storm cellar out?" Mitch asked.

Hannah shook her head. "No. I mean, I guess yes, it's possible, but no I don't think she did. I was home to visit a lot when she was first diagnosed." She hesitated for a moment. "And I remember one time when I was visiting, she'd gone down to get some peaches to make a pie."

"But you didn't go with her," Simon pushed.

"No." Hannah shook her head. "She didn't need me to go with her. Plus, she knew I didn't like it down there. She never asked me to go after things for her. She was independent."

"She was," Mitch confirmed.

"Ms. Miller, somebody has completely cleaned out the cellar."

She shook her head. "It wasn't me."

"Someone did," he insisted. "What's more, it looks like someone has been using it as a storage space. There are marks in the dirt that would indicate heavy stacks of boxes or crates. You're certain your grandmother never used it for storage? Christmas decorations and the like?"

She shook her head. "You saw the attic."

"We did," he concluded.

Placing his hands on his hips, Simon drew in a deep breath, then blew it out as he surveyed the small fenced-in yard. Nodding to the gate at the side of the house, he asked, "Do you keep the gate locked?"

She shook her head. "I've never had reason to."

Suddenly the veil of shock lifted, and reality started to settle in. A car crept past on the street out front. No doubt, word of the police raid on the local florist shop had spread. A motorcycle rumbled to a noisy stop. Hannah cringed as she forced herself to give voice to Simon Taylor's suspicions.

"You think somebody's been coming in and using my storm shelter to store…things?"

"Hannah, darlin'?" A man's voice rang out from the side of the house. "Hannah? You here?"

She frowned and turned to Mitch. "Is…?"

The police chief's bushy brows rose. "Russell Whitman?" he called out, keeping his querying stare locked on her.

A second later, a man appeared at the gate Agent Taylor had been asking about. Russ Whitman was handsome in the craggy outdoorsman sort of way. A local success story, Russ had taken an active role in his father's construction company, then expanded their reach into all forms of real estate development. But, despite his impeccable clothes, expensive haircut and over-the-top manners, Russ always looked like he had a leer and wolf whistle at the ready.

"Hey, uh, Russ," she called back. "I'm kind of in the middle of something." She gestured to Mitch, who straightened and started across the yard to intercept her visitor before he could lift the latch. "Can I, uh, catch up with you later? I still need to get ready for the service."

Russ smirked at Mitch's approach, then leaned over the fence to eyeball the agents from the state police. "You sure you don't need some help? Looked like you had some trouble at the store."

"No. There's no trouble." Hannah flushed, her cheeks and ears flaming at the attention focused on her. Russ Whitman had been friendly to her since she returned to Eureka Springs, but she wouldn't have called him a friend. He ran with a crowd significantly louder than her choice of companions. "I'm fine," she called back, her tone short. Then she added a swift, "Thank you," for good measure.

"Well, all right, then," Russ called, his tone dubious. "Take care."

Mitch held his post at the gate as they waited for Russ to leave, then turned back with a nod to Special Agent Taylor. "All clear."

Simon Taylor looked over at his second-in-command, who simply shrugged in response. Blowing out a breath, he let his shoulders drop. "Ms. Miller, either you're in this up to your neck, or somebody has been using both your website and your storm cellar to facilitate an illegal moonshine business."

"I can't believe this is happening," she whispered. "What's happening?"

Simon Taylor stepped directly into her line of vision before answering, "I don't know, but I intend to stay here until I get answers to those questions."

Chapter Four

Simon pulled his tortoiseshell reading glasses from his nose and tossed them onto the built-in desk in the motel room he'd rented immediately after leaving Hannah Miller's house. Suzee's SleepInn was a cosmetically renovated motor court with painted paneling on the walls and carpet he could only hope had been replaced in the last decade. But it was a couple blocks from Flora's Florals, which meant it was close to Hannah Miller's place as well.

Good strategy, he thought with a wry smirk.

Pinching the bridge of his nose between his thumb and his forefinger, he stretched his neck forward and exhaled loudly. He hadn't had a dressing down like the one his commanding officer had delivered that evening since his academy days.

But he couldn't blame his superiors for being upset. He was upset. He'd been so sure they finally had a bead on the bootlegging scheme, he managed to convince the brass at State Police Headquarters and his counterparts with ATF to go along with his plan on little more than his word and a whole sheaf of datasets Simon knew none of them would ever actually study.

And now, his raid had gone belly-up, his theory was full

of holes and his credibility ranked right up there with snake oil salesmen.

Rolling his shoulders back, he sat up straight and gave his head a shake. There was no point in getting bogged down in recriminations. They hadn't been wrong about the website, even if he was beginning to think Hannah Miller truly had nothing to do with the e-commerce platform currently running on the site she'd set up years ago.

He'd missed checking one of the most rudimentary aspects of cybersecurity. Sure, they pinpointed the uptick in traffic to the site, but he made the spurious assumption the owner of the domain name was the one driving traffic.

It was a rookie mistake.

With a sigh, he picked up the reading glasses and scowled at the lenses. They were smudged beyond reason. Pulling the tail of his shirt free, he cleaned them as he replayed the day's events and tried to formulate a plan for moving forward. On his own.

Unwilling to stake the careers of the team he'd so scrupulously assembled on any more hunches, Simon had sent his agents back to Little Rock. Their counterparts from ATF had already returned to their offices, and he had no doubt the story of the flower shop raid raced like wildfire through both agencies.

But he couldn't bring himself to leave. Not when they were this close. He'd spent the last thirty minutes arguing his case with his boss. Thankfully, Commander Brenner was a lifelong fisherman and didn't believe in cutting bait too soon. He'd put up a token resistance. He warned the cost of the room at Suzee's SleepInn might bounce back on Simon if he didn't come up with something concrete.

But Simon wasn't worried about nailing things down.

Once he realized the error he'd made, he'd set Emma Parker on researching the security on the Flora's Florals website. It was being manipulated by someone. He needed to track down the hosting platform, then work his way back to determining who was accessing the domain and hosting the control panels. Once they eliminated the IP addresses connected to Hannah Miller and her shop, they could start hunting down the real perpetrator.

But first, he needed to rule her out beyond a doubt.

Sliding the glasses back onto his face, he leaned in and peered at the columns of data splashed across the spreadsheet. If anyone was going to be able to uncover it and find out what the original routing was, it would be Emma Parker.

Simon had the utmost faith in his team. He had handpicked each member of the Cyber Crimes Division himself. And though some would argue he lacked people skills, he didn't come up short when it came to identifying talent in others. No one was better at tracking invisible footprints through cyberspace than Emma.

For now, all he could do was wait. And work off an assumption, a practice he despised but would embrace as part of his penance. How had he failed to check the cyber trail more thoroughly before going in guns drawn and, thankfully, not blazing?

The spreadsheet contained an itemized list of transactions taken place over the last thirty days. Whoever was running this outfit kept it on the down-low. Orders were steady but nothing excessive enough to draw too much attention. At least, not in the beginning. In the past few months, the quantities had been increasing and the shipments more far-flung.

From what they were able to piece together, the floral arrangements offered on the site corresponded to cases of liquor. Wyatt Dawson was the one who saw the pattern emerging. An order for a dozen roses would equal a case of booze. The three dozen "anniversary special" arrangement was theoretically three cases. The all-rose funeral spray equaled five cases.

And only one item was being offered. Whiskey. This was the South after all. Untaxed and unregulated whiskey still appealed to a large sector of the population who resented any government "interference" in their lives.

Though many people believed it to be a thing of the past, modern moonshining was still a thriving business. Many had taken family recipes above board, applying for the appropriate licenses, setting up facilities, meeting health and safety standards, and most importantly paying the taxes required by the state and federal governments to legally distribute alcoholic beverages.

But it was no secret more than a few were operating undercover. Like the one they uncovered here in Eureka Springs, they used legitimate businesses as fronts, and took full advantage of the expanded logistics offered by global shipping. They were decent-sized operations with a longtime following and, now with the boom in e-commerce, a growing demographic customer base. Illegal liquor now flowed over state lines and was creeping like kudzu into areas well beyond a day's drive in a hopped-up muscle car.

Simon sighed and turned away from his computer, his concentration too splintered to make sense of what he was reading. He closed his eyes and tipped his head back. But rather than clearing his mind, he brought up the image of the Flora's Florals online order form.

They'd be able to determine the simple click form that came with the site had been manipulated to populate with fake shipping information. The delivery addresses were all local, but the buyers were scattered all over, and it looked like whoever was running the site had switched the two. If this turned out to be a correct assumption, they weren't simply looking at a few cases straying across the borders into Missouri, Texas and Oklahoma. Some of these orders they suspected shipped as far north as Minnesota and west to Utah.

Turning back to his screen, Simon placed a filter on the headings of the spreadsheet and sorted the orders by state. While many of the products seemed to be shipping within Arkansas and into Missouri, Oklahoma and Texas, some also ran to Louisiana, Mississippi, Tennessee and Kentucky.

"Who ships Arkansas whiskey into Tennessee and Kentucky?" he grumbled as he scrolled through the information.

Beside him, his phone buzzed and Simon jumped, startled from his musings. The ID on the screen showed Emma Parker calling, so he swiped to accept the call.

Before he even said a word she said, "I don't even know how we've missed this, Chief," in such a tone of self-disgust he couldn't bring himself to pile on.

"Me either," he commiserated.

"I should have run the backlog. I should have tested IP addresses—"

"Should haves aren't going to get us anywhere," Simon said brusquely. "Any of us should have thought to do those things and we didn't. Plus, when we started looking at this, all the orders were coming from in state."

"The killer is always inside the house," Emma muttered bitterly.

"Excuse me?" Simon sat up straighter, his mind flashing back to the stricken look on Hannah Miller's face when she realized someone had been using the storm cellar under her house without her knowledge. He didn't blame her. She was a woman living alone, and the discovery had to feel like a violation.

"Nothing. A stupid horror movie joke," Emma said dismissively. "Never mind."

Simon took no offense at the explanation. His team was used to him not quite understanding their jokes.

"Anyway, I'm on the case now," she assured him. "I'll let you know as soon as I hit on anything concrete, but judging from the patterns I'm seeing right now, I think your theory about somebody hijacking this account might be right. It was dormant for months after it was first created, but then it went live about eighteen months ago. We saw a steady stream of in-state orders in the beginning, as you know, but now they've expanded."

Simon nodded, removed his glasses again and tossed them aside. "We're going to work with the buying and shipping information for now, but I need you to try to get a lead on who's running this site and where they are logging in."

"On it," Emma assured him. "Did you tell the flower lady not to mess with it until we get a better handle on what's happening?"

Simon looked up, his breath tangling in his throat. "Uh, yeah," he lied, then shot from his chair to pace the room.

Would Hannah Miller try to go in and shut down the site? It was possible. She had a heck of a scare that afternoon, no thanks to him. Emma was right. He needed to warn her not to take the site offline. They needed it to be active to trace it.

"Great. I'll keep working on collecting IP data and get back to you as soon as we can make sense of any of it."

"Thanks. Talk soon," he said, then ended the call without further comment.

Simon stalked over to the window. Suzee's SleepInn wasn't only close to Hannah Miller's shop and residence, it was literally down the street from the funeral home where he assumed she was at the moment.

Pushing back the curtain, he stared down from the second-floor room into a parking lot. Directly across the street was a strip mall with the antique shop and flea market on one end, and a storefront boasting funnel cakes and frozen yogurt on the other. The flashing Open sign of a tobacco outlet blared into the dusky evening. Turning to his right, he cast his gaze down the street to the low-slung brick building the police chief had pointed out to him as the funeral home, where the services for Grace Templeton were being held.

Hannah was there. He could slip in like someone coming to pay their respects and warn her not to change anything on the site. It wouldn't take long, and he'd keep his head down. Only Chief Faulk would know who he was.

Simon couldn't see much from his vantage point, but judging from the gleam of metal under newly lit streetlights, he had to guess the turnout for the funeral was proportional for a life well lived. He would be another face in the crowd.

But the thought of crashing a funeral had him curling his fidgety fingers into a fist. He turned away from the funeral parlor and cast his eye on the cinder block building on the lot adjacent to the motel. A flashing roadside sign invited passersby to stop at Downshift for a cold draft beer, and reminded riders that bikers were always welcome.

Simon took in the dozen or so motorcycles already parked in the lot and let the curtain fall back into place. No shocker there. Eureka Springs had long been known as a haven for motorcycle enthusiasts. The scenic vistas and winding roads spreading like tendrils through the Ozark Mountains made them an idyllic ride.

Or so he'd heard.

Simon had never been much of one for cycling of any kind, motorized or not. Making his way back to the desk, he plucked a bottle of soda from the ice bucket where he'd placed it to keep cool.

He was going to have to apologize to Hannah Miller, he reasoned as he twisted the cap on the plastic bottle. And though he had no difficulty in making his apologies to his superior officers and counterparts at ATF, Simon found himself balking at the notion. Not because she was undeserving, but because he didn't want her to think any less of him than she already did.

He took a deep drink from the bottle, replaced the cap and plunged it back into the ice bucket. Then, without allowing himself to think too hard about what he needed to do, Simon tucked his shirt back in, grabbed the tie he'd tossed onto the room's worn easy chair and started reassembling himself.

In the morning, he would need to go out to buy more clothing and some personal items, but for now he figured he'd do well enough. He hesitated, his hand hovering over his state police windbreaker he'd worn earlier but decided against it. The last thing he wanted was to draw attention to himself.

Grabbing his wallet, phone and key card, Simon exited the motel room, pulling the door firmly shut behind him. As he descended the exterior staircase, a half dozen motorcycles roared into the lot for the bar next door. Ignoring their rumble, he took off in the opposite direction.

As he approached the funeral home, he saw he hadn't been wrong in his assessment of the crowd. The small parking lot was packed. A few knots of mourners gathered in various positions away from the entrance, sharing cigarettes and local gossip. Simon kept his head down as he walked past them.

"I swear it looked like they were raiding the place, but seriously, what can one hope to find in the florist shop? Maybe she's smuggling rare tropical flowers from South America or something?" a woman with teased brown hair said with a snort of disbelief.

"Not judging by the arrangements in there," a shorter blonde woman wearing a flowing dress that skimmed her ankles replied. "I swear the poor girl didn't inherit one ounce of her grandma's talent. Have you ever seen flowers more bland and boring? And carnations? Really?"

Simon slowed, but he didn't allow himself to be derailed. Let the small-town gossips do their thing, he counseled himself. All he had to do was keep his eyes and ears open. Towns like Eureka Springs drew tourists from in state and out, but the locals were a static lot. And their idle chatter may become one of his most valuable assets.

Slipping past them as unobtrusively as possible, Simon headed for the front entrance. The place was as dated as Suzee's SleepInn, but the crowd inside was impressive. He wove his way through groups of people, overhearing their conversations, taking in the aroma of overcooked coffee and the eclectic mix of mourners assembled in the main parlor. There were women in pearls and tailored dresses speaking to others who wore macramé sweaters and clunky leather sandals. Men clad in suits chatted with others wearing camouflage or even motorcycle leathers.

A few people lingered near the guest book, so Simon gave it a wide berth. When he entered the main viewing room, he noted there was no official receiving line. Grace Templeton died alone. The notion gave him a moment of pause, but then he spotted a few people lined up to greet friends and neighbors as they came through.

Police Chief Mitchell Faulk headed the line. Beside him, Hannah Miller stood speaking to another young woman around her age. Simon recognized her as the person Hannah had asked to call the police chief earlier. There was a younger man looking highly uncomfortable in an ill-fitting suit standing on the other side of Hannah's friend.

About a half dozen people were queued to pass in front of the casket. Simon fell into step behind them, but as they grew closer, he grew fidgety. He didn't know this woman, and though he was sorry for her untimely passing, stopping at her coffin seemed heinously disingenuous. Thankfully, the woman at the front of the line paused to kneel, folding her hands in prayer. He made a split decision to skip ahead to the chief of police.

"Chief Faulk," he said, extending his hand to Mitchell Faulk.

If the other man was surprised to see him there, he didn't show it. Simon made a mental note never to get talked into a poker game involving local law enforcement. "Agent Taylor," the older man said gruffly.

Simon glanced over his shoulder at the mourners scattered throughout the seating area and shook his head. "Simon is fine. Call me Simon."

The two men locked eyes, and Simon knew the chief understood what he was asking.

"We didn't expect to see you here, Mr. Taylor," the chief said in a jovial tone. Hannah was deep in conversation with the woman next to her. The police chief threw an elbow eligible for a flagrant foul, and Hannah jumped.

Her attention swiveled to him, and her eyes widened almost comically.

Chief Faulk continued, "Look, Hannah, your friend Simon Taylor is here," he said in a stilted tone.

Hannah Miller gaped at him. "I… Uh, why?" she stammered.

Simon thrust his hand out for her to shake. "I wanted to pay my respects. And to apologize for the grave mistake I made earlier today."

The young man at the end of the small receiving line snickered. "Grave mistake. Ha," he guffawed. Then he nudged Hannah's friend. "Get it? A grave mistake, and this is a funeral."

The petite woman beside Hannah rolled her eyes. "Yeah, I get it, Micah." She turned her attention to Simon, her dark eyes blazing. "I don't think this is the appropriate time or place for gallows humor."

Simon shook his head, as much to clear his own confusion as to deny the implication he meant any disrespect. "My apologies. I didn't mean to—"

"What are you doing here?" Hannah cut in.

"I wanted to say I'm sorry," he hastened to assure her. Then glancing around the room at the clusters of people speaking in low voices, he remembered the cutting remarks the woman outside made and straightened. "The flowers are lovely. Elegant. Understated. They're…" He paused, searching for more superlatives to heap on, but coming up empty, he shook his head and settled for, "Beautiful."

"Thank you. I appreciate you coming," she said in a clipped tone.

Simon glanced over his shoulder to see the woman who'd knelt in prayer straightening and turning to approach Chief

Faulk. He needed to say what he had to say before anyone else came near. "I'll be staying in town for a few days. I need to ask you not to touch your website."

"What?" Hannah wrinkled her forehead with consternation. "Age—"

"Simon," he interjected, casting a nervous glance at the woman behind him.

"Simon," Hannah said, adding a hefty dollop of acidity to his name. "I can assure you I don't plan to go home this evening and update a website we haven't used in years."

"It's important," he insisted, unperturbed by her obvious annoyance. "We need it to stay up and running as it is."

"What's going on?" the woman beside Hannah interjected.

Hannah exhaled a gusty sigh. "This is Mia Jones. She owns Hot Buns Bakery. We've been best friends since we were kids," Hannah said, touching her friend's arm to reassure her. "Mia, this is Simon Taylor. He came into the shop today with some questions."

Simon wouldn't have thought it was possible, but the other woman's glare intensified tenfold. "I thought you looked familiar," she said in a clipped tone.

"I'm also an old friend of Hannah's," he blurted. When both women raised their eyebrows in astonishment, he blundered on with his ad-libbed cover story. "From, uh, school." He punctuated the statement with a grimace. "College."

After sharing a glance, the two women decided to have mercy on him and roll with his fib. "Thanks for coming, Simon," Hannah said, making it clear she didn't want to prolong this charade of a conversation. "I appreciate your advice, and I promise we will talk more about this another time."

Simon met her gaze, then nodded solemnly. "Thank you. Another time."

Feeling shored up, he gave Hannah and her friend Mia another nod before moving on. Before he could escape, the younger man thrust his hand out to greet him.

"I'm Micah. Mia's younger brother," he said gruffly. His flat delivery made it clear this was not the first time he had said these words over the course of the evening.

Simon glanced back at the casket and then turned to the younger man. "Were you and Mrs. Templeton related?"

Micah shook his head. "No, man. But Mrs. T used to be real tight with our grandma and Hannah's. She doesn't have any family left, so I guess we're kind of it."

Simon digested that with the slight incline of his head. "Nice of you to be here for her. My condolences." He gave the man's hand another firm shake, then dropped it.

His eyes fixed on the exit sign, he made his way through the crowds gathered there, picking up snippets of conversation as he moved along.

"Wilder than the March hare," one woman said, directing her attention to young Micah Jones. "Poor Mia has her hands full trying to keep him on the straight and narrow."

As he skirted a group of men with their hands thrust deep in their pockets, Simon heard one say, "Yeah, well, Whitman's building it. Means it's going to be the highest possible cost and the lowest possible quality." The man chuckled at his own joke.

"Best not let him hear you saying such things," a man with a goatee said in an undertone.

Simon slowed his steps, hoping to catch more of the conversation without being too obvious about eavesdropping. To his disappointment, talk turned to Razorbacks football.

He was passing through the bottleneck formed at the entrance to the viewing room when he spotted the man who called over the fence at Hannah's house that afternoon. Something Whitman. This was the guy the other men were talking about. He searched his mind for the other man's first name but came up empty. Pulling his phone from his pocket, he opened his notes app and typed in: Whitman?

"I'm not sure exactly what the commotion was," the man was saying as Simon approached the exit. Thankfully, he was too involved in keeping his audience captive to pay much attention to Simon.

As he pushed through the door, he heard the other man say, "From what I hear it sounds like some kind of drug bust gone wrong. Can you imagine? Hannah Miller of all people," he said with a laugh. "They busted in the wrong door for sure."

Having heard enough about the day's misadventures, Simon rushed out into the evening. Head down and hands tucked in his pockets, he strode past the whispering cliques without pausing to pick up any gossip. The moment he reached the edge of the parking lot, he set his sights on Suzee's SleepInn, determined to shut himself into his room and not come out until he had something more concrete to offer Hannah Miller by way of apology.

Chapter Five

Hannah stooped to give Beauregard's ears a reassuring scratch as she closed her front door. "Hey, sugar baby," she croaked.

Her voice was hoarse, her back and feet hurt, and a tension headache radiated from the base of her skull into her shoulders. But with a wiggle and a lick, Beau managed to wipe away about 75 percent of her complaints. His warm, furry body snuggled up against her on her bed would take care of the rest.

"Come on, baby boy. We'll take a trip out back, then you can sleep with me tonight. Would you like a snuggle? Huh? Sound good?" she babbled as she led the dog through to the back door. Flipping the switch to illuminate the backyard floodlight, she made a mental note to investigate motion sensor lighting.

She'd changed little about the house since moving back to take care of her grandmother, feeling safe and secure in her hometown again. Now she could see she was living in a fool's paradise. Unwilling to venture into her own backyard, she hovered on the threshold as her best boy darted around the yard, making sure he hit all his favorite spots and inspected any new scents accumulated since his last patrol.

She purposely didn't look in the direction of the storm cellar. It was too much to think someone could have been using the space for heaven only knew what. Bootlegging, Simon Taylor had said. Who knew bootleggers even existed anymore?

Special Agent Simon Taylor did apparently, she thought, twisting her mouth into a smirk. And he thought she had something to do with the people running illegal liquor to who knows where. She couldn't even remember the last time she left Carroll County. Hannah took a step back into the kitchen, giving herself a little more distance from the worn wooden doors that led to the dugout beneath her house.

Violated. She felt violated. Everything she thought was secure had been trampled. Her home, her business, her integrity, all of it.

Logically, she was aware Simon Taylor had absolutely no way of knowing who she was or what she would be up to, but still, she couldn't help but feel affronted by the notion she'd been involved in such activities. Mitch Faulk's assessment of her as a teetotaler had been slightly overstated, but not by much. When she was younger and the wounds from her parents' deaths still fresh, she'd been more rigid in her beliefs. But, as with everything, time had softened not only the wound but her stance on people who chose to imbibe.

Mia had played a big role in her growth. Mia and years of working with a therapist to come to grips with her grief and the excessive boundaries she'd erected around her life to maintain an illusion of control. She knew now the only thing a person could control in life was how she reacted to the obstacles thrown into her path. But it rankled to have her name linked to something so distasteful.

Bracing her hands on the door frame, she leaned out and

gave a sharp whistle. "Come on, sugar Beau," she called into the night. "Who wants a snack?"

The question always did the trick. As much as Beauregard loved exploring his territory, he loved the prospect of food even more. The dog bounded across the yard, up the steps and through the door, his pink tongue lolling at the side of his mouth and his eyes bright with anticipation. She gave his head a rub and his ears a scratch before giving his flank a solid pat.

"Who's a good boy?"

Beauregard dropped his rump to the floor with a thump. Hannah chuckled as she reached into the jar where she kept dog biscuits. "You're right, my sweet Beau baby is a very good boy," she crooned as she offered him the treat.

The dog snarfed it down with all the grace of an overexcited alligator, but Hannah didn't worry about the mess. When it came to food, Beau also came with a handy-dandy vacuum setting. Whatever crumbs she scattered, he picked up on a subsequent scour.

"I'm going to brush my teeth," she announced, falling into her usual pattern of conversing with her pet as if he were a human. "Come in when you get everything cleaned up," she said, then turned toward her bedroom.

The house was a mess. Evidence of the afternoon's search was everywhere. Oh, the agents had been respectful. Careful, even. But Hannah could see how everything was slightly off.

The books she kept neatly stacked on her nightstand were slightly fanned out rather than neatly aligned. Her dust ruffle was caught under the bed rail at the foot of the bed. The dog bed where Beauregard slept most nights was at least six inches out of position. When she opened her closet to kick off the low-heeled pumps she'd worn to the funeral home, she noted her shoes had not been placed back on their rack the way she kept them.

With a frustrated grunt, she dropped to her knees and quickly set about reordering her footwear. While she appreciated that they didn't simply leave everything in a jumble, the fact they put them back incorrectly felt like as much of an insult. She switched a pair of sneakers with some blue suede penny loafers she bought on a whim but rarely had occasion to wear. When she was satisfied with the arrangement, she added the low-heeled pumps in their proper place, then rose to her feet with a tired groan.

Alerted by the commotion, Beauregard wandered into the room but kept his distance, his gaze wary.

The dog stayed close to the bedroom door as she moved around the room setting things to rights. The books were straightened, her jewelry box moved back to the right side of her dresser. A quick peek inside told her they had gone through its contents, but she simply didn't have the energy to straighten it before bedtime. Instead, she settled for putting Beauregard's bed back in its proper spot before yanking an oversize T-shirt from her bureau drawer and padding off to the bathroom to shed the rest of the day.

Water ran in the sink. At last, she let her mind drift as she brushed her teeth. A low rumble in the distance caught her attention. She switched off the water and cocked her head. She hadn't seen thunderstorms in the day's weather forecast, but that didn't mean anything. The weather in the Ozarks could be capricious.

As the noise grew louder, she paused in her brushing. Rather than dissipating, the rumble continued to grow more ominous. Then it clicked. A motorcycle was passing by. Reassured, Hannah turned the water back on and continued with her bedtime routine.

With the bathroom light switched off and her bedside lamp on, she pulled back her duvet, folding it neatly in half at the foot of the bed, then crawled between the sheets. Piling the pillows behind her, she selected a book from the stack, then gave the mattress two firm pats. "Want to come up, my Beau?" she called to her dog.

Beau didn't have to be asked twice. Nights spent on the bed were a special treat, and Beauregard was the sort of guy to take full advantage.

The moment his warm body settled against her leg, she opened the book and tried to pick up where she'd left off. She was two paragraphs in before she noticed the growl of another motorcycle rumbling past.

Hannah looked up with a frown. Bikers loved Eureka Springs, and the town loved their two-wheeled friends. Motorcycle tourism brought a lot of business to the town, and like any business owner, she appreciated their patronage. Over the years she'd grown used to the roar and rumble of the bikes, but tonight a creepy sensation crawled up her spine. The gathering of bikers in the area sometimes also brought trouble.

Placing her finger in the book, she closed it and turned toward the window. It was late. She lived on a quiet side street. *Who is cruising the area at this time of night?* Most of the cyclists stuck close to the main drag. There they frequented the restaurants, bars and other businesses that stayed open late to cater to them.

When the engine noise floated away, she shook her head and opened her book again. The day's events had clearly left her rattled. She needed time to relax and unwind.

She read another two pages when the same low, growing motor pierced her concentration. Lowering her book again, she glared at the window.

Her blinds were closed, of course, so she couldn't see who was cruising her street. Since her light was on, she dared not sneak a peek. Instead, she held her breath until the noise died away. Beauregard huffed and sighed in his sleep, shifting his girth to press more firmly against her leg. It was his way of telling her it was time for her to settle down.

Hannah smiled and reached down to give his silky head a soft stroke. "You're right, bud," she whispered to the sleeping dog. "Time to call it a day."

She set her book neatly atop the stack, checked to make sure her phone was plugged in and charging, then reached for the switch on the lamp.

Five minutes later the motorcycle was back.

Tossing back the covers, she swung her legs from the bed and crept over to the window. Holding the edge of the blinds back an inch, she peered out into the darkness. She saw no headlight, nor taillight, but her neighbors' porch lights and the occasional streetlamp reflected off a large, powerful bike.

Hannah frowned. It looked too ungainly to be able to move at such a low speed. And why were they riding with no lights on? Squinting to try to get a better view, she noted the rider was dressed in black from head to toe. Not unusual, she had to concede, but creepy.

She stepped back from the window, knotting her fingers as she weighed what she'd seen versus the slamming of her heart against her rib cage. On the bed, Beauregard thumped his tail twice as if asking her if everything was all right.

Biting her lip, she turned back to the bed and gave the dog a reassuring pat even as she said, "I have no idea."

She walked back to the bedside table and picked up her phone, her thumb poised to swipe the screen. But who was she going to call, Mitch Faulk? And what would she say? *Hey, Mitch, someone's riding past my house with no lights on?* While probably an offense worthy of a ticket, it was hardly a crime serious enough to warrant rousting the police chief.

She set the phone down, then sat on the side of the bed. She was on edge. She was looking for any little thing to be wrong. She was looking for trouble where there wasn't any, she chastised herself. She needed to let it go.

Hannah decided to climb back into bed and turn on a meditation from her LYYF app. Cara Beckett's soothing voice was sure to help her drift off to sleep. Tomorrow would be a better day. She'd get some motion sensors set up for outside the house, then call her therapist and talk through her feelings about the search. Get it all out there before the fear had a chance to take root.

With the new plan in place, Hannah slipped back between the sheets, rearranged her pillows to lie flat, selected a meditation session geared to encouraging deep sleep and gave Beau a gentle stroke to reassure him she was settling in for the night.

The soothing noises of water and songbirds caught the dog's attention, and he lifted his heavy head. "Not real birds," she reassured him.

Then, as if taking her word for it, he dropped his head back onto his paws and fell immediately back into a deep sleep.

Hannah lay staring at the ceiling. "Lucky dog," she murmured.

Beau responded with a sniffle snort and smacked his lips.

Barely three minutes passed before she heard the growl of the engine again.

She sprung from the bed, yanked the charging cord from her phone and stalked over to the window to peer out again. This time she split the slats with two fingers and stared directly into the night. It was the same rider on the same bike. Still riding with no lights on. They appeared to be looking for something. Or possibly someone.

The second they passed, Hannah spun on her heel and trotted in the direction of the kitchen. Simon Taylor's business card lay on the counter near the coffeepot, where she'd left it that afternoon. Without hesitating, she dialed the number marked mobile and tapped her foot on the cool tile floor as she waited for the call to connect.

"Taylor," he answered.

His voice was rough, as if she'd roused him from sleep. A quick glance at the clock on her stove showed her it was barely 10:00 p.m., but she imagined Simon Taylor had as big a day as she had in many ways.

"Someone's riding past my house on a motorcycle," she blurted without introduction or preamble.

"Excuse me?" He sounded bewildered, though his tone made it clear she'd captured his attention.

"Someone is riding past my house on a motorcycle at very slow speed and with their lights turned out," she repeated, adding the last to emphasize her reason for concern.

"Ms. Miller?" Simon Taylor asked, his tone cautious.

"Yes. This is Hannah Miller, and someone is riding past my house on a motorcycle with no lights on. Repeatedly. They're wearing all black, and it's dark out there, and it's freaking me out," she said, her voice rising. "I know motorcycles are thick on the ground around here, but I don't exactly live on a street that lends itself to cruising."

"Right." He cleared his throat. "I see what you're saying." He paused for a moment and then asked, "Have they stopped? Do you feel unsafe?"

"No, they haven't stopped, but yes I feel unsafe," she snapped. "As you so kindly pointed out to me earlier today, somebody's been violating my property without my knowledge and now I'm being…surveilled?"

"I understand," he said briskly.

"Unless this is one of your people," she accused. "Do you have somebody keeping an eye on me?"

"No," he answered quickly and emphatically enough to make her believe him. "No, ma'am. Not at all."

"I don't know whether that should make me feel relieved or terrified," she responded honestly.

"Do you want me to call the police? Have you called the police?"

"No. What would I tell them? Someone's driving past my house slow and creepy and with no lights on, but they haven't done anything illegal…except maybe driving with no lights on," she demanded.

"I take your point," he answered. There was a pause and then he said, "I don't hear the dog barking."

"He only barks if someone approaches the house," she explained.

"And nobody has approached your house itself, am I correct?" he asked, sounding markedly more alert.

"Correct."

"Okay," he continued, drawing the word out. "Um, do you want me to come over?"

He asked the question with such cautious disbelief Hannah was tempted to answer in the affirmative, to see if he would do it. But no, he was a stranger as well, so what possible comfort could he bring to her doorstep?

"No," she responded quietly. "I guess I wanted someone to know."

"I don't mind," he said quick enough to almost reassure her. "If it would make you feel better, I would be happy to come over and check the area around the house."

"Thank you, but no. I have Beauregard, and I'm sure you're exhausted. I know we are."

"Have they driven by since we've been on the phone?" Simon asked.

Hannah raised her head. Had they? She hadn't been listening for the motor; she'd been too busy sparring with the man who'd turned her life upside down. "I don't know. I'm in the kitchen. The bedroom is in the front of the house, so I guess I hear it more clearly there."

"Go back in there," he ordered.

Hannah didn't have the energy to bristle at his brusque command. Instead, she picked up his business card and padded back to the bedroom. True to form, Beauregard lay on his side, snoring prodigiously. She sat down on the edge of the bed, propped the card against the stack of books and plugged her phone into the charger again.

"Okay, I'm in here."

"Is that the motorcycle?" he asked.

Hannah listened for a moment, then shook her head with a chuckle. "Oh, no. That's Beau. He snores."

"Ah."

There was an awkward pause, and Hannah suddenly felt compelled to fill it. "So, you found a place to stay in town?"

"Yes, it was no problem."

"If there's one thing we've got plenty of, it's delightful bed and breakfasts."

"I opted for a motel. I don't like the...uh, forced camaraderie of a bed and breakfast."

She snickered softly. "I understand," she assured him. "While I'm all for free snacks, I don't understand why they have to come with a social hour."

"Precisely."

"Which motel?" she asked, curious to see which of the generic chain hotels he'd chosen over the town's more charming options. "Don't tell me you were brave and booked a room at the Crescent," she teased, referring to one of the town's famously haunted hotels.

"No," he said with a dry chuckle. "But for the record, I'm not afraid of ghosts."

"Neither am I," she assured him.

"Only phantom motorcyclists," he said gruffly.

As if on cue, Hannah caught the rumble of exhaust and jumped up, but her phone cord held her back. "Hang on," she said as she tried to free herself from the cord. "Sorry, my phone is ancient, and I have to plug it in whenever I can because it has no battery life." Hurrying to the window, she pulled the blinds aside and openly stared at the rider cruising past at a slow speed. "Okay, he's back."

"What can you tell me?" he prompted.

"No lights. Dressed all in black. The streetlights reflect, so probably leather?"

"Helmet?"

"Yes. Full helmet with a visor," she reported.

"And the bike? Can you tell anything about the bike?"

Hannah reared back slightly. "Uh, it's big?"

"Is the rider sitting more upright or leaning down low on the handlebars?" he asked.

"Uh, upright."

"Are you catching reflections off the bike? Color? See any chrome?"

"Uh, no, nothing shiny. It's possible it's black or another dark color."

The bleep of a patrol car's warning siren nearly made her jump out of her skin. The whirl of blue lights dancing across the houses spurred the biker into gear. His engine roared as he gunned it, easily slipping away from the patrol car that had crept up on him.

"Wha—" Hannah gaped as she listened to the motorcycle roaring off in the distance. "Did you—"

"I sent a text to a friend with the Carroll County Sheriff's Department. He asked dispatch to send a car by," he explained.

"I can't believe you sent someone," she said, backing away from the window as if the officer in the patrol car might turn his attention to her next.

"You felt uncomfortable. Their job is to check out anything suspicious," he reasoned. "I would have called the local police, but I figured Mitchell Faulk had enough of me for one day."

A soft laugh escaped her. "You and me both. When I was leaving after the service, he told me to go home, go straight to bed and try not to cause any more trouble today. I guess I got two out of three."

"You didn't cause this trouble," Simon retorted. His voice was low and gruff, and Hannah realized for the first time since she stepped foot in her home, she felt safe.

"Thank you," she said, dropping down on the edge of the

bed hard enough to startle Beauregard. The dog sent her an offended glare, which she returned. "I guess I'm discovering Beau isn't as much of a guard dog as I thought."

There was a moment's hesitation on his end, and Hannah smiled, certain he was going to agree with her assessment.

But then he said, "He might not be good on the perimeter, but I doubt he'd let anybody get to you."

"Right," she concurred, stroking her dog's impossibly soft ears. The pause in their conversation lasted a beat too long. Hannah was trying to figure out how to wriggle out of the conversation politely, but Simon beat her to it.

"Hopefully, our friend on the bike will find a better route to cruise, but if he doesn't you can call me back."

She glanced at the card she'd propped against her to-be-read pile and felt her cheeks warm. "I'm sure that did the trick. Thank you again."

"You're welcome." He cleared his throat softly, and she caught herself holding her breath, waiting to hear what he would say next.

"I'll be by the shop first thing in the morning, and we can discuss the website issue then," he informed her, his tone brusque and businesslike.

Hannah's lips parted, and the breath escaped her on a long, deflating exhale. "Fine. Great," she fumbled. "See you then."

"See you then," he confirmed.

Then, before either of them could end the call, she rushed out another, "Thank you."

"No trouble at all."

Hannah's brows drew together as three short beeps indicated the end of the phone call. With a breathy laugh of self-derision, she grabbed the power cord for the phone and plugged it back in before falling back onto her pillow.

Disgruntled by the disturbance, Beauregard stretched and stood, then gave her a long, pitying look before jumping down off her bed and reclaiming his own.

"Fine," she called into the darkened room. "You weren't doing me any good anyway."

Her dog turned himself around a few times, then settled onto his bed with a huff. Hannah blinked at the ceiling, wondering how a person could feel so wired and exhausted all at the same time. She turned toward her nightstand. The home screen on her phone had dimmed, but in the soft glow she caught sight of the crisp, white business card with its embossed state police shield.

With a sigh, she closed her eyes and exhaled, giving herself over to the pull of utter exhaustion.

Chapter Six

The following morning, Simon couldn't help feeling hopeful. Emma Parker had managed to pinpoint three different IP addresses in the Eureka Springs area. Unfortunately, one traced to the local library, and two others to fast-food outlets. Whoever was accessing the website was doing so from public spaces, but they weren't attempting to reroute or mask their location. Which meant he and his team hadn't been running down a blind alley when they decided to zero in on this quirky little town.

Though he knew from checking the website Flora's Florals didn't open until 9:00 a.m., Simon found it difficult to keep himself occupied. By 8:30 a.m. he was walking past the line of storefronts, his sights set on the plate glass window with the flaking gilt window paint. The interior was dark. A faint glow emanated from the refrigerated case where the flowers were stored, but there were no signs of life inside.

Other than the plants.

He lingered in the recessed entry. The front door was flanked by small display areas packed with lush green foliage. He wondered idly if the specimens on display were even real. He couldn't imagine what it would take to keep every plant looking its best. There had been some mention of silk arrangements on the website. Since silk flowers were part of the original layout Hannah had created for her grandmother, it was entirely possible Hannah had carried on offering them in the store as well.

Simon shoved his hands into the pockets of the still creased khaki pants he'd picked up at the super center that morning, along with a few other essentials. The golf shirt he wore was not his usual style, but in a town like Eureka Springs he figured the casual look would blend in better than his typical business attire.

He squinted into the morning sun, taking in the surrounding shops. One appeared to be dedicated entirely to yarn, a notion Simon found hard to wrap his head around. Could a person make a living selling nothing but yarn? Next to the yarn shop there was what appeared to be an old-fashioned newsstand crammed into a narrow space. A few newspapers and magazines were on display, but most of the front was taken up by a selection of candy, gum, snacks and souvenirs.

To kill a little time, Simon wandered over and selected a pack of chewing gum from the rack.

"Be all for ya?" the bearded gentleman seated behind the counter asked, barely looking up from his phone screen.

"Yes, sir," Simon said, placing the pack of gum atop the narrow counter and then fishing his wallet from his back pocket.

The other man made change for his five-dollar bill, tearing his gaze from the phone, and handed it over with little more than a glance. "Have a good day."

"You too." Simon pocketed his change and the pack of gum and decided to peek in to see if any lights had come on at Flora's.

No luck.

The scent of cinnamon caught his attention, and he turned in its direction. Walking purposely to the end of the block, he caught sight of a brightly lit corner bakery that appeared to be serving half the population of the tiny town. Though he'd indulged in a drive-through breakfast sandwich prior to picking up supplies at the supermarket, Simon followed his nose, helpless to resist.

Bells chimed as he opened the heavy wooden door set perpendicular to the streetcorner. The scent of fresh-brewed coffee and cinnamon assailed him full force, and his stomach let out an audible growl. Simon ducked his head in embarrassment as he walked his way through the crowd to where a line had formed at the counter. Two women in their early twenties ran back and forth behind the display case, calling out customer names, frothing milk for fancy coffees and pulling delectable bakery treats from the glass display case with practiced efficiency.

He watched in fascination as they worked around one another, each moving from one task to another without a bit of hesitation and without colliding into each other or even spilling a drop of coffee.

The line inched forward, and as people shifted Simon caught sight of the woman taking the orders. It was Hannah's friend. The one she'd introduced him to at the funeral home the night before. Mindy? Millie? Micah? No, Micah was the brother, he recalled almost instantly. Micah and…

One of the women gathering orders called back to the counter. "Mia? Was a triple espresso on the last order?"

"Yep. Triple shot," the woman behind the register replied without hesitation.

"Thank you," the girl working the coffee machine replied cheerfully.

"Mia," he said under his breath. Mia Jones. His brain provided the full name once it had been given the prompt.

Mia Jones was Hannah Miller's best friend. She had to know who he was and why he'd been in the florist's shop the previous day. She probably also knew Hannah didn't know him from her college days.

Suddenly the orange juice and sausage-and-egg biscuit he'd consumed that morning curdled in his stomach. Simon glanced around the busy café, feeling claustrophobic. He made a show of glancing at his watch, then checking out the number of people in line in front of him.

Then, confident he had put on a good enough show, he darted an apologetic glance at the guy behind him and murmured, "I'm gonna be late," before ducking out of line and heading for the door.

As he stepped back out on the sidewalk, Simon could only hope the café had been busy enough for Mia Jones to not notice either his arrival or departure.

A soft squeaking noise above his head caught his attention, and he looked up to find a cut wooden sign in the shape of a cinnamon roll swinging from a wrought iron arm outside the door. The words *Hot Buns* were written across it in black script. He'd been so drawn in by the scent of coffee and pastry, he hadn't noticed it on his way in.

Satisfied he escaped a close call with the suspicious best friend, he hurried back down the block to await Hannah's arrival.

Flora's was still dark when he got there. He checked his watch again and saw it was a good ten minutes past the store's posted opening time. Pulling his phone from his pocket, he tapped until he pulled up his recent call activity and found Hannah Miller's number from the previous evening. Stepping into the alcove of the doorway, he leaned against the locked door and debated.

Someone had been casing Hannah Miller's house the previous night. Maybe she had a hard time sleeping after they talked. Or maybe mystery rider had come back. His thumb hovered over the button that would place the call. He was still dithering when someone spoke behind him.

"Good morning. I guess you weren't kidding when you said you'd be by today," Hannah said, her tone dry, but a small smile played at the corners of her mouth.

"You're late," he blurted.

She blinked, then let out a soft chuckle of disbelief as she shook her head. "Gee, I hope I don't lose your business," she said acerbically.

Realizing his tone must not have matched the worry he felt, Simon did his best to add, "I only meant, um, I thought you opened at nine."

"Nine-ish," she said, smirking at him as she moved to insert her key into the lock on the front door. "Most days I'm here earlier, but I had a hard time sleeping last night."

Simon was not pleased to hear he'd been right. He took a step closer as she pulled the door open. "Did the motorcyclist come back?" he demanded.

Hannah shook her head. "No. At least not that I know of," she amended. "I crashed not long after we talked. I was… restless, I guess."

"Understandable."

He followed her into the shop, hanging back as she went through what was clearly her usual morning routine. Lights were turned on, as was a cash register straight out of the 1990s. He watched in fascination as she punched keys on the ancient machine, and it began to spew a long strip of tape from its printer.

She looked over and caught him staring. Simon saw the color rise in her cheeks as she gestured to the cash register. "Works perfectly well, so I didn't see the point of swapping it out." She gestured to an up-to-date credit card point-of-sale terminal. "Most of our business is done over the phone with a credit card or fed through one of the online distribution networks via email."

"Makes sense."

Hannah turned away from him without another word and continued with her opening tasks. He grimaced slightly as she swept up some of the detritus from the previous afternoon's search. In the walk-in cooler, she plucked several damaged stems from the buckets, then plunged them into the large open trash can next to the workbench. Simon was moving in her direction when she began working the trash liner free from its rim, another apology teed up and ready to go.

"Let me get this out," she said, yanking the fifty-gallon bag from the massive bin. "There's nothing worse than the smell of rotting foliage."

Before he could offer to take the trash out for her, she had the bag tied and was dragging it toward the back door. Simon rushed over as she disengaged the locks. "Let me help."

"I've got it," she assured him. "I do this every day."

"But I can help," he argued.

"I don't need your help," she replied. "At least not with the trash. Let me get this out, then you can tell me what you figured out."

Simon stood rooted to the spot as she pushed out into the alley behind the shop. He reminded himself she had every reason to be upset, but still, it stung. He'd explained what they were looking for and why they approached the way they had, but it didn't undo the damage. He'd been wrong. They both knew now. What more was there for him to tell her about the raid? It was bad enough he'd probably take some razzing for it for years to come.

He stood his ground, his hands buried deep in his pockets and lips thinned into a tight line as he waited for her to return. But the sound of a motorcycle rumbling to a stop in the alley jolted him from his sulk. He heard her trade greetings with someone, but the stilted familiarity in the exchange didn't sit right with him.

Simon pushed open the back door to find Hannah standing next to a man straddling a bright cherry-red racing bike. They were exchanging pleasantries, but he could tell by the stiffness in Hannah's stance she wasn't completely at ease.

Simon could see flashing white teeth set in a deeply tanned face. It wasn't until the two of them turned their attention toward him that he realized he'd seen the man before.

The developer guy who'd come by Hannah's house, he prompted his brain. He was drawing a blank on the name, but he could read the man's intentions clear as day. He thought he had some kind of claim on Hannah Miller.

And for all Simon knew, he might.

He racked his brain for the guy's name, but Hannah beat him to it with a breezy introduction. "Oh, this is Simon," she said, gesturing to him with an exaggeratedly casual wave.

The man on the bike extended a hand. "Hey, there, Simon. Russell Whitman, Whitman Development."

He shook the man's hand, but offered no more than a gruff, "Nice to meet you."

"I hear you and Hannah were off at school together,"

Whitman said, the assessing light in his eyes belying his jovial tone.

"Did you?" Simon forced a short laugh, then glanced over at Hannah.

She shrugged. "Small town."

"No kidding," Simon muttered.

"I hear a lot about what goes on around here," Whitman bragged. "I have a number of business interests around the area, so I'm always moving around talking to people, getting the lowdown."

"Oh, so you probably heard Simon and some guys who work for him came up yesterday to check out the place for me," Hannah said, her halting delivery undercutting her story. She wasn't any better at lying than Simon was.

"Check out the place for you?" Whitman propped his helmet on the cycle's tank and, straddling the bike to hold it steady, leaned over it, a rakish grin spreading across his face. "What's there to investigate? It's a flower shop. It's got a lock on the front door and a lock on the back door and not much else," he said, his tone cocky and condescending. "I keep trying to tell Han she needs to put some better security in, but she isn't one for change," he said with a chuckle. "Are you, Han?"

"Han-nah," she corrected, putting extra emphasis on the second syllable. "And I don't see the point in pouring more money into the shop when I'm not even sure I'm going to hang on to the place, but with what happened to Mrs. Templeton..." She trailed off with a sad grimace.

"Why wouldn't you keep it?" Whitman asked, his face a mask of appalled disbelief. "You've got an established business. Even if you don't wanna run it full-time, you could hire some part-time workers to help you out with the hours. You don't want to give up a toehold in the community."

"Yes, well, like I said, I haven't decided what I'm going to do yet," Hannah answered briskly, making it clear she had no intention of discussing her future with the man on the bike.

"Well, whatever you do, I'm sure you're going to be great at it," the man said with all the sincerity of a used car salesman. "But I sure hope you decide to keep it because we'd hate to lose you around here."

"Lose me?" Hannah raised both eyebrows. "I didn't say I was moving. I said I was debating whether to maintain the business."

Whitman gave a large, toothy smile. "There's a relief," he said as he opened the throttle on the bike a smidge. "Listen, gotta run. Tons of things to do today," he said as if she had been the one to lure him into the back alley for a chat. "You take care, Han."

Then he turned to Simon and raised a hand. "Nice to meet you, man. Maybe I'll see you if you decide to come through town again."

"Maybe," Simon replied but found he couldn't muster a smile for the man smirking at them.

"Bye, Russ," Hannah said with little inflection. Then she turned and marched back toward the back door. "Come on, Simon, I'll show you some of the stuff."

The motorcycle roared to life, and Simon bristled at being called to heel in front of the other man, but he followed her through the back door.

The moment the latch caught, he threw the bolt and turned to look at her. "Are you involved with Mr. Whitman?" he asked, keeping his tone as neutral as he possibly could.

Hannah looked genuinely taken aback by the question.

"What? Me and Russ?" She wagged her head hard. "No. No, I'm not involved with Russ Whitman," she said with such derision Simon found her antipathy toward the man fascinating.

"It was a simple question."

"And I gave you a simple answer," she retorted quickly. "I realize we don't know each other well, but I can assure you I am not the kind of woman Russ Whitman is interested in. Never have been, never will be."

"Have you known him long?"

"Since I came to live here." She dropped down onto the stool behind the workbench. "We all went to high school together. Russ was a year ahead of us. Me and Mia," she clarified.

Simon nodded. "Mia Jones?" he prompted.

"Yes. You met her last night."

"You said she was your best friend?"

"Is," she corrected with a nod. "Mia and her family lived next door to my grandmother until we were in high school."

"Did they move away?"

"To the other side of town," she explained. "Mia's mom inherited some land from her parents, and they built their dream home on it."

She said this with a hint of irony. "You did not like their new home?" Simon asked, fishing for the bit of rancor he sensed in her tone.

Hannah shook her head, then shrugged. "No. It was nice. Lovely. I hated they moved my friend away from me."

"Do you think her parents did it on purpose?" he prompted.

"No. But that doesn't mean I wasn't bitter about it all the same. Nobody could claim I was going to be a bad influence on their kid. I was the town goody-goody, remember?"

He nodded. "Did you and Mia grow apart after the move?"

"No." She smiled. "Mia and I have always been friends. Things grew a little more distant when we were off at college, but once we were both back in town, we picked up right where we left off."

"She owns the bakery?"

She nodded, then tipped her head in the direction of the corner shop. "At the end of the block."

"And does she live around here too?"

Hannah shook her head. "No. Mia and Micah's dad died of a heart attack five years ago. Mia moved home to help her mom with everything, then ended up staying. They all still live in the house he built for them."

"And she opened a bakery?"

Hannah nodded. "Her grandmother's recipe. Everyone in the county loved Miss Verna's cinnamon buns. She sold out at every bake sale, won every fair she entered and handed out batches of them as gifts at Christmas."

He'd been led down the street by his nose by the scent of those rolls, but he didn't want to admit he'd ditched the line at her best friend's bakery. So he settled for a hum of acknowledgment. "Good, huh?"

"Better than good," Hannah said as she continued moving around the workspace, setting things to rights.

"And how's business for you?" he asked.

She smirked and picked up a small spiral notebook kept next to an old cordless phone and answering machine combo. "Let's see," she said, pressing a button beside the flashing red light on the machine.

"Hannah, dear, it's Marjorie Huffins. I wanted to tell you the arrangements you made for Grace were lovely. Your grandma would be so proud," a woman crooned in a shaky voice. "But I heard last night you had some trouble at the shop. Nothing serious, I hope. Call if you need anything at all."

There was a click, and the machine beeped to indicate the end of the message. Hannah rolled her eyes and huffed as the next message began. It was from a man named Walt Able and seemed to be a fishing expedition about the previous day's raid. There were two more calls from "concerned" friends and neighbors before the machine reset itself.

"I guess the hot item of the day is gossip," she said wryly, placing the notebook back in its spot.

"I am sorry for the trouble we have caused you," he said gruffly.

"Can't stuff a genie back in the bottle," she said, turning away to boot up a desktop computer that looked to be of a similar vintage as all the other electronics in the store.

One thing appeared to be certain—Hannah Miller was not a tech junkie. He watched as she opened an email server and exhaled a long, slow sigh as she began entering notes into an online calendar.

"Okay," she said in a slightly brighter tone. "I have some arrangements to finish out for a banquet at the Basin Park Hotel. Can we use our delivery van now?" she asked, looking up at him for confirmation.

"Yes, it should be fine."

"Great. Give me a few minutes to get them lined out, and I'll text Micah to see if he can run them over," she said, heading for the walk-in.

She emerged a minute later pushing a cart with a dozen glass bowls jam-packed with pink roses. Hannah disappeared back into the refrigerator and came out with a handful of long stems bearing spear-like whitish-green flowers. He watched as she cut them to the desired length, then ruthlessly stripped off foliage. Then she jabbed a few of the stems into the tightly packed rose arrangements, adding the slightest bit of height and a neutral foil for the pale pink blooms.

Simon watched as she worked, fascinated by both her efficiency and her creative eye. The smaller flowers somehow gave the elegant clusters of roses a less formal and more natural look. They looked wild. As if they'd sprung up amid the roses in her garden, and she'd done nothing more than clip them and drop them into vases.

"Beautiful," he murmured when she stepped back to assess her work.

She turned with a little half smile. "Thank you."

"What are those?" he asked, pointing to the flowers she hadn't used.

"Oh. They're a variety of a snapdragon." Her smile widened. "I like to add something unexpected here and there."

"It works," he said, surveying her work with a frown.

The night before, some woman had called her creations boring. But they weren't. They might not be splashy, or over-the-top, but they were interesting. Like their creator.

Reminded of his visit to the funeral home, he asked, "Will Mrs. Templeton's funeral take place today?"

She nodded. "A graveside service this afternoon."

"I didn't mean to intrude last night," he began. "It occurred to me you might want to take a look at the website yourself, and I—"

She held up a hand to stop him. "I understand."

He was saved from responding when the front door opened and the tantalizing scent of cinnamon wafted in.

"Special delivery," a woman called out, and Simon took an involuntary step back.

"You are a goddess," Hannah answered.

"I brought sustenance," Mia Jones announced as she breezed past him into the workroom. "Ooh! Pretty," she said, admiring the centerpieces as she deposited a bakery box and a coffee cup on the counter. She reached out to stroke one of the snapdragon stalks. "I like this."

"Thanks," Hannah said warmly. "You remember, uh, Simon," she said, drawing her friend's attention to him.

Mia Jones turned slowly, one eyebrow arched as she gave him a once-over. "Simon? Your friend from college I never heard of until he and some buddies stormed into your shop yesterday afternoon?" she asked knowingly. "The one you didn't want to talk about last night?"

"Yes," Hannah replied, offering no further explanations.

Mia glanced from him to Hannah then back again. "Hi, Hannah's friend Simon from school," she said with deliberate condescension. "Sorry, I only brought coffee for Hannah. Guess you shouldn't have given up your spot in line at Hot Buns earlier."

"I, uh…" He paused to clear his throat. "I didn't want to miss meeting Hannah."

"Mmm-hmm," Mia said, turning back to Hannah with a dismissive sniff. "I guess this isn't a good time to get the scoop on what's going on either," she said with a wry twist of her lips.

Thankfully, Hannah chose to change the subject. "Hey, I texted Micah to see if he could deliver these for me, but he hasn't answered."

Mia's lips thinned into a line. "Oh, he didn't answer because my dear brother got an offer he couldn't refuse last night, leaving his only sister and her bestie high and dry this morning."

"An offer he couldn't refuse?" Hannah asked with a laugh. "He was propositioned at Mrs. Templeton's visitation?"

"Yep," Mia said with a grave nod.

"By whom?" Hannah asked.

Mia's expression darkened. "By Russ Whitman."

"Russ?"

"Russ told him he could start full-time as of today, meaning you and I are nothing more than the dirt under our little Micah's work boots."

"Russell Whitman?" Simon interjected. "The guy who came by earlier?"

"He came by here?" Mia asked as Hannah was answering. "Yes."

Simon took a moment to digest the information. "The guy gets around."

Mia let out a bark of laughter. "Oh, Friend-Simon-No-One-Has-Ever-Heard-Of-Before, you don't know the half of it."

Chapter Seven

"Why do I get the feeling neither of you two ladies is terribly enthralled by Mr. Whitman?" Simon asked.

"We don't dislike Russ," Hannah was quick to assure him.

"He's not for us," Mia chimed in, as if that explained everything he needed to know about the man.

Hannah smirked at her friend, then turned her attention back to Simon. "Russ has always considered himself a big shot."

"No doubt about it," Mia said dryly.

"I got the same impression," Simon confirmed.

"You have to understand," Hannah was quick to rush in. "Russ's dad started a successful construction company when we were kids. By the time we got to high school, the Whitmans were one of the wealthier families in town."

"Russ has always thought he was God's gift," Mia said.

"And his parents did nothing to disabuse him of the notion," Hannah finished for her. "He always had the nicest truck, the best clothes and cash to throw around."

"He also threw the biggest parties," Mia said, shooting her friend a sidelong glance. "Wildest parties. More out of hand than any teenager had any business hosting."

Simon shifted his gaze to her, but Hannah shrugged. "I wasn't invited."

"He seems friendly enough with you," Simon pointed out.

"Russ is friendly with everybody," Mia supplied. "As far as he's concerned, each person he speaks to in a day is a connection, and each connection can somehow benefit him."

Hannah gave her friend a perplexed glance. "Cynical much?"

"I'm a realist," Mia shot back.

"And now your brother is going to work for him?" Simon asked, his gaze darting between the two women.

"Apparently," Mia said, biting the word off short.

"Micah's been trying to get on at Whitman Development full-time for a long time. Other than summer work and the odd jobs he's done for them, he doesn't have a lot of experience other than working for me or Mia," Hannah explained. "It's been tough for him to find a toehold on anything permanent over there."

"He's worked for them before?"

"Russ would call him in to work temporary crews or for an extra pair of hands in the busy season, but when it came to parlaying into a regular job, he always had some reason or another not to bring Micah on," Mia said with a disapproving sniff. "Not that I mind. But I don't like some of the guys Russ has running his crews."

Simon perked up. "Oh?"

Mia shook her head as if dismissing her last statement. "Nothing in particular. Russ likes to hire his buddies, and you know what they say about birds of a feather."

"Slick?" Simon asked.

"Not exactly." Hannah shot a warning glance at Mia, then shifted gears. "Anyway, if this job is for real, I'm happy for Micah." Mia gave a soft grunt, and Hannah looked her friend directly in the eye. "We're going to be happy for him. There's no way you and I could ever afford to pay him what he could make working for Russ."

Mia glanced down at the tile floor and scuffed the toe of her worn sneaker. "I suppose so," she said at last. Blowing out an exasperated breath, she flashed a tired smile. "I've got to get back. I'm one person down this morning." She pushed away from the counter and wrapped an arm around Hannah's shoulders, giving her a squeeze. "Sorry about the deliveries. I'd help, but I'm guessing they need these before lunch," she said, gesturing to the roses.

"No worries. I'll deliver them myself." Hannah returned her friend's side hug. "Are you going to Mrs. T's graveside service?"

Mia broke away, shaking her head. "I can't. I need to prep for tomorrow, and my mom has an appointment with Dr. Bertram at four o'clock."

"Okay. Let me know if I can do anything to help," Hannah said, waving her friend off.

Mia sauntered to the front door, raising a hand above her head in a wave without turning to look back. "We all know there's no help for me," she called back. "You should ask Simon-the-Friend-Nobody's-Heard-of-Before to help you with the deliveries."

She paused at the door, and Hannah nearly burst out laughing when she caught the look her best friend sent the man. She was half-surprised Simon didn't duck. "It's the least he can do," Mia called out as she stepped into the bright sunlight.

Hannah chuckled and shook her head as she turned back to the cart. "She's a mess."

"A whirlwind," Simon concurred.

Hannah glanced over at him. "One of the nicer words people have used to describe her."

"I am happy to help you make whatever stops you need to make," he offered, his speech halting and oddly uncertain.

She cast him a sidelong glance. "It *is* the least you could do," she said pointedly. "And, while we do this, you could fill me in on what your team discovered."

Working in unison they boxed and loaded the delicate centerpieces into the ancient white delivery van still parked in the alley. As they drove to the historic hotel downtown, Simon asked questions about her business and the town in general but steered clear of addressing his suspicions about how her website, and possibly her storm cellar, was being used. She wasn't sure if she should be grateful for the reprieve, or annoyed he was avoiding the topic, but she let it slide for the moment. She'd spent enough time dwelling on the subject the previous night to leave her yawning and fuzzy headed.

Once the centerpieces were safely delivered to the catering manager at the hotel, they climbed back into the van and Hannah started the engine. Warm air blew from the vents. She adjusted them to point directly at her face, hoping cooler air would be soon to follow.

"The air conditioning isn't as efficient as it used to be," she apologized.

Simon shrugged, looking unperturbed and curiously unruffled by either the heat or the activity.

Curious, she stared at him for a moment until he met her gaze. "Do you sweat?" she asked in a teasingly acerbic tone.

He gave a short laugh. "Yes, I do. You should have seen me sweating when I realized all the assumptions I made on a case I have been working on for months were grievously incorrect and I embarrassed myself in front of my own people and a federal agency." He shrugged. "It may be hot out there, but it's a lot cooler than it is in Little Rock right now. Literally and professionally. So, I am happy to be here."

"I see."

He waved her sympathy away. "And frankly, I liked helping you. Most of my work takes place behind a desk, so it's good to move around."

Hannah laughed. "You try working a job where you're on your feet most of the day. You'll change your tune."

"Have you always wanted to be a florist?"

There was something disarmingly innocent in the way he asked the question. Had this man led a raid on her business and home without doing at least some rudimentary research on her? It wasn't as if she was well-known, but like everyone else she had an online presence.

"No."

The one-word answer seemed to startle him. He twisted in the passenger seat to study her. "No?"

"The shop was my grandmother's, Simon. She was the one who was the florist." She spoke slowly, as if waiting for him to catch up. But his expression remained blankly curious. "I studied architecture and design. I planned to build buildings, not bouquets."

"I remember reading that somewhere, but I thought maybe you were using the design part of your education in the floral…realm," he said, speaking slowly and circling his hand as if to gather his thoughts. "And now that I say it out loud, I feel like a fool."

Hannah smiled then. "How about you? Have you always wanted to be a cybercrime investigator?"

"Ha." He shook his head, then began to nod slowly. "Well, I always wanted to be a policeman, but that was not the path my parents wanted me to take. The internet was in its infancy when I was in school, and I was fascinated by it. I ended up studying computer science, and ironically enough spent an hour speaking to a representative from the state police academy at the senior job fair."

"I bet your parents didn't appreciate being thwarted," she teased as she put the van in gear.

"They were a little put out at first," he admitted, a smile tinging his voice. "Thankfully, they got over it."

"And now you're the head of the whole shebang," she commented.

"If by whole shebang you mean a team of six agents including myself, yes," he said with a wry smile.

"Your own division," she said, unwilling to allow him to discount his accomplishment. She paused a beat, then plunged ahead. "Are you going to tell me what your team found, or are we going to chitchat all day?"

"Believe it or not, no one's ever accused me of being overly chatty," he said sardonically. "Can I get you to call a couple of members of my team and tell them you think I chitchat?"

"Simon," she prompted.

"We believe whoever is using your website is working here in town," he said, getting down to the brass tacks. "The IP addresses we've identified so far have all been in the Eureka Springs area. Most of them are in public areas—the library, fast-food places, chain coffee shops—that sort of thing."

"Makes me wonder if it is somebody local," Hannah

mused. "Those of us who live here tend to make a point of shopping local small businesses whenever possible."

"Right, but they wouldn't do if they were trying to remain anonymous," he pointed out. "If they were frequenting local establishments, it would be a lot easier to pin it down. By using the national chains, their data can be lost in the shuffle of hundreds of customers per day."

"True," she conceded.

"We're still tracking it. We've got months of data to comb through, and we're hoping at some point someone gets lazy and uses a private connection or a personal hot spot."

"But the odds of it happening are probably slim if they have any brains at all," she said grimly. Gnawing on her bottom lip, she steered through the streets on autopilot. "If whoever is doing this was smart enough to co-opt an unused website, they're also savvy enough to hide in plain sight."

"They would also have to be someone close enough to know the website was not being used," he countered.

"How would someone know?" she asked as she switched on her blinker.

"Hard to say for certain, but it is probably easy to assume they knew you or your grandmother and you were not utilizing the site." She caught his glance out of the corner of her eye. "Any ideas on who it could be?"

Hannah pulled a grim face. "Almost anyone. I set it all up as a surprise for my gran, thinking she'd be excited to have a new way to drum up business." A soft, sad laugh escaped her as she turned into the alley behind the shop. "She was not."

"Why?"

"Gran was the original troglodyte. She hated the hand-me-down computer I brought in. Wouldn't even use it to email me. She barely tolerated the answering machine, and only had a cash register because some of the national services requiring receipt reporting would not accept handwritten tickets."

"I see."

"And now you know how I came to inherit a shop full of outdated office equipment," she said, pulling to a halt in the spot where she parked the van. "You and your whiz kid pals are trying to figure out who might have known Gran hated technology. The answer is everyone," she said grimly.

"I get you," he assured her. "But we can get more out of the data. Business has been picking up on the site," Simon said, reaching to unlatch his seat belt. "They may back off if word of our visit gets around. Then again, business is picking up and they may be too greedy to back off. If that's the case, they could get sloppy," he added.

"Let's hope—" She froze, her gaze riveted to the back door of the shop. "Did I not lock the back door?" she wondered aloud.

Simon's head jerked up, and he peered through the windshield at the steel door standing slightly ajar. Hannah jolted when she felt his hand on her arm, holding her in place. "You did," he said without hesitation. "Stay here."

She could only stare in shock as the mild-mannered man who had been sitting beside her moments before reached down, pulled up the leg of his pressed khaki pants and pulled a gun from a holster strapped to his leg.

Hannah was still trying to pick her jaw up off the floor when he opened the passenger door and slid out, closing it carefully behind him, making as little noise as possible. His back against the wall of the building, he approached the back door with his weapon held high, muzzle pointed to the sky.

"Oh my…" she said as she watched him dart around the

narrow opening in the door to put the slab of steel between him and whoever might be inside.

She stared wide-eyed, willing him to look up at her. When he did, she waved her hand frantically, begging him to come back to the safety of the van. He ignored her, raising his free hand in a motion cautioning her to stay put.

Hannah watched as he gripped the edge of the door and pulled it slowly open, using it as a buffer until the opening was wide enough to allow him to enter. Simon swung around, and she watched with her heart in her throat as he lowered his weapon and aimed it into her storeroom.

A flash of memory jolted her. Men in windbreakers bursting through the same door the day before. How had they unlocked it? Was it locked? She cringed, recalling how she'd carried an armful of boxes out the door maybe an hour before her uninvited guests appeared. She'd simply dropped them next to the dumpster and strolled back into the shop, fully intending to break them down later.

A glance to her left confirmed the boxes were still there. But Simon was not. He was going into her shop with his gun drawn again. This time, not to catch her, but to protect her.

"No," she whispered, startled by his decisive step into the path of danger.

Through the rolled-up windows she heard him shout at anyone who might be inside, ordering them to drop their weapons and identifying himself as a police officer. He repeated the warning before he began to move cautiously into the back room.

Panic scrambled up her throat and escaped as a hoarse cry. "No!" she croaked as she grappled with the door handle.

Before she could think her actions through, she was out of the van and running after him. Breathless from fear and exertion, she grasped the edge of the door with both hands and peered into the dimly lit space. When they'd left, she had turned off the storefront lights and put out a sign notifying customers she was out making deliveries. But they'd left the workroom lights on, and from what she could see the place was empty.

Simon raised his weapon, then turned to glower at her over his shoulder. "I told you to stay put."

"I couldn't let you come in here alone."

"It's my job," he said flatly. "Now step back."

The command made it clear he was in no mood for argument, so she did what he asked. Peering around the edge of the door, she watched as he checked the walk-in, then made a complete circuit of the retail space before coming back to the workroom.

He must have been satisfied the shop was empty, because he bent to holster his gun. "You can come in now," he called out brusquely.

"I can't believe you ran in here," she said as she stepped back across the threshold.

He shot her a quelling look. "I can't believe *you* ran in here," he shot back. "Does it look like anything is missing?"

She turned in a slow circle. As far as she could tell nothing looked to be out of place. There were some scraps on the workbench she didn't get cleared up before they left to deliver the centerpieces, but nothing was broken, nothing out of place, and now she thought of it, she hadn't noticed any scratch marks or gouges on the back door.

Simon must have been thinking along the same lines because he asked her, "Who else has keys?"

"Keys?" she repeated, still bewildered and wondering if she had only imagined locking the door behind them.

"Someone used a key and came through the back door," he concluded. "I didn't see any sign of forced entry."

"Me neither," she admitted.

"Keys?"

Hannah bit the inside of her cheek as she searched her mind for the information he sought. "I know I gave Mia a set for emergencies," she began haltingly. "But I don't recall giving any to anyone else. Mia and Micah were the only people who've ever helped me out with the shop."

"No part-time employees? Past employees?"

She continued shaking her head to ward off his suspicions. "It was me and my grandmother. When I went off to school, she started asking Micah to help here and there, and Mrs. Templeton would step in if she was in a pinch," she recalled.

"Did Mrs. Templeton have keys?" he asked.

Hannah held her hands up in a helpless gesture. "I suppose so. She must have. I never thought about it."

"You said Mrs. Templeton was robbed?" he prompted.

Hannah felt a bolt of cold streak down her spine as the implication of his question sank in. "Yes," she said, barely managing to squeak the word out.

"I'm assuming the local police inventoried her shop?" he asked.

Hannah shrugged. "I don't know what the procedure was," she said, her voice cracking. "All I know is they found her in there, tied to a chair. Alone."

Simon nodded as he digested this information. "I'll call Chief Faulk and ask if any sets of keys not belonging to her establishment were found on the premises."

"You think somebody went into Grace Templeton's store to rob her and took whatever spare sets of keys she had laying around?"

"It's a possibility I can't dismiss," Simon said, planting his hands on his hips and turning in a slow circle. "Mia has keys, Mrs. Templeton, and anyone else?"

"Me," she hazarded. "I keep an extra set at home."

"We'll need to make sure your second set is accounted for as well. Would you reach out to Mia?"

Hannah wet her lips as she patted her pockets. "I guess I left my phone in the van," she said, starting toward the back door again.

"Hold up," he barked.

She stopped in her tracks and turned to look at him.

"You're not going out there alone."

"You came in here alone," she retorted.

Simon sighed. "I don't want to argue with you."

As a concession, she gave a short laugh. "Okay, then I won't pretend I'm not grateful for an armed escort."

They stepped through the open door into the alley once again. Simon turned back to inspect the door and its frame. "Yeah, someone had a key."

Hannah closed her eyes and saw herself locking the door behind them when they left. Simon had been rolling the cart filled with boxed centerpieces across the broken asphalt, and she cringed at every bump. But she also remembered the cool metal of the door under her palm as she turned her key in the lock.

She had locked the door. And someone had unlocked it.

Turning on her heel, she started toward the van. Agitation was outweighed by anger by the time she pulled her phone from the console. Simon came up beside her as she called her best friend.

Mia picked up on the third ring. "What's up? I'm kind of slammed here."

"Yeah, sorry. I forgot it's lunchtime. I need you to check to see if you have the keys to the shop handy when you have a minute," Hannah said, trying to sound casual.

Mia laughed. "Did you lock yourself out?"

"No, the police asked me to account for all sets of keys for the shop, and I wanted to ask before I forgot," she said, shooting Simon a glance.

"Easy enough to check now. I keep them in the register." Hannah heard the beep of keys being struck and the faint *ka-thunk* of a cash drawer springing open. "Yep, still got them. Do you need me to bring them to you? I can after the lunch rush," she offered.

Hannah met Simon's gaze, and he shook his head.

"No. Hang on to them. If they need them for some reason, we'll come and get them."

"Sounds good," Mia replied briskly.

"Thanks—"

Hannah huffed a laugh as the phone beeped in her ear. Mia didn't take time to chat when there were customers to be served.

Meeting Simon's steady gaze, she pulled her keys from the van and hit the button to lock the doors, then slammed the driver's door shut. "Come with me."

He followed her back toward the steel door. But rather than opening it, she inserted her key and turned the bolt. Looking back over her shoulder she cocked an eyebrow. "Locked, correct?"

He inclined his head. "Yes."

"Come up to the house, and we'll eliminate another set. I need to get ready for Mrs. Templeton's graveside service."

To her surprise, Simon shook his head, plowing his hands deep in his pockets as he took a step back. "No, you go on ahead. Let me know if you have them. I know you have things to do, and so do I."

Hannah took in the grim set of his mouth. His eyes were dark with determination and his focus was already somewhere else. But enough trepidation roiled in her gut to make her toss any false bravado she had to the wind. Hannah wasn't crazy about the idea of walking into her house alone. Not after this.

"What if somebody has broken into my house?"

Simon jerked as if drawn back from some faraway place. "You're right," he said gruffly. "I'll walk you home. That way we can both move on with our business without worrying."

Hannah was about to brush him off with some bluster about being able to handle herself, but she was too shaken by the events of the past few days to even pretend not to be scared. Instead, she nodded in the direction of her house and jingled her keys in her hand.

"Thanks," she said softly. "And there's no need to worry. Deliver me to Beauregard and I'll be fine from there."

Chapter Eight

Simon paced his hotel room. He'd called a meeting with his team. It was due to begin in less than ten minutes, but something was nagging him, and he couldn't quite put his finger on what it was. All he knew for certain was it was important and it was something he needed the other members of the cybercrime team to go over for him before he presented it to anyone else. He couldn't trust himself to see the path forward after the previous day's debacle.

Restless, he walked over to the window and pulled the curtain aside again. The parking lot of Suzee's SleepInn had emptied shortly before noon, but business at the Downshift Bar and Grill seemed to be booming. Two shiny muscle cars, one a classic in canary yellow, the other a newer model Challenger in coral red, sat parked beside a cinder block storage building in the back.

A half dozen motorcycles were lined up on the side of the building facing the motel. He could only assume there were more on the other side. As he stood gazing at the window, three more riders pulled into the lot. They wore leather from head to toe despite the heat of the day, but no helmets. Simon shook his head, wondering how someone could justify the disconnect.

"Why worry about a little road rash when your head could be crushed like a melon?" he asked aloud.

The question bounced off the window back at him. As the riders parked, he noticed the emblem sewn into the backs of their jackets. The background sported the jagged outline of a mountain range, but this rendition was far craggier than the rounded edges of the tree-covered Ozark Mountains. It was embellished with an overlay of back-to-back *R*s. The words Ridge Riders encircled the emblem at the top and bottom.

On impulse Simon pulled his phone from his pocket, opened up the camera app and zoomed in as best he could before snapping a photo of the jacket.

"Ridge Riders," he murmured to himself as he moved back to the desk.

A quick internet query informed him the Ridge Riders were a motorcycle club that started in the Blue Ridge Mountains and boasted chapters in multiple states.

He made a note to do further research on the group, then went back to the window to see if the bikes parked in the lot gave any indication there were more members of the same club inside the tavern.

Squinting into the afternoon sunlight, Simon made a mental note to pick up a pair of field glasses the next time he went to the superstore. The motorcycles in the parking lot varied in size and power, but they had one thing in common. These were serious bikes. There were no off-road bikes or small engine cycles as far as he could see. These were rides meant to go far distances.

Using the camera on his phone, he zoomed in on the leather saddlebags attached to another bike and spotted the double *R* logo stitched into the flap.

His phone beeped, alerting him it was almost time to

start the conference call, and Simon lowered it with a sigh. Watching the comings and goings of members of a motorcycle club wasn't going to get him any closer to breaking up this bootlegging ring. Unless they were employing bike trailers, it would be impossible to deliver cases of liquor on a motorcycle.

Walking back over to the desk, he set his phone next to his laptop and took his seat. Once he was settled, he opened the line to the conference call and waited for his team to assemble.

They came in all at once, the two women murmuring to one another as Wyatt and Tom tossed jibes back and forth. Simon closed his eyes and envisioned the water-stained drop ceiling in the small conference room they used at headquarters. For about half a second, he wished he was there in person. Then, Wyatt Dawson spoke up.

"Hey, boss, you wanna come back here and take some of this heat?" he asked with a laconic drawl. "It's tough when a guy can't even pour himself a cup of coffee without some jerk jumping out and telling me they're raiding the break room."

Simon gave an involuntary snort. "No. I'll let you handle them, Dawson."

Emma Parker chuckled. "Wow, I think Wyatt called you a chicken, chief."

"I'm not saying he's a chicken," Wyatt shot back. "I'm only saying he is missing out on all the fun."

"You're the only one who thinks getting razzed by everybody at headquarters is a good time," Special Agent Tom Vance, one of the newer additions to their team, grumbled.

"He's perverse," Emma said primly.

Simon cleared his throat meaningfully, and they abandoned their byplay.

"I do apologize to you for any heat you're taking for my mistake," Simon began, sitting up ramrod straight.

"It was *our* mistake," Emma was quick to chime in. "Every one of us should have thought to check where the activity was coming from on the back end of the website."

"Either way, we're on the right track now," Simon said crisply. "Anything interesting in terms of access?"

"Uh, yes, sir." Special Agent Caitlin Ross, the newest member of his team, spoke up, a quiver of nerves in her voice. "We haven't been able to trace activity back to a residence or private IP, but we have been able to pinpoint access made through a few local businesses."

Simon grabbed his pen and pulled the tablet he'd been taking notes on earlier closer to him. "Can you give me the names of the businesses?"

"Cuppa Joe Coffee, the Crescent Hotel, Hot Buns Bakery, Mother's Tea Room and Sandwich Shop, and a place called Downshift Bar and Grill?" she recited.

Simon glanced over at his window. "Do bars usually offer public Wi-Fi access?" he asked his team.

There were murmurs of both yes and no on the other end, but then someone said the word *trivia* and the naysayers conceded.

Wyatt spoke up. "It's entirely possible. A lot of bars run trivia nights and source software programs to generate the questions and answers. Sometimes they have the players enter their responses on their phones."

"Yeah, but isn't it usually on paper?" Tom Vance asked. "I know at Bankshotz they block the Wi-Fi so you can't search the internet for answers."

There was more general discussion around the table, and

at last Simon cut in. "Okay, so it's possible a bar has Wi-Fi, but maybe it's not public."

"Or they may share the password only with their regulars if it's a local place," Caitlin suggested.

"I've seen two of these businesses," Simon replied. "I'll take a closer look at them, but it sounds like our perp is still using places easily accessed by the public."

"They've certainly been careful to do so," Emma Parker said. "I haven't been able to hit a hot spot or anything that could be traced back to an individual."

"Is it possible one of the owners of one of these businesses could be involved?" Wyatt asked.

Simon pulled up the image of Mia Jones behind her counter this morning, a five-foot-nothing spitfire of a woman wearing a sticky sunflower-print apron. He wanted to shake his head but stopped himself. The last thing he could afford to do would be to dismiss any possibility out of hand. "I'll look into it," he assured them.

"I ran the backgrounds you asked for," Emma told him. "I've already sent you dossiers on Hannah Miller, Mia Jones, Micah Jones and Mitchell Faulk," she continued. "I'm still waiting on some information to come back on the Whitman guy you asked about. I'll send it along as soon as I get it."

"Thank you."

"As of last night, we have 273 cases moving," Wyatt told him.

"Did you have a chance to double-check my theory about the delivery addresses?" Simon asked.

"Yes, and I believe you're right." Simon heard the rustle of papers and then Wyatt was back. "I've targeted five of the addresses from the orders placed the night before last. I'm not sure what the shipping window is, so I picked three here in the Little Rock area we might have a better chance of monitoring."

"Good thinking. We're going to have to be careful on this front," Simon warned him. "People have so many types of products shipped to them. We can't risk trying to force a sneak peek at somebody's dog food delivery."

"I'm going to watch it for a period of time," Wyatt said gruffly. "I want to make sure we're not seeing patterns we want to see. Any of the addresses shipping to this area in the coming days will be under surveillance."

"From a distance," Simon cautioned.

"Yes, sir."

"Great. Thank you for your work on this. I'll look over the dossiers and see what I can find out about some of the local businesses. I'll also see if there are any orders coming from persons in the immediate area and try to do the same surveillance on this end."

"Sir?" Emma Parker called out.

"Yes?"

"I've been looking at the datasets Wyatt has been working on. I think we're on the right track with the delivery piece. I'm also convinced at some point our perp is going to have to access the website from someplace inconvenient. I promise you, we're going to have eyes on it when they do."

Simon paused for a moment, tapping his pen against the notepad as he searched for the right thing to say to keep his team focused and on track. But great words of wisdom were beyond him, so he simply said, "I think so too. And thank you."

He cleared his throat and straightened up in his chair. "Anyone have anything else?"

At the general negative response, he leaned closer to his

phone case, prepared to cut the call off. "Okay, I'll check in with you later."

Without another word he ended the call. Turning back to his computer, he scanned the information on the Ridge Riders again, then closed the window. He wasn't here to pick fights with bikers. He was here to deal with another sort of trafficking altogether.

An email from Emma sat in his inbox with four pdf attachments. Unable to resist slaking his own curiosity, he clicked on Hannah Miller's first.

None of the information contained in the report surprised him. Hannah had given most of it up herself. Her parents had been killed in a car accident when she was young, she'd gone to live with her maternal grandmother in Eureka Springs, went off to school at Fayetteville, then directly into their master's degree program. Emma even included her transcripts. From what he could tell, she finished her program remotely when her grandmother was diagnosed with cancer. At which time, Hannah moved back to Eureka Springs to assist with her grandmother's floral shop and take care of the woman who raised her.

He breezed through Mia Jones's information. Other than learning about her culinary and food service training at a college in Little Rock, there wasn't much there. Her brother, on the other hand, had been in his share of trouble. Mostly little stuff—property damage and a couple fender benders when he was a teenager, but he'd picked up a speeding ticket with a bonus charge of riding a motorcycle without the proper classification on his driver's license the previous summer.

He was making note of the violation when a series of engines fired to life outside the motel. Simon abandoned his notes and made for the window. The three he'd seen pull in earlier had all mounted, as well as a few others parked at the front of the building. The angle wasn't great, but he didn't bother hiding his interest behind the curtain. The men below were too intent on their impending departure to even look in his direction.

He was squinting at the logo on the back of the third rider's jacket, trying to make out any additional details, when movement beyond the driveway the bar shared with the motel snagged his attention.

Russell Whitman.

A jolt of recognition shot through him. The man was still dressed in the same dark-wash jeans and snug T-shirt he'd worn in the alley behind Flora's Florals this morning, but the bike was different.

Simon was no expert on motorcycles, but he could tell the difference between a racing bike and a chopper. He watched as Whitman raised a hand in farewell, then turned his bike toward the back of the Downshift. He was about to abandon his spot at the window and take off for the motel's back stairwell when he saw the man slow to a stop behind a red-orange Dodge Challenger.

A moment later, the back door of the bar swung open wide and a tall, lithe brunette with a full sleeve of tattoos sauntered out. She held something large and flat in one hand, waving it back and forth as if fanning herself. It looked like some kind of soft leather portfolio, but he couldn't tell for certain. On instinct, Simon dashed over to snatch his phone from the desk. The moment he was back at the window, he began snapping photos.

Once the woman was within arm's reach of Whitman, he snatched the zippered pouch from her hand. Then, he used the same arm to haul her closer. In the time it took for the two of them to exchange a long, torrid kiss, Simon was able to zoom in on what she'd handed over. Whitman was holding an old-fashioned bank bag. The kind businesses used to use to drop cash deposits into overnight repositories.

He drew back from the window, frowning at the magnified photo on his screen in puzzlement. Did Whitman own a stake in the bar next door?

Simon's attention was drawn back to the scene playing out below. The last of the three bikers who'd been departing pulled into traffic with a roar. The couple at the back of the building broke their kiss but did not pull apart.

Simon watched as the woman smiled warmly at the man straddling the powerful bike. She ran her fingers through Whitman's close-cropped hair. It was a gesture as oddly possessive as the way he'd reached for her. These two people knew one another intimately.

Frowning, Simon resisted the urge to avert his gaze from the tender moment playing out below. Whatever the two of them were discussing, their interaction seemed easy and even lighthearted. With this woman, Whitman displayed little of the overbearing solicitude he'd displayed in his interactions with Hannah.

Hannah.

Did Russ Whitman have his eye on her? It was entirely possible Simon read the signals wrong. He was never the best at picking up on undercurrents or nonverbal cues, but it sure seemed like he was interested in Hannah. He scowled and looked away when the man pulled this new woman in for another long, hard kiss.

Only the rev of the bike's motor drew his attention back. The woman stepped back as the powerful machine lurched forward. Whitman drove past the storage building, then hooked a sharp right. Seconds later, Simon spotted him zipping down the narrow fire lane that ran behind the establishments lining the main drag.

He moved his attention back to the parking lot, only to find the woman from the bar had backed up to lean against the cinder block wall of the building. She pulled something from her back pocket and stuck it in her mouth. Even in bright sunlight he could see the LED glow of the vape cartridge as she took a deep pull. A cloud of vapor curled around her head like a halo, but she still gazed off in the direction of Whitman's departure.

Simon stayed put, hoping for a better look at her face when she turned to go back in, but minutes later the back door opened again and a dark-haired man wearing jeans, clunky boots and a grimy work shirt exited. Simon blinked twice, trying to reconcile the differences between this disheveled young man and the one who'd worn a suit and shook his hand the previous night.

His mouth agape, Simon stared as the woman gestured to the coral-colored car. Before he could fully process the man's arrival on the scene, the woman tossed a set of keys to the newcomer and disappeared through the back door.

Simon cursed softly under his breath when she got away without him getting a good glimpse, but he figured he could always venture into the Downshift if he needed to get a better look. He was too absorbed in watching the guy heading toward the shiny muscle car.

The moment he slid behind the wheel, Micah Jones looked up, a wide grin splitting his beard-stubbled face as the muscle car's engine rumbled to life.

Once Mia Jones's little brother cleared the parking lot, Simon gathered his wallet, keys and phone. He knew there was no chance of catching up to the guy, but the town wasn't very big. There were only two main highways intersecting in town, and Micah had headed south.

Pulling out of the lot, Simon headed away from downtown, hoping this time his hunch proved to be correct. He didn't have to go far before he spotted the flashy sports car parked in a bay at a coin-operated car wash. Simon pulled into a gas station across the highway and parked so he had eyes on his mark.

Drumming his fingers on the steering wheel, he tried to fit the pieces together. Russ Whitman had some kind of stake in the Downshift Bar and Grill, he reasoned. And he also had a relationship with the woman who drove the Challenger, based on the interaction he'd witnessed between them. Mia said Micah had finally landed a job with Whitman Development, but it was possible the younger man was working for Whitman himself, and not necessarily working construction. And while Whitman might give off a sort of smarmy vibe, Simon had no real reason to believe the man was up to anything more than playing the field.

Still.

He clicked his tongue with impatience as Micah ran through every option available at the self-service wash with a seemingly endless supply of quarters. Picking up his phone, he called Wyatt Dawson.

"Dawson," the agent answered.

"I need you to look into something for me," Simon said without preamble.

"Shoot," Wyatt said gamely.

"The Ridge Riders. It's a motorcycle club. Looks like they're operating around here," Simon said, his gaze glued to Micah Jones.

"Aren't there a few of those up there? It's a popular area for bikers."

"Yes, it is," Simon conceded. "But I want some info on this group. Anything you can find on their activities in the state."

"You want to know how well they do on toy drives?" Wyatt asked, his tone sardonic.

"More like the opposite end of the good deeds spectrum," Simon replied.

At last, Micah put the wand back in its metal sleeve, and Simon almost groaned with relief. Surely there had to be more to this errand than a quick wash and wax, he hoped. Then, he blew out a long gush of frustration when Micah reached into the car and pulled out a large chamois cloth.

"You okay, boss?"

"I'm fine," Simon answered, sitting up straighter. "Getting antsy to find something concrete."

"I might have something for you to mess with," Wyatt began, his tone cautious.

"What?"

"It's a hunch at this point," his agent cautioned.

"What is?"

"I was trying to cross-reference some of the names on the orders, and it turns out, most of the hits I have so far belong to people who live there. Or, I should say, lived there, in some cases."

Simon tore his attention from the activities at the carwash and stared at the in-dash display as if he could somehow see Dawson through the screen. He couldn't, of course, so he was forced to use his words to put the pieces together.

"You're saying the shipments we believe to be going all

over the mid-south are being addressed to residents of Eureka Springs?"

"It's harder to track now most people don't use landlines, but yeah, according to some public records I've accessed. I've only confirmed about a dozen or so…"

Wyatt continued, talking about different databases and the number they'd need to confirm before they could claim a reasonable sample, but Simon was way ahead of him.

"Send it to me," he ordered.

"What?"

"Send me the list of names. I'm here. It will be easier for me to track people down."

"If you're sure," Wyatt hedged, sounding uncertain.

"I am."

His head jerked up when a flash of reddish orange zipped past his window. Micah had finished his wash and wax and, thankfully, driven straight across the street and pulled in at one of the pumps rather than taking off while Simon was focused elsewhere.

He felt a tingle of anticipation at the base of his skull. They were getting closer. He could feel it in his bones. And, no matter what his commander said about his expense report, Simon knew staying on in town would prove to be invaluable.

"This is good stuff, Dawson," he said, eyes fixed on the Challenger in his rearview mirror. "I've made some contacts here. Send me what you have, and I'll track them down," he instructed, then ended the call.

Sure enough, when Micah Jones was done filling the tank, he revved the engine and punched the accelerator as he pulled away from the pump. Simon put his car in gear and pulled out of his space as the younger man sat at the exit, waiting for traffic on Highway 62 to open enough to pull out.

Simon smirked when the kid made a point of leaving a streak of tread behind when he left. He was clearly having the time of his life driving the boss's girlfriend's hot rod, but Simon found he couldn't begrudge him the cheap thrills. Micah was heading back toward downtown. Simon hung back, allowing another car to turn onto the highway between them as he followed him back to Downshift.

Pulling into Suzee's SleepInn on the opposite side of the motel, Simon cruised around the back of the building in time to see the Challenger parked in its original spot and Micah happily twirling the key fob as he made his way to the back door.

Simon waited until Micah disappeared into the back of the bar before making use of the same fire lane Russ Whitman had earlier. Though, as he instructed his navigation system to take him to Eureka Springs Police Department, he doubted they were heading for the same place.

Chapter Nine

Hannah was settled in on the sofa with Beauregard when the doorbell rang. As if shot from a cannon, the dog launched from the cushion beside her, jostling her arm and causing Hannah to spill icy cold cola down the front of her favorite Razorbacks T-shirt. White, of course.

"Gah! Darn it, Beau!" she cried as she leaped to her feet.

The dog's incessant barking was maddening. Sticky soda plastered her shirt to her chest, likely soaking through the thin fabric. She pulled it away from her skin as she started for the door. Beauregard stood with his legs braced wide and his gaze focused solely on the doorknob, as if daring whoever was on the other side to attempt to turn it.

"Beauregard, stop," she cried in exasperation. "You're making my ears ring."

Her dog did not relent. He kept up a steady stream of intimidatingly deep barks until she nudged him aside and pulled the lace curtain on the sidelight to see who might be visiting at this hour.

Simon Taylor stood on her welcome mat, a crease furrowing his brows and a pizza box balanced on his open palm.

Hannah glanced down at the mess splattered down her

shirt and grimaced. "Great. Great," she said as she wedged herself between her dog and the door and disengaged the locks.

The moment she swung the door open a few inches, Beau stopped barking, took a few steps back and settled for a low growl. She cut him an exasperated glance. "Coward," she chided.

"I'm sorry. I didn't even think about upsetting your dog." Simon shook his head. "I should have called first."

"It wouldn't have mattered. Mia comes over almost every day and she receives the same type of greeting," she informed him.

"I come bearing gifts," he said, offering up the pizza box.

Hannah opened the door wider and took it from him. "The price of admission." She turned on her heel and left him to close the door after himself. As she passed her dog, she glowered down at him. "You're doing laundry this week, Beau."

"Your dog helps with the laundry?" Simon asked as he followed her into the cozy living room.

Hannah set the box on the coffee table. "Unfortunately, no. He is completely useless when it comes to everyday household tasks."

"I wouldn't say completely useless," Simon said, smiling down at the dog who was now giving the corner of the box a hopeful sniff. "He's a good deterrent with that big bark of his."

Hannah bit her lip as she studied the man. What was he doing here? And why was he bringing pizza?

"I'm not one to reject gift pizza, but you've already apologized. Multiple times."

He shifted his weight, looking uncomfortable amid her

grandmother's English chintz decor. "It's, uh, part apology, part bribe."

Intrigued, she gestured to the sofa and an adjacent armchair. "Take a seat. I'm going to go change, then we can debate how effective Beau is at his job, and you can tell me what it is you're trying to bribe me to do."

As if sensing a kindred spirit, Beau moved closer to Simon. She softened a little inside when the man automatically reached down to scratch behind the Labrador's silky ears. "Go ahead. I'll give him some pointers and things to look out for," Simon assured her with such an earnest expression she wasn't entirely certain he was joking.

But the shirt had to go. "Be right back."

Questions swirled in her head as she rushed into her bedroom and yanked another shirt from the drawer. She ducked into the bathroom to sponge the sticky drink from her skin, then quickly slipped into the dry shirt.

By the time she reemerged, Beauregard was staring deep into Simon Taylor's eyes as if the man held the key to all the world's secrets.

"So, it's not only knocking you need to listen for," Simon was saying. "Thumps and bumps and scrapes count too," he informed the dog. "Your territory doesn't start at the door, buddy. You're in charge of the whole property, all the way from the sidewalk to your back fence, you got me?"

Beauregard tilted his head so adorably Hannah had to clamp a hand over her mouth to keep a soft "aw" from escaping.

Simon looked up then, and for a second, she understood exactly why her dog was so enthralled by the man. His eyes were pools of concern and sincerity. His expression was so guileless, she had a hard time believing he'd be skeptical enough to be an effective investigator. And yeah, this man led an entire team of the state's most techno savvy investigators.

She gave herself a small shake, then pointed to the half-empty glass of soda on the table. "You want a Coke?" she asked.

Simon nodded. "Sure." Then, falling into the vernacular of the region, he asked, "What kind do you have?"

She turned and walked toward the kitchen. "Sprite, Dr Pepper, yellow sports drink and, of course, Coca-Cola," she offered.

"A Dr Pepper would be great," he replied.

Hannah busied herself by pulling down a fresh glass and filling it with cubes of ice. "Mia tells me in other parts of the country they don't call other soft drinks Cokes," she said by way of making conversation.

"I have also heard this rumor," he replied.

"What I don't get is where they even got soda or pop from," she said as she poured his drink of choice over the crackling cubes of ice.

"Though I have to admit I love it when people come in from up north and a waitress asks them what kind of Coke they'd like," she admitted.

Simon came to join her in the kitchen and Hannah smiled as she handed him the glass. She snagged another can to replenish her spilled drink, then asked, "What kind of pizza did you bring?"

"I played it safe and went with pepperoni, but then I realized you might be vegetarian, so if there's something you'd prefer I'd be happy to pick up another one."

Hannah shooed him toward the living room. "Pepperoni works fine." She gathered two small plates and a handful of paper napkins before following. "I'll basically eat anything on a pizza except for fruit."

"Fruit?" he asked as he returned to his seat next to the dog.

"Some people put pineapple on pizza," she said, wrinkling her nose.

"I thought that was the Canadian thing."

Hannah laughed. "Canadian? I thought they called it Hawaiian?"

Simon shrugged. "I have a Canadian friend who loves it, but I'm with you. No pineapple on pizza."

They flipped open the box, and Hannah surveyed the thin-crust pepperoni pie in front of her. It was cut into squares rather than wedges, and her mouth watered. "If this is a bribe, I want you to know I'm going to eat all the crispy edges and the corners."

He gestured for her to proceed. "Have at it."

Hannah plucked all four of the small corner squares from the pizza and added them to her plate. "What are you bribing me to do?"

Simon helped himself to a single edge piece, then took a crustless square from the center. "You know most people would have asked what the bribe entailed before accepting the payment," he pointed out.

"Beau and I had resigned ourselves to eating peanut butter sandwiches for dinner because I'm too tired to cook. At this point I would have considered swapping the dog for the pizza," she said, pinning her beloved beast with a playfully stern look.

"I doubt you would."

"So, what's the catch?" she asked, waving her slice around before taking a large bite.

"No catch," he assured her. "I'm looking for some help. I

came from a meeting with Mitch Faulk, and from what he has told me I think we might be on to something. I wanted to get your feedback as well."

"My feedback?" She gave a soft snort and shook her head. "I thought you guys were the professionals."

"We are, but they need someone who's more of an insider to help with this."

"I don't see how you get to be more of an insider than Mitch Faulk," Hannah mumbled through stuffed cheeks.

"He was a great help, but apparently this is his wedding anniversary, and his wife informed him it would be their last if he didn't make it home by six o'clock."

"Ah, gotcha." She picked up another corner piece and pointed the edge of the crust at him. "I am your default."

"Not at all. I planned to come and talk to you either way, but you might be able to help confirm some of what Mitch told me, as well as shed some light on some other things."

Hannah took a sip from her glass, then loaded two more squares of pizza onto her plate before plucking a napkin from the stack. "What have you got?"

"One of my agents had a theory the names of the addressees coming through on the website might be the names of residents. Mitch was able to confirm they were locals at one time, but they are now dead. My team in Little Rock is working on confirming them through public records, but as the police chief so kindly pointed out, one business in town provides arrangements for most of the funerals in town. He thought you might be able to confirm my theory."

She sat up a little straighter. "They're using the names of people who have passed away?" she asked, aghast.

Simon nodded. "That's our guess. When I ran it past

Mitch, there were a few he couldn't remember, but yeah, he thinks so too," he said with a shrug.

"Wouldn't deaths be part of the public records?" she asked. "When I try to look up anybody's address on the internet there are dozens of services offering to sell me all the vital statistics I want," she pointed out.

"Yes, but the information isn't always as easy to access as they make it look on television, and those private databases are not always accurate."

"You know, if you want the most accurate information, we probably need to talk to Gavin over at the funeral home. He literally knows where the bodies are buried."

Simon inclined his head and reached for another slice of pizza. "I may if I can't get enough information on my own, but at this juncture I would prefer not to tip my hand to too many people in the area."

Hannah leaned back, her eyes opening wide as his meaning sank in. "Oh, I get you."

"I've been thinking about it, and I'd like to stick with the story about us being friends from college if we can," he said, glancing down as he toyed with the food on his plate. "It's much easier to get information from people when they don't know you're with the police."

"I don't understand why anyone wouldn't want to cooperate," Hannah said, shaking her head in disbelief.

A wry smile lifted the corner of his mouth. "They may not want to cooperate because they're involved. Or they may not want to cooperate because they don't like government interference." He shrugged. "Or, some people mainly want to help, but they get nervous and start to tell you everything they think you need to know, and it muddies the waters."

"I see."

"And I think it might be better for you in some ways if we were to keep up the ruse."

"Better for me?" Hannah placed the sliver of pizza she'd been nibbling onto her plate, then lowered it to her lap. "How so?"

"Have you and Russell Whitman ever been involved?" he asked bluntly.

Hannah's jaw dropped and her eyebrows rose. "Excuse me?"

"I only ask because he seems to be interested in you, but you don't seem to think it's a possibility. I didn't know if maybe there was some history beyond being classmates once upon a time." He paused for a moment. "Or maybe something you didn't want your friend to know?"

He asked the last question so hesitantly, she nearly burst out laughing at the absurdity of the notion. "You think I wouldn't tell Mia if I had a thing with Russ Whitman?"

Simon's brows furrowed together, and his expression darkened. "Is the guy such a prize?"

"Weren't you listening when we told you about him?" she asked in exasperation. "Russ Whitman doesn't go for women like me."

"He seems to be hanging around a lot lately," Simon pointed out.

She shook her head and raised a palm in a helpless gesture. "Your guess is as good as mine."

"My guess comes down to two possibilities," he said with brisk efficiency. "Either there's a personal relationship between the two of you, or he has a professional interest in your business."

Hannah scoffed and set her plate down on the coffee table with a plunk. "And the answer is neither," she informed him stiffly. "I have never had any sort of personal relationship with Russ, nor does he have any interest in Flora's Florals. You're barking up the wrong tree," she insisted.

As if he'd been given a cue, Beauregard raised his head and replied with a sharp bark. Hannah chuckled and plucked a bit of pizza crust off her plate. "Easy there, killer," she said as she offered the bit of contraband to the dog.

"You're not the only one susceptible to bribes," Simon commented.

"We both have a weakness for pizza," she informed him.

"You say Russ Whitman isn't interested in women like you," Simon repeated blithely. "Do you know what kind of women he is interested in?"

Hannah picked up her plate again, giving her head a small shake as she lifted a slice to her lips. "To be honest, I never paid much attention," she said before taking a healthy bite. "I mean," she mumbled as she chewed, "he and Darla Ott have had an on-again, off-again thing going on since we were in school, but I get the impression it's always been casual on both sides."

"Darla Ott?" Simon prompted.

"Yeah, she was in the same class as me and Mia," Hannah said. "We didn't run in the same circles though."

"I take it she was the one going to all the wild parties young Russ was throwing?"

Hannah nodded. "Precisely. Darla was always a little bit…" She paused, wanting to choose her words carefully, as she was not one to tear down other women. "Darla had a tough upbringing," she began. "And it probably explains why she wasn't the kindest girl in our class," she said, picking and choosing each word with care.

"She bullied you," Simon replied in a flat tone.

"No. I mean, yes," Hannah said, ending with a laugh. "But not only me. Everyone. Darla was kind of the queen bee, seeing as how she was Russ's girlfriend and all. Plus, she's beautiful," she said with a little chuckle. "I mean, like guys tripping over their tongues trying to talk to her beautiful," she explained. "She has this big mane of gorgeous dark hair, and she's sleek and edgy. She's one of those people who looks exciting and glamorous in jeans and a T-shirt."

She glanced down at the wrinkled shirt she'd pulled from her dresser and frowned. She was certain Darla could even make her TACO CAT shirt look cool.

"Tattoos?" Simon asked, jolting her from her thoughts.

Hannah blinked twice, wondering if he was reading her mind. "Well, yes. She started getting tattoos when we were seniors in high school. Way before most of the other kids could get permission from their parents. And now she has this intricate…" She trailed off, gesturing to the length of her own arm with a slice of pizza.

"Sleeve?"

Hannah used the slice to point at him again. "Somehow, she totally pulls it off. On Darla it's chic and alluring. I would look ridiculous." She ended with a shrug.

"You said she had kind of a rough upbringing," he prompted.

Hannah nodded. "I don't know the details, of course. We weren't friends. But from what I heard, she lived with her mom down in Little Rock, but her mom got into some trouble. She ended up bouncing between a couple of foster homes before they were able to get her placed with her paternal grandmother here in town."

"Did you know her grandmother?"

"Yes." She swallowed a lump in her throat and then added, "Martha Ott, Grace Templeton and my own grandmother were all close. Unfortunately, Mrs. Ott passed away not long after we graduated high school. She left her house and a little bit of money to Darla."

"And Darla stayed in town?" he asked.

Hannah set her plate aside and took a drink from her glass. "Yes. She bought a restaurant." She paused. "It's more of a bar that serves a little bit of food. You've probably passed it. It's right near downtown. It's called the—"

"The Downshift," he supplied.

Hannah blinked. "Yes. How did you know?"

Simon gave her a lopsided smile. "I'm staying at Suzee's SleepInn. The Downshift is next door."

"So, you saw her. That's how you knew she had tattoos," Hannah concluded.

Simon nodded. "She was speaking to Russ Whitman this afternoon. They looked to be more than friendly."

"Ah, they're on again," Hannah said, lifting her glass in a toast. "Best of luck to her this time."

"What does that mean?" he asked.

Hannah raised her shoulder and let it fall. "Sorry. I'm being a little snarky," she confessed.

"About?" he prompted.

"Russ," she answered, as if it should have been obvious. "I always figured she was hanging around waiting for him to come around once and for all. But he's never going to marry her. His parents would have a conniption." She wiped her fingertips on a paper napkin. "If she hadn't been so mean to everyone back in school, I might almost feel sorry for her, but from what I've seen of her in the years since, Darla hasn't changed much."

"Do you think Russ Whitman owns an interest in her business?"

She shot him an exasperated look. "The guy is a real estate developer, not an investment broker. Why do you think he owns a chunk of everybody's business?"

Simon blew out a breath. "It's a place to start. First thing they teach us in detective school is follow the money. I was fishing to see if he had any financial interest at stake."

"I can't tell you whether he has a piece of the Downshift. I wouldn't be surprised, I guess. But if he is her partner in the business, he's probably a silent one. Like I said, his parents are conscious of their standing in the community, and I don't think they would approve."

"Gotcha."

Simon set his own plate atop the closed pizza box, and Beauregard let out a soft whimper, his adoring gaze straying to the uneaten bits left on the plate. As if taking his cues from her dog, Simon shot her a baleful look.

"Are you the only one allowed to give handouts?"

Hannah eyed his plate. "No pepperoni. He'll spend the whole night burping, or worse."

They watched as Simon carefully wiped the excess tomato sauce from a bit of uneaten pizza, then replaced a tiny sliver of cheese before feeding it to the dog. "You're a good guy," he said gruffly, giving Beau an ear scratch.

Hannah caught herself beginning to melt and promptly changed the subject. "Tell me about the names," she urged.

"Oh, yeah," he said as he pulled some folded sheets of paper from his back pocket. "I put marks by the ones we've been able to identify as having lived here or near Eureka Springs."

"How are they giving these names? Filling out a form?" Hannah asked, tucking her hair behind her ear as she bent to study the list.

"Yes. The mailing addresses given in the ship-to section

of the web form don't exist. It took us forever to figure out they were using the sender information as the delivery location. We believe the names are people from the area, but as you can see, the addresses they give are all over the place."

Hannah pointed to one of the lines. "Edna Brownwood?"

"You know her?"

"Knew," Hannah corrected. "She was my third-grade teacher. I think Mrs. Brownwood passed away five or ten years ago though." She traced her finger across the page to the address associated with her name. "Atchison, Kansas?" Hannah looked up at him, baffled. "Mrs. Brownwood lived over on Third Street."

Simon sat forward, lacing his fingers between his knees and bracing his elbows on his thighs. "Exactly. We're trying to deconstruct the information they are using on the website and use it to track down orders as they deliver."

"Are you having any luck?"

"Ask me again in a couple of days."

"You're pulling this information off the website daily?"

"Yes. When we started digging, there were only a few orders placed each day. A few months ago it ticked up to about a dozen or so, but lately we're seeing upward of thirty. Plus, they're shipping to addresses farther and farther away."

"And you need help determining if the names are a cover for whoever is actually placing the order."

"Exactly."

"I can help you," she said with a decisive nod. "Bring me your list tomorrow, and I'll go through it."

Simon gave Beau's head a gentle pat but didn't meet her gaze. "I appreciate your willingness to help, particularly given how we, uh, how this all started."

Hannah smiled, charmed by his awkwardness. "Well, you

did pay me," she said, gesturing to the pizza box. "Beau and I are keeping the leftovers."

He smirked as he smoothed his palms down his pants, then pushed to his feet. "Yeah, well, it is appreciated."

Hannah and Beau stood to walk him out. "Hey, what are old friends for?"

Chapter Ten

The latest dataset Wyatt Dawson sent filled Simon's computer screen, but his thoughts were far, far away.

Well, not far.

He was only six or seven blocks away. When he picked up the pizza to take to Hannah Miller's house, he hadn't envisioned himself sitting down and sharing it with her. In his mind, it had been far more transactional. He'd hand over the pizza, and she'd agree to help him track down the anomalies in their data.

Of course, it wasn't unusual for his brain to fail to connect the dots in a social situation. Agents Dawson and Parker were always giving him a subtle nudge when some sort of nicety was necessary. His old friend from college Max Hughes had always been blunt with Simon about what he considered his shortcomings in the people skills department. Simon was never perturbed by these cues. He knew they were always given with the best of intentions. He wondered if Max was here, if he'd have foreseen the implications of showing up at a woman's door unannounced but bearing food.

Simon sat back, and the uncomfortable desk chair creaked ominously. He stretched his hands high and let his head fall back. He could hear shouts of greeting and the rumble of motorcycles through the ancient single-paned window. He didn't need to look to know the Downshift was doing a brisk business across the parking lot.

Good for Darla Ott, he thought with a grim smile.

He laced his fingers together and leaned from side to side. A door slammed somewhere down the corridor. Every thirty minutes or so he heard the ice machine down the hall run through a cycle. The hum of the air conditioner under the window did little to dampen the noise surrounding him.

Suzee's SleepInn might as well have been built out of cardboard and duct tape.

Simon thought longingly of his apartment back in Little Rock. What he wouldn't give for some black-out blinds and good insulation. In all the years he lived there he didn't think he'd ever heard more than the occasional thump of a heavy object being dropped in the unit above his.

What was even more surprising was the fact the hustle and bustle surrounding Suzee's SleepInn wasn't making him uptight. He was usually sensitive to stimulus, but for some reason he was okay here.

More than okay. Simon felt like he was at the precipice of something big. Like his toes were nudging the starting line and he was poised, waiting for the pistol to go off.

He knew in his gut he was closer than he had been in the days before the team he assembled busted into Hannah's flower shop. He'd felt none of this prickling tingle when he got his counterpart at ATF to sign off on the plan to surprise the owner of the website. He'd been confident in his data and able to lay out a clear, concise pattern of reasoning. The others on their joint task force were equally convinced he was on to something. But he'd been missing a crucial element.

Certainty.

He'd been confident walking into his last task force meeting, but he hadn't felt like this. He was on the right path now. He was certain of it. And he was learning certainty was so much more potent than confidence. Confidence sprung from a belief in oneself. Certainty was founded in fact.

He lowered his arms and stared at his laptop, but rather than the elaborate spreadsheet Wyatt compiled daily, he saw the facts as he'd presented them to his team.

Fact: the orders coming through the website were being monitored regularly.

Fact: whoever had set it up had purposely misused the form fields to make tracing the deliveries even more difficult.

Fact: his team had followed the pattern used in the bogus ship-to information and confirmed Eureka Springs, the location of the shop whose site was being used, as the point of origin.

Simon rose from the chair and began to pace a U-shaped path around the double bed in the center of the room. He always thought better when he could move. His place in Little Rock backed up to a wooded park known for its hiking trails. He did some of his best thinking while stepping over tree roots and kicking aside pinecones. But he could make this work.

He managed four laps back and forth before it came to him. They could place an order through the website. All they had to do was figure out whether the names being used included some kind of code.

With Mitch and Hannah's help, hopefully they'd be able to nail this down quickly. Simon stopped in his path and turned back to the desk. Leaning over his computer, he highlighted the names on the most recent order and copied them. He dropped the list into a blank document, then stepped back, staring at the screen as if willing it to give up its secrets.

They were not alphabetical. Nor could he see any patterns between surnames, first names or even combinations of initials. His gut told him it wasn't the names that were important, but something binding them together.

Frustrated, he turned away from the page and began to pace again.

It was possible they were related in another way, but given the now hundreds of names that had been used on previous orders, it would not be an easy pattern to nail down.

"They're all dead," he murmured to himself.

He moved to the window and stared out into the parking lot. One of the lights in the motel's retro sign flickered. The tint darkening the windows of the Downshift was no competition for the neon beer signs dangling in each rectangular opening. His gaze caught on one advertising an Arkansas microbrewery, but his mind raced with possibilities.

Had they all been members of the same club? Attended the same church? Buried in the same cemetery?

The last one struck him as a possibility. Someone could be collecting names from gravestones. He went back to the computer and typed in a quick note.

Cemetery?

How else did people connect?

Picking up his pen, he twirled it between his fingers. School, of course, he figured. But almost as quickly, he dismissed the thought. If these people were all dead, they'd have left school long ago. He was about to take a turn by the nightstand when the missing piece fell into place.

They could have been classmates.

His heart rate sped up as he pondered the notion. It would

be easy, he reasoned. All someone had to do was pull out some old yearbooks and choose names at random. There could be some still alive, but if one went back far enough...

Simon recalled Hannah saying one of the names belonged to her teacher in primary school who had passed away some years ago.

How could they narrow the pool down? he asked himself. It wasn't like schools published lists of their graduates by year in public records. And who was to say if they even graduated? No, the school thing was a hunch. But maybe Hannah or Mitch could help determine whether it was a good hunch.

Satisfied he'd hit on a couple viable ways their perpetrators might be selecting the names, Simon moved back to the desk and sat down in front of the spreadsheet again. They'd determined the shipping addresses entered in the form were all in the Eureka Springs area, but none of them were streets or numbers on streets that existed.

"They made it look like they were delivering flowers locally," Simon murmured. He tapped the pen rhythmically. "They picked names of locals they knew were deceased to send flowers to other dead people at addresses that don't exist," he said aloud.

Hearing it put that way, Simon couldn't help but admire the forethought that had gone into this enterprise. It was a clever cover game.

He picked up his phone, thinking he might call Hannah and run the theory past her, but an email appeared in his inbox. It was from Emma Parker and the subject line read "Whitman."

Brows raised, he opened the message. The body of the email read "Interesting guy." Simon gave a soft snort of a laugh, then clicked on the file she'd attached.

Several pages of information appeared. The first document was a simple background check, the kind a potential employer might run when bringing in a new hire. The next was not so easily obtained. One of the perks of bringing a talented hacker onto his team, he thought as he read through a list of offenses expunged from Russell Whitman's record.

Most were committed when he was a teenager and sealed. Simon wasn't shocked by anything he read. It was a litany of the usual stuff for a kid with too much of everything—petty theft, vandalism, damage to public property, underage consumption of alcoholic beverages, and the like. Once he was out from under the protection of the juvenile court system, Whitman seemed to wise up.

Or he became more selective about the risks he took.

There'd been a DUI in his early twenties. He'd paid a thousand-dollar fine and was ordered to perform two hundred hours of community service. It appeared he carried out his sentence to the judge's satisfaction. He'd been involved in an altercation with another man and charged with public intoxication and disorderly conduct. When Simon dug a little deeper, he found a pdf of the police report taken from the incident. It sounded like Whitman could have been charged with assault as well, but the other man involved refused to press charges.

He skimmed a couple of articles Emma had pulled from profiles published in regional and trade publications. In both articles, Whitman extolled the virtues of life in the Ozarks, and waxed poetic about his affinity for motorcycles. Both features were accompanied by photos of the man in question. They each used what appeared to be his professional headshot, but the trade publication showed images of Russ poring over blueprints with another man on a job site, and the regional publication had a photo of him astride a large matte-black motorcycle.

Simon was about to click open the next document when something snagged on a memory, and he went back to the photo. An all-black motorcycle. And Whitman was dressed in black leather from head to toe. Simon used the track pad on his laptop to zoom in on various aspects of the man's attire.

The jacket he wore didn't appear to have any emblems or embellishments, but it was clearly high-quality. As were the leather trousers. Simon frowned at the man's feet. The lug-soled boots looked as if they'd never touched pavement. But there, high on the upper part of his left boot, he spotted it. The double *R* logo of the Ridge Riders was engraved into the leather.

"Well, hello," Simon murmured, squinting to get a better look.

Once he was certain he hadn't imagined the logo, he made a note to have Wyatt add the Whitman wrinkle into his investigation of the motorcycle club. He was setting his pen down when a ruckus erupted outside.

Pushing back, he hurried over to the window and saw three men standing with their backs to the motel. Two wore Ridge Riders jackets, the other wore jeans and a black T-shirt. They were leaning in, in a clear attempt to intimidate a fourth man who was facing off with them. He was big and burly and clearly not about to back down from whatever fight the trio had in mind. Simon was reaching for his phone, badge and gun when their raised voices escalated into shouts.

The man in the T-shirt was walking away from the confrontation, his head held high and his swagger unmistakable.

Russ Whitman.

Simon was nearly to the exterior staircase when he heard a motorcycle fire up, its driver revving the engine in agitation. He circled the landing in time to see the low-slung bike Whitman had been riding earlier tear out of the parking lot. The big man shouted something about running home to daddy after him, but the growl of the motor drowned out any bite the insult might have held.

Simon paused at the bottom of the stairs, his service weapon in his hand, and eyeballed the remaining men. A few more words were exchanged, then the big guy turned his back on the two men in the jackets and stomped back toward the entrance to the bar.

The guys left behind stayed planted for a moment, as if they had no idea what to do next. Then, with a shrug, one gestured to a cluster of bikes parked along the side of the building. A minute later, they mounted their rides and took off, heading in the same direction Whitman had gone.

He was about to head back up to his room when the back door of the Downshift swung open, and Darla Ott stepped out into the humid night. She paced back and forth a couple times before pulling her vape from a back pocket and tipping her head back. She hugged herself as she pulled deeply on the cartridge. When she lowered her head, she caught him watching her.

A smirk tilted her full mouth, and she cocked her head. "Evenin'," she called across the cracked asphalt.

Simon was suddenly conscious of his service weapon held tight in his grip. "Hello," he replied.

"I think the floor show is over," she said, nodding to his hand.

"I was, uh…" He paused, searching for the appropriate word. "Concerned."

Her lips curved into a smile, and she gave a slow nod, unwinding her arms. "I get ya. But these guys are mostly bluster. Don't let them worry you," she said as she reached for the door handle.

"I'll, um…" He pointed up to the second floor of the motel with his free hand. "I'll head up."

"Sleep tight," she sang out. He was halfway up the staircase when she said, "I'll call you if I need you… Hannah's friend from college."

His steps slowed as the realization that word of his visit to their town had spread. He kept his head down, lingering in the stairwell until he heard the *ka-thunk* of the metal door closing.

The following morning, Simon stopped at Hot Buns Bakery before heading to the flower shop. He stood patiently in line, but when he got up to the counter, he didn't even have a chance to order. Mia pushed a cup of coffee and a small bakery box at him. "Deliver these for me, will ya?"

"I'm, uh, okay." He opened his wallet and pulled out a twenty. "Can I get a roll too?"

"It's in there," she said, tapping the lid. "Now go before the coffee gets cold."

"How much do I owe you?"

She shot him an incredulous look. "I don't charge my best friend for her morning jolt."

"Yeah, but—"

She huffed, ruffling a strand of hair that escaped her headband. "You're a cop, aren't you? Everyone knows cops don't pay," she said with a smirk.

"This one does," he said, stiffening.

"Simon, go," she said, exasperated. "You're holding up the line."

He relented, taking the cup and box with a murmured, "Thanks," then headed out on his errand.

Hannah was at the front counter when he came in, cordless phone cradled between her shoulder and ear. "One dozen," she said into the phone. With a jerk of her thumb, she indicated he should head for the back. "With baby's breath and greenery in a vase," she said as if repeating the customer's request.

He watched as she scribbled something into her notebook.

"I'll have it ready in about thirty minutes, Mr. Pressler," she promised, then disconnected the call. "Oh, you are my savior," she said as she walked into the back room, her gaze locked on the coffee cup.

"Busy morning?" he asked as he slid the cup in her direction.

She shrugged and shook her head, prying the lid from the cup to blow across the milky brew's surface before taking a cautious sip. "Milton Pressler has his eye on a new lady down at the community center."

"And he's taking her flowers," he concluded. "Nice."

Her lips twitched at the corner. "He is nice," she said with a knowing gleam in her eye. "He's also the biggest player in the over-seventy crowd. Last month, it was an orchid in a pot for Millicent Graves."

"Oh." He pulled a grimace. "She didn't like it?"

"Loved it. But she broke her hip at Seniors' Swing Dancing. She's in rehab, and Milton doesn't have time to let the grass grow under his feet." She paused, pinning him with a somber look as she added, "His words, not mine."

Simon chuckled. "Well. Good for Milton, I guess."

"Millie's better off without him," Hannah pronounced. "Even if he is one of my best customers." She took a bigger slurp of her coffee, then replaced the lid. "Let me grab some stuff from the cooler."

Simon eyed the untouched bakery box as she walked away. "Mia sent over cinnamon buns too," he called after her.

"Go ahead and start without me, but prepare to be ruined for any other cinnamon roll," she called back.

Simon smiled at the boast. "I haven't had a wide sampling of cinnamon rolls, but I am certain I will be impressed."

He opened the box and saw two huge rolls nestled into its cardboard confines. Cream cheese frosting oozed over the sides and into the swirling crevices. His mouth watered at the scent rising from the box. They were warm from the oven. Desperate to get his hands on one but feeling strange about eating without her, he turned in a slow circle, looking for some paper towels or something he could use to wipe his sticky hands.

"There are forks in the drawer by the sink," Hannah said as she emerged with a five-gallon bucket filled with roses, greenery and the little branches with clusters of tiny white flowers often seen in rose bouquets.

He moved over to the drawer she indicated and found several plastic-wrapped packages of utensils accumulated from various take-out establishments. He grabbed two, pleased to note they included napkins, and returned to the workbench as she was setting a clear glass vase on the surface.

"So, I was thinking about the name thing last night," Hannah said as she began snipping the ends of the rose stems.

"Makes two of us," Simon said as he tossed the packets of plasticware down beside the box. "These are warm, you know," he said, hoping to entice her into abandoning the order so he wouldn't feel like a heel for starting without her.

Hannah smiled. "Don't wait on me. This will only take a few minutes."

Simon didn't need to be told again. He tore open one of the packets, extracted the fork and plunged it into the outer layer of a cinnamon roll. "What were you thinking about the names?" he asked as he hacked off a decent hunk of the sticky bun.

"I'm thinking they have to have something in common," she said as she began dropping red roses into the vase.

"I was thinking the same thing too," he said, lifting a napkin to his mouth as he chewed.

"Not sure what it would be," she said with a shrug, starting in on the fronds of greenery.

Dispirited by her admission, Simon finagled another bite of the delicious sweet roll from the box and shoved it into his mouth. He chewed thoughtfully for a moment. He wiped his fingers on the scrap of napkin as he swallowed, then leaned forward to catch her attention.

"Darla Ott knows who I am," he said bluntly.

Hannah looked up at the non sequitur. Lifting a single brow she asked, "Does she, now? Are you famous?"

"Apparently, I am known as Hannah's friend from college," he replied. "Didn't take long for it to get around."

She shook her head in a mockery of dismay but smiled. "It never does." She continued with her snipping and arranging, now adding sprigs of the tiny white flowers between the red and green filling the vase.

"What's that stuff called?" he asked, stabbing his fork into his roll once more.

She paused, then held up the stem. "This?"

"Yeah. I don't think I've ever known," he admitted.

"This is baby's breath. People like it in rose bouquets because it offsets the color and fills in the spaces between the blooms making the bouquet look lush."

He nodded. "I figured it was some kind of filler."

Hannah gave a soft gasp. "Baby's breath is not filler," she shot back. "It's a flower in its own right and used in all sorts of floral applications."

Grasping his fork between his thumb and forefinger he held up his hands in surrender. "I meant no offense."

"I'm not sure baby's breath would accept your apology," she answered with a sniff.

"I know nothing about flowers," he admitted.

"Clearly."

"I know I've always seen it mixed in with roses."

"And yet you know the rose," she announced with a dramatic sigh. "So many flowers in the world, but most men never look beyond the rose."

Simon shook his head, knowing he'd never win this battle, so he plunged his fork back into his breakfast. "Apparently Milton did at least once."

Hannah barked a laugh. "Touché."

She added a few more stems of the baby's breath, then stepped back to survey her work. "So, what did you and Darla get to chatting about?"

Simon paused with a hunk of cinnamon roll halfway to his mouth. He wasn't entirely certain, but he thought he picked up a sharp edge in her question. "We didn't talk," he said gruffly. "I overheard a confrontation in the parking lot of the Downshift last night and went out to see if I should intervene."

Her head snapped up and her eyes met his. "The answer to that question is no," she said, as if he had suggested something preposterous.

It was Simon's turn to pin her with an unrepentant stare. "I am a police officer," he reminded her. "If I hear trouble brewing, it's not only wise for me to attempt to diffuse it, but also my duty."

A pale pink flush crept into her cheeks, but she didn't look away. "I only meant the people who patronize the Downshift aren't always respectful of the law."

Simon placed his half-eaten bite back into the box. "I am aware of the dangers of my job," he stated quietly.

"I thought your job was investigating internet crimes," she retorted.

Simon noted her flush deepening even as she spoke. She knew she insulted him, but she was too darn stubborn to walk it back. But rather than offend him, her mulishness only made her more intriguing.

"I attended and graduated from the same training academy every other state police officer attends. I excelled there," he added. "Many of us have specialties within the law enforcement field. Mine happens to be cybercrime, but it doesn't mean I'm unable to handle myself in other situations."

Hannah blew out a breath, pushing the arrangement of vibrant red roses to the side. She was clearly agitated as she snatched up the other set of plastic-wrapped utensils. Her lips thinned into a line as she tore the cellophane, spilling the fork and knife onto the work surface.

He grimaced when she pierced the pristine cinnamon roll with the tines in a vicious thrust. With a brutal twist of the fork, she freed a healthy piece of gooey cinnamon-and-icing-drenched pastry and shoved it into her mouth.

"Sorry," she mumbled through stuffed cheeks.

Simon couldn't help but chuckle as he picked up the bite he'd abandoned and popped it into his own mouth. "It's all right," he replied in the same manner. "I didn't talk with her," he said after gulping the bite down. "Whatever was happening had broken up by the time I got down there. She saw me as I was turning to go back up to my room and called me 'Hannah's friend from college.'"

"At least we know the story is sticking."

"I guess we should be thankful for small favors."

"What were you thinking about the names?" she asked.

"I had a couple of ideas. It could be someone simply walking through the cemetery pulling names from gravestones," he hazarded.

Hannah nodded as she chewed, then wrinkled her nose as she shook her head in dismissal. "Sounds like something out of a TV detective show."

Simon snorted. "You'd be shocked by how many people get their ideas from TV and movies," he said. "We're usually not talking about criminal masterminds."

"But these ones kind of are, aren't they?" she prodded. "I mean, they've been clever."

Simon conceded the point with a nod. "My other thought was classmates," he told her.

She paused with a chunk of roll stuck to the end of her fork, then gestured from him to her. "You mean like us?"

"I was thinking people who went to school together for real. Somebody could be pulling names from old yearbooks," he said, wondering how this theory would strike her.

Hannah popped the morsel into her mouth and chewed slowly. It was all Simon could do not to stare. At last, she gave a slow nod, pointing the tip of her fork at him. "Sounds right," she said, speaking slowly. "Some of the people on the list you showed me would have been contemporaries."

"I have a new list today," he informed her.

At that, she tossed her fork into the lid of the box, reached in and picked up the remainder of her cinnamon bun. "If that's the case, we'd better get a move on checking them out." Then she saluted him with the sticky mess and proceeded to take a huge bite out of it, smearing icing and cinnamon onto her cheeks in the process.

He found himself staring at her mouth, mesmerized by the gusto with which she chewed. "I'm not sure how—"

She waved his hesitance away. "I am. I know who to ask."

Twenty minutes later, an older gentleman wearing salmon-colored golf pants and a turquoise polo shirt pushed through the door, and he watched as Hannah turned on the charm for her best customer. "Hey, Milton. How'd you like to help me and my friend Simon out with a bit of a mystery?"

Chapter Eleven

The following morning, Hannah was putting together boutonnieres for Lacy Callahan's wedding when Mia pushed through the door. Her friend's usually sunny disposition was leaning more toward overcast. But years of experience had taught her not to ask. Mia's moods were like storm fronts. Most of the time they blew through quickly and her natural positivity reappeared. Occasionally, they settled in and the gloom held on for days.

She made up for the lack of light in her friend's eyes by fixing a bright smile on her own face. "There is the woman I worship," she called out.

Mia paused at the entrance to the workroom. "Where's your sidekick?"

"Huh?"

"Your friend Simon from college?" Mia prompted, a snarky edge in her voice. "He didn't come in this morning."

"He, uh, he had some work," Hannah replied.

As far as she knew, it was the truth. After speaking with Milton about the names he was researching, both Simon and Hannah were convinced they were on to something with the classmates angle. He'd taken off not long after the older man left to go a-courting—as he put it—promising to call when he knew more.

She hadn't heard from him since.

And for some reason, not hearing from him felt strange. As if all it took to work his way into her life was a botched raid, a shared pizza and a mutual appreciation for Mia's cinnamon rolls. Hannah scowled as she lifted the lid on the box Mia placed on the counter. Two warm-from-the-oven buns were nestled so tightly into its confines, the frosting had run together, making them look conjoined.

She closed the lid and pushed the box aside. "I'll have mine after I finish these."

Mia scowled as she picked up one of the finished boutonnieres. "What are these for?"

Hannah said only, "Lacy Callahan," by way of explanation.

Mia nodded her understanding, then twirled the tiny arrangement between her fingers. It was a snow-white rose, but rather than the usual sprig of greenery and wrap, Lacy—a scratch golfer—had insisted they surround the stem with colorful golf tees instead.

"How are they supposed to pin these on?" she asked.

Hannah shrugged. "Through the ribbon, I guess. I'm including the long pins, but I wouldn't be surprised if Lacy used a divot tool to poke holes in their jackets."

Mia snorted out a laugh, and Hannah was relieved to catch a glimpse of her friend's smile. She picked up the coffee cup and took a small sip. "What's up, my Mia? You look sad."

When Mia's dark eyes met hers, Hannah could see her friend had moved beyond sad straight to troubled. "I'm worried about Micah."

Hannah resisted the urge to sigh. She loved Micah as if

he were her own brother, but the boy attracted trouble like static electricity. "What's happened?"

Mia shook her head. "Nothing's happened. He's acting different, is all. It's been a weird couple of days since he started working for Whitman."

"Okay," Hannah said slowly. Mentally, she ran through different possibilities for Micah's change in temperament. "Different how?"

Mia shrugged. "Belligerent," she said with a twist of a smile. "But that's not anything new." Her friend heaved a heavy sigh. "Yesterday when he came home, he was so mean to Mama, and you know how she thinks the sun rises and sets on him. Most days he's the only person she recognizes," she said, her voice choking with tears.

Hannah scooted around the edge of the workbench and wrapped her friend up in a tight hug. "I'm sorry," she murmured into Mia's dark hair. "I know you're carrying so much. I wish he'd grow up and help you bear the load a little bit."

Mia pulled away, wiping her eyes with the backs of her hands. "You and me both," she said in a strangled voice. "And I've tried to reason with him. I've tried to make him understand I can't handle the stress of worrying about him. I already spend all my time worrying about Mama and the business and keeping the bills paid and a roof over our heads."

Hannah rubbed her friend's upper arms briskly. "I know you do. And you know I'd do anything to help you."

"Oh, I know," Mia replied softly. "I wish my brother felt the same way."

"Well," Hannah said, searching for a silver lining at the edges of this dark cloud. "Maybe working this job for Whitman will pay him enough that he can help contribute to some of those household expenses."

"Oh, I've mentioned it," Mia said with a bitter little laugh. "The first time I did, he told me he was planning on saving up to move out. Said he was too old to be living with his mama and his bossy big sister."

The snide edge to Mia's tone was as foreign to Hannah's ears as a different language. But before she could talk, her friend plowed ahead.

"Last night, when I asked him what he's been doing running around town at all hours of the day and night for Russ Whitman, he tells me he's doing it because it's his job and he's trying to help out."

"What do you think he's been up to?" Hannah asked warily.

"I think he's been hanging out at job sites all day acting like he's learning whatever skills, then going to the Downshift with all those degenerates after he gets off work. He keeps trying to weasel his way in with the Ridge Riders, and it makes me sick to my stomach even thinking about it."

"The Ridge Riders?" Hannah repeated. "Because of your dad, do you think?"

Matthew Jones had been one of the charter members of the Arkansas chapter of the Ridge Riders. Back in the day, the club was civic-minded—sponsoring highway clean-up projects and collecting clothing, household goods and toys for families in need. But as the younger members of the group came into leadership positions, the Riders became more of a social club than a philanthropic group.

"Maybe." Mia looked on the brink of tears, but simply shrugged. "He's fixing up Daddy's old Honda," she said with a sniff. "And it's not like I can tell him not to. He's got as much right to the bike as I do, and heaven knows I'm not going to be riding it. But I don't like him hanging out with those guys." She wrinkled her nose in distaste. "I know the Riders used to do a lot of work around the community and raise a lot of money for the kids and all," she said, as if fending off an argument. "But you and I also know things have changed. These days, they get into as much mischief as they do good deeds."

"I get you," Hannah assured her.

"And I don't know if anyone has been by here to talk to you, but Mrs. Hopkins told me Tyler Fresnel came into her shop the other day to pick up his grandmother's yarn order, and he and some other guy from the Ridge Riders were talking about how folks were working with the police on setting up a neighborhood watch."

"Are they?" Hannah asked, interest piqued.

"I don't know, but these guys scared poor Mrs. Hopkins. Well, not Tyler, but the other guy. She said he kept staring at her and talking about how people around here don't need to go blabbing to the police when the Riders are around."

"What does that mean? Were they taking care of Grace Templeton?"

"Poor Mrs. T," Mia murmured. "I can't stop thinking about how scared she must have been."

"I know. Me too," Hannah agreed.

"So, yeah, the thing with Micah and the Riders makes me nervous."

"Totally understand."

Mia heaved a heavy sigh. "He says it's me trying to be over controlling as usual," she said with a dismissive wave of her hand. "And I know he's twenty-two, and he's going to do the things twenty-two-year-old guys do," she continued.

"But he took the pretty sky-blue gas tank Daddy had on the bike and painted it this ugly flat black, and I can't help thinking his color choices are reflecting what he's feeling inside."

Hannah's brows shot up. "What he's feeling inside?" she repeated. Mia was not the type for fanciful notions. Or even feelings. She had her hands too full of real life to deal with problems she couldn't wrap them around. "Do you think he's depressed?"

Mia gave an indelicate snort. "Depressed? No. I think he thinks he's a tough guy, and I got news for him. I can still put a whoopin' on him."

Hannah chuckled. Once upon a time it had been true. She and Mia had bossed poor Micah around as if he'd been put on this earth to do their bidding. But Mia refused to acknowledge the growth spurt her baby brother went through in high school. He was nearly a foot taller and fifty or sixty pounds heavier than her petite friend.

"I'm not sure threats are going to get you anywhere with him right now," Hannah said with an amused smile. She nodded to the pastry box. "You're so sweet with everyone else. Have you tried talking nice to him?"

Mia fixed her with a dead-eyed stare. "I don't have to talk nice to him. He's my sibling."

Hannah raised both hands in surrender. "I'll have to take your word," she said dryly. Then, after a moment's thought she asked, "Flat black? Like a matte finish?"

Mia nodded, pulling a face. "He says it's all the thing now. You know how you see cars with the blacked-out emblems where they used to be chrome? I think it has something to do with video games," she said dismissively.

"Huh."

Hannah closed her eyes as she sipped from her cup again,

trying to envision the rider who'd been cruising past her house the other night. Could it have been Micah? Wouldn't she have recognized him? She turned away, moving to the drawer where she kept leftover silverware packets, afraid Mia might be able to read her thoughts.

"Though your friend Simon from college…" Mia began, then let the sentence dangle in the air between them.

Relieved at the change of subject, Hannah grabbed one of the plastic-wrapped packages and turned back to the workbench. "Yes?" she asked, drawing the word out.

"Tell me about him," Mia prompted, tipping her chin up in challenge.

Hannah freed the fork and knife from their packaging and began slicing off hunks of gooey cinnamon roll. "What do you want to know?"

"Is he single?" Mia asked without missing a beat.

It wasn't until that moment Hannah realized she had absolutely no clue whether anyone was waiting at home for Special Agent Simon Taylor. She got the impression he was single, but you never knew. Still, for the sake of their cover story, she picked the option she preferred.

"Yes."

"And he chose to come to visit now because…" Mia made a circular motion with her hand, encouraging Hannah to fill in the blanks.

But Hannah didn't have a reason she could give her friend would buy. "He came here because he's working on a case."

"A case that involves him and a bunch of guys in windbreakers storming into your shop?"

When Hannah hesitated, Mia turned and pointed to the bench on the opposite side of the street. A reed-thin older man dressed in baggy cotton shorts and a white T-shirt with a pocket on the front sat watching as people moved from store to store.

"You know Vern Lindquist sits there all day every day. We all saw those guys come in here the other day, and Vern said it looked like they were coming in to arrest you. Now why would your good friend Simon from school raid your shop?" Mia asked, fixing her with a penetrating gaze.

The only response Hannah could muster was a whispered, "Vern." She closed her eyes amid the mortification and tried to focus on drawing even breaths.

"You don't need to worry about Vern. I already told them he was mistaken. You know he doesn't see as well as he used to," Mia said, planting a hand on her hip. "But he wasn't the only one and it's hard to miss the initials on those jackets. People are wonderin' what you're mixed up in, Hannah."

"I swear I haven't done anything wrong," Hannah assured her.

Mia burst out laughing. "You? Oh, honey, I know you haven't done anything wrong," she said through her chortles. "I want to know how they got the wrong shop." She leaned in conspiratorially. "You know if I suspected anyone, it's Laurel Mercer," she confided in a low tone.

"Laurel Mercer?" Hannah asked, picturing the trim, stylish woman who moved to Eureka Springs a few years before. She opened a designer women's wear shop called Taupe two doors down from Flora's Florals and seemed perfectly friendly whenever Hannah spoke with her. "Why?"

"Because no one in this town wears that much beige," Mia said, as if the answer should have been obvious.

Hannah laughed. "Remember when the sign first went up, Vern thought it was going to be a wig shop," she recalled.

"Toupee!" they cried at the same time, then broke into gales of laughter.

Hannah was wiping a tear from the corner of her eye when the front door swung open and Simon Taylor strode in, looking like a man on a mission. But when he spotted Mia, he drew up short.

Hoping to cover the moment of awkwardness, she said, "Hello, friend-from-college Simon. Friend-from-childhood Mia brought us some hot buns."

"Good morning," Simon said, inclining his head with the greeting. "I didn't mean to interrupt."

"You're fine," Hannah assured him. "Grab a fork and dig in while I get these boutonnieres boxed up."

Simon did as he was instructed, and by the time he returned to the workbench, he wore his usual placidly interested expression. Hannah's hand trembled slightly as she nestled one of the tiny arrangements in the bed of tissue paper she'd used as a cushion in the long white florist's box. When had she started reading Simon Taylor's expressions? she wondered.

"What's happening?" he asked as he freed his fork from the package. But before either she or Mia could answer, his gaze snagged on the roses surrounded by golf tees. "What are those for?"

"A wedding," Hannah answered.

"I take it he's big into golf?"

Mia gave a scoffing laugh, but Hannah pinned him with a stare. "He's marrying a woman who plays on the LPGA tour."

"Oh." His ears reddened, and he winced as he met her eyes. "Boy, I'm blowing it on assumptions this week, aren't I?"

"Your instincts may be a little off," she said, softening the criticism with a wan smile. She nodded to the box. "Maybe your blood sugar is low."

Mia laughed, drumming her hands on the work surface before turning away. "I'd better get back. Enjoy the sugar rush, Friend-Simon-From-College." She blew a kiss at Hannah, then started for the door. "Thanks for the whine."

"Anytime," Hannah called, watching as her friend bustled out onto the sidewalk.

She turned back to Simon and found him staring at her with a puckered brow. "I thought you didn't drink."

"I don't," she confirmed, frowning in confusion.

"She said you had wine," he said, pointing toward the door with his fork.

Realization dawned and she laughed. "Oh. No, not wine," she told him. "Whine with an *h*."

"Oh." He nodded, turning his attention to the cinnamon roll. "Everything okay?" he asked when she resumed packing up the flowers.

Hannah paused, weighing whether she should say anything to Simon about Mia's concerns regarding Micah.

"Do you know anything about a motorcycle club called the Ridge Riders?"

The question startled her so much, she jumped. Whipping her head up, she pierced him with a hard stare. "What?"

Simon popped a bite of roll into his mouth and chewed, humming his appreciation before swallowing it. "The Ridge Riders. They are a motorcycle club with chapters in various states. I've seen some of their members pulling in over at the Downshift."

Hannah exhaled slowly, still thinking about Micah and

his propensity for stumbling into trouble. "Yeah, I know who they are. Why are you asking about them?"

"I'm wondering if Russ Whitman is a member," he said, stabbing his fork into the roll again.

"Russ?" The name popped out of her mouth before she could stop it.

Simon paused in his dissection of his breakfast and looked over at her. Her cheeks burned. She knew she was turning bright red but ignored the heat.

"I—I don't know," she stammered. "If he is, he isn't about to go flaunting it," she assured him. "His parents are still very much in control of the company business, and no matter what Russ does to expand it, he's not about to do anything that would go against his parents' wishes."

Simon nodded as he lined up his next bite. "Like dating Darla Ott."

"Exactly. Another thing that would not go over well with his folks."

"But he's a grown man," Simon said almost conversationally. "It must chafe. I mean, technically, he could do anything he wants, and his parents can't stop him."

"True, but you've never met Russell Sr. He's a heavy-handed man."

Simon looked at her with interest. "Heavy-handed as in abusive?"

She shook her head. "I have no knowledge of any physical abuse. I meant overbearing. Relentlessly so. Most people bend over backward to make sure they don't get on his bad side."

"And you think he'd hold his son to the same standard? Sounds like they let him run wild as a kid," Simon commented.

"I know he would. We've all seen it. Even Mrs. Whitman

rarely goes against his wishes, and she's the one who brought the money to the marriage."

"I thought Senior started a construction company?" Simon asked.

Hannah fitted the lid onto the florist box, then gave it a little tap for emphasis. "He did. With the money from his wife's family." She gave him a tired smile. "There are some men who simply can't abide the notion of the world thinking they didn't pull themselves up by their own bootstraps. Russell Whitman Sr. is one of those men."

She picked up the box and carried it toward the cooler. He must have been waiting to pull the conversation back because the moment she stepped out he pounced.

"So, you don't know if Russ Whitman is somehow affiliated with the Ridge Riders, but it's possible," he persisted.

Hannah began to clear debris from the work surface. "Sure, anything is possible. But what makes you think he is? Other than the fact he hangs out at the Downshift," she added.

Simon took his phone out of his pocket and pulled up his photos. Hannah tipped her head to the side as she studied a posed photograph of Russ Whitman. "Where did you get this from?"

"It was accompanying a feature in one of the local magazines."

"This proves nothing. Everyone knows Russ likes to ride motorcycles. He has a few of them and is always zipping around town. He says it's easier to get from job site to job site on a bike."

Simon pressed a blunt finger to the phone screen. "Look at his boots," he said as he spread his fingers apart to zoom in on the man's ankle. "See there? Engraved into the leather? Looks like the Ridge Riders logo."

Hannah squinted, then pursed her lips as she spotted the impression he described. "Yeah, possibly," she conceded.

He zoomed out and refocused on the motorcycle. "Does this look like the bike someone was riding past your house the other night?"

Hannah's breath caught in her throat. She pressed her hand to her chest and used the other to tuck her hair behind her ear as she leaned in to take a closer look at the photo. "It's all blacked out," she murmured.

"Very on trend," Simon said blandly. "We see a lot of vehicles with blacked-out trim these days."

Hannah met his eyes directly. "I was so scared," she began, then cut herself off before she went too far.

Misunderstanding, Simon pulled the phone away and stepped closer to her. "I know you were," he answered gruffly. "I didn't mean to upset you. I was—"

She shook her head hard. "I don't mean I was scared then," she interrupted. "I mean I was," she adjusted. "I was scared because Mia told me something that had me wondering about her brother, Micah."

Simon leaned back on his heels, his eyebrows shooting high. "Micah? Why were you worried about Micah?"

"Okay, I'm not sure if I'm supposed to say anything about this, and I'm probably breaking about fifty different friend codes here," she said in the rush.

"If it has anything you think might be pertinent to the case, then I need you to tell me," he insisted.

"I don't know if it's pertinent to your case. I also don't know why you're asking me about the Ridge Riders. All I know is apparently people are riding around on blacked-out motorcycles these days." She pinned him with a hard stare, hoping he would be able to read between the lines.

After an excruciating minute, his dark eyes widened before narrowing in consternation. "Does Micah Jones ride a matte-black bike?"

"I've heard he's refurbishing his father's old motorcycle," she informed him stiffly. "Mia mentioned something about a paint job, but I don't know if the bike is even running."

Simon nodded slowly. "Okay, then. Let's try to focus on what you saw that night. You said it was a big bike," he prompted. "Do you know if the bike Micah Jones is refurbishing is as big as this one?" he said, holding up the photo of Russ Whitman astride his motorcycle.

Hannah took in Russ's black-on-black ensemble, then shifted her gaze to the powerful machine between his legs. Relief flooded her as she realized Mr. Jones's old motorcycle was nothing more than a plain old road bike. And it would be older than Micah. Russ's cycle was large and menacing.

She shook her head. "Micah's bike would be a twenty-year-old Honda." She shrugged. "I have no idea how big those were in comparison, but whoever was cruising past my house the other night was riding something more along the lines of whatever this is," she said, gesturing to his phone.

"Do you think you would have recognized Russ Whitman if he'd been the rider the other night?" Simon asked.

Hannah wanted to cast her doubts in Russ's direction rather than Micah's, but when she closed her eyes and visualized the rider passing so slowly under the streetlight, she knew in her gut it was not Russ.

"No, it wasn't Russ. Whoever was riding past my house was not as big as Russ," she said, pointing to Whitman's photo.

"Not as tall? As muscular?" he pressed.

"Both. Either," she said with a shrug. Then something else occurred to her. "Hey, the rider wore a helmet."

Simon frowned. "Yes."

"Russ never wears a helmet when he rides," Hannah informed him.

"Helmets are not required by law."

Hannah gave a sharp bitter laugh. "I know. But most serious riders wear them, right?"

"I suppose," he conceded. "Not wearing one is reckless," Simon said stiffly.

"Russ is the type of guy who likes to see everything, but more than that he wants to be seen. Even if he put a helmet on, it sure wouldn't have the full visor," she said dismissively.

Simon turned the phone back to himself and inspected the photo carefully before setting it on the workbench. "Were you worried about Micah Jones keeping an eye on your house?"

Hannah took a half step back. "Yes and no," she answered at last. "Yes, because I know Micah wants to get in with the Ridge Riders," she said slowly, lifting her gaze to meet his.

"He does?"

She grimaced as she shrugged. "He's a kid who lost his father young and is now losing his mother to early-onset dementia. He's looking for someone to follow."

"And he went to work for Russ Whitman," Simon concluded grimly.

"Yes, but that doesn't mean anything. And the job at Whitman Development can only be a good thing. He can learn some skills he could take with him anywhere. Micah has been drifting. Maybe a steady job will give him some direction."

Whatever hope she had of her wishes coming true dissipated when Simon's lips thinned into a tight line. He knew something. He knew something about Micah he wasn't telling her.

A surge of frustration rose inside of her. "What?" she snapped. "What aren't you telling me?"

"It isn't that I'm not telling you something," he began slowly. "I'm not sure what I saw means anything."

"What did you see?"

"I saw Micah Jones taking Darla Ott's car to be washed and filled," he told her. "I've seen him around town during the day. I don't think he's working at a Whitman construction site. I think he may be working as Russell Whitman's... As his...assistant."

"Errand boy," Hannah corrected.

"I'm not certain Whitman—"

Hannah held up a hand to stop him, recalling what Mia said about Micah coming home at all hours. "I don't think you're wrong," she informed Simon. "I was only correcting your terminology."

"You said the rider was smaller than Russ. How would it be compared to Micah?"

Hannah closed her eyes as a lance of pain burst through her stomach. "Oh, God." She curled her lips in and bit down, trying to hold back the hot rush of tears crawling up her throat. Lowering her head, she shook it. "But the bike."

"It's possible Whitman let him ride one of his bikes," Simon pointed out.

"But why?"

"As a reward, maybe? Or a bribe?" Simon hazarded. "Or maybe he told Micah someone needed to keep an eye on your place for your safety," he said slowly, as if warming to the idea. "It's possible Whitman asked Micah to watch out for you because people were poking around your business and your house," he said grimly. "Maybe Whitman convinced your best friend's brother you were in danger, then he offered the use of one of his bikes as an enticement."

Hannah lifted a hand to her mouth, her eyes flooding with horrified tears as his theory struck home. She could see it all. Micah would want to protect her. Russ would know exactly what buttons to push. But why was Russ so worried about what went on at her house?

"Do you think Micah was the one using my cellar?" she whispered.

"He may know who was," Simon said as he tore a piece of paper towel from the roll by the sink. He carefully folded it into a neat square, then used it to staunch the flow of her tears. "We're putting a new hasp and padlock on those doors today. No one will be able to get in there without you knowing," he assured her.

"But how did I not know before?" she demanded, her voice cracking.

"They were probably in and out of there while you were at work," he reasoned. "I doubt they would have risked going in there if you were at home. They know you have a dog, and they wouldn't have wanted him to alert you."

A memory of Mr. Blaine, her next-door neighbor, complaining about the noise Beauregard made during the day hit her like a club to the head.

"Oh, God. You're right. One of the neighbors told me Beau was barking a lot, but I thought he was being a grumpy old man."

"I confirmed the theory about the names. They all graduated in 1954," Simon told her solemnly.

"Most of them would be about ninety now," Hannah said softly.

"If they're still alive." He pulled a folded sheet of paper from his pocket and flattened it on the work surface. "I went by the school district office this morning, and they were able to pull some records for me."

Hannah stared down at the names listed for each graduating class from the school's opening in 1951 through 1962. As she scanned the page, familiar surnames started to jump out at her. She touched the tip of one finger to a checkmark beside Alvin Ardell's name. "What are these?"

"Those are the ones I can confirm they have already used."

Her eyes widened as she took in the number of checked-off names. "So many."

"Too many," he agreed. "We're getting close."

"How can I help?" she asked, looking him square in the eye.

"I'm going to get an updated list tonight. My team is already tracking a few deliveries, so I'll get updates on those, but I was thinking…"

"Yes?" she asked encouragingly.

His expression brightened, his eyes aglow with the thrill of the hunt. "How do you feel about helping me set a trap?"

Chapter Twelve

Simon sat back, giving Hannah the space she needed to pore over the list he had Wyatt send the night before. Every time she moved her head, her hair slipped out from behind her ear. He had to curl his fingers into his palm to resist reaching out to touch it. Thankfully, Hannah had zero patience for the wayward locks. She swept the strands back before he could surrender to the impulse.

"There's a Matthias Kinnan on here," she murmured to herself. "I wonder if he's any relation to Jacob Kinnan."

Though he knew his input wasn't necessary, Simon couldn't help asking, "Jacob Kinnan? Friend of yours?"

She gave a huff of a laugh. "Hardly. But he was Russ Whitman's best friend in high school."

"Are they still good friends?"

Hannah looked up then, wrinkling her nose in concentration. "I suppose in a way," she said at last.

"In what way?"

"I wouldn't say Jacob's as much a friend as he is a toady."

"A toady? Whitman hired Micah to be his errand boy when he already has a toady on staff?"

She gave him a lopsided smile. "Do you suppose they have the same job description?"

He raised his eyebrows in challenge. "You tell me."

She paused to give the question thought. "I would put Jacob more in the category of First Lieutenant," she said after a moment's thought. "Russ likes to maintain a certain image in the community. Jacob helps him keep his hands clean by doing Russ's dirty work."

Simon nodded his understanding. "Ah, more muscle than toady," he concluded.

She pointed at him, then turned her attention back to the list. "Exactly."

"Do you recognize the surnames of any of the others on the list?" he asked, curious.

She looked up again. "Well, yeah, quite a few. The town isn't big," she added, as if this conclusion should have been obvious to him.

"Would you be able to tell if any of the other names on the list have connections to Whitman?"

She studied him for a moment, her bottom lip caught between her teeth. Simon had to break eye contact first. All Simon could think about was her poor abused lip. He needed to be thinking about breaking this case open.

"You think there's a connection between Russ Whitman, the Ridge Riders and the names they're using on the orders?"

He shrugged. "I realize it can't be a one-to-one correlation given the number of orders," he began. "But I have to admit I wouldn't mind finding something to connect them."

She studied him for a moment. "Because you don't like Russ?"

Simon opened his mouth to answer but then clamped it shut again. "It's not a matter of whether I like the man or not," he said, choosing his words carefully. "I suspect him."

"Why?"

"Too many coincidences. You say you don't have any sort of social relationship with him, and yet he's paid an awful lot of attention to you lately."

Hannah sat back in her chair and crossed her arms over her chest. "And that strikes you as odd?"

It was his turn to laugh. "It struck you as odd," he reminded her. "You're the one who told me he doesn't usually pay attention to women like you. And yet, for the last few days he's certainly been making his presence known."

Hannah didn't answer right away. Instead, she picked up the pen she'd been using to mark off names that had already been used and tapped it against the paper. "I'm sure there are connections," she said at last. "But we need somebody who's more familiar with the Riders to be able to tell us who may be related to current members of the club. I can name a few offhand because I see them wearing gear around town, but I don't frequent places like the Downshift and I don't ride myself, so I am not a good resource."

"Do you know someone who would be?" he probed. "Someone we could trust?"

Hannah ducked her head, then licked her lips before answering. "Someone I would trust with my life," she said quietly.

When her gaze met his he knew exactly who she meant. "Mia?"

She nodded slowly. "Her dad was one of the founding members of the local chapter. Most of the older guys have drifted away from the club, but a few still go by the house to check on her mom and help her out with stuff." She tapped the pen nervously. "Things have changed with the club, and a lot of the older guys don't like it."

"Do you think she'd be willing to help?"

Hannah picked up her phone. "We can ask. The bakery closes at two, and she usually does prep for the next day right after she locks the door."

He thought she was about to call her, but she hesitated, her thumb hovering millimeters over the screen.

"I hate to pile anything else on her," she said quietly. "She has enough to worry about with her mom and Micah."

"What's the issue with her mom?"

Hannah put the phone down again. "Early-onset dementia," she said grimly. "Mia has a woman who comes to stay with her mom while she's at work, but Micah isn't much help, and she's trying to keep the bakery going…"

"Maybe she'd let us come bounce some things off her as she preps? We can leave Micah out of the conversation if you think it'll help. Focus on the members of the Ridge Riders she knows and any connections we can find to the names we know have been used."

She tapped the screen with her fingernail as she considered his suggestion. Then, to his relief, she picked up the phone and made the call.

At exactly 2:15 p.m., Mia opened the back door of the bakery to let them in. "Hey," she said as they filed past her. "I hope you don't think you can hang out here and not work."

Simon glanced back over his shoulder. "I'm willing to help, but I can't guarantee good results."

"I can," Mia assured him. "Step into my laboratory."

She pronounced the word dramatically, like they used to do in old horror movies. Simon couldn't help but smile as he followed the two women into the large kitchen. The walls were painted a stark white. The work surfaces and appliances gleamed. There was an island in the center that appeared to be topped with marble. The entire room was spotlessly clean and ruthlessly organized. It was the antithesis of the chaotic vibrancy he'd experienced in the front of the store.

"This is where the magic happens."

Simon eyed the two industrial mixers churning away on the other side of the room. They were far from new but seemed to be journeying away without a hitch. He turned in a slow circle, taking it all in.

"Impressive," he said when he met Mia's steady gaze.

"It is, isn't it?" she said with an impish smile. "I dreamed of having a place like this since I was a little girl."

Simon nodded. "Well done." He gave her a lopsided smile. "I don't have to tell you I'm halfway to being an addict."

She tipped her head to the side. "Only halfway?" She gave him a stern frown. "Remind me to give you one of my pecan sticky buns tomorrow morning. They'll tip you right over the edge."

When he turned to look at Hannah, she simply shrugged. "Only the strong survive. I hope you have a good workout routine."

Mia spun away from them to pull a few plastic food service containers down from a shelf. "You two go on flirting. I'm going to start getting this next batch ready to roll."

"We're not flirting," Hannah said with an exasperated huff.

"You should be," Mia shot back. "Now, tell me what brings you to my humble establishment?"

Simon and Hannah exchanged a look, and then she gave him the nod to proceed. "I assume you know I work for the Arkansas State Police," he began.

"The windbreaker the first day tipped it off," she responded.

"Then you've probably figured out it's not a coincidence I'm visiting Eureka Springs," he concluded.

Mia rolled her eyes as she pulled down an enormous bottle of vanilla and carried it to the workstation. "Given this is the first I've ever heard of a friend from college named Simon, I figured it wasn't purely a social call." She set the jug aside and turned to look at him, her hand planted on her hip. "You guys weren't exactly subtle busting in on poor Hannah here," she reminded him.

"I realize," he admitted.

"Then why don't you give me the skinny on what you're really doing here, and why y'all need my help," she said, casting a sidelong glance at Hannah.

"I set up a website for my grandmother a few years ago," Hannah informed her. "I wanted her to start taking orders online, but she was never interested. She liked doing things the way she did them," she said, her mouth twisted into a sad smile. "I got it set up and built a shell of a website with an order form I downloaded from the site builder, but we never went any further with it."

Mia plucked a large silicone spatula from a pottery jar on the work surface and tapped its handle against the counter a couple of times. "I seem to remember you working on a website. You should have known Flora Fontaine wasn't going to have anything to do with your internet folderol," she said with a laugh.

"Yeah, I should have known," Hannah conceded. "I forgot about the site, and it's just been…out there. I must have set the domain up to renew on the company credit card and never noticed the charges."

Mia sniffed. "Sounds about right."

"Anyway," Hannah said, a tinge of impatience entering her tone. "Apparently the site has been hacked, and someone's been using it for another type of business."

She caught Mia's full attention. "What kind of business?" she asked warily.

Hannah glanced at him as if handing over the baton. "Bootlegging," Simon replied.

He watched her reaction carefully but didn't offer anything more. Her puzzled frown spoke volumes. "Bootlegging? Like moonshine?"

Taking a deep breath, he forged ahead. "Yes." He pulled the papers he and Hannah had been going over and placed them on the work surface. "We believe there's a growing bootlegging business running whiskey out of Eureka Springs using the Flora's Florals website as its online portal."

Mia's eyes widened. She pointed the business end of the utensil at Hannah. "Is he trying to tell me someone is using the website you built for your gran as some kind of Moonshine-Depot-dot-com?"

Hannah nodded. "Looks like it."

"We didn't know if Ms. Miller was involved," Simon said, trying to keep his recitation as factual as possible. When Mia began to sputter, he held up a hand to stop her. "It quickly became apparent she is not."

"Of course she isn't," Mia snapped.

"He had no way of knowing whether I was or not," Hannah reminded her friend.

Her quick defense of his frankly indefensible raid on her business shot a warm rush of pleasure rippling through him. "We quickly understood we were off base with our assessment," he continued.

"Way off base," Mia commented.

"Anyway," Hannah interjected. "We've figured out they are using the names of former residents as pseudonyms for the people buying the booze. Now we're trying to figure out if maybe some of those people had ties to folks still living here in town."

Mia blinked, absorbing the information coming at her. "All right. Well, I suppose it would make sense some would," she ventured. "But you wouldn't need my help figuring as much out. You know as many people around town as I do."

Simon was about to speak up to clarify when Hannah reached over and grasped his forearm. He was still staring down at her delicate fingers wrapped tightly around his wrist when she spoke.

"More specifically, we're wondering if those families might have ties to the Ridge Riders," she said, gentling her tone ever so slightly.

"The Ridge Riders?" Mia repeated, her expression blank.

The two women stood there, locked in some sort of silent communication. Simon grappled for the right thing to say but came up empty. Instead, he opted to hang back and see how the conversation played out.

"You know a lot more about the club than I do," Hannah said to Mia.

"What makes you think they're involved?"

"Russ Whitman has been hanging around a lot lately," Hannah said, still maintaining eye contact.

"And what's that supposed to mean?" Mia asked, a touch of defensiveness entering her tone.

"It's common knowledge Russ is the leader of the Ridge Riders," Hannah said bluntly.

Simon glanced over at Hannah before quickly shifting his attention to Mia for her reaction.

"Is it?" Mia asked without inflection.

"Maybe not officially, but I think we all know who's calling the shots these days."

"The members of the club are good people," Mia said stiffly.

"All of them?" Hannah asked. Exhaling a loud gust, she leaned in and tapped the papers he'd placed on the work surface. "Mia, I've found at least a half dozen people on this list who were related to people I know to be members of the club. It's entirely possible we're barking up the wrong tree, but I don't know enough about the membership to be able to say if there's significantly more."

Feeling uncomfortable as a bystander to this standoff, Simon decided it was time for him to step up. "We're only trying to find out if there is enough of a correlation for it to be worth pursuing," he assured her. "If you can't find any more than the six Hannah was able to identify, then we let this line of investigation drop."

"But, Mia, if this is happening, and the riders are involved, don't you want to find out now rather than later?"

Simon found himself glancing from one woman to the other, trying to parse the subtext of the question but coming up empty.

"Don't you want to stop this now before it spreads to other members of our community?" Hannah asked her softly.

The three of them stood still as the mixers whirred behind them. Just when Simon thought Mia might tell them both to leave, she snatched the papers from her counter as quick as a snake striking.

"Of course, you know this doesn't prove anything," she said dismissively. "Half the people in this town are related to each other in one way or another," she muttered under her breath as she began scanning the list. Then she slowly lowered the papers to the counter and leaned over them, her finger pressed to the margin beside one of the names Hannah had not yet checked off.

Simon wanted to ask if the person might correspond to one of the current members of the motorcycle club, but the intensity of Mia's perusal stopped him in his tracks. A second finger came down beside another name, then her breath caught on a hitch.

"Hand me a pen," she ordered, nodding in the direction of a small desk set up with a phone and a laptop.

Hannah went over and plucked a ballpoint pen from the coffee mug being used as a pencil cup and carried it over to the work surface, handing it over to her friend as if presenting a ceremonial sword.

When Mia looked up, Simon could see her eyes were bright with unshed tears. Biting the inside of his cheek, he looked down at his shoes frantically, scrambling for the right thing to say or do at what felt like a pivotal moment. Thankfully, Hannah beat him to it.

"It's only a list of names. A place to start. It doesn't prove anything," she said softly. "But it may lead to preventing future issues."

He looked up in time to see Mia nod and swallow hard. She took the pen Hannah offered and quickly began checking off names on the list. By the time she was done, she had marked nearly half of the previous night's orders.

"Russ isn't officially any part of the Ridge Riders," she said in a raspy voice.

"But not for wanting," Hannah retorted. "We all know they do whatever he wants."

"I know," Mia said in the husky voice. Then she turned and fell into her friend's open arms. "Oh, Hannah, what am I going to do with him?"

Simon stared at them, confused by the question. "What is Russ Whitman to you?" he asked. The two women turned to look at him in unison, their expressions of incredulity easy to read but hard to decipher. "What? What am I missing?"

"It's not Russ she's worried about," Hannah informed him stiffly. "It's Micah."

"Micah? Is he with the club?" Simon asked.

"No," Mia answered a shade too quickly.

"No," Hannah echoed in a softer tone.

Simon watched as the two women's eyes locked, and he could almost see the unspoken communication arcing like electricity between them. He focused on Hannah. "Tell me what I need to know."

"Micah is not part of the Ridge Riders," she said without sparing him a glance. "But he would like to be."

"Hannah—" Mia said, a pleading note entering her tone.

But Hannah didn't stop. "He'd like to be because Mia and Micah's dad was important in the group. And we're afraid he wants it so much he'd do anything they asked to get in."

"Do you know exactly what your brother is doing for Whitman Development?" Simon asked.

Mia dropped her gaze, wet her lips, then shook her head. "No. I mean, I assumed he'd be working on a job site. He's done some roofing work for them before." She looked up again, but her gaze went straight to Hannah. "Do you know what he's doing for them?"

Hannah shook her head. "No. Not for certain."

At last, she turned her attention to him. "Do you?"

"Not for certain," he parroted, "but I have a hunch."

"Is it better than the hunch that brought you and the windbreaker brigade up here from Little Rock?"

Oddly enough Simon was happy to see some of her sass come back. "I hope so."

She squared her shoulders and turned to face him, her chin up. "Hit me with it."

"I've seen him around town. He seems to be working directly for Russ Whitman. Odd jobs, errands, you know, like an assistant."

"Errands?" Mia repeated, incredulous. She shot a glance at Hannah and then back to him. "Are you telling me my brother stopped helping with our family businesses so he could run errands for Russ Whitman?"

There was a charged pause, and Simon wasn't exactly sure how to fill it.

"If you think about it, it's not so different from what you and I had him doing," Hannah said at last. "I suppose it's cooler to do it for Russ."

They lapsed into silence again, and Simon found himself growing antsy at the tension filling the room. He did the only thing he knew to do—he acted like a cop.

"Do you know where your brother went after the visitation for Grace Templeton?"

Mia turned a puzzled frown on him. "Where he went?" She bit her lip as if searching her memory and gave her head a shake. "I went home right after because Shelley Tompkins was sitting with Mama so we could attend, but Micah said he was going to catch up with some of his friends."

"Do you know if your brother owns a set of motorcycle leathers?" he asked.

Mia's eyes narrowed. "Yes, I know," she hedged. "Why?"

"Does he?" he persisted.

"Yes," she answered. "But why are you asking?"

"Mia," Hannah interrupted. "He's asking because it's important."

"Yes, he does," her friend retorted stiffly.

"And Micah still has a black helmet with a full visor, doesn't he?"

Mia nodded, then began to shake her head vigorously. "Yeah, sure he does, but what does it matter when he doesn't have a bike to ride? Daddy's isn't running."

"Are you sure?" Simon prodded.

"Yes, I'm sure. I see it parked in the garage every night when I pull in." She turned on her heel and stomped over to the mixers. Simon and Hannah exchanged a quick glance as she punched buttons and pulled a lever to shut them down. When she turned back to them, her hands were planted on her hips. "What are you getting at?"

"I didn't tell you because I didn't want to worry you," Hannah began, "but the night of Mrs. Templeton's visitation there was a guy on a motorcycle cruising past my house at regular intervals."

"And you think it was Micah?" Mia asked with an incredulous laugh. "He doesn't have a motorcycle."

Simon stepped in. "Russ Whitman has been hanging around Hannah more than usual lately, hasn't he?"

Mia shot him a testy look, then gave a grudging nod. "So?"

"Someone has been using Hannah's website to process orders for illegally distilled spirits," he reminded her. "We also have reason to believe someone has been using the storm cellar at her house without her knowledge."

"What? How?" Her startled gaze swiveled to Hannah.

"Probably while I was at work. Remember me telling you Mr. Blaine was complaining about Beau barking all the time during the day?"

"And you think it was Micah?"

"No," Hannah answered her in a rush. "I mean, if anyone's

going in my yard, I hope it's Micah, but no," she assured her friend. "But the bike the guy was riding past my house looked an awful lot like one of Russ's bikes. But the person riding it wasn't Russ," she stated with certainty. "Whoever was on the bike was smaller and he wore a helmet. A full helmet with a visor."

The two women stared at one another. "Russ doesn't wear a helmet," Mia murmured.

"Ever," Hannah confirmed.

Mia caught her upper lip between her teeth as she digested this information. "You think Micah was riding past your house on one of Russ's bikes? Micah would never do anything to hurt you or scare you. You know he wouldn't," Mia argued.

"I do know," Hannah reassured her.

"I'm thinking Whitman asked him to do it to protect Hannah," Simon interjected. "I think he played on Micah's relationship with Hannah to make him worry, then graciously allowed him to borrow one of his bikes to keep an eye on her place."

Mia exhaled loudly. Closing her eyes, she murmured, "Okay, I'd buy that. But why were they keeping an eye on Hannah's house?"

"I think they may have been storing some of their merchandise in her cellar," Simon said bluntly. "Either that or using it as a sort of staging area for preparing their shipments."

Mia pressed the heel of her hand to her forehead. "This is all too much."

"It's a lot," he conceded. "It's also nothing more than conjecture at this point. I need to gather evidence, and I need to find the ties that will bind the story together."

Hannah gestured to the list that lay abandoned on the work surface. "Can you give us the names of the current members of the Riders who would match up with these customer names?" she asked quietly. "This is all I'll ask. If you'll give us those names, then Simon can talk to Mitch Faulk and they can delve into it deeper from there," Hannah assured her.

Mia stared deep into Hannah's eyes, and for a heart-stopping moment Simon feared she might refuse. But then she walked back over to the table, picked up the pen and started writing down names.

Five minutes later, he had the list tucked carefully in his pocket. He stepped out the back door into the alley, leaving the two women alone, and leaned against the sun-warmed brick wall. As always, he felt drained by the emotionally charged confrontation. He closed his eyes and tried to concentrate on the case, but his mind was a jumble.

The *ka-thunk* of the heavy-duty door latch startled him. He jumped to attention when the metal door swung open, and Hannah stuck her head out. "Hey."

"Hey," he replied, pushing a hand through his hair. "You ready?"

"Actually, I think I want to stay here a little longer. Can you head over to see Mitch? I'll meet you after I run home to let Beau out."

Simon nodded. "Okay." He jerked his chin in the direction of the bakery. "Is she all right?"

"Will be," Hannah assured him. "You go on and start with Mitch. I'll meet you there in about a half hour."

Relieved not to stop and be stuck between two best friends at odds, Simon shoved his hands in his pockets and nodded. "Sounds good."

The moment the heavy door closed behind her he headed

for the mouth of the alley. His state-issued SUV was parked on the side street. He headed straight for it without glancing over his shoulder to see if anyone had been watching.

Chapter Thirteen

Hannah stood inside the bakery, taking a moment to catch her breath before going back in to finish the conversation she needed to have with her best friend, but she dreaded instigating it. Asking questions about the Ridge Riders and Micah had been hard, but now she had to push on a bruise Hannah knew for certain never quite healed.

She inhaled deeply, then exhaled to a count of eight, exactly as she'd learned from a woman named Cara Beckett, whose soothing voice welcomed her to the meditation app she had downloaded when her gran's health took a bad turn. Closing her eyes, she whispered, "Okay. Okay," in a weak attempt to buck herself up.

"Are you?"

The question startled her. She opened her eyes to find Mia standing in the doorway to the kitchen, her arms crossed snug over her chest.

"I am," Hannah answered cautiously. "Are you?"

"Yeah," Mia replied after taking a beat to consider the question.

"Are *we*?" Hannah asked, pushing away from the door to close the distance between herself and the person who was the closest thing to family she had left in this world.

Mia's posture softened, even if her expression remained somber. "We will always be okay."

The statement gave Hannah the boost of confidence she needed. "Even if I ask about Mr. Unmentionable?"

Mia glanced away, wetting her lips before giving a brief nod, then turning back to her kitchen. "Come back in here. I won't let this batch get away from me. Not on his account."

Hannah did as she was told. Silence hummed around them as Mia worked the dough she'd turned out of the mixers. When it became apparent Mia was going to force her to ask, Hannah fell back against the door of the stainless steel fridge and pressed her hand to her belly to quell the butterflies setting her on edge.

"Was he on the list?" she asked, unable to bring herself to say the man's name out loud.

Mia nodded but did not look up from her work.

Hannah exhaled. Mia's ex-boyfriend Tucker Jenkins had once been a fixture in both their lives. He and Mia began dating not long after she turned sixteen and remained exclusive until their early twenties. Or, at least, exclusive as far as Mia was aware. Tucker had a much more flexible definition of the word.

"You know about Tucker's family," Mia said in a low voice.

Hannah nodded in response. Everyone in Carroll County knew about the Jenkins brothers. There were three branches of the family tree sprawled across Benton, Washington and Carroll counties, and each one more rotten than the last.

"Do you think he's involved?" Hannah asked, though she was certain she already knew the answer.

Mia flipped and patted the dough, gently spreading it on the flour-coated surface. She picked up a large roller and gave it a generous dusting as well, but paused before going to work on the dough in earnest. "They're proud of the family business, you know," she said, casting a challenging look over her shoulder.

The Jenkins boys, as Tucker's father and brothers were collectively known, were all employed by legitimate businesses, but everyone in the northwest corridor knew they made the real money by being the area's premier providers of homemade hooch and locally sourced marijuana. Tucker's parents divorced when the kids were in fourth grade, and his mother found religion in a big way not long after. By the time he reached middle school, Tucker Jenkins no longer had much of a relationship with his father or uncles, but that didn't mean he was immune from being lumped in with the rest of them.

"I know," Hannah replied calmly. "But Tucker always said he wanted nothing to do with it," she reminded Mia.

"He didn't," she said with a shrug. Then, she brought the rolling pin down on the poor, innocent dough with a brutal thump. "And then, I guess he did." She began rolling the dough with ruthless efficiency. "I mean, how would I know what Tucker gets up to these days?"

"Mia—"

"I don't want to know," Mia said, nipping Hannah's sympathy in the bud. "It's been years. I'd barely know him anymore."

Hannah clamped her mouth shut. She knew the last bit certainly wasn't true. Hannah had seen Tucker not long ago herself, and he was still as handsome as ever—even if he was rough around the edges.

"Do you still hear from his mama?" she asked. Ms. Eileen had been genuinely heartbroken when Tucker and Mia split up and had tried on multiple occasions to intervene with both her son and Mia, but to no avail.

Mia shook her head. "We all moved on."

Squelching her own doubts, Hannah moved to stand next to her friend. "You did a good thing today," she said quietly.

There was the merest hesitation when Mia switched directions on the dough. "Did I?" she asked, her voice barely more than a whisper.

"You did," Hannah stated emphatically. "How many times have you told me your daddy would have hated what the Riders have become? And Bruce and Will and some of his old friends. Aren't they always complaining to you about how things are run these days?"

Mia curled her lips inward and nodded quickly, blinking furiously. She pushed the dough to its limits with a final stroke, then turned to face Hannah. "They're the ones telling me to keep Micah out of it, but how am I supposed to stop him? He's grown. It's not like I can ground him," she complained.

"I know." Hannah placed a comforting hand on her friend's back. "But maybe, with Simon's help, we can find a way to…help get the Riders back on a smooth road."

Mia gave a sharp bark of a laugh. "Good luck." Then she turned her face to her, her eyes wet with unshed tears. "I mean it," she said softly. "I wish you and your friend from school Simon good luck, because if my baby brother is involved in any of this, I don't see how I'm going to have the energy or the inclination to pull his ungrateful behind out of the fire this time."

"I get you," Hannah assured her.

Mia set her rolling pin aside, then jerked her head toward

the door. "Go on and get out of here. I have work to do and you're distracting me."

Thankful for the reprieve, Hannah waved and beat a path to the door. When she stepped into the alley, she caught sight of a dusty white pickup parked at the far end of it and turned in the opposite direction.

Checking the time on her phone, she took off up the hill at a brisk clip. The conversation with Mia had eaten into the thirty minutes she'd promised Simon, but there was no reason for her to hurry to police headquarters. She didn't doubt Mitch would have no trouble filling Simon in on the members of the club.

By the time she reached the next block, her breath was coming faster and her steps moving slower. As she did most every night, she made a silent vow to take Beauregard out for more walks. She'd fallen back on letting him race around the yard because it was easier, but evening walks would benefit them both.

As she reached her own block, she noted the neat edging around Mr. Blaine's lawn and made a mental note to take time to cut her grass and deadhead the rosebushes her gran had been so meticulous about. Her shoulders slumped when she took in how leggy the shrubs had become. "The cobbler's kid has no shoes," she muttered under her breath.

"Hannah?"

Her steps faltered when she heard Mr. Blaine's screen door slap against its frame. Cringing, she forced herself to stop, plastering a friendly smile on her face before making a full pivot.

"Hi, Mr. Blaine," she called, lifting a hand to wave to the older man.

"Listen, I know you're busy with your grandmother's shop

and all, but if you're going to have work done on the house, you should leave a key with me. It isn't safe for a woman living alone to let people come and go whenever they please, even if you have a dog for protection," he chided. "Plus, keeping your neighbors apprised of any upheaval is simply good manners. You know I can't work in the middle of chaos," he said, waving a hand in the direction of his garage slash workshop.

Mr. Blaine built novelty birdhouses he sold in various gift shops and flea markets in town, and he was the stereotype of the temperamental artist when it came to needing peace and quiet to create. Keeping her smile glued in place, she nodded and began to inch closer to her house. "I will, Mr. Blaine," she assured him.

The older man served a harrumph along with his glower. "At least that fool mutt of yours has finally worn himself out. I swear, he was barkin' a blue streak all morning."

"I'm sorry, Mr. Blaine," she called dutifully. "I'll keep working with him, I promise."

She even raised her hand as if taking an oath. But she didn't turn away. She didn't dare. Her grandmother taught her never to turn her back on an elder, and Hannah wasn't about to get haunted on grumpy Mr. Blaine's account.

"See you do," he admonished. Then, having vented enough for one day, he turned and went back into his house, the ancient screen door slapping shut behind him.

She exhaled a long gust of air, then spun around to do the same. But when she looked up, she found her own screen door clinging by its lower hinges and the oak door with its frosted glass standing wide open.

Without thinking, she sprinted across her scraggly lawn

and up the steps, calling for her dog. "Beau?" She skidded to a stop in the foyer. "Beauregard?"

But there were no barks of greeting. No skittering of toenails on polished oak floors. Not even the whine of a dog who'd taken refuge under a bed. Beauregard was not there.

The house stood still. Lifeless. As it had in the days after Gran's death. She didn't need to check every room to know her dog was gone. But gone where? How?

She glanced back at the broken screen door. It had been latched and locked the night before. She herself had left via the back door after letting Beau out to do his morning business. Without a thought for her own safety, Hannah charged through the house, glancing into every room she passed to be certain.

Her dog was gone.

Her door was broken.

Work done on the house.

She stopped in her tracks and rewound Mr. Blaine's litany of complaints to the beginning.

Had someone come into her house posing as a workman?

She ran through to the kitchen. Nothing was out of place. Nothing missing or even moved, that she could tell. Still, she pulled a knife from the wooden block beside the stove and crept to the back door.

It was closed, but unlocked, though she knew for a fact she'd twisted the thumb lock on the knob before blowing Beau kisses goodbye this morning. Opening it cautiously, she held the knife high, ready to strike if someone popped out at her from nowhere.

Then, she remembered there was a place someone might be hiding. A place where someone had hidden something before.

The storm cellar.

She yanked open the door and poked her head out. The afternoon sunlight glinted off the new heavy-duty hasp and padlock Simon had installed the previous day. Her breath caught as she pictured him kneeling on the peeling wood door, his hair falling over his damp forehead as he drove screws into the age-softened wood using the screwdriver from Gran's junk drawer.

Maybe that was where Beauregard was.

She ran down the steps and over to the cellar doors. It wasn't until she went to dig her keys from her pocket that she remembered the knife she held. Hannah dropped it to the ground as she yanked the key ring free.

"Please, please, please," she murmured as she fumbled for the shiny new key with numb, trembling fingers. "Please be here, my sweet Beau baby," she said as she dropped down to grab hold of the padlock.

But he wasn't.

She knew he wasn't there before she popped the lock. Still, she unhooked it and threw back the lever on the hasp, grunting as she hauled one of the doors open. The darn thing didn't even have the decency to creak. Whoever had been breaking into her cellar had oiled the hinges.

"Beau?" she called into the blank darkness.

But her dog was not there. A sob rose in her throat. She tried to call for him again, but his name came out in a croak. Stumbling to her feet, she let the heavy padlock drop into the abyss. She turned in a wide, frantic circle, scanning the yard and all the neighbors' yards as she freed her phone from her back pocket.

Someone had come into her house and stolen her dog. Poor, sweet, nervous Beauregard with his big-dog bark and his spindly legs. They'd either taken him or turned him out into the streets.

Either way, this madness had gone too far.

Rage clawed its way up through her fear and confusion. Stumbling away from the storm cellar, she made her way to the gate she'd used to let herself out that morning. It was closed, but the U-shaped latch stood propped on its hinge. He could have pushed his way out, she reasoned. She gave it a shove. But even though its hinges had also been oiled, it did not swing shut behind her.

Standing in her side yard, she pressed her hand to her thumping heart. It beat so loud she was certain the whole neighborhood could hear it. She cast a glance at her nosy neighbor's garage workshop and wondered how the man could hear her dog barking from inside her house but had somehow been completely oblivious to total strangers tromping through her yard and into her cellar in broad daylight.

She was about to storm over there to ask him when she heard the opening chords of a Pink Floyd song blasting from the depths of his workshop. Hannah backed up a step when the high-pitched screech of a power saw joined the cacophony. She stared goggle-eyed at the side of the garage, stunned by the man's audacity.

Making her way back toward the front of the house, she cupped one hand around her mouth and shouted "Beau!" in case the dog had simply gotten scared and bolted. But looking up and down the sidewalk, she saw no sign of movement. Frustrated beyond freaking out, she swiped at her phone until she pulled up Simon's number.

He answered with a brisk, "Hey. Are you on your way over? Listen, I need you to—"

But she quickly interrupted him. "No, I can't. It's Beau.

He's gone. I came home and Beau is gone. I can't believe this. Who would kidnap my dog?"

"Whoa. Wait. What?" he interrupted. "Where are you?"

She threw her hand up as she stalked up her front porch stairs again. "I'm at my house. I came home and my screen door is ripped off the hinges and my front door is wide open," she said, staring at the doors as if they were responsible for her situation. "And when I went in, Beau was gone."

"Wait. You went in?" he asked.

Incredulity dripped from every syllable, and she did not have one ounce of patience for his judgmental tone.

"Yes, I went in. This is my house. I was looking for my dog—"

"Someone could have been in there," he shot back.

Hannah swallowed a lump of pure annoyance. Sure, the thought occurred to her. Of course, she'd been all the way in the kitchen before she gave a thought to her own safety, but still, now was not the time for a lecture. She wasn't at fault here. She was not the one who was missing.

"Beauregard is gone," she repeated. "Someone came into my house and either took my dog or scared him so badly he took off." She planted a hand on her hip. "Are you going to help me?"

"Of course I am," Simon answered.

She heard the tinge of hurt in his tone and pushed her hand into her hair. He hadn't hesitated. Or told her Beau was only a dog. Or even asked where she'd looked for him already. He'd simply said he was coming to help. Choking back tears, she forced out the only word she could think of.

"Hurry."

She paced the length of the porch, then, unable to simply stand there and wait, she strode to the entry. Annoyance and anger rippled through her as she reached past the cockeyed screen door and yanked the front door closed. She was coming down the porch steps when she saw a white pickup truck slow to a crawl at the curb.

The logo for Whitman Development was painted on the door. She couldn't quite make out who the driver was until the passenger window slid down and he leaned across the seat to call to her.

"Hannah? Hey, Han?" Russ Whitman shouted.

She wanted to wave him off. To tell him to leave her alone once and for all. She was busy. She was rapidly edging toward frantic.

"Did your dog get out?" he asked, yelling to be heard over the truck's powerful motor.

Hannah froze for a second. Then she took off down the steps at a sprint. "Yes!" She dashed across her ungroomed lawn as the music blaring from Mr. Blaine's workshop rose to a crescendo. "Have you seen him?" she panted, practically falling into the open window of Russ's truck.

He nodded. "He was running toward the shop." He stretched across the cab of the truck and yanked on the door handle. "Get in. We'll catch up to him."

Hannah didn't hesitate. Beauregard was skittish on his best days. If he was panicked, it was unlikely he'd allow himself to be corralled by anyone but her. "Okay, thanks," she said, pulling the door open and practically hurling herself into the seat.

She was pulling the seat belt across her body when Russ cranked the wheel and made a tire-squealing U-turn in the middle of the street. Hannah grabbed the door handle to steady herself, a nervous laugh bubbling out of her as he pointed the nose of the truck toward the center of town.

No doubt alerted by the squeal of rubber on asphalt, Mr. Blaine stepped out of his garage as Russ punched the accelerator. Thrust back in her seat, Hannah couldn't do more than raise a hand in a wave of apology, before returning to her efforts to secure her safety belt.

"I appreciate this," she said, breathless.

"Not a problem."

Russ's response was brusque, but he was scanning both sides of the street as he drove. "I don't know how he got out," she said, releasing some of her nerves with her babble. "I came home to take him for a walk, and he was…gone."

He nodded, then held his hand out, palm up. "Let me see your phone," he said, giving his fingers an encouraging waggle.

She frowned down at his hand. "My phone? Why?"

"There's an app," he answered abruptly.

Pulling her phone from her pocket again, she swiped to get to her home screen. "An app for lost animals?" she asked, bowing her head and squinting as she searched for the icon that would lead her to the app store.

Before she could ask what the app was called, Russ snatched the phone from her hands and tossed it out the open window.

"Wha—what are you doing?" she asked, twisting in her seat to look back at the pavement, aghast.

But when she turned back to look at him, her indignation froze into a hard lump of fear.

Russ had a gun.

A sleek, scary-looking handgun rested on his denim-clad thigh, his hand placed casually atop it.

"Don't have a hissy fit," he warned her.

Hannah tried to swallow, but her mouth had run dry.

She dragged her tongue over her lips as she leaned heavily against the door. If she hadn't been such a law-abiding priss and buckled herself in, she might have thrown herself out of the truck. She'd read an article about how Cara Beckett, her favorite meditation leader, had done something like that in a carjacking situation. But Hannah had never been quick to think on her feet.

She bit her lip as he rolled through a stop sign, barely slowing to check for traffic. When he accelerated past the turn that would take them to the shop, she forced herself to accept what was happening. Beau may or may not have been kidnapped, but she was.

"What are you doing, Russ?" she asked, wincing at the quaver in her voice.

"Your friend Simon from college," he said, his voice low and nasty. "He's DEA?"

Hannah's heart thudded hard against her breastbone. But she shoved down the panic. He asked a simple question, and she had no need to lie to answer him. "What? No."

"But he's a cop," he replied, unfazed.

"He works for the state police," she said, keeping the details as vague as possible. "He's an IT guy. A computer nerd," she added, hoping to appeal to Russ's innate sense of superiority.

"A computer nerd," he said with a derisive sneer. "Well, I think your computer nerd pal has been sticking his cursor where it doesn't belong."

"How do you mean?"

She clung to the door as he hooked a sharp right onto the main road. If there was any act she could sell, it was the innocent one. So many of her fellow classmates mistook her principles for naivete. She wasn't above using it to her advantage when she could. But before she could get more of an explanation from him, he turned right again, bumping into the rutted parking lot between Suzee's SleepInn and the Downshift.

Letting out a soft groan, she bit the inside of her cheek. He whipped the truck into the handicapped parking spot closest to the door, and they jerked to a stop. He twisted in his seat to glare at her. All traces of his smooth, handsome facade were stripped away down to an ugly sneer.

"Billy Aikens got arrested down in Little Rock last night, and I'm pretty sure your computer nerd friend had something to do with it. Now, I'm not worried about old Billy, because he can handle himself, and what he can't fix, I can." He jabbed a thumb into his chest. "But I don't need you and your pal messing with my business, you got me?"

Hannah made her eyes go wide. "Your business?" she repeated, all innocence. "Did something happen at one of the building sites?"

Russ rolled his eyes, then lifted the gun from his lap. "Get out and come around the front of the truck. I want you to open my door for me."

She stared at him, dumbfounded by the request. "Open your door for you? Why?"

He smirked and lifted his weapon. It was pointed directly at her. "Why? Why else? So I can look at you, sweetheart."

Heart thudding, Hannah opened the door and stepped down from the truck. The asphalt was cracked and strewn with shards of broken glass and cigarette butts. She closed the door with a slam, but the burst of temper only seemed to amuse Russ. He grinned and kept the muzzle of the gun trained on her. Her mind raced as she skirted the grill of the truck. She could feel the heat rising from the engine. Russ opened his own door before she even cleared the bumper and shifted his position so the gun remained pointed at her chest as he slid out of the driver's seat. He let the door close softly behind him with the motor still running.

"Aren't you going to turn it off?" she asked as he closed the gap between them, lowering the gun so it was concealed between them.

"Don't worry about it." He jerked his chin toward the entrance to the bar. "Go on in."

Hannah turned and trudged toward the door, noting how the matte black paint was peeling in places and the pull handle was worn to a dull sheen. The Downshift looked seedy for a bar that had a steady stream of business. And she knew it had done well at first, because Hannah's grandmother had promised her friend she'd keep an eye on Darla after her grandmother's death, and Gran had kept her word. But maybe things hadn't been going as well in the years since Gran's health started to decline.

Hannah yanked open the door. She had no idea whether the bar made money or not. After all, it wasn't like Darla Ott was the type to join the chamber of commerce, and they were hardly friends.

She stepped into the vestibule and drew up short, needing a moment for her eyes to adjust to the dim interior. Russ quickly closed the distance between them, and she felt the business end of his gun press into her back.

"Keep going," he said, leaning down to speak directly into her ear.

"Hannah," a guy to her right called out, clearly shocked to see her in the Downshift.

She turned her head in time to see Micah slide off a bar

stool, his forehead creased with concern. "What are you doing here?"

"Hey, Micah, buddy," Russ interjected before she could answer. "Hannah's here to pick up some paperwork, but could you do me a favor? I left the truck running out front. I need to get it back to the Saddle Creek site. There are permits in the glove box. Would you run it out there for me?" He propelled Hannah past the boy she'd known since he was a toddler. He gave Micah a friendly nudge with his elbow as they passed. "You know this stuff with the city never stops."

"Sure thing, boss." Micah nodded eagerly, his gaze fixed on Russ, as trusting as a puppy. "See you later, Hannah," he called, then took off for the door at a trot.

"Head for the back," Russ instructed. "We'll borrow Darla's office for our little chat."

Hannah's head swiveled as she made her way through the bar. Though she knew at least three-quarters of the patrons, not one of them met her gaze as they passed, the cowards. When they reached the dark hall that led to the bathrooms and a closed door she assumed was the office, she hesitated. Russ gave her a shove in the direction of the closed door, then sauntered up behind her. He used the barrel of his gun to knock twice.

A minute passed before Darla opened the door, looking annoyed by the interruption. Then, she realized exactly who Russ had dragged into her bar and she began shaking her head. Hard.

"Nope. Nuh-uh," Darla began. "I don't know what this is, but I want no part of it."

But Russ ignored her refusal. "Darla, sugar, I hope you don't mind if Hannah and I borrow your office for a bit."

He gave Hannah a shove, practically pushing her into the other woman's arms. Darla caught her, then quickly let go.

"No. No way. I don't know what you think you're doing here, but no," she protested.

"Sorry, darlin', no choice," Russ said, grabbing Darla by the elbow. "But, hey, why don't you stay here with her while I attend to some things? It'll give you two girls time to catch up," he said as he reached around the door and fiddled with one of the locks on the inside.

The next thing Hannah knew, he stepped out of the office and slammed the door. Hannah and Darla stared at one another in astonishment, only jolting from it when they heard the thunk of a dead bolt sliding home. Hannah stared at the keyed lock mounted above the doorknob, shock turning to horror.

"Oh, well, now that was a damn fool thing to do, Junior," Darla muttered, glaring at the door. Turning to Hannah, she shook her head in disgust. "I swear, the man doesn't have the sense God gave a goose."

Chapter Fourteen

Simon's mind started racing the minute he stepped into Mitch Faulk's office and found Wyatt Dawson and another man he'd never met waiting for him. "What are you doing here?" he asked his second-in-command.

Dawson nodded to the stranger sitting beside him, then gestured to the police chief. "We were filling Chief Faulk in on the interesting development we had this morning." He paused, then turned to look Simon in the eye.

Simon blinked slowly. "What interesting development?" he asked stiffly.

Wyatt frowned. "Didn't you read the email I sent?"

"I've been busy," Simon replied, instantly defensive.

He'd been so wrapped up in unraveling the connection between the fake names being used on the orders and the Ridge Riders, he'd completely ignored his email notifications, figuring his team would call or text if anything important happened. Apparently, he figured wrong. But he only had himself to blame. Years of training his agents to avoid interrupting his concentration had taken hold. They all knew he preferred to have reports sent to him via email. Texts and phone calls were to be initiated by him, or as a matter of life and death.

"We caught a guy named William Aikens making a delivery to one of the addresses we had targeted this morning."

"How did you know he wasn't a legitimate delivery driver?" Simon asked.

"The house he was delivering to is on the market and confirmed unoccupied by the listing realtor. Aikens was driving an unmarked white van, and the shirt he wore had a Whitman Development logo on it." Wyatt gestured to the man beside him. "The trooper blocked the driveway before Aikens could leave. He notified me, and I notified Agent Lyle at ATF. They confirmed the package to be suspicious."

"How?" Simon asked, turning his attention to the ATF man.

"He wasn't delivering a cardboard box. These guys deliver in a wooden crate. It's a selling point with their customers. A handmade crate filled with straw to cushion the glass bottles. We've seen similar packaging in product confiscated in other areas."

"I see."

"William Aikens is a resident of Eureka Springs," Wyatt Dawson informed him. "Agent Lyle here and I thought it would be a good thing if we came up to meet with you and Chief Faulk in person. You weren't at your motel, so we came here." Dawson straightened. "We got here about three minutes before you walked in."

Simon shot a glance at the police chief, who simply nodded in confirmation. "Where are we?" he asked, trying to get a good grip on what was happening.

"We'll need a lot more than one bird in hand," Agent Lyle reminded them.

Simon looked at Mitch Faulk. "Do you know this Aikens guy?"

Mitch inclined his head. "Not as *William* Aikens, but yes. Billy grew up here in the area. He's also a member of the Ridge Riders," he confirmed, clearly anticipating Simon's next question.

"Is he talking?" Simon asked Wyatt.

"Not yet, but I have a feeling it won't take much to get him to change his mind. He doesn't seem particularly thrilled to have been sent on this errand."

Simon turned back to Mitch. "How old is this Aikens guy?"

The police chief shrugged. "A little older than me," he said gruffly.

"So, he's one of the old-school Ridge Riders?" Simon pushed. "Would he have been around the club when it was forming?"

Mitch pondered the possibility for a moment, then nodded. "It's possible. He may have been one of the younger guys when they started up. I can tell you a lot of the older fellas aren't particularly happy with the direction the club has been going for the last few years."

Simon felt the list of names he'd worked on with Hannah and Mia burning a hole in his pocket, but he wanted to get some answers from the police chief himself before he revealed their suspicions.

"Who's the top dog?" Simon asked.

Mitch chuckled. "On paper? It's a guy named Tom Jenkins."

Simon couldn't suppress his surprise at hearing the name. He's thought for sure Russ Whitman would be the man calling the shots. "Jenkins?"

Faulk waved his hand as if the name was not important. "I said on paper," he repeated in an impatient tone. "Jenkinses are a dime a dozen around here. They pop up like weeds. He's not your problem. Well, I take it back. He's a part of the problem," he conceded, "but he's not the head of it."

"Who is?" Simon asked bluntly.

Mitch fell back in his chair and crossed his arms over his chest. "I don't think it's going to come as a surprise to you. If you were to take a guess as to who is running the show with the Ridge Riders, who would you say?"

"Russ Whitman," Simon said without hesitation.

"Bingo." The police chief pointed both index fingers at Simon like pistols. "Got it in one."

Simon pulled the folded sheet of paper from his pocket and was unfolding it when his phone rang. He yanked it from his belt, studiously ignoring Wyatt's raised eyebrows. Hannah's name and number appeared. She was likely calling to tell him she was on her way over, but he didn't want her walking into this meeting. He was still conducting an active investigation, and no matter how helpful she was, she was a civilian.

"Hey. Are you on your way over?" he asked, pivoting away from the other men for a modicum of privacy. He wasn't sure how Hannah would take being told to stay away, but he had a hunch it would not go down well. "Listen, I need you to—"

She cut him off with some semi-coherent story about her dog running away. He was trying to keep up, but she was upset and rambling about kidnapping and her screen door, and he was having a hard time making sense of it. Holding up a finger, he stepped out of Chief Faulk's office, his senses coming fully online when she said she'd gone into her house alone when someone had clearly broken in.

"Wait. You went in?" he asked, stupefied by her audacity.

"Yes, I went in. This is my house. I was looking for my dog—"

"Someone could have been in there," he shot back.

"Beauregard is gone," she repeated. "Someone came into my house and either took my dog or scared him so badly he took off." She paused only for a second before asking him the one thing he'd never deny her. "Are you going to help me?"

"Of course I am," Simon answered.

She whispered only the word, "Hurry," before ending the call.

Gripping his phone, Simon cast about for a second, weighing what he should do versus what he wanted to do. He should go back into the office and continue working on his case, but he wouldn't. Couldn't.

Striding back into the office, he walked to the desk and flattened the piece of paper that seemed so important mere minutes before. "Hannah and Mia Jones helped me connect some dots earlier. I think you're right about the older members being discontented." He straightened, then hooked a thumb over his shoulder. "I've got to go. Someone broke into Hannah's house, and she wants me to come check it out."

Mitch Faulk shot from his chair. "Broke into her house?"

"Hannah Miller?" Wyatt asked at the same time.

Beside him, Agent Lyle stiffened. He'd no doubt heard a lot about the botched raid on the flower shop. But Simon didn't have time for explanations. Hannah had asked him to hurry.

"I'm going to go check it out, and I'll be right back," he insisted.

"Let me send a patrol car," Mitch offered.

Simon shook his head, knowing Hannah would hate any undue attention brought to the situation. "No, I can handle it." He pointed to the list. "Look over the names on the list, will you? And bring these guys up to speed? I'll be back as soon as I can."

Before anyone could detain him a second longer, he turned and started for the door. The Eureka Springs Police Department was headquartered outside of the city limits. Frustrated and in a hurry to get to Hannah, Simon jabbed at his GPS, hoping to find a more direct route to downtown, but the highway seemed to be the best answer, even if it was a bit circuitous.

Despite the AC blasting straight at him, a fine sheen of sweat dampened the back of his shirt by the time he turned onto Hannah's street. He blew out a relieved breath when he saw the spot at the curb in front of her house. Whipping the SUV into the open space, he scowled as he scanned the front porch.

The door to the house was closed, but the screen door was indeed ripped off one hinge. He bailed from the driver's seat, half expecting to be greeted by the sound of her calling her dog's name. Instead, he was treated to an earful of the Grateful Dead blaring from the garage next door.

Jogging up the porch steps, he peered into one of the windows, but the house appeared to be still and dark. "Hannah?" he called out as he moved the broken screen door aside. He got no answer, so he tested the knob on the inner door. It turned easily. He swore softly under his breath. "Learn to lock your doors," he muttered as he stepped into the entry.

"Hannah?" he called even louder.

But the house was empty. He could feel its emptiness pulsing around him like an ache.

A quick check at the living room and dining room proved his assessment to be correct. He started down the short hallway. "Hannah?" he called again in case she was tucked away in one of the bedrooms.

He started at the far end of the hall. This room was clearly the primary bedroom. He could tell by the fine coat of dust on its furnishings it was likely her grandmother's room. He took a quick peek into the en suite bathroom, then started back down the hall, where he checked the main bath and then finally peered into Hannah's room.

A tufted dog bed lay cozied up to the footboard. The duvet had been pulled up tight and tucked beneath her pillows. Simon was oddly pleased to note the lack of decorative throw pillows in the room. He never understood them, and for some reason felt he might understand Hannah better for her lack of them. The room was mostly in order. It certainly hadn't been ransacked.

Satisfied she wasn't anywhere in the house, he headed for the kitchen door. The wooden steps leading down into the yard were every bit as worn and warped as they'd been on his first visit. The grass was still spotty in areas and strewn with discarded dog toys and abandoned balls. When he glanced to his right, he saw the cellar. One of the cellar doors lay open wide. He paused, then bent to withdraw his gun from the ankle holster he wore.

"Hannah?" he called cautiously, allowing the gun to lead as he approached the storm cellar.

Still, no answer came.

Simon reached the opening and peered down into the darkness. "Hannah," he called again, this time with far more snap in his tone.

She wasn't there.

She'd come home to find her dog missing, asked him to help her find him, and now she was gone as well.

"What the—" Simon's muttered curse was cut off when the gleam of something shiny caught his attention.

He leaned down and peered at what looked to be a kitchen knife abandoned in the overgrown grass. "Oh no," he said, taking off for the back door again.

He swung through the door into the kitchen and began searching frantically through the drawers for where she might keep her knives. He made it to the last drawer before he looked up and noticed the large wooden block placed beside the stove. One slot was empty.

His eyes locked on the empty space, Simon shook his head in denial. "No, no, no," he muttered, then he turned and sprinted back out of the house again.

The knife abandoned in the grass appeared to match the others in the set. He left it where it lay and knelt to inspect it closely. There didn't appear to be any blood or other incriminating evidence on the blade.

"You looking for Hannah?" a gravelly old voice called to him.

Simon looked up to see an older man with hair buzzed into a militaristic crew cut leaning over the chain-link fence. He wore a faded T-shirt featuring the cover art from an old Led Zeppelin album, jean shorts sagging to his knobby knees and a pair of Birkenstocks. With socks.

Simon's brain was still trying to reconcile the haircut with his fashion choices, but he couldn't make it all add up. "Who are you?" he called to the stranger.

The buzz cut dude frowned and jerked a thumb toward the house next door. "I'm her neighbor. Who are you?"

Simon pulled the slender wallet holding his credentials from his back pocket and surreptitiously placed his service revolver back in its holster as he rose from the grass.

"Special Agent Simon Taylor, Arkansas State Police," he announced, holding up his badge and identification card as he walked toward the man. "And you are Mr.—"

"Blaine. Andrew Blaine," he provided.

"Mr. Blaine, have you seen Ms. Miller this afternoon?"

The older man nodded. "She came home a little while ago, then went tearing around here yelling for her dog. I was trying to get some work done in my workshop," he said, nodding to the garage. "I tell you, sometimes I gotta turn the music up so loud to focus on what I'm doing over all the racket over here."

Simon snapped the slim leather wallet shut and tucked it back in his pocket. "What kind of commotion did you hear?"

The older man shrugged. "All kinds. She's got guys coming in and out of here all the time. They're always making quite a ruckus, and then that dog of hers barks and barks and barks his fool head off."

"You saw people over here today?" Simon pounced.

"Yeah." Mr. Blaine wiped his hands on his jeans and then shook his head. "They left early. Before she got home. Thank goodness, because the dog finally stopped barking."

"Did you speak to Ms. Miller when she got home?"

"You bet I did. Told her if she was going to have work people in and out of here all the time, she needed to let somebody know so we can keep an eye on things. It's a safety issue for the whole neighborhood to let people come and go willy-nilly."

Simon nodded. "And did Ms. Miller tell you her dog was missing?"

"Missing?" The older man shook his head adamantly.

"I tell you he wasn't missing. He was barking all day. The whole time those people were here."

"Did you get a look at the men who were here?" Simon pursued.

"Well, sure, not that there was much remarkable about them," Mr. Blaine offered. "A couple of white guys. Young, probably in their twenties. Sounded like they were tearing something out over here."

"And did Ms. Miller say anything to you about those workmen?" Simon asked.

Mr. Blaine shook his head. "No, but I figured they worked for one of the local construction companies. Not long after she got home, I saw Hannah climbing into a truck with the young Whitman fella, and the two of them took off."

A cold shiver of dread streaked down Simon's back. "You saw Hannah leave with Russell Whitman?" he asked.

The older man nodded. "Sure did. The fool laid a patch of rubber out in the road for no good reason," he said, shaking his head again. "I know they have money to burn, but even the Whitmans don't need to be wasting perfectly good tire tread. That boy is always showing off."

"Did you see which way they were headed?" Simon demanded.

Blaine extended an arm in the direction toward downtown. "They went that way."

"Toward downtown," Simon confirmed.

"Yep."

Simon took hold of the gate and used it to brush the man aside as he stepped through. "Thank you so much for your help," he said as he strode past the nosy neighbor and down across the lawn, his sights set on his own vehicle.

He almost reached the driver's door when Blaine called

after him. "Never had so much trouble when her gran was alive. Miss Flora was a right proper lady. Wish I could say the same for her granddaughter," the old curmudgeon called out.

Simon paused, his hand on the door handle. "Her granddaughter is ten times better than any person I've met in this town so far," he said as he climbed into the SUV. Pulling out of the space, Simon cranked the wheel and left a patch of rubber of his own to punctuate the sentiment.

"Russ Whitman," he grumbled in disbelief. "Why would she get in a truck with Russ Whitman?"

He slowed for the stop sign at the bottom of the hill. As he was checking for cross traffic, the late afternoon sunlight flashed off a glass screen lying in the road. He pressed the accelerator but then jammed on the brakes. Throwing the SUV into Park, he bailed out of the seat and jogged back over the street. Sure enough, the flash he'd seen was the shattered face of a cell phone. Cautiously, he squatted down and gave the screen a gentle tap. A strangled groan rose in his throat as he saw the fractured image of a spindly yellow Lab smiling at the camera.

"Beau," he said, then snatched up the phone.

Not sure where to go or what to do next, Simon turned and got back into his car and steered toward Flora's Florals. As he came around the corner, he spotted Mia Jones in her flour-dusted clothes kneeling at the mouth of the alley, petting a short-haired yellow dog.

He jerked the car to a stop, then wheeled it into the alley. "Is that Beauregard?"

Mia looked up, her brow furrowed in confusion. "Yeah, it is," she replied. "I don't know what he's doing here."

"Can you take care of him? Make sure he doesn't run off again?"

Mia's confusion morphed into outright concern. "Run off? Beauregard would never run off." She smoothed her hand along the dog's cheek, then scratched reassuringly behind his ear. "He's scared to leave the yard. Hannah practically drags him every time she tries to walk him on a leash."

"He got out today," Simon said grimly. "And I have a feeling he may have been bait for a trap."

"A trap? What do you mean? Set by who?"

"Hannah's neighbor told me he saw her get into a truck with Russ Whitman," Simon informed her. "I'm going looking for them, but it will be a big relief if I could tell her you have Beauregard."

Mia nodded as she stood, her finger hooked through the dog's collar. "Of course. But Russ Whitman? Do you even know where to go look for him?"

Simon gave her a level look. "I figured I'd start at the Downshift unless you have a better suggestion."

"No. That was exactly what I was going to suggest," she said with an encouraging nod. "Don't you worry about this guy, Simon. Go get our girl."

Simon pulled into the cratered lot of the Downshift and parked his truck directly behind a line of motorcycles. Several of the bikes proudly displayed Ridge Riders stickers and artwork painted onto pipes and fuel tanks, but only one had embossed leather saddlebags. His eyes locked on the front door, he pulled his phone from his belt and dialed Wyatt Dawson.

"Dawson," Wyatt answered. "Where you at, boss?"

"I'm about to walk into the Downshift. I know it won't mean much to you, but it will to Mitch Faulk. I'll explain more later, but right now all you need to know is Hannah Miller has been taken."

"Taken?" Wyatt echoed. "As in abducted?"

"As in I believe the leader of the Ridge Riders has her and is planning to use her as a bargaining chip." He eyed the door warily and said, "I think he has her at the Downshift. This seems to be their main hangout. I'm probably going to need backup, but I'm going to tell you right now I'm not waiting for it."

"Wait, Simon—"

Wyatt's use of his given name was a clear indicator of the man's level of anxiety, but Simon couldn't wait any longer.

"Get the scoop from Mitch. Tell him to bring some of his guys or whoever he can round up," Simon instructed. "I'm going in."

He ended the call, put the phone back in its clip and reached for the door handle.

The interior of the Downshift matched its squat, gloomy exterior to perfection. The glow of the neon beer signs in the windows shot arrays of color along the walls, but any other lighting in the place came from several mounted televisions.

He'd taken exactly two steps into the bar proper before a big burly fellow dressed in riding chaps swung his legs off the bar stool he was sitting on and stretched them out to block Simon's path.

"Howdy, stranger," the big man said in an overly friendly tone. "Something we can do for you?"

"I'm looking for someone," Simon replied brusquely. He started to step over the man's legs when another hand wrapped around his upper arm.

"I don't think this is your kind of bar, mister," the man who gripped his arm said in a low growl.

"Take your hand off me before you regret it," Simon returned.

"I don't believe in regrets," the man said, tightening his grip.

Simon swallowed a sigh. "I warned you."

He dipped his head, moving closer to the man holding his arm. The moment the other man's grip slid down to Simon's forearm, Simon turned to face him, stepped into his space, then struck a single, definitive blow directly above the man's wrist.

A bone snapped, and the man howled with pain and indignation. Several others in the room rose to their feet. But before they could converge on him, someone called out, "Hold up."

He swung around to see Russ Whitman seated at one of the low tables running parallel to the bar. Their eyes met, and Whitman raised his hands and gave Simon a slow clap.

"Impressive," he called. "Jujitsu?"

"Where is she?" Simon demanded.

"Who?"

"You know who. Hannah. Where is she?"

"We know you're with the state police. She said you were a computer nerd for them, but someone down in Little Rock is holding one of our own for no good reason and you just broke poor Bart's arm." A smirk twitched the corner of Whitman's mouth, but he squelched it. "Wanna play *Let's Make a Deal*, Hannah's-Friend-From-College-Simon?"

"Where is she?"

"She's fine," Whitman relied with a jerk of his chin. "Let Billy Aikens go."

"This is only going to get worse for you," Simon warned.

"You forget you're not in Little Rock anymore, friend Simon," Whitman said mockingly. "You aren't the law in this neck of the woods."

"Mitch Faulk and the others are on their way," Simon informed him.

Whitman held his hands up as if surrendering. "Oh no. Mitch Faulk? Ooh, I'm scared."

Simon's blood ran cold at the mockery. What if the chief of police was not the ally Simon believed him to be?

Russ rose from his chair. "I think you've caused enough trouble here. You'd better leave."

The moment the words left the man's mouth, Simon shot back, "I'm not leaving without Hannah."

"I beg to differ," Whitman replied, then nodded at the men who'd closed in behind Simon during their standoff. "Go on back to Little Rock, Hannah's-Friend-From-College-Simon. There's nothing for you here."

The next thing Simon knew, he was being lifted off his feet by three men and hauled toward the door. He kicked and thrashed, but the harder he fought, the more they laughed.

"Now, be careful, boys," Whitman called after them. "He's an officer of the law, and you don't want to be brought up on assault charges, do you?"

A wave of uproarious laughter followed them from the bar. The men carrying him took a few steps out into the parking lot before dropping him to the asphalt. Two of them laughed and slapped one another on the back as they returned to the bar, but the third stayed behind.

Simon rolled to a crouched position, bracing himself to take the man on one-on-one, but the blow he was expecting never came.

He looked up to find a man not much younger than himself staring at him, clearly at war with himself. Seeing his opening, he pounced. "Where is she?" he asked, breathless.

The man hooked a thumb over his shoulder. "In the back. Darla's keeping an eye on her."

Simon frowned as he digested the information. Then he

noticed the name sewn onto a patch on the man's work shirt. He nodded, then straightened as the man turned to walk back into the bar.

"Thank you, Tucker," Simon called after him.

The other man didn't turn around. He simply paused with his hand gripping the door handle. "Tell Mia I said, 'Hey,'" he said gruffly, then he flashed a sad smile before disappearing back into the bar.

Simon looked around, thankful only the passing traffic witnessed his humiliation.

He might be a desk jockey, but he was no slouch when it came to hand-to-hand fighting, as the thug in the bar could attest. He was also a certified sharpshooter, but his skill with a rifle wasn't going to do him any good here. He'd brought this on himself, he reasoned as he turned away from the door and stomped in the direction of Suzee's SleepInn. He was one man up against a bar filled with bikers. What had he been thinking, rushing in there without backup?

He pushed a hand through his hair in frustration as he pulled his phone from his belt and rounded the corner of the building. The call he placed was answered on the first ring.

"I've got a hostage situation here and I need backup, and if you're not going to provide it, I suggest you get some for yourself, because I will come for you next," he warned the police chief.

"Turn around," Mitchell Faulk growled in response.

When he did, what he saw almost made him drop his phone. Hannah was standing at the back of the parking lot with Darla Ott, the two women scowling at the building as if plotting to take it apart brick by brick.

Behind them, three patrol cars and a couple of unmarked vehicles nosed their way down the fire lane. The first patrol car stopped beyond the storage building, and the chief of police himself slid out of the passenger seat.

He nodded to Hannah and Darla, then smirked at Simon. "Looks like your hostage has done rescued herself. Oh, and your boys back there say they got Billy Aikens to roll on young Russell."

Simon registered the words the man was speaking, but he only had eyes for the woman standing beyond the chief. When she met his gaze, he called out the only thing he could say to reassure her.

"Beauregard is safe. Mia has him."

Hannah compressed her lips for a second, then swallowed hard as she nodded. "Great. Then let's go get this guy, because Darla and me, we're tired of being pushed around by Russ Whitman."

Chapter Fifteen

"I cannot believe he was cocky enough to think I wouldn't keep a spare set of keys on me," Darla muttered as she pulled a ring from the pocket of her snug blue jeans.

Hannah goggled at her in amazement. "You have another key?"

Darla rolled her eyes. "Honey, half the time this place is complete chaos. I keep one on me, one inside the door, and another in the till." She paused and looked down at the keys in her palm. "When I was six, my mama locked me in a closet for more than a day," she said quietly.

"I'm sorry," Hannah said softly.

Then, lifting her chin in defiance, Darla looked at Hannah with a raised eyebrow. "I'm never getting locked in anywhere ever again. And if he's fool enough to think I'm so far gone for him that I'll take the heat on a false imprisonment charge, he's delusional." She shook her head as she rounded the desk and pulled open a drawer.

Hannah's heartbeat stuttered when she saw Darla pull a small handgun from the drawer and test its weight in her palm. She must have looked as horrified as she felt because Darla waved the hand holding her keys. "No, don't freak.

This is only to get us out of here." She paused for a moment, then nodded. "Follow my lead."

Hannah stood close behind the other woman as she turned the key in the lock. Thankfully, some uproar in the bar covered the sound of the bolt sliding back. Darla opened the office door a crack and peered into the dim hallway.

"Looks like some kind of fight going on," she said in a low voice. Then, jerking her head to the side, she stepped into the hallway.

Hannah followed close on her heels, her pulse racing as Darla turned back to relock the door from the outside. Then, she made a shooing motion, pointing Hannah to the end of the corridor. Darla stepped past her, impatience rippling off her in waves.

The patrons in the bar gave a collective cheer, but Darla kept moving toward the end of the hall. More shouts from the barroom covered the sound of them opening the back door. Hannah hesitated on the threshold, momentarily blinded by the slanting gold sunlight.

Darla's hand closed around her wrist and yanked her into the parking lot. Hannah watched as the other woman caught the heavy steel door seconds before it slammed shut. Holding the handle, she made certain it closed softly but securely behind them.

"Those jerks better not trash my bar," Darla growled, pulling Hannah along toward a small outbuilding in the back. "I promise you, if they break so much as a beer sign, I'm sending the bill right to Russ's daddy."

"He doesn't deserve you," Hannah panted.

"Tell me something I don't know," Darla shot back. When she stopped, she whirled to face Hannah. "I mean it. What's going on with you and the cop guy? I need to know what I don't know. Is it going to be trouble for me and my business?"

Hannah shook her head. "No. I mean, I don't think so," she amended. "I don't think it has anything to do with you."

"But obviously Russ is involved," Darla said, crossing her arms over her chest. "What were you doing with him?"

Hannah's eyes widened, then narrowed into a glower. "What was I doing with him?" she repeated. "Someone broke into my house and stole my dog. Then, Mr. Always-Lurking-Around-the-Corner-Russ shows up and says he saw Beau running loose. I got in the truck, and the next thing I know he's tossing my phone out the window and pointing a gun at me," she said, indignation flaring into rage. "He kidnapped my dog, then he kidnapped me. That's what I was doing with him."

"How can someone so clever be so stupid at the same time?" Darla wondered aloud. "I mean, did he think I was going to let him keep you in my office?"

"I don't know what he was—" Hannah trailed off when she spotted a familiar figure coming around the side of the building. She sidestepped Darla, staring in disbelief. "Simon?" she asked, but he couldn't hear her.

Then, she became aware of the small parade of vehicles coming down the lane behind the bar. The first one pulled to a stop, and Mitch Faulk got out. He nodded to her and to Darla as if they were passing one another in the supermarket, then continued toward Simon.

Hannah glanced over her shoulder and caught Darla's wary expression. This time, she reached for the other woman, her fingers closing gently around Darla's slender wrist. "Come on. Let's go find out what's going on."

Darla glanced down at Hannah's hand but didn't resist.

"Yeah. Let's see what your friend from school Simon has been up to," she agreed.

"Simon?" she called again.

He stared directly back at her. "Beauregard is safe. Mia has him."

Hannah compressed her lips for a second, then swallowed hard as she nodded. "Great. Then let's go get this guy, because Darla and me, we're tired of being pushed around by Russ Whitman."

By the time they reached Mitch and Simon, the rest of their contingent caught up to them. Hannah had to shush one of the approaching officers because she was still trying to piece together what was going on.

"Whitman is in there with a bunch of other Ridge Riders. I thought he had..." He trailed off with a gesture in her direction. "I thought he had Ms. Miller holed up in there, so I went in, but I couldn't get anything out of him."

Darla's brows shot up. "You went in there alone?"

"I was in there," Hannah said at the exact same time.

She turned to Mitch. "Russ Whitman tricked me into getting into his truck. He then proceeded to take my phone and toss it out the window, then pulled a gun on me. He brought me here and locked me in the office with Darla." When she finished her recitation, she planted her hands on her hips. "What charges can I press?"

Mitch blinked, then gave a huff of a laugh. "Sounds like you've got a lot, but let's see what Simon's guys have. I'm betting we can come up with more."

Darla stepped in beside her. "He's been skimming money from construction draws and using it to buy his way into businesses around town. He says his *partnership*—" she emphasized the word with air quotes "—comes with a special protection package, courtesy of the Riders."

Hannah turned to gape at the other woman. "Are you kidding me?"

"Nope." Darla wrapped her arms around her middle and looked down at the broken asphalt at her feet. "He helped me out when I was in a jam a couple years ago."

"And that's when the club started hanging here more," Hannah concluded.

"Holy moly," Chief Faulk said under his breath. "Kidnapping, imprisonment, terroristic threatening, assault with a deadly weapon, extortion." He ticked the possibilities off on his fingers. "Not to mention damage to property," he added. He eyed Darla warily. "Would anyone testify to the extortion?"

She shrugged. "I would. And I bet others will too. They're tired of his attitude."

Mitch turned to Simon. "What have your people got?"

But Simon wasn't listening. He was too busy dissecting her with laser beam blue eyes. "Did you say he pulled a gun on you?"

Simon twitched, and with cat-like reflexes, Mitch reached out and caught Simon's arm. Hannah was glad, because it looked like he was about to go storming back into the bar.

"Save it," he barked. Then, Mitch turned to one of the agents who'd been with Simon the day they raided her flower shop. "Agent Dawson, what did you get?"

"Emma Parker got Billy Aikens to talk, and he had a lot to say about Russ Whitman," the agent informed Simon.

He smirked as Simon seemed to snap out of his thoughts. "How much?"

The agent pulled out his phone and began to read. "Liquor made by someone named Jenkins—"

"More than one of those," Darla interjected, her tone dry.

"The, quote, computer thing, unquote, was set up by someone named Tucker," he continued.

Hannah's breath caught, and her hand flew to her mouth, but she stifled her exclamation.

"Emma said everything Aikens told her circled back around to this Whitman guy and how he ruined the Ridge Riders."

Simon's gaze met hers, and Hannah nodded. "Billy is one of the guys who has been around awhile."

"Sounds like we have enough to pick him up," Mitch said with a nod.

"There's more," Dawson said, turning to Mitch again. "He said someone named Jacob Kinnan locked someone named Templeton into a storeroom?" His eyebrows dipped, then rose as he read from his notes. "Do you know what that means?"

"I know exactly what it means," Mitch said grimly. Their eyes met, and he nodded to Hannah. "I'll take care of him."

Simon grimaced, then glanced at the half dozen officers around them. "How? We'd have to have a tactical unit on hand to get Whitman out of there. He's got at least two dozen guys in there."

"Nope. Uh-uh," Darla said, wagging her head emphatically. "You are not bringing some sort of SWAT team in here to tear my place up," she insisted.

Simon turned his attention to the woman standing beside Hannah. "Any other ideas?"

Darla rolled her eyes. "I swear, men think we're the ones who overthink things," she said, then turned on her heel. "Spread out, fellas. You're about to get overrun by cockroaches."

They watched as she crossed back to the rear door, pulled it open a few inches, then reached inside and gave something a hard jerk.

An ear-splitting buzz screeched from inside the building. Almost immediately, patrons started spilling out the front and back of the bar. Mitch quickly directed his officers to cover both doors.

"Russ will go out the front," Darla shouted to them, "but grab as many as you want. I can promise you they're all guilty of something."

As if to punctuate the sentiment, Darla stuck her booted foot out and tripped one of the bikers coming out the back door. The two behind him tripped over the prone body. She looked up, and her eyes met Hannah's, a wide grin splitting her beautiful face.

"See? It's easy."

Hannah felt a hand on her arm and almost jerked away from the grasp, but then Simon spoke in a low, urgent tone. "Don't move." When she turned to look at him, he darted a look at the front of the building, then added a belated, "Please."

"Go," she told him before he sprinted to the front of the building.

Darla walked up beside her as she watched Simon run into the melee at the front of the building. "You going to let your friend Simon handle this on his own?" she asked, crossing her arms over her chest.

"What am I supposed to do? Simon's going to arrest him."

Letting out an exasperated huff, Darla hooked an arm through hers and tugged her forward. "Honey, you need to learn to think about the big picture. The possibility of getting arrested isn't going to scare Russ one bit. You know his daddy will get him the best lawyers money can buy." She sent Hannah a sly smile as they approached the growing crowd. "But you know what might give him a moment of pause?"

Hannah looked down at their linked arms, then at the woman who clearly had not outgrown being the most vengeful girl in school. "Seeing you and me together?" she guessed.

Darla grinned. "See? You're not as sweet as you want everyone to think you are."

"And you aren't as mean as you want people to think you are," Hannah retorted. "You didn't have to get me out of there."

Darla snorted and drew to a stop at the corner of the building, scanning the crowd spilling out into the parking lot. "Oh yes, I did. You think I want a big stick-in-the-mud hanging out in my bar? You'll try to reform all my customers."

Hannah rolled her eyes. "I'm not a crusader."

"Once a SADD girl, always a SADD girl," Darla teased.

Hannah elbowed her in the ribs, but she was the one who gasped when she saw one of the ATF agents placing Tucker Jenkins in handcuffs. As if reading her mind, Darla squeezed her arm to her side. "She's better off without him," she said quietly. "He's not the same guy he used to be."

"I know," Hannah whispered. "Mia does too."

They fell silent, sobered as they watched officers and agents move in to confront various patrons. Two county patrol cars pulled into the lot. She searched the crowd, her heart hammering as she strained to catch sight of Simon or Russ, but she couldn't spot either of them.

Two of Mitch's officers pushed past them, heading for the front door. That's when she saw Simon and Wyatt Dawson duck into the dark interior of the bar behind them. Minutes later, the Eureka Springs officers held a surly-looking man with a scraggly beard cuffed between them.

"Is that—" she began.

"Good," Darla interrupted. "I cannot believe Jacob Kinnan tied that poor old lady up and left her there."

Hannah swallowed the lump of rage and sadness rising in her throat at the thought of the boy she once knew contributing to the early demise of a woman she loved. "Yeah, I can't either."

"The years have not been kind to Jacob," Darla said, just loud enough for the man to hear as they hauled him past. "Looking rough, and not in a tough-guy way," she added, speaking louder so he could catch every word. Satisfied, she crossed her arms over her chest. "Never liked that guy."

Hannah looked over at her. "You know if Jacob was the one who went after Mrs. Templeton, it was probably because Russ told him to," she said, a note of caution creeping into her tone.

"Of course it was," Darla replied without missing a beat. "Jacob Kinnan never had an original thought in his life. At least, not any good ones."

As if the mention of his name summoned them, Russ Whitman sauntered out of the Downshift flanked by Simon and Agent Dawson, his hands cuffed behind his back. The man smiled as if he didn't have a care in the world, and the sight of those cosmetically whitened teeth made Hannah want to punch him in the mouth.

He was calling greetings and reassurances to his sycophants as they led him through the crowd. Thankfully, his promises of lawyers and bail money were drowned out by sirens as the fire department arrived on scene.

Darla heaved a sigh. "I'm going to get fined for a false

alarm," she said, scowling at her now empty bar. "Maybe pulling the alarm wasn't the best idea."

Hannah tore her gaze from the sight of Simon pressing Russ's head down to place him in the back seat of one of the county patrol cars. For the first time Hannah could remember, Darla looked fidgety and uncertain.

"It was a great idea," Hannah reassured her. "And if you get fined, which I doubt you will since you were aiding a police operation, I'll pay half."

Darla gave a soft chuckle. "I might hold you to that," she warned. Gesturing to various members of the Ridge Riders being tucked into official vehicles, she said, "This might put a dent in business for a while."

Hannah nodded, unable to refute her assessment, but she wasn't worried about Darla. If the woman was one thing, she was a survivor. "You'll figure it out, I'm sure."

"I will."

The first of the patrol cars were pulling away from the scene when a white Whitman Development pickup pulled into the adjacent lot. She swiveled around, scanning the remaining crowd for Simon, but coming up empty.

"Looking for your friend from college?" Darla asked in a teasing tone.

But Hannah was beyond playing it cool at this point. "Yes. I don't see him anywhere. Do you think he left in the car with Russ?"

Darla shook her head. "No, the tall dark-haired guy went with him."

Then Hannah was distracted from her search by the sight of Mia's Subaru bumping across the parking lot. She pulled in right next to the Whitman Development truck and jerked to a stop.

A spate of ferocious-sounding barks cut through the chaos, and she spun on her heel. Squinting, she could make out the shadow of her dog sitting in Mia's passenger seat, a safety belt pulled across his wriggling body in a futile attempt to restrain him.

"Beau!" Without a backward glance, she took off, her sights set on her best friend and her dog. But before she could reach the passenger window, Simon appeared from behind the pickup truck.

Hannah skidded to a stop, her gaze locked on him as Beau continued to bark beside them. "There you are," she panted.

He gestured to Mia's car. "I figured you might need some backup too."

Mia opened the driver door and rose, holding on to the door like she may need a shield as she stared at what was left of the crowd outside the Downshift. "Whoa. What's going on?"

Hannah opened her mouth to answer, but clamped it shut again. She had no idea where to begin.

"Pet your dog," Mia said, shooting an annoyed glance at poor Beau. "He's making my ears bleed."

Hannah reached through the partially open window and gave Beau several firm, reassuring strokes. "It's okay, my little love," she cooed, staring into his wide brown eyes. "I'm okay. You're okay."

Someone opened the door of the pickup truck beside her, but Hannah was too focused on calming her dog to care.

"Mia?"

Her best friend's name came out in barely more than a croak. Hannah turned and saw Micah standing beside the truck, his face white with panic. Out of the corner of her eye,

Hannah saw Simon step closer when Mia dashed around the front of her car to get to her brother.

"What are you doing here?" she demanded.

"I, uh…" he stammered, his gaze drifting to the scene at the Downshift. "I was running an errand for Russ, but… what is this?" he asked, gesturing to the bar patrons who were not being detained.

Denim-and leather-clad men and a few women stood talking in small knots. Occasionally one peeled off and headed for a vehicle to make their escape, but most seemed to be waiting for the okay from the fire department to go back inside.

Yanking her arm out of the window, Hannah whirled on the man she'd known since he was a boy. "He had a gun pointed at my back, Micah."

Micah stumbled back a step, and Mia froze, her arm outstretched toward her brother.

Mia recovered first. "What?"

"Russ had a gun pressing into my back when he walked me into the Downshift, and who was the first person I saw there?" Hannah asked, gesturing to Micah. "But you weren't any help to me, were you?"

Micah began shaking his head furiously. "No. I didn't know. I just saw you there, and then Russ asked me to run the per—"

"Russ asked you to run," Hannah shot back. "And that's all it took."

"Hannah, I swear, I didn't know. Why would he have a gun pointed at you?" Micah argued.

"Were you over at Hannah's house this afternoon?" Simon interrupted. "Did you go into her storm cellar?"

"Today?" Micah asked. "No. Why?"

Simon raised an eyebrow. "Were you in her storm cellar another day?" he persisted.

"Just to get the stuff she was donating to the rummage sale," he said, shifting his gaze from Simon to Hannah and finally to his sister. "Jacob said she told him she wanted all the old stuff from her grandma's cellar cleaned out. I know she hates going in there."

"What kind of stuff did you take out of there?" Simon asked.

Micah shrugged. "Well, there were a bunch of really heavy crates of canning jars. But we also took out some old shelves, and a few jars of fruit preserves Miss Flora left behind." He turned back to Hannah. "It didn't take long."

Mia let out a strangled sob, then pressed her fist to her lips to stop any more sound from escaping.

"What day did you do this?" Simon asked.

"Just a few days ago," Micah answered, his expression eager to please. "Tuesday? Wednesday?"

"Was it the day of Mrs. Templeton's visitation?" Hannah asked softly.

Micah's face lit, and he pointed to her. "Yes. Jacob said we had to hurry so it would be a surprise for Hannah when she came home from work. She was so upset about Mrs. T, and I figured it would be one less thing for her to worry about, you know?" He shrugged. "We finished up, then I went home to shower and change. It didn't take long."

Simon stepped closer, then so did Mia. Hannah closed her eyes for a moment, hoping she wouldn't need to get between the two of them.

"Micah, did you ever use the flower shop's van to do things other than deliver flowers?"

"Now, hold on—" Mia began.

But Micah was nodding, as eager to please Simon as he had been Russ. "Oh, all the time. But Hannah knew," he interjected. "I'd help people move, or if they needed something hauled over to Bentonville or down to Harrison."

"Did Russ Whitman ever ask you to haul anything in the van?" Simon asked.

Micah didn't answer right away, but a mottled red flush crept up his neck. "Yeah, maybe," he answered evasively.

"Do you remember what he asked to deliver?" Simon persisted.

"Don't answer that," Mia snapped. She whirled on Simon. "We want a lawyer."

Micah shook his head in disbelief. "A lawyer? For dropping a couple boxes off at ExpressShip?"

Hannah couldn't let him go on. "Micah, stop," she insisted, stepping closer to Mia and glaring at Simon. "There's more going on here than you know."

The younger man gestured to the fire truck pulling away from the bar. "Obviously."

Hannah waded into the heavy silence that fell over them. "Micah, did Russ Whitman ever ask you to keep an eye on me?" she asked softly.

Micah's troubled gaze flew to hers. "Only because we were worried about you."

Before anyone could say any more, Simon turned to Mia. "We're going to have to talk with him. You can have a lawyer present if you want, but the more he cooperates, the better off he'll be."

"We want a lawyer," she insisted.

"I guess I want a lawyer," Micah mimicked, shooting his sister a bewildered glance.

Simon nodded, then waved one of the Eureka Springs officers over. "Would you take Mr. Jones in for me? It's just for questioning, but he wants his attorney present." He then turned back to Mia. "Go ahead and call someone in, but if my gut is correct, I don't think your brother had extensive knowledge of what was going on."

"Hey, I know things," Micah objected.

Mia elbowed him sharply in the ribs as the patrolman took hold of his arm. "Please," she implored. "Stay quiet. Okay? Don't talk to anyone until we have someone there for you."

"Okay, geez," Micah said, rubbing the spot where she jabbed him as the officer led him away.

Mia turned back to Simon. "You'll have to forgive me if I'm not all in on trusting your gut instincts these days," she said, aiming a pointed look at Hannah.

"Hey," Hannah objected.

But Simon raised his hand to stop her. "No. She's right. And he does need an attorney," he added in a hushed tone. "If only to save him from himself."

He turned to Hannah. "I have to go." She stared at him, uncomprehending why he was stating the obvious. Then he added, "We're transporting Whitman and Tucker to Little Rock tonight." He cast a glance in the direction of Mia and Micah huddled near the patrol car, then met her gaze again. "I'm glad you're safe."

Hannah gulped. Until he mentioned Little Rock, it hadn't occurred to her he'd be leaving. For good. All she could manage was a soft, "Oh."

He gave her a wan smile. "I'll be in touch. I'm sure there will be details about the website—"

She batted away his concerns for the site she'd forgotten even existed with a wave. "Use it. Take it down. I don't care." She wrapped her arms tightly around her torso and ducked her head as she spoke the last bit. It was a lie, but it was the only defense she had against the fear she'd never see this man again.

Then, to her surprise, Simon reached out and tucked her hair behind her ear. "I have to go," he repeated, his tone wooden.

"I know."

She looked up through her lashes as he stepped back. He was staring at her with unsettling intensity. As if trying to memorize her. Tugging up her last surge of defiance, she lifted her chin and met his unwavering gaze. "See you, Friend-Simon-From-College," she said, her voice husky.

"See you soon," he answered.

He turned and walked away before she could ask what he meant by soon. She watched as he climbed into the SUV parked behind a row of bikes, then pulled away without so much as a backward glance.

Epilogue

Hannah was finishing an orchid wrist corsage for Milton Pressler's latest conquest when the bell above the door rang. "I'll have it ready for you in a second, Mr. Pressler."

She checked to be certain the delicate blooms were firmly affixed to the circlet of elastic lace, then popped the corsage into a clear plastic box.

"Milton has a new one on the hook?" a familiar voice asked.

Hannah whirled and found Simon Taylor standing in the doorway. "Simon," she breathed.

He inclined his head. "Ms. Miller."

She stiffened at his formal greeting. "You in town to pick up more of the local reprobates to help make your case?" She tried to keep the hurt out of her tone but failed miserably.

According to Mitch Faulk, Simon had been back twice in the weeks since apprehending Russ Whitman at the Downshift. Both times it had been to make further arrests, but not once had he attempted to talk to her, much less see her. She'd tried to tell herself she had no reason to be hurt, but as the days passed, she realized reason had very little to do with what she was feeling.

"No, I came to see you," he answered simply.

"I gave Agent Parker access to all my hosting information and released the domain name as of its next renewal," she said, setting the box with its beautiful corsage back on the workbench. "Thank you for helping Mia and Micah navigate all this," she said, folding her hands in front of her.

Micah had pled guilty to a misdemeanor charge of aiding in the commission of a crime, and in exchange for information he provided concerning the Ridge Riders' various activities, he was given a one-year suspended sentence and probation. He was living under Mia's watchful eye and working at Fuller's Lumber Yard when not pitching in at the bakery or driving deliveries.

"He provided us with some good information."

"She said you really went to bat for him. For what it's worth, I truly do believe Micah had no idea what he was doing. For the most part," she amended.

In the middle of it all, Micah confessed to having a duplicate copy of the key to Hannah's store made because he was tired of having to ask his big sister for everything. He'd come to the shop to snag the keys to the van the day Hannah and Simon were delivering centerpieces. When he realized it wasn't available, he'd ducked out the back door, but hadn't realized it locked with a different key. Scared he'd be spotted if he unlocked the front door a second time, he took off, figuring he could come back for the van later.

Not as comfortable with silence as Simon was, she asked, "Is there something I can do for you?"

"Micah tells me you are selling the business," he said at the same time.

"Maisey Jenkins has been training with me," she said with a slow nod. "She's got a good eye. I think she'll do well with it."

"Jenkins, as in…" He trailed off, raising a brow.

"She's a young woman trying to get out from under the shadow of a bunch of troublemaking men," she retorted.

She could practically see the gears turning in his head, but in the end he said only, "I understand."

Hannah could tell he was dying to ask where young Maisey would get the money to buy a business, but sometimes it was better for everyone if some questions remained unanswered.

"What will you do?" he asked.

"I've applied for a couple of design internships. I'm years behind in getting any kind of practical experience, but with the money from the sale of the shop, I can afford to be unpaid labor for a little while."

"Oh."

He seemed taken aback by the notion of her pursuing a career beyond creating floral bouquets, and Hannah found she liked surprising him. In truth, she'd surprised herself when she clicked on the link for the first application.

The fact was, something about Simon's departure had shaken something loose in her. Mia said it was almost as if she'd forgotten people were free to come and go as they pleased. And Hannah figured it was high time she started doing what pleased her, rather than staying stuck in one place.

"Yes. I'm hoping to hear from them soon," she said, feeling smug about her decisions.

"Are they internships around here?" he asked with a perplexed frown.

She laughed, tickled by the realization that Simon was having as hard a time picturing her anywhere else as she had. Shaking her head, she said, "One is in Bentonville, the other in Little Rock. I'm looking at another opportunity in Tulsa, but I'm not sure about it."

"You'd have to cross state lines," he said gravely.

"Well, yes, plus I'm not certain I want to design mausoleums."

"Mausoleums?" he echoed.

She shrugged. "Someone has to do it. This firm in Tulsa does all the spec work for smaller monument companies."

"Huh."

Hannah laughed. She had the exact same response when she first read the listing.

Unable to suppress her smile, she sat on the stool and allowed herself a minute to set aside her hurt feelings and simply drink him in. His hair looked freshly trimmed and was neatly combed. His starched white shirt and dark pants suited him far better than the khakis and casual shirts he'd picked up in town. His collar was open, but she had no doubt there was a discarded tie in his vehicle. He looked every inch the plainclothes cop. A vibe she found devastatingly appealing.

She drew a deep breath and boosted her faltering smile. "So, what brings you in today? Is it college reunion time already?"

"I said I'd see you soon," he reminded her.

"Oh. Is this soon?" she asked, pinning him with an arch stare.

To her delight, he squirmed a bit.

"I wanted to come sooner, but things were…hectic," he said gruffly.

"Understandable." She nodded encouragingly. "You know, I did replace my broken phone."

"I didn't want to talk to you on the phone."

He answered quickly enough for her to know it was the

truth, but it stung more than a little. She stiffened, then stood up from the stool so she could look him in the eye. "Why are you here, Simon?"

The direct question seemed to throw him. "I'm here to see you."

"You want to see me, but you don't want to talk to me?"

"Yes. I mean, no," he corrected, shaking his head. "I want to do both."

"But you couldn't be bothered to call," she shot back.

"I didn't think a phone call would be enough."

She blinked, surprised. "Enough?"

"I didn't want to call and talk about our days. I didn't want our every conversation to devolve into a never-ending analysis of what went down up here. I didn't want to play catch up," he said, exasperated.

Planting her hands on her hips, she glared at him. "Well, then, what did you want to do?"

When he moved, his steps were sure and decisive. He closed the distance between them, and before she had a chance to catch her breath, his mouth was on hers.

The kiss was hard at first. Like he was stamping her lips with an imprint of all his pent-up frustrations and unarticulated need. Then, his hand slid up her nape into her hair and the kiss softened, melting into nothing but untempered hunger and yearning.

When they broke for air, Simon pressed his forehead to hers, his long fingers knotted in her hair, his thumb stroking the sensitive spot behind her ear.

"Oh," she breathed. "I get it now."

"Do you?" he asked, his chest heaving against hers.

"I'm not sure. Better try again."

He took her mouth again, but this time she met him there,

giving as good as she got and taking everything she wanted from the kiss.

Then the bell above the door rang, and the two of them jumped apart like scalded cats.

"So sorry to interrupt," Milton Pressler boomed. The smile on his wrinkled face said he was far more tickled to have caught them at it than sorry to disrupt their embrace. "I only wanted to pick up my order, but I can come back."

Hannah scrambled to grab the plastic box containing the corsage. "I have it right here."

"Oh, wonderful! It's lovely. I'm sure Irene will love it," he enthused. "What do I owe you, dear?"

Still fuzzy-headed from the kiss, Hannah waved him off. "You're my best customer. This one's on me."

The old man mimed a little jig, then picked up the box. "Thank you, darling girl," he said with a wide smile. "Now, I'm off to do a little canoodling of my own. As you were," he said with a cheerful wave. As he tottered his way to the door, he began singing, "Love is in the air—"

Hannah's face flamed, but when she sneaked a peek at Simon, she found him watching her with that now familiar intensity. He reached for her before the door was even closed.

"Simon—" she protested weakly.

"I hope you get the job in Little Rock," he said, still gazing at her with undisguised greed.

She smiled and let him pull her into his arms, winding hers around his neck. "You do?"

"Yes. It would be so much better than Bentonville," he said gravely.

"Oh?" She tilted her head to the side, perfectly aligned for another one of those searing kisses. "How so?"

"Well, for starters, you already have a friend in Little Rock," he said encouragingly.

"You mean my friend Simon from college?" she asked, feeling flirtatious.

"Yes," he replied with his customary directness. "But he's hoping you want to be more than friends," he whispered, his mouth millimeters from hers.

"He is?" she breathed.

"So much more," he answered, then sealed his intentions with a kiss.

* * * * *

COMING SOON!

We really hope you enjoyed reading this book. If you're looking for more romance be sure to head to the shops when new books are available on

Thursday 19th June

To see which titles are coming soon, please visit
millsandboon.co.uk/nextmonth

MILLS & BOON

OUT NOW!

ROMANCE ON DUTY

UNDERCOVER Passion

3 BOOKS IN ONE

CINDI MYERS JO LEIGH SARAH M. ANDERSON

Available at
millsandboon.co.uk

MILLS & BOON

LET'S TALK
Romance

For exclusive extracts, competitions and special offers, find us online:

- **f** MillsandBoon
- **X** @MillsandBoon
- **◉** @MillsandBoonUK
- **♪** @MillsandBoonUK

Get in touch on 01413 063 232

> For all the latest titles coming soon, visit
> **millsandboon.co.uk/nextmonth**